KILLING MONICA

KILLING MONICA

CANDACE BUSHNELL

GRAND CENTRAL
PUBLISHING

NEW YORK   BOSTON

Grand Central Publishing
Hachette Book Group
1290 Avenue of the Americas
New York, NY 10104

HachetteBookGroup.com

Printed in the United States of America

RRD-C

First Edition: June 2015
10 9 8 7 6 5 4 3 2 1

Grand Central Publishing is a division of Hachette Book Group, Inc.
The Grand Central Publishing name and logo is a trademark of Hachette Book Group, Inc.

The Hachette Speakers Bureau provides a wide range of authors for speaking events. To find out more, go to www.hachettespeakersbureau.com or call (866) 376-6591.

The publisher is not responsible for websites (or their content) that are not owned by the publisher.

Library of Congress Cataloging-in-Publication Data

Bushnell, Candace.
Killing Monica / Candace Bushnell. — First edition.
pages cm
ISBN 978-0-446-55790-0 (hardcover) — ISBN 978-1-4555-3037-3 (large print) — ISBN 978-1-60788-913-7 (audio download) 1. Women authors—Fiction. I. Title.
PS3552.U8229K55 2015
813'.54—dc23
2015010911
ISBN 978-1-4555-5856-8 (int'l edition)

To Angie "Pangie" Silverstein

PART ONE

PROLOGUE

I T WAS SUMMER, and Monica was everywhere again.

She was there, in the supermarket, on the rack of tabloids between displays of candy and sugarless gum at the checkout counter. And there, on the side of the bus kiosk. And there, on the cover of the fashion magazines in the salon. She was all over the morning shows, recommending what to wear, store, or toss from your summer wardrobe. She was with you in the backseat of the taxi, on the screen in front of your knees, telling you where to go, what to see, and what to buy. Selling, always selling. But mostly, what she was selling was happiness.

And she still looked great doing it. Her skin, soft and flawless, was radiant. Her cheeks resembled peaches. And her hair: masses and masses of it in pure twenty-four-karat color.

On June 1, like clockwork, Monica's image began to go up on the billboard overlooking the designer boutiques in Soho. First a strip of her hair appeared, followed by the smooth, high forehead, and then the eyes: the irises an almost translucent light green encircled by a band of dark gold hazel. And then the mouth: perched on her face like a sweet strawberry surprise, lips open, smiling. Monica was happy. So very, very happy. You looked at her, and suddenly you wanted to *be* her.

Unless, of course, you *were* her. Or had once been a version of

1

her—in the past. But now you are frazzled, beaten down, and your skin looks like crap. Your eyes are bloodshot. There is something sticky in your hair.

Pandy looked at the top of Monica's head and thought, *Just two more days. Three or four at the most.* She could do this. She could *win.*

She reminded herself that she had won before. *With* Monica.

Silly, charming, madcap Monica; the beloved heroine of four Monica books and four Monica movies.

Pandy had conjured up Monica as a child, for the entertainment of herself and her younger sister, Hellenor. Monica had hair the color of yellow marigolds, and she had quickly turned into their favorite creation, becoming the star of a series of notebooks called *Monica: A Girl's Guide to Being a Girl.*

When Pandy left home, moved to New York, and became a struggling writer, naturally she figured she was leaving Monica behind.

But she was wrong.

Because one night, when the third book she'd written had been rejected, when she'd had to borrow money to pay her rent, when the man she thought she was seeing turned out to be seeing someone else—she suddenly remembered Monica.

Monica. The goldenest of golden girls. On the outside, anyway. But what only Pandy knew was that when she'd created Monica, she'd been at the lowest point in her life.

Monica was the answer to her despair.

Pandy got up, walked to the window, and frowned. The billboard was two blocks away. The sun moved behind Monica's head, and once again Pandy found herself standing in Monica's shadow.

∽

"Henry," she'd said to her agent, leaning over his desk. "You and I both know I can't write Monica forever. Not that I have anything *against* Monica. I love her. We all do. And I'm grateful to her. I know I'd be a fool to turn down money on a sure thing to take a chance on the unknown. But I've got a million stories in my head. I need uncharted territory. I need to be..." She'd paused. "Scared."

Perhaps she shouldn't have been so glib.

"Uh-huh," Henry said, and smiled patiently. Every year or so she went through this phase of not wanting to write about Monica; of wanting to go back to writing something "serious" and "meaningful." She would write a hundred or so pages of this "different" book, and inevitably return to Monica.

Because, as Henry pointed out, she *was* Monica.

But this time *was* different. She didn't give up after a hundred pages.

She couldn't. She had to succeed.

Over both Monica and her soon-to-be ex-husband, Jonny Balaga.

⌖

The sun was now high behind Monica's head. Pandy realized that her image was still not complete. They had yet to attach her leg.

Perhaps they were changing her shoe.

Pandy smiled, suddenly feeling sentimental about Monica. She remembered the first time she'd watched the billboard go up. She'd been so excited, she'd insisted that SondraBeth Schnowzer, the actress who played Monica in the film versions of the books, come over and watch with her as it progressed. The two of them had sat there for hours, as rapt as if the universe had conspired to give them this gift—their own private movie about their very own lives.

And when the billboard was finally complete, when Monica's leg had at last been raised, revealing her famous neon blue spike-heeled bootie, they had looked at each other and screamed:

"It's you! It's you!"

"No, it's you! That part is definitely you!"

Leading to the inevitable conclusion: "It's *both of us*!"

And then SondraBeth had walked to the window and said, "Monica? I've a feeling we're not in Montana anymore."

Pandy felt a sudden stab of yearning, not just for Monica, but for SondraBeth Schnowzer, too. This desire to see her former best friend again—to laugh giddily as if the entire world were their playground—was confusing. SondraBeth had dealt her a terrible blow, and they hadn't spoken for years. Ever since that moment in the ladies' room when SondraBeth had warned her about Jonny.

Sondra*Bitch*, she'd thought.

And now both Jonny and SondraBeth Schnowzer were dead to her.

And that was the essential problem with Monica. Monica made it look easy when it wasn't. No one ever asked the legions of Monica lovers to consider the years of struggle and hard work it would have taken Monica to *become* Monica; the self-doubt, the self-loathing, the fear, the sheer amount of energy required to set a goal and keep at it day after day, with no immediate reward in sight and the possibility that it might never materialize at all. On the other hand, who wanted reality? Reality was depressing. And *free*.

☙

Pandy was almost finished writing by the time the entire billboard went up and she'd seen her name in those crisp white letters. Smaller and smaller each year, perhaps, but nevertheless, still there:

BASED ON THE BOOKS BY P.J. WALLIS

Pandy looked back at the billboard and frowned. Monica's leg was still missing. It had never been late before.

Maybe it was a sign?

She hit SEND.

And then the landline began ringing. Only a few people had the number, including Henry and her divorce lawyer, Hiram.

Hopefully, it was Henry. But she'd happily take Hiram.

"Hello?" Pandy said into the receiver.

"Congratulations!" a man bellowed.

"What?" *Who is this?* she almost asked.

"You, young lady, are free."

"Hiram?"

"He's agreed to it all."

"He *has?*"

"Yup."

"What about the numbers?"

"What we wanted."

"Ohmigod!" Pandy shrieked.

"I knew I'd make you happy," Hiram purred. "Remember the first day I met you? Remember what I told you? 'My wife and daughters *just love Monica.*' I promised I'd do right by you."

"And you *have.* And I'm *so* grateful." And then a second thought: "Did he actually sign? On the dotted line?"

"You mean, with the *actual* John Hancock? No, he did not. Nevertheless, he verbally agreed. And when you verbally agree in front of four of New York City's top thousand-dollar-an-hour litigators, you do not go back on your word. Let's just say we gave him a little talking-to, and he's agreed to see things our way."

Pandy laughed nervously. "You mean, my way."

"Your way, our way, it's all the same way, isn't it?"

"Well, golly," Pandy said. "I wasn't expecting this to happen so *soon.*"

"I know. After all the hell he's put you through. Put *us* through. I've never seen anything like it, and I've seen everything. One of my guys canceled his vacation to get the paperwork finished. *His* daughters love Monica, too."

"Thank God for Monica." Pandy paused and inhaled deeply as reality began to set in. "In that case, I suppose Jonny will be wanting his check."

Hiram laughed. "I suppose he will. But don't think about the money. Go out and celebrate. You are now officially free from that asshole."

Hiram hung up.

For a moment Pandy could only stand there, dazed.

Divorced.

Free.

Suddenly the world came rushing back to her in all its Technicolor glory.

CHAPTER ONE

P J WALLIS! Is that really you? And what the hell are you wearing?" screamed Suzette as she came barreling into the loft, followed by a posse of Pandy's twelve closest girlfriends.

"I'm back!" Pandy shrieked, removing the silver-sequined cardboard top hat from her head and giving a little bow. Suzette grabbed her around the shoulders, and they jumped up and down like ten-year-olds.

"I need a drink," Meghan announced. "These divorce parties make me nervous. What if it happens to *me*?"

"It will inevitably happen to you, and then you will get one of these." Suzette thrust her left hand under Meghan's nose so she could get a closer look at the large yellow stone. "Ten carats. Unfortunately the guy who comes with it is eighty and has liver spots, but if he wants to pretend he's younger than he is, who am I to object?"

"But you're not young, either," Meghan pointed out. "You're nearly—"

"Shhhh." Suzette glared at Meghan as Pandy—right on cue—cooed at the ring in wonder.

"You're engaged?"

"Not all of us have been under a rock for the past two years," Suzette quipped as the elevator doors opened and six more women spilled out.

"Champagne in the bathtub, cupcakes in the kitchen, cigarettes in the living room," Pandy said by way of greeting.

"What about cock? Do we get cock in the bedroom?" one of the women screamed, sending the others into peals of nervous laughter.

"Do you think Jonny thought you spent too much time working?" asked Angie. Pandy laughed and put her arm around Angie's slight shoulders. "Of course I spent too much time working," she said loudly, as much for herself as for the benefit of the crowd. "What woman isn't forced to spend 'too much time working' these days? And if men don't like it, too bad. If you're in a relationship with *me*, I come with a career. Just like Jonny came with *his* career."

"And all those restaurants," Nancy interjected, breezing by.

Pandy smiled stiffly. "He doesn't actually own those restaurants."

"Do you just totally *hate him* right now?" Amanda was on the verge of a gossip orgasm.

"Let's just say I will never do *that* again."

The elevator door opened and another gaggle of women rushed out.

"Pandy!" Portia screamed. "Look at you! You're so brave. Standing there in that skintight silver dress and looking like a goddess!"

"Is it true?" shrieked Brittney. "I heard he tried to get money out of you from *Monica*. How could he do that? He didn't even *know you* when you started writing *Monica*."

"Ladies, please," Pandy addressed her rapt audience. "When it comes to divorce, what's fair and logical is the first thing that goes right out the window. Jonny was threatening to go after the rights to *Monica*. He thought I'd be so terrified he might get them, I'd give him the loft instead."

"So what did you give him?" Portia chirped. "Not the loft. And certainly not Monica."

"You gave him money, didn't you?" Suzette scolded. "Oh, I knew this would happen. Didn't I tell you this would happen?" She looked around at the women closest to her, who nodded. "I predicted this," she continued. "I said, 'Pandy is such a softy, you just watch. She'll end up giving him all her money.'"

For a moment, Pandy grimaced—if only her friends knew how true that was. But hopefully, with the success of her new book, no one would need to know the truth about anything, including her marriage.

"But he's got tons of his *own* money!" Meghan cried.

"Not as much as you'd think," Nancy chimed in. "Those chefs have all their income tied up in the real estate for their restaurants."

"Do you think he was having an affair?" Angie asked breathlessly.

Pandy smiled queasily. Angie was the most naïve of her friends—surely she'd heard the rumors of Jonny's infidelities. But Pandy had already had quite a bit of champagne, and feeling puckish, she said, "Let me put it this way. If he *wasn't* having an affair, it wasn't from lack of *trying*." She guffawed loudly.

The party had officially begun.

By seven p.m., the loft was packed. The air was filled with steam from various inhalers, along with actual cigarette and marijuana smoke. Strewn around the loft were cracked plastic cocktail glasses, sticky napkins, and empty bottles of champagne. In the midst of their celebration, Henry arrived.

"Look, Cary Grant is here!" Pandy heard Portia shout. Followed by Suzette's curt reply:

"Cary Grant is dead. That's Pandy's *agent*."

"Any word?" Pandy screamed, rushing toward him with so much enthusiasm, she knocked over several drinks in the process.

"On what?" Henry asked, coolly raising his eyebrows as he surveyed the room. Almost imperceptibly, he shook his head.

"On The Book. Hello? Remember The Book? That thing I've been writing for the last two years?" Pandy waved her hands in front of his face.

Henry didn't blink. "If I had word, you'd be the first to know." He squeezed Pandy's shoulder reassuringly. He stayed another five whole minutes before he was forced to flee, claiming he didn't want to end up in a meat sandwich between Suzette and Nancy.

"A new Monica book?" cried Angie. Despite the booty-shaking beat now blaring from the speakers, she'd somehow managed to overhear Pandy's conversation.

"I knew it!" Brittney shrieked. "Now that Pandy's divorced, Monica will have to get divorced, too."

"Then she can try online dating."

"And a matchmaker. That would be hilarious."

"What would be even more hilarious would be watching Monica try to arrange a date by *texting.*"

"And then she can date some hot young studs. With their own hair and actual muscles."

"I don't know about you," Amanda added, "but now that I'm dating younger guys, I personally can't stand men my age anymore. It's fine if you're already with one, but otherwise—"

"I agree. If I want to look at an old guy, I can look at my husband!"

"I suppose you could, if you ever saw him!"

"And what is *that* supposed to mean?"

Texting? Divorce? A matchmaker? No. That isn't Monica, Pandy thought.

She had to stop this.

"Hold on!" she shouted. "Monica *isn't* getting divorced."

"But everything that happens to you happens to Monica, right?" Brittney squawked.

"Not anymore," Pandy declared, suddenly remembering her new, very un-Monica book and how it would force the critics to finally take her seriously. This was something that would *never* happen to Monica. No one took Monica seriously at all.

And could you blame them? Look at *her* right now. Look at her *friends*: Portia was sitting on the kitchen counter, her too-short dress riding up her thighs, while Nancy was inadvertently sloshing champagne on the front of Angie's shirt and extolling the virtues of vaginal steaming.

Pandy held up her hand for order. "As a matter of fact, I *do* have a new book coming out."

"When?"

"I don't really know. I just finished it. Last week, as a matter of fact."

"Pandemonia James Wallis," Suzette crowed. "You naughty girl. Why didn't you tell us before? Now we can stop celebrating your divorce, and start celebrating your new book." She held up a bottle of champagne. "To PJ!"

"To Monica!"

"To PJ *and* Monica!"

Pandy groaned. She pushed through the crowd to the couch. "I have an announcement—"

"You have a new boyfriend!" Amanda gasped.

For a moment, Pandy put her face in her hands. Then she climbed onto the couch, standing precariously with one foot on the cushion and one foot on the arm for balance. As she was climbing, she noticed that the sun was about to set.

"Hello! Over here!" she said, waving her arms. Most of the women were no longer paying attention.

"Hello! Me here. Wanting to say something!"

Suzette heard her voice, turned around, and shushed the crowd. "Our hostess wants to say something."

"Hey, Pandy's talking."

"Be po*lite*."

As the noise level dropped, Pandy was quite sure she heard the words "needs Botox" and "still totally naïve about Jonny," although not necessarily in that order. Then Angie handed her an open bottle of champagne, and Pandy took a swig and gave it back. She touched her mouth with her fingertips.

"I have an announcement," she repeated, scanning the room. Everyone was listening now. "I can't tell you how much it means to me that you're all here. You all know how much I love you!"

"Awww."

"We love you, too, Goobers."

Pandy bowed her head in thanks, waiting for them to settle down.

"I want to thank all of you for coming. Because this *is* a celebration. A celebration of not only moving forward, but also of letting go of the past." Pandy glanced back at the billboard. The sun had set, and for the moment, Monica had disappeared.

"One of the things I learned during this divorce," Pandy continued, "is that I probably never should have gotten married in the first place. But then my insecurities got the better of me. No matter how stupid it is, if you've never been married, it's all you can think about. It's always there, in the back of your mind: 'What's wrong with me? How come no one's ever wanted *me*?' And it's important not to get caught up in society's expectations—"

"Cock in the bedroom!" someone shouted.

Pandy laughed. "In any case, what I've realized is that I have to grow up. Which means I can't keep on being Monica."

"Oh, go on," Nancy hooted. "You *are* Monica."

Pandy shook her head. "Not anymore. I don't want to be. Partly because if I stay like Monica, I'm going to end up with another Jonny."

"Forget about Jonny. You were too good for him."

"Men will be lining up to meet you. You'll see," Suzette cackled.

"No." Pandy playfully pointed her finger at Suzette. "They line up to meet *you*. But that's sort of the problem. If you have a man, great. But it shouldn't *have* to be about men. And we *already know this*. But sometimes it takes getting divorced to learn that lesson all over again."

Pandy's mouth was suddenly dry. She motioned to Angie for the bottle. While she drank, she heard Brittney ask, "Did Jonny really have fourteen suitcases full of knives?"

"Shhhh," Nancy said.

"And so," Pandy said quickly, "I will keep this short. I *do* have a new book coming out, and it is *not* about Monica. It's what I'm calling a 'me' book. Meaning it's the book I've always wanted to write, and I've finally taken the chance to write it. I hope you're not disappointed. About Monica." She paused. "And the fact that I definitely don't have a new man—"

"We're almost out of champagne!" Portia screamed as if a nuclear bomb were about to go off.

"Music!" Meghan shouted. "What happened to the music?"

Pandy picked up her sequined top hat and placed it on her head. As she turned to step off the couch, the lights that bathed Monica's image every evening at eight p.m. sharp suddenly flooded her face.

Pandy took a step backward. The heel of her shoe caught in one of the tears in the cracked leather.

She went down.

Chapter Two

EYES FIRMLY shut, Pandy rolled over, determined not to face what she knew was out there: the light.

The *morning*. Why, oh why couldn't morning ever come when you wanted it to? Why were these things always out of one's control?

She felt around her face for her eye mask. Her fingers sensed padded foam covered in slick silk. But the straps felt wrong. For starters, there seemed to be too many. And the thing reeked. Of expensive perfume—

Pandy gasped, hinged upright into a sitting position, and flung the offending garment to the floor. She caught her breath and moaned. A band of pain radiated from the top of one ear to the other, as if her head were caught in a vise. The pain was bad, but that was to be expected. She'd had too much to drink—everyone had had too much to drink—and she hadn't thrown a party in ages. She'd known she would wake up with a Godzilla of a hangover—one that, as she liked to say, could destroy tall buildings in New York. Mysteriously, however, this expected pain was accompanied by a more sinister sensation: a spongy, pulsating throb on the back of her head.

Like being tapped, again and again, by a small and very annoying elf wielding a tiny hammer.

Pandy's exploring fingers discovered a lump the size of a large marble. She grimaced. She remembered falling off the couch. And then what?

She leaned over the side of the bed. What she'd thought was her eye mask was a hot pink bra with cups the size of cantaloupes. Suzette's? Or Meghan's? They'd both gone to the same plastic surgeon. Pandy dropped it back onto the floor. Damn friends. They'd gotten drunk, and all of a sudden they'd started trying on each other's clothes.

The phone rang. The landline, not her device. Making it harder to ignore.

Pandy stared at the phone. Its incessant ringing was incomprehensible. Why was it so loud? Who was calling? She groaned and gritted her teeth. There was only one person who could possibly be calling this early in the morning after a major party the night before.

"Hello, Henry." Her voice cracked on the first word, but by the time she got out "Henry," she had managed to infuse his name with a passable imitation of the living.

Henry wouldn't be fooled; he was all too familiar with how she lost her voice when she'd had too much to drink. He'd warned her about it many times on book tours: "If you have a glass of wine with every blogger who wants to interview you, not only will you have consumed the equivalent of six bottles of wine, but you will also have no voice. Meaning you cannot talk. Meaning you cannot tell all these journalists how fabulous your new Monica book is. Meaning, what is the point of you being on a book tour at all?"

"Funny, it never feels like six bottles," she'd said musingly.

Henry had thrown up his hands at such idiocy.

"Good morning," he said now. His greeting was surprisingly pleasant, but also, Pandy noted, slightly artificial.

"Henry?" She shifted on the sheet. Tiny unidentifiable particles were pressing into her thighs. She wriggled around and extracted something that looked like a colorful shard of plastic. She examined it while gripping the phone tightly in her other hand.

"What are you doing today?" he asked with unexpected cheer. "Are you busy?"

"Why?" Pandy asked cautiously as she examined the particle between her fingers. It was a dried piece of cupcake frosting. She flicked it away.

"I was thinking it might be nice to get together. Meet in my office for a change. We haven't done that in a while."

"Today?" Pandy laughed. "But I just saw you last night."

"Indeed you did. Sadly, I wasn't there to witness what happened after I departed, but I suppose it doesn't matter. Someone and their party are all over Instalife today."

"You don't say." Pandy suppressed a hiccup.

Photos, she suddenly recalled. That's why everyone was exchanging clothes.

A terrible possibility began to dawn as Pandy felt around the bed for her glasses. If what she feared were true, she would need to be upright for what Henry would no doubt tell her next. She found her glasses, untangled one leg from the sheet, and swung her foot off the bed.

"The pictures," she hissed. "How bad are they?"

"Depends on what one calls 'bad.'"

Pandy lowered her other foot and stepped on Suzette's bra. "Damn." She took another step. Crunch. Another spot of cupcake frosting. Her goddamned friends! "There wasn't—nobody was—"

"Sober?" Henry chuckled nastily. "No. They certainly were not."

Pandy sighed. "Not *sober*. *Naked*. No one was naked, were they?" She took a step toward the window and saw a pair of black Spanx draped over a lamp. Why would anyone take those off? "Because there seems to be a lot of clothing left behind." She continued to move around the bedroom, just like an object that "once in motion, stays in motion." An aphorism learned from the arthritis ads on daytime television. She took a breath.

"And really, Henry. What's up with Suzette and that huge yellow diamond? Who needs ten carats? What's wrong with three? Honestly, what can seven extra carats do that three can't?"

Henry paused. Pandy gingerly lifted the edge of the Spanx between thumb and forefinger. "And don't say 'blow job,'" she added.

"I wasn't going to say anything at all."

"Good. I hope *I'm* not in these ridiculous pictures." Picking up steam, she pulled on her plaid pajama pants. Catching a glimpse of herself in the mirror, she had a sudden new thought:

"That's why you called," she said, recalling that comment about Botox. "I look old, don't I?"

"I didn't call to talk about your wrinkles."

"Good. Whose wrinkles should we talk about instead?"

Flames of sunlight were licking the edges of the blackout shades. "Listen to me," Pandy groaned. "I'm a lousy human being."

"All human beings are lousy by definition," Henry said patiently. Then he added, "Speaking of which, I wanted to talk to you about your new book."

"My book?" Pandy had barely closed her mouth when Henry dropped the bomb.

"It's all over Instalife."

Pandy yanked open the shades. The sun shot into her eyes, momentarily blinding her. "Fuck." She dropped the phone. A piece broke off, exposing the batteries. Pandy clamped her hand over the wiring and brought the phone back to her ear.

"It's on Page Six. And *People!*" hollered Henry, who was given to random bursts of shouting.

Pandy was suddenly annoyed. "That's *it*? I thought you were calling because you'd had word."

Henry ignored this, continuing as he read the headlines aloud: "'PJ Wallis: Uncoupled and Un-Monica'ed.'"

"Hey. That's good!" Pandy exclaimed. "Very good. Word of the book is already spreading."

She stuck her feet into a dusty pair of velvet loafers she hadn't seen in ages. The loafers came from the far reaches of her closet—meaning the clothing exchange must have been more extensive than she'd imagined.

"Anyway," she continued, shuffling into the living room, "who cares? In fact," she added, "I'm glad. Maybe when my publishers see that the book is all over Instalife, they'll actually get off their asses and read it. Christ. The school year isn't even over. Surely everyone in publishing can't already be on summer vacation?"

"They're not on summer vacation," Henry said ominously.

"Good. Then they can read it. It's been over a week." She was tempted to add, *And don't call me until they have read it*, but she caught herself. She pressed her thumb sharply into her right temple. She mustn't let her hangover turn her into a demanding ogre.

"Gotta go," Pandy said quickly. She hung up and tossed the phone onto the couch, batteries dangling like viscera from the handset.

∞

Moving slowly into the kitchen, Pandy encountered a telltale flat white box on the counter. It contained two slices of cold pepperoni pizza.

The sight of the pizza made Pandy unaccountably happy. Balancing a slice on her open palm, she slid the floppy triangle onto the rack in Jonny's pizza oven. She turned the control to five hundred degrees and made herself a cup of tea. Discovering a cache of neatly folded plastic grocery bags in the pantry, she tried to stuff the pizza box into a bag, but it wouldn't fit. She gave up and went to work on cleaning up the living room instead.

Plastic cups—some empty, others still containing fluid and floating cigarette butts—went into one empty grocery bag after another. Pandy discovered a couple of stray cigarettes behind one of the couch cushions. She lit a cigarette and leaned out the half-open window, trying to blow the smoke through the opening. The first rush of nicotine almost made her retch, but she fought the impulse and smoked it down to the filter. As she was lighting another, she smelled something burning. She raced to the kitchen and yanked open the pizza oven as black smoke billowed into her face. She coughed, slammed the door, turned the oven off, and ran the butt under the tap.

She grabbed another plastic bag and headed into the bathroom.

Several empty bottles of expensive pink champagne—both Pandy's and, of course, Monica's signature drink—were floating on a scrim of dirty water in what had been last night's enormous ice bucket. Bobbing among the debris like a bad apple was a curious piece of cushioned green plastic. Pandy picked it up. It was a green cartoon frog with large yellow eyes and two flexible feet on either side.

The frog was attached to something stiff and unyielding. Pandy turned it over. On the other side was a black screen. The frog was a child's waterproof cell phone cover.

But whose? Pandy frowned. Was it possible someone had brought a child to the party, and she hadn't noticed?

She tapped the screen. An image appeared: Portia on a tropical beach, holding the hands of two adorable towheaded children.

Oh, right. Portia had children. Pandy suddenly pictured Portia at the beach with her kids. Portia was worried they might lose their cell phones in the water. And so she had bought them all these funny floating cell phone covers at the resort's gift shop. Pandy could smell the fresh green scent of locally made straw hats hanging on a rack near the cash register; could feel the goose bumps rising on her upper arms as she walked from the stifling heat into the sharp cold of the shop's air-conditioning.

When was the last time she'd gone on a tropical vacation?

Years ago. Six, to be exact. When she'd gone to that island with SondraBeth Schnowzer. And Doug Stone had turned up.

Water under the bridge, Pandy thought as she opened the tub drain and watched the dirty water disappear.

What wasn't disappearing, however, was her hangover. She searched for aspirin and, finding none, realized she was going to have to venture outside.

∽

Exiting her building, Pandy stood on the sidewalk looking up and down the street. She caught a whiff of cotton candy, meaning the San Geronimo festival was in full swing. Continuing down Mercer Street, Pandy skirted a large patch of dirt from the never-ending construction of a nearby building. It had been under construction for so long, Pandy could remember making out with a guy in front of it when she'd first bought her loft and had yet to meet Jonny.

Belascue. That was the guy's name. He was an artist; a painter. He'd been really good, too.

If only she'd ended up with Belascue instead of Jonny, she thought. But this fantasy was short-lived. When she'd finally had sex with Belascue, he'd freaked out and said he didn't want to have a relationship. Now, at age forty-nine, she'd heard he still didn't have a proper girlfriend.

Thank God she'd never gotten too involved with Belascue. This reminder—of having dodged at least one bullet from her past—gave Pandy renewed hope. Enough to encourage her to head down the deserted street.

Wandering past the still-darkened shop windows, Pandy realized it was not yet ten a.m. If she were still writing, the hour wouldn't have mattered. Other than the fact that she always felt like there wasn't enough of it, when she was writing, time wasn't relevant.

But now that she'd finished her book, once again, time mattered. And the problem with time was that you had to *do things* with it.

She went into the pharmacy, bought a large bottle of Advil, and wondered if she ought to stop by her bank to begin the process of getting Jonny his check. How did that even work? Could you write out a personal check for such a large amount?

22

At the thought of the amount—seven figures—her stomach heaved, bringing up a rancid trickle of bile. What she could do with that money! The divorce settlement was twice the cost of Suzette's ring; enough to buy a twenty-carat diamond instead. Possibly even a pink one. She could have the biggest pink diamond ring in all of New York City for the amount she was going to have to pay Jonny to be rid of him at last.

Pandy grimaced. Best not to think about it.

She strolled to the newsstand, where Kenny, the proprietor, was counting money behind a Plexiglas barrier. He grinned, exposing a gold tooth. "You're back," he said.

"Oh. I've been—" Pandy broke off, not sure how to explain the months that had disappeared while she'd been writing.

"I got the brand-new magazines. Hot gossip. Just came in this morning."

Pandy nodded automatically. "That's great." And then remembering *why* she was at the newsstand in the first place—*Jonny, his check, a massive hangover*, all adding up to *stress*—she mumbled, "I'll take a pack of Marlboro Lights."

"You smoking again?" Kenny exclaimed.

"Only today."

"One of those days, huh?" he asked.

Pandy nodded again, feeling an ache from the nasty bump on the back of her head. When Kenny turned away to get the cigarettes, she glanced down at the magazines. Besides *Vogue* and *Elle*, Sondra-Beth Schnowzer had made the covers of three tabloids. They were all proclaiming she'd been dumped again, this time by her latest love interest, a handsome French model. SondraBeth's romantic transgressions were listed in bullet points on the side of her head: *Spends all her time working; obsessed with her strict schedule*; and worst of all: *Has no friends.* "Here you go," Kenny said, beaming, as he handed her the cigarettes.

Pandy walked half a block before she stopped to light one. She looked up to find that she was standing smack in front of the former entrance to Joules. There was the bamboo curtain, now reduced to a few pieces of dirty string; behind it, the long and treacherous walk down the narrow alley and then down damp cellar stairs into what had once been the most fabulous nightclub in the world.

For a moment, Pandy could literally smell it.

That *smell*. It hit you as soon as you entered Joules Place. The odor of money. And drugs. The harsh metallic scent of a million chemicals in a million deals in a million grams of cocaine. The sweet-sour stink of tobacco and marijuana smoke absorbed into the walls and the carpets. The aroma that brought back a million memories, a million conversations, a million hopes and desires; the belief that maybe this time the meaning of life *would* be found at the end of a straw.

And flash: There was Joules himself to welcome you in his navy-blue blazer and cravat. Genuine Eurotrash, a true aristocrat whose father had left Joules his title and his pile of debts.

And flash: There was SondraBeth, her voice husky with drink and drugs and cigarettes, whispering, "Joules, it's me," on one of those long nights back when they were best friends. Back when they were called "PandaBeth." Back when a legendary singer played with his band, and PandaBeth sang backup. Back when PandaBeth held court at the corner stall in the bathroom. Back when PandaBeth got free drinks from the mob guys like Freddie the Rat, who kept Joules supplied with everything from bar napkins to coke. Back when PandaBeth might do or say anything; when there was a razor-sharp edge to their riotous shenanigans; when Pandy would wake with a gluey disgust the next afternoon, racked with guilt over conduct that was clearly drunk and disorderly in the mind of any sane person.

She'd be wincing in shame—"I can't believe I can't believe"— and SondraBeth would be laughing, her hair a matted tangle, her outfit from the night before torn and covered with mysterious stains, as if at some point during the evening she literally had rolled in a gutter.

And SondraBeth would say, "Guilt is a useless emotion. The past is the past, even if it was just an hour ago..."

Pandy shook her head and laughed. Compared to those nights at Joules, last evening's party was nothing. *And thank God for that*, she thought as she headed to the park.

⚭

The park was in full bloom, the leaves on the trees a brilliant emerald green. Daffodils blared their yellow trumpets from neat beds. Spring had passed into summer while she'd been holed up, wrestling with that bear of a book. There had been so many times when she'd wanted to give up. But she'd kept going, fueled by a fierce desire to prove herself. The fact that she was battling Jonny as well had only made her determination greater.

Pandy took a seat on a freshly painted bench near the dog run, inhaling the pungent odor of earth mixed with a vague chemical smell that rose from the dusty air. She absentmindedly rubbed the bump on the back of her head and heard a groan of frustration.

She looked up to see a young woman struggling to maneuver a baby stroller and a small dog through the gate. Pandy sprang up to help her, holding open the gate so they could pass.

"Thank you," the woman said gratefully. Pandy smiled and went back to her bench, recalling the tired cliché that finishing a book was like giving birth. It wasn't wrong: A friend had described the pain of childbirth as so intense as to be incomprehensible, during which there was no normal interpretation of time. What felt like ten minutes was actually ten hours. And then once you had the baby in your arms, you immediately forgot all about the agonizing process.

It was the same with writing a book. Once the manuscript was finished—once you'd printed the page with those final words, *The End*—you forgot about the struggle and felt only joy. Unlike a baby, however, your opinion about your "child" wasn't the one that really mattered.

She wrinkled her nose, trying to prevent her sunglasses from falling off the tip. It wasn't until the publisher had called your agent—or better, you—to say how much they loved the book and how brilliant it was and what a genius you were, that you could finally relax. Only then could you take a breath, knowing that soon they'd be processing your check.

The check that would then allow you to pay your asshole of an ex-husband to get out of your life forever.

Best not to think about it, Pandy reminded herself as she picked up her cell phone.

Immediately it began flashing and buzzing as a series of alerts and notifications rolled across the screen like a swarm of locusts.

She tapped on the pretty white bird in the blue square.

She had five hundred new Twitter followers. That was odd. It usually took weeks to accumulate that many new fans. She checked her notifications and suddenly understood why Henry had been in such a panic. There were dozens of tweets and retweets about her new, un-Monica novel—including several requests for interviews, along with encouraging missives from fans. "Can't wait to bite into yur new book like a big crunchy chocolate chip cookie," StripeSavage had tweeted.

What? Oh no, Pandy thought. It wasn't that kind of book. Should she inform StripeSavage? Or leave it alone? She hoped StripeSavage wouldn't be disappointed.

"Wonder what SondraBeth Schnowzer will think?" another fan had inquired.

To which Pandy was tempted to reply: *No need to worry about SondraBeth Schnowzer*. This was true. According to Google, Sondra-Beth was worth eighty million dollars. This Pandy believed, despite the fact that according to Google, she *herself* was worth the astronomical sum of forty million—when in fact, the truth was at least one decimal point away. This hadn't stopped Jonny from trying to use this erroneous information against her at the beginning of their divorce, however.

"She's worth forty million!" Jonny had screamed.

"There is no evidence of this money. There is no record of it in bank statements, tax returns, or payment stubs," Hiram replied.

"*It's on the internet,*" Jonny had retorted.

Pandy shook her head in disgust.

She looked down at her phone and tapped in her usual response regarding SondraBeth: "Luv Her!" followed by three sparkling emoji hearts in Day-Glo colors.

She moved on to her texts. Several friends had sent photos from the party; there were group shots, and one of Pandy lying on the floor with her legs up in the air. There was a close-up of Suzette's enormous ring, which she in turn had posted to Instalife. The photo had more than ten thousand likes.

And finally, a text from Henry: "Where are you? Call me."

Pandy rolled her eyes. She was still feeling annoyed with Henry.

The first few notes of the theme song from the Monica movies suddenly began playing, indicating that she had an actual phone call. Expecting Henry, she was relieved to see it was Suzette.

"Honey, is that *you?*" Suzette screeched.

"Who else would it be?"

Pandy suddenly remembered Portia's phone. "I have Portia's phone," she announced.

"Good. You can bring it to the Pool Club."

Pandy looked at the time: ten fifteen. "Are you already there?" She paused, considered the implications, then added, "Please don't tell me you guys stayed up all night."

"We didn't."

"I was in bed by midnight!" Portia screamed in the background.

"The question is, who was in bed *with* you?" Suzette quipped. "Honey, come to the pool. Now. We've already ordered a bottle of champagne."

"I don't have my bathing suit," Pandy protested mildly.

"Then go buy one, silly," Suzette hooted and hung up.

Pandy was barely out of the store when all of a sudden, there it was, roped to the top of a long flatbed truck that was blocking the street: Monica's missing leg.

"Hey!" Pandy said, waving to the drivers. Two men in white coveralls had gotten out of the truck and were hoisting themselves onto the flatbed.

"What took you so long?" Pandy asked.

"Huh?" The older guy glared.

"Monica's leg. It's late."

"You one of them Monica fans?" the older guy said, sounding slightly annoyed, as if he'd had his fill of Monica fans already.

"I am indeed," Pandy said proudly. She considered telling them who she was—Monica's creator—but decided against it. They probably wouldn't believe her anyway. Instead, she said crisply, "Carry on, men," as if she were a queen, and they were her loyal subjects.

The knot of pain in her solar plexus eased. Pandy expelled a great huff of air as she remembered that she didn't need Monica anymore. She had her new book. Her entire future was riding on it and she hoped that, just like Monica, it would be a hit.

Meaning everything was going to be just fine, she thought happily as she raised her hand to hail a taxi.

Chapter Three

T HE POOL CLUB was located on the rooftop of a recently reno-
vated flophouse hotel on the West Side Highway. Smiling to
herself as she rode up in the sleek elevator, Pandy remembered when
she'd first come to the city and her sunbathing had taken place on
"Tar Beach"—the roof of her walk-up apartment building. Somehow,
during the two years in which she'd been working on The Book, these
pool clubs had sprung up like mushrooms all over lower Manhattan.

The club was already packed when Pandy arrived just after
eleven—so much so that an unsuspecting tourist might think she
was in another city, possibly Miami or Las Vegas.

"There you are!" Portia exclaimed as Pandy wove through lounge
chairs covered with towels, bits of clothing, suntan lotion, and bags
spilling computers and magazines. And so many young people. The
girls in bikinis with flat stomachs and competitive breasts. The arro-
gant young men talking loudly on their devices, as if they were all so
very important.

"Here." Suzette picked up a pile of magazines from the chaise
next to her and motioned for Pandy to sit down.

Pandy eased herself onto the terry-cloth cover. She took off her
sunglasses and glowered at a skinny, hairy man with two doting
young women a few feet away. "Why are there so many people here?
It's Thursday; doesn't anyone have to work?"

"Thursday is the new Sunday." Suzette passed Pandy a handful of necklaces made of plastic beads in gold, purple, and green. "San Geronimo festival," she purred. "When I woke up this morning, my son had strung them all over the apartment."

"It's a celebration," Portia said, sitting up. She twisted around to remove a bottle from an ice bucket on a stand next to her. "Champagne?" she asked.

"Of course she wants champagne," Suzette said. "Look at her."

"I have your phone," Pandy said to Portia.

Portia pounced on it. "What about your agent?" she asked.

"My agent?" Pandy sputtered as she took a sip of the fizzy drink.

Suzette rolled her eyes and lay back. "All morning she's been talking about Henry. And you. 'Why doesn't Pandy date her agent? He's so cute,'" she said in a mimicking voice.

"Henry?" Pandy picked up several strands of beads and slung them around her neck.

"He's a real pretty boy. You have to admit that," Suzette said.

"When I saw you talking to him at the party, I said to Suzette, 'Those two look like they could go together.' You know?" Portia added.

"*Henry?*" Pandy screeched.

"He's gay," Suzette said. "Has to be."

Pandy reddened and shrugged.

"And besides, she's not going to date her agent," Suzette added dismissively. "No one dates their agent. It isn't done."

"I thought SondraBeth Schnowzer dated her agent. The guy with the funny name. PP?"

Pandy sat up. "He wasn't her agent," she muttered. "He was the head of the studio." Determined to get off the topic, Pandy turned to Portia. "How are you here in the middle of the day? I thought you had a job."

"I was let go." Portia shrugged.

Pandy gasped. "Again?"

"Again." Portia smiled.

"How much time off do you have this time?"

"A year. At full salary. I'll start looking for another job in nine months. In the meantime, I'm going to travel."

"So far she's only made it to the Pool Club, though," Suzette said.

"Hey, guys. If it weren't for you, I'd be in Rio right now." Portia giggled.

"Oh, please." Suzette rolled her eyes. "The South of France."

"Saint-Tropez is totally boring in June," Portia said dismissively.

"How about Switzerland?" Pandy asked.

Suzette stared at Pandy. "Who goes to Switzerland in the summer?"

"I do," Pandy replied, rubbing suntan lotion on her arms. "Or I want to, anyway. I went there once in July. For a wedding. We stayed in one of those castle hotels. And the beds—triple down pillows and comforters. Like sleeping on a cloud. And the mountains! I kept thinking I was in *The Sound of Music*. There was this piano player, and I started singing Burt Bacharach songs. Johnny Depp was there, and supposedly he was so horrified by my singing that he left."

"The room?" Portia asked.

"The *hotel*," Pandy said. "Supposedly he checked out that evening."

"What about your house in the country? Why don't you go there?" Suzette asked.

"*That* place?" Portia said with a grimace.

"Come on, Portia," Suzette said. "It's Pandy's family house. She grew up there."

"I don't mean to insult anyone's family, but that place is creepy. No cell service, no Wi-Fi, not even cable. And nothing to do. And all those spooky portraits of your ancestors..."

"Portia. *Please*," Suzette said sharply. She leaned back and closed her eyes. "In any case, I had a *great* time there. We dressed up in old clothes and played charades. And croquet. Remember?"

"Old-lady games." Portia sneered.

"What's the name of the town again?" Suzette asked in a polite tone intended to silence Portia.

"Wallis," Pandy said. "But it's not really a town. It's a hamlet."

"And isn't it someplace historic, like your family seat?" Suzette asked encouragingly.

"Hello? Her last name is Wallis, and she comes from Wallis. What do you think?" Portia yawned, bored with the discussion.

"*I've* got a family seat," Suzette cackled. "It's called my big fat juicy *ass*."

"Another bottle of champagne, ladies?" A harried young man in a white shirt and crisp khakis lifted the bottle and poured the last few drops into Pandy's glass.

"Thank you," Pandy said with excessive gratitude. She finished the glass and got up to change into her new bathing suit.

⌒

When she returned, Suzette and Portia were tearing through the pile of magazines. "Here," Portia said, handing Pandy the magazine *Connected*. SondraBeth Schnowzer was on the cover, dressed in sharp white jeans and towering platform shoes, her hand held up to her face as if to block the paparazzi.

"Trash. All trash," Portia added. She held up another magazine and shook it for emphasis. "I have to say, I do love reading my trash in an actual magazine, though, because then I can throw it out after I've read it. I can literally throw the trash into the trash, and that makes me feel good."

"Maybe you should get a job with the city. Picking up trash," Pandy murmured.

"What is up with this poor woman?" Suzette demanded, snatching up the tabloid with SondraBeth on the cover. "Why does everyone call her romantic poison? She's gorgeous. Why can't *she* find a man?"

"Doug Stone, remember?" Portia said. "I read that he dumped her right before the wedding. And when you've been rejected by one of the biggest movie stars in the world, there's nowhere to go but down." She chortled and turned to Pandy. "Didn't you date Doug Stone once?"

Pandy flushed. "Not really."

Suzette waved at the waiter. "That's right, you and SondraBeth used to be friends."

Pandy's hand shook slightly as she poured herself more champagne. "Sort of," she said vaguely.

"Doug Stone." Portia sighed. "And what about his third leg?" she asked wickedly.

"*What?*" Pandy laughed.

Suzette sighed. "She wants to know how big his cock was."

"You know, I honestly can't remember."

"Good girl." Suzette lifted the hand with the yellow diamond and patted Pandy's shoulder. "Don't kiss and tell. It's true for men and it's true for ladies, too." She looked sharply at Portia.

"I'm not the one who claims to be a lady." Portia laughed. Pawing through the pile of magazines, she shook her head. "Christ. Sondra-Beth Schnowzer is everywhere. Everyone *knows* she's Monica. You'd think she'd have enough with the endless publicity."

"*Pandy* is Monica. SondraBeth is a pale imitation. Although I have to say, she does look good," Suzette added, flipping through *Vogue*. She stopped at a photograph of SondraBeth and held up the magazine so they could all get a look.

SondraBeth was in a seemingly impossible position, half kneeling, her head ducked alluringly as her green-gold eyes twinkled at the camera. She was wearing a crystal-bejeweled catsuit, and there were sparkles in her hair. She looked like a gorgeous piece of jewelry.

Pandy couldn't tear her eyes away.

Portia snatched the magazine out of Suzette's hand. She looked from the image back to Pandy. "Well," she said triumphantly. "You were right. You're definitely not Monica anymore." A beat, then she added: "You need airbrushing!"

"Can I get you ladies something else?" the waiter asked.

"How about some airbrushing?" Pandy asked, as Suzette and Portia screamed with laughter.

⤳

It was past two when Pandy picked up her phone and saw that she had three texts from Henry. She held up her phone so that it glinted annoyingly in the sun. "My goddamned agent," she said loudly. "Why won't he leave me alone? Doesn't he know I'm *busy*?" Without bothering to read his texts, she wrote, "Yes?"

Henry immediately replied: "Have you read my texts?"

"No," Pandy sent back. She put the phone down and lay on her stomach, resting her chin over the edge of the chaise. She closed her eyes and allowed her thoughts to wander. The mechanical bleeps of other people's devices turned into the sound of crickets; the hum of conversation became the lazy buzz of bees. As she was drifting off, a vision came to her of a smattering of reddish freckles marching like ants across the bridge of a turned-up nose.

She lifted her head with a start. The freckles belonged to Sondra-Beth Schnowzer.

She tried to push the image away, but it was too late. SondraBeth was lifting her gold aviator sunglasses, lowering her gaze to focus on Pandy. And there it was: the smile.

Monica's smile.

Pandy shook it off and sat up sharply, her sudden movement causing the world to spin ever so slightly.

She glanced around. The pool was quieter now, the heat having driven away all but the die-hard sunbathers. Suzette was sleeping. Portia was at the bar, in the middle of an animated conversation with someone Pandy couldn't see.

Suzette's reading glasses had fallen into the space between the two chaises. Pandy picked them up, put them on, and read Henry's texts.

"Call me."

"Where are you?"

"We need to talk."

And finally, "Where and when can I meet you?"

Pandy shot up. She was suddenly wide awake and stone-cold sober. Henry had *had word*. That was why he wanted to see her.

Her hand trembled as she tapped in his number, walking briskly to the shaded awning at the far end of the pool. The phone rang and rang, until it went to voice mail.

"Damn," Pandy said aloud, hanging up. She immediately sent him a text: "Do they LOVE it?"

"Where are you?" came the reply.

"Pool Club." She was tempted to add, "Answer your damn phone," but couldn't be bothered to tap in all the letters.

"On my way!" Henry wrote back. He'd added an exclamation point; that meant it had to be good news. Suddenly feeling giddy with anticipation, Pandy hurried toward her friends, waving her phone in the air.

The club was filling up again, this time with mothers and children who must have just gotten out of school. Pandy skipped around a toddler wearing so many flotation devices, he looked like a small astronaut.

"Henry's coming!" Pandy said to Suzette, who was now awake due to the screams of the many children who appeared to have taken over the club. "I think it's good news."

Unable to contain her excitement, Pandy began pacing, circling around the nest of deck chairs as she mumbled incoherently. "After all this...I can't believe...*Ohmigod.*" Overcome, she had to sit down.

"Honey, are you all right?" Suzette asked.

Pandy put her hand to her chest. She wished she could explain to her friends how important this was, but she knew they'd never quite understand. She vigorously nodded her head instead. "Where *is* Henry?" she cried out impatiently.

"Henry's coming?" Portia asked, strolling over with a drink in a plastic martini glass sloshing onto her hand. She looked at Pandy assessingly. "Doll, you're all sweaty. Why don't you take a dip in the pool?"

"Don't want *Henry* to see you all sweaty like that," Suzette joked pointedly.

"Maybe I will," Pandy replied, realizing that the excitement of her impending triumph had indeed made her perspire. She grabbed her cell phone and walked to the edge of the water. Unable to bear the suspense any longer, she tapped in Henry's number.

He picked up after the first ring.

"Henry," she said eagerly. "They *do* love it, right?"

"We'll talk about it when I get there."

"When you *get here*? What's that supposed to—"

What felt like a giant sponge slammed into the back of Pandy's knees. She took a step forward, her arm swinging upward to correct her balance. The toddler in the astronaut suit rolled past her and splashed into the water as Pandy watched her cell phone plunge into the pool.

As her phone hit the bottom, the realization that Henry had bad news dropped like a brick into the pit of her stomach. Motioning wildly, she stumbled back to her friends. "I need a phone!" she screamed.

"Why?" Portia asked.

"I need to call Henry."

"I thought he was coming *here*."

"I need to know. Before he gets here." Pandy choked out the words, reaching for Portia's phone and dialing.

And then the sun must have gone behind a cloud because a shadow began to darken Pandy's vision. A wave of nausea caused her knees to buckle as she dropped onto the chaise and Portia's phone fell out of her hand.

"Sweetheart. Are you all right?" Portia bleated as Suzette picked up the phone and held it to her ear.

"Henry?" Suzette asked.

She looked over at Pandy and nodded. "I see. Yes, I will," she said briskly, and hung up.

"*Whadhesay?*" Pandy screamed.

"He'll be here any minute. He's hired a car."

"A car?" Pandy asked in confusion. Black and white squares began pinwheeling in front of her.

"I don't understand. What just happened?" Portia demanded, talking over Pandy as if she weren't there.

"I think her book just got rejected," Suzette said in a stage whisper.

"What?" Portia gasped.

"Her new book," Suzette hissed. She made a slicing motion across her throat.

"Ohmigod," Portia screeched. She paused, then added, "Is that *all?*"

"What do you mean, is that all? Isn't that *enough?*" Suzette's voice rose.

Portia shrugged. "I thought maybe Jonny wasn't going to give her a divorce. Or he wanted even more money."

Pandy struggled to sit up. "He's giving me the divorce!" she shouted.

"Well, then. There's no problem, is there?" Portia continued blithely as she draped a towel over Pandy's shoulders. "If it's only the book—you can just write another one, right?"

"Oh, good. Here comes Henry now," Suzette exclaimed with false cheer.

"Pandy?" Henry asked, leaning over her.

Pandy was now frozen in place, her hands soldered over her eyes.

Henry peeled back her little finger and then slowly pulled her hands away.

"The book?" Pandy gasped.

"I'm sorry," Henry said, as Pandy's throat closed in terror.

∽

It took a stiff slug of vodka before Pandy was able to speak again.

She swayed on her barstool, alternating between sobs of grief and valiant reassurances. "It doesn't matter!" "It's all for a reason!" And most of all: "It will all be *all right*." In between these statements were longer moments that felt like some sort of punctuation that would never end: a very long dash, for instance.

She wanted to crawl into the deepest and darkest of holes; to tunnel lower than she'd ever gone before—where, naturally, she would curl up and die.

But as the people around her wouldn't allow that sort of behavior, Pandy went along with their plan:

Yes, she did agree that it might be a good time to take a couple of days off.

Yes, she had been holed up for a very long time.

And yes! She *had* been dealing with a huge amount of stress. Particularly with Jonny. People couldn't believe what he had put her through.

So, yes, she would go to her house in Wallis to recover, especially after these last few months in New York. Henry would join her tomorrow morning *at the latest*.

And so she went willingly into the town car Henry had hired to transport her to Wallis.

She didn't ask Henry how or why all this seemed to have been arranged in advance, being too confused to ask questions.

"Goodbye!" She waved out the window to her friends.

She raised the window and leaned back against the seat. The blast of cold air-conditioning in the car met the day's heat, and a cloud of steam began to form. Pointing her finger, Pandy briefly held it to her temple. Then she lowered it. Aiming it at the foggy glass window instead, she wrote two words:

HELP ME.

Rescued by Suzette, her device came back to life and began vibrating, releasing those buoyant Monica notes into the air like happy-face balloons. Pandy put her hand over the machine to silence it. She looked past the angry line of cars on the other side of the West Side Highway. A sleek white boat, sails trimming the wind, raced across the spackled surface of the river.

For a moment, she pretended she was in Miami.

The fantasy was short-lived. Looming ahead was a second Monica billboard—another reminder of her disastrous failure.

What no one knew was that without her new book, she couldn't pay Jonny.

Meaning she, PJ Wallis, was finished. Monica had won after all.

And then she frowned. Like the first billboard, this Monica also lacked her leg.

Despite the circumstances, the sight caused her to convulse with mad, wild laughter. She suddenly had a crazy urge to call SondraBeth Schnowzer to tell her that Monica's leg was still missing.

SondraBeth was the only person in the world who would have appreciated the hilarity of the situation.

The car rounded the corner, and Pandy took one last look at the billboard as her laughter turned to tears. And for the first time in a long time, Pandy remembered how different it had once been, nine years ago when it was new and fresh and exciting...

And how it had all started when she'd said those four fateful words:

"I want that girl."

PART TWO

Chapter Four

I want *that* girl!" Pandy had exclaimed.

She was in Los Angeles, sitting in the backseat of a town car, when she'd seen the billboard. It was hanging over Sunset right near the Chateau Marmont, where Pandy was headed after another dispiriting round of auditions for the lead role of Monica.

All of a sudden, the car had come around the curve after Doheny, and there she was: masses of hair fluttering behind her like the American flag; shining green-gold eyes looking out over the flattened landscape of the universe. In her arms was a golden wolf pup.

Then the tagline: WHAT IF DOGS CAN SEE STARS, TOO?

"Her!" she screamed, pointing up at the billboard as they passed by. "That girl."

The driver laughed. "She's a model."

"So what?"

Handsome and genial, the driver laughed again. "It's the same old story. Everyone who comes to Hollywood has the same dream. They think they're going to discover some unknown talent. Some gorgeous model who turns out to be a movie star in disguise."

Pandy smiled. "And isn't that your story, too? A movie star in a gorgeous male model's body?"

The driver glanced back at her in his rearview mirror. He laughed toothily, appreciating her humor. "I guess you could say that."

For a second she could see The Girl's reflection in his mirrored shades.

And then she was gone, and in the next moment, the driver was pulling into the driveway of the Chateau Marmont.

The studio had flown Pandy out to Los Angeles for the casting of Monica, and Pandy had been given the star treatment: a car and driver at her disposal, and bungalow 1 at the Chateau. Bungalow 1 may or may not have been the room where John Belushi died; the staff was vague on the particulars. In any case, the large, dark apartment was enormous. It included two bedrooms, a kitchen, and a terrace shielded from the pool by a chain-link fence woven with thick greenery. Not surprisingly, given its history, there was something unsettling about the place. The first evening, sitting in the front room on the orange fuzzy-caterpillar couch, the TV an arm's length away, Pandy had thought, *You could go crazy here.*

Well, she wouldn't be the first, she thought now, getting out of the car and slotting her key into the private door that led to the pool and the bungalow. Throwing her stuff onto the caterpillar chaise, she rushed upstairs and flung open the windows, looking past the brown haze on the horizon and trying not to think about the word "no." A word that was to showbiz as smog was to LA.

"No."

"No?"

"Noooo."

And, of course:

"NO!"

That last "no" had been hers. Delivered just that afternoon at the end of another fruitless casting session, when the studio people tried to convince her to let Lala Grinada play Monica. Lala had the limpest blond hair Pandy had ever seen, and she looked like someone who would starve herself under the slightest bit of pressure. And she was British.

No, Pandy thought. Lala Grinada was not going to play Monica. She leaned out the window and, by craning her head sharply to the left, discovered that she could just catch a glimpse of The Girl on the billboard.

And then, as if it were a sign from the Hollywood gods themselves, the buzzer rang and Pandy rushed downstairs, breathlessly opening the door to discover a waiter holding a tray with a bottle of champagne. Propped against the glittering condensation on the silver ice bucket was a gray envelope bearing the name *PJ Wallis*. Written in block letters and underlined twice.

Pandy shook off the droplets and ripped open the envelope. Inside was a single heavy card, on which a note was written in the same block lettering: *Hope you've enjoyed your stay in LA so far. Looking forward to our meeting tomorrow!* It was signed with two letters: PP.

Peter Pepper, the head of the studio that was making *Monica*.

Who calls himself PP—Pee-Pee? Pandy wondered as she slid the letter back into the envelope.

PP, she knew, wanted to talk about casting.

This was good. She wanted to talk about casting, too.

The part of Monica had been offered to several well-known actresses, all of whom had turned it down for various reasons. One claimed she didn't understand the character. Another was worried that Monica wasn't likable. Yet another insisted she couldn't use bad language, take drugs, or be rejected by a man on-screen.

No actress who was any good wanted to play Monica. And the ones who wanted to play her weren't good enough.

Pandy picked up the phone. "Can I have two vodka cranberries with ice and a bacon cheeseburger, medium rare?"

"Just one person," she clarified. Then: "*One* person. *Two* drinks. I'm thirsty."

Pandy put the phone down.

"I need that girl," she said aloud.

⌒

The next morning, before the meeting with PP, Pandy risked her life crossing Sunset to get to the newsstand across from the Chateau. The road forked oddly, and anything in the intersection was potential roadkill. Pandy darted, stopped, darted. She imagined herself as John Belushi in *Animal House*.

She bought a pile of magazines and two packs of cigarettes, just in case.

⌒

"I hear you haven't liked anyone so far," PP said, leaning back in his conference room chair.

PP was a squarish man with a squarish head and smooth dark hair that resembled the sort of plastic coif favored by action figures. He had thick, blocky thighs that strained against the fine fabric of his black suit pants. He always sat with his legs apart.

"If you're referring to Lala Grinada, you're right," Pandy said boldly.

PP—Pee-Pee—scanned the faces around the conference table, taking his time to pause at each one before he said, "Lala Grinada would never be right for this. Whose bad idea was that?" He tilted back in his chair.

"The agency," someone said.

"Actually, there *is* someone I'd like to see," Pandy interjected. "She looks right for the part, anyway."

"Looks are something," agreed one of the other executives—a second- or third-in-command, Pandy guessed. "Who is it?"

"Her." Pandy laid out the array of magazines, turning to the pages that featured The Girl in a variety of ads—lingerie, fine jewelry, and perfume.

"*Her?*" someone asked incredulously.

"Is she the one with the—"

"The name? Yes. That ridiculous name that no one can remember."

"SondraBeth Schnowzer."

"How would that look in the titles?"

"Terrible."

"What kind of name is that, anyway?"

"Austrian, maybe. Like Schwarzenegger."

"*Schnowzer*," someone said in Arnold Schwarzenegger's voice.

There was benign laughter around the table.

"Sorry, darling," someone said to Pandy.

"Hold on." PP raised his hands from behind his head as his chair's front wheels dropped to the floor. His dark eyes caught Pandy's.

"It's not that crazy," PP said, addressing the room. "I happen to know she's taking acting classes. Roger?"

Roger quickly looked down at his BlackBerry and tapped out a message. In a moment there was a light rap and the blond wood door opened a crack.

"Come in," PP answered.

"I just wanted to give this to Roger," a young woman said, making herself invisible as she handed Roger a piece of paper.

Roger scanned the document, then raised his sparse eyebrows as if impressed. "She has some real credits here. Mostly indie movies, but lots of them."

"Indie movies. Meaning she's a relative unknown. I love that." PP pushed back from the table and stood up. "Interesting. Okay. Go," he said, shooing them all away with his fingers.

Pandy lingered a moment as the others left the room.

"Thanks," she said.

"You are just terrific!" PP suddenly exploded, and before Pandy had a chance to react, he embraced her in a bear hug.

Roger was waiting for her on the other side of the door.

"That was it," he said, walking her down the hall. "You got the hug."

"The hug?" Pandy asked, clutching the magazines to her chest.

"It's a sign. PP likes you."

"And that means what, exactly?"

"You've got a meeting with SondraBeth Schnowzer."

Pandy stopped and stared at him as he paused to hold open the heavy glass doors that led to the elevator bank.

"I don't even know what that means."

"You'll meet her, get to know her a little. If you still think she's right, PP will make sure she gets an audition."

"Wow," Pandy said. "That's it? It's that easy?"

"Hollywood is an easy place when you know the right people."

"Great!" Pandy enthused. "So when can I meet her?"

"Right now," Roger said, pressing the button for the elevator. "The car will take you to a salon near the Chateau. SondraBeth will be there. She wants to get her hair done or something."

A disturbing thought occurred to Pandy. "Is she high-maintenance?"

Roger shrugged and gave an exaggerated smirk. And in that moment, Pandy's heart sank. She suddenly understood that this so-called meeting with SondraBeth Schnowzer was merely an indulgence, the studio's way of making the author of the book feel special. When the meeting led nowhere—as they apparently suspected it would—the studio would go back to doing whatever it was they planned to do from the beginning. They would do it with impunity, and they wouldn't think twice about doing it without her.

As Pandy got into the elevator, she decided that wasn't going to happen.

The salon was in a small shopping center on Sunset, a few blocks from the hotel. When the car pulled up, Pandy spotted SondraBeth on the sidewalk, head bent over cupped hands.

She was lighting a cigarette.

She was wearing a fringed suede jacket that looked expensive, possibly Ralph Lauren.

She had on a pair of men's pea-green trousers. She'd rolled the waist down to reveal the silver-gray lining and the tops of her hip bones.

As Pandy got out of the car, SondraBeth glanced over hopefully. She was still looking hopeful as she took in Pandy's appearance: her long, swinging hair, stylishly short yellow skirt, and fancy black-and-white patent leather heels. A front tooth pulled back the edge of SondraBeth's lower lip as a look of dismay crossed her face. It was quickly replaced with a grin. "Hey," SondraBeth said, as if she, too, were in on the joke. "I'll bet you can't even get me this job." She tossed her head as if it didn't matter.

Pandy laughed. "I'll bet I can."

SondraBeth got the cigarette lit. She exhaled a stream of smoke without taking those topaz-green eyes off Pandy. She shrugged. "If you can't, it's not your fault. I deal with this bullshit every day."

"Listen," Pandy said quickly. "I hate salons—and my hotel's right up the street." Sensing a skittishness on the part of The Girl, she tried to make the invitation sound casual. "I've got a bottle of champagne in the fridge."

She needn't have worried. At the word "champagne," Sondra-Beth suddenly relaxed, dropping her cigarette and grinding it under a gray-and-white snakeskin cowboy boot.

"Now, that sounds like a plan," SondraBeth replied eagerly. "Champagne. It's the best offer I've had all day."

"I'm at the Chateau."

SondraBeth smirked. "I figured."

"Bungalow One," Pandy added.

She got back into her car. When she went to close the door, her hands were shaking.

❦

"D'you mind if I wash my face?" SondraBeth asked as she entered the bungalow a few minutes later.

"Not at all." Pandy went into the hallway that led to the kitchen and opened the door to the powder room. "In here."

"I just want to wash off my makeup." SondraBeth stepped inside the bathroom.

"No problem." Pandy smiled broadly as if to reassure her. "I'll open the champagne. PP sent the bottle last night."

"Why doesn't that surprise me?" SondraBeth stuck her head out, emitted a loud "HA!" and slammed the door shut behind her.

Pandy went into the kitchen. She took PP's bottle from the refrigerator and carried it and two glasses out to the terrace, placing them on a filigreed metal table with an umbrella poking out of the top.

"Hey!" SondraBeth reappeared, rubbing her face with a hand towel. She walked toward Pandy, a ray of sunlight illuminating the reddish freckles marching across the bridge of her nose like ants. "Sorry for using the bathroom. It's just that I didn't get a chance to take my makeup off." She laughed and carelessly dropped the towel onto an empty seat. "I left a shoot early so I could get to meet you."

"Oh." This, Pandy wasn't expecting. "You didn't have to do that."

"Oh, yes I did." SondraBeth raised her glass of champagne. "To meeting you. Fuck Hollywood."

Pandy laughed and sat down. "Is it really that bad?"

SondraBeth hooted, plopping into the chair next to Pandy and resting her boots on the table. "It's just like in the movies," she said with a sneer.

"How do you know PP, anyway?" Pandy asked casually.

"You mean…" SondraBeth leaned back in her chair, and suddenly she *was* PP, right down to the way he yawned ever so slightly before he dropped his arms from behind his head.

"You mean *that* PP?" she asked.

"How do you do that?" Pandy cooed with appropriate awe.

SondraBeth shrugged. "I can imitate anyone. Always could, ever since I was a kid. When you grow up on a cattle ranch in Montana—" She broke off and chuckled, waggling her fingers at Pandy. "For a while, I actually wanted to be a stand-up comic. Like Ellen. Can you believe it?" She raised her eyebrows, as if this idea was now impossible to contemplate. "But then I discovered it's a helluva lot easier to stand in front of a camera, where all anyone wants you to do is look 'purty.' Besides, the first thing you learn as a woman when you come to Hollywood is that you've got to choose: pretty or funny. Because no one will let you be both."

"Wow," Pandy said.

"I *know*," SondraBeth replied, lifting one leg and tugging on the heel of her cowboy boot. "As a matter of fact, when my agent told me that PP himself had suggested the meeting, I almost said no. I mean, why bother? Lemme put it this way—every woman under a certain age in Hollywood knows PP. You could say he's 'dated' a few friends of mine. But when my agent told me I was meeting *you*, that changed everything."

She yanked off the boot and expertly tossed it through the open door and right into the kitchen sink. "I was on the girls' basketball team. And the baseball team. I probably would have been on the football team if they would've let me."

"You don't say," Pandy replied admiringly. It was no wonder, she decided, that SondraBeth was having a hard time in Hollywood. It was difficult to reconcile this gorgeous creature with the tomboy attitude.

"Anyway," SondraBeth continued, taking off her other boot. "I didn't mean to imply that PP is a *total* asshole. Unlike most of these guys in LA. At least he's interested in making projects that are good.

At least he doesn't have to wake up in the morning and say to some-one, 'Today you are playing a vampire.'"

Pandy laughed. "So did you sleep with him or not? And if you did, how was he?"

SondraBeth howled as she tossed her other boot. "D'you think I'd be sitting here if I *had* slept with him? 'Cause he's one of those guys who only cares about the chase. That's why I wasn't going to bother to come. But when I found out it was about Monica—" She suddenly jumped up, hurried into the apartment, and returned carrying a bat-tered copy of *Monica*. "When I told my friend Allie I was meeting you, she freaked out. She drove all the way to the shoot to get me your book; said if I didn't get you to sign it, she'd never talk to me again."

"No danger of that." Pandy held out her hand for the book. "Of course I'll sign it."

"Damn," SondraBeth said, shaking her empty cigarette box. "I'm outta smokes."

"There's a brand-new pack in the kitchen." Pandy opened the dog-eared paperback and flipped through the pages. She noted that several passages were underlined. She looked back at SondraBeth, who was leaning into the refrigerator, assessing the contents.

"What's your friend's name again?" Pandy called out.

"Oh." SondraBeth stood up. "You don't have to make it out to her. Just sign it."

"Sure." Pandy smiled, guessing the book actually belonged to SondraBeth.

SondraBeth returned with two lit cigarettes, and handed one to Pandy.

"How would you play me, anyway?" Pandy asked, leaning back on one elbow as she raised the cigarette to her mouth. She took a puff, imagining herself as Spielberg.

"*You?*" SondraBeth asked. "PJ Wallis-you, or Monica-you?"

"I'm not sure." Pandy blew the smoke out in a plume.

"You're easy," SondraBeth said, springing to her feet. Jutting out her head and adopting Pandy's slump—a result of all those hours hunched over a computer—she began waving her cigarette. "Now look here, PP," she said, in a close approximation of Pandy's voice. "I've had enough of you and your Hollywood bullshit. From now on, I'm in charge. And I'm telling you, I want SondraBeth Schnowzer!"

And then the pièce de résistance: She stomped her foot.

"Oooooh." Pandy put her hands over her face and groaned in mock horror. "Do I really look like that?"

SondraBeth sat down and contorted herself into a pretzel. "It's all about posture," she said, fluttering her right arm like a wing.

"How would you play Monica, then?"

SondraBeth lifted her head and suddenly, there it was: the smile. The delighted grin that made you momentarily forget the frustrations of your own life; made you want to be—or at least be *with*—this beautiful, happy creature instead.

"I've got a great idea." SondraBeth pounded the table in glee. "Let's have a party."

And then, like the legions of guests before them, Pandy and SondraBeth went a little crazy.

Leaving the hotel, SondraBeth nearly crashed her car in the intersection; when Pandy pointed to the Liquor Locker half a block away, SondraBeth made an illegal U-turn that left them both hysterical with relieved laughter. Then, when they got back to the Chateau and opened the trunk, they were even more hysterical about the amount of alcohol they'd bought. This led to the inevitable conclusion that they must invite everyone they knew in LA to drink it.

For Pandy, this meant mostly displaced New Yorkers: writers working for comedians, sexy magazine girls in the midst of creating "an LA office," and a couple of disgruntled literary writers who were determined to show New York, mostly by drinking too much, that they didn't give a shit about it. They all came, along with Sondra-

Beth's friends: two bona fide up-and-coming movie stars, a hot young director, more models and actors, a musician who insisted on driving his motorcycle into the suite, and a very tall transvestite. And then, like those brave marines, they kept on coming: more showbiz folks who were staying in the hotel, a few acquaintances from New York who happened to be in LA, and several film executives who had heard about the party and decided to stop by.

At some point, Pandy remembered SondraBeth coming toward her with PP himself in tow. "Here's Pandy," she said. And with a glance back at PP, she hissed delightedly, "For a minute, he thought I was *you*."

Pandy woke up the next morning dramatically hung over. Her contact lenses were glued to her eyeballs; she had to feel around for the saline solution and pour half the bottle into her eyes before she could see. Once she could, she was relieved to discover that the bedding, including the duvet and the six down pillows, was mostly untouched. At first she was annoyed—apparently no one had been interested in her enough to at least *try* to get her into bed. Then a freight train came roaring into the tunnel that was her head.

When the train passed, she shook her head and heard music softly wafting up the stairs. The buzzer rang, and a voice called out, "Who ordered the poached eggs?"

Grabbing a robe from the bathroom, Pandy proceeded cautiously down the stairs.

"There you are," SondraBeth said, coming out of the kitchen. "Your poached eggs have arrived. I guess you must have ordered them last night."

Pandy stared at her blankly, unable to process what she was seeing. SondraBeth was wearing one of her dresses, which was incomprehensible, as she had to be at least two sizes larger than Pandy. Nevertheless, she'd somehow managed to squeeze herself into Pandy's best dress, a one-of-a-kind piece that Pandy had bought at an exclusive sample sale to which only ten women had been invited. The seams under the arms were straining against the silk fabric in an effort to contain SondraBeth's breasts.

"Hope you don't mind," SondraBeth said, giving Pandy a brilliant smile. "I crashed in the second bedroom. Didn't want to drive. That was one helluva party, sista."

"Yes, it certainly was," Pandy said carefully, eyeing her dress.

"Want some coffee?" SondraBeth raised her arm to remove a mug from an upper shelf. Terrified the seam would rip, Pandy quickly brushed past her to grab the cup.

SondraBeth poured out coffee, and then, barely able to contain her excitement, motioned Pandy into the front room. "Want to see something crazy?" she asked, pointing at the fuzzy caterpillar couch. "Look at *that*."

Pandy immediately forgot all about her dress.

Lying facedown was a youngish man, tanned and shirtless, a flop of dark brown hair with blond roots brushing his shoulder. Pandy inhaled sharply.

"Doug Stone." SondraBeth giggled. "Now *there's* a guy who really knows how to live up to his name. On the other hand, he's gorgeous, so who cares?"

Pandy took a step closer. "He's *so* gorgeous, I can barely stand to look at him." She sighed longingly.

SondraBeth cocked her head in surprise. "You certainly looked at him plenty last night."

"I did?"

"You were making out with him. For, like, an hour. Don't you remember?"

Pandy thought back through the hazy snippets she could recall. "No."

"How could you forget a thing like that?" SondraBeth scolded. "In any case, I wouldn't get too upset about it. He probably doesn't remember, either."

"Thanks a lot," Pandy groaned. She took another look at Doug Stone and scratched her ear. "Do you think room service knows how to remove a body?"

SondraBeth laughed. "I'd try housekeeping instead."

∞

The next day, SondraBeth auditioned for the part of Monica in front of several people from the studio, including PP and Roger.

Pandy didn't go. She was nervous for SondraBeth, but mostly, she was embarrassed. During the full day it had taken her to recover, Pandy realized that no doubt everyone else would turn out to be right, and SondraBeth wouldn't be able to act at all. And then PP would be annoyed with her for wasting his time, and SondraBeth would be devastated. Pandy would have to deal with that startled, hopeless, beaten-down expression she saw on the faces of all the actresses who'd auditioned and knew they weren't getting the part. Pandy would have to walk SondraBeth to the door, where they would say their goodbyes and never see each other again.

And that would be that. Recovering from the party and its aftermath—four hours of housekeeping's cleaning the room, Doug Stone's insistence on staying for breakfast and ordering enough room service for three people, SondraBeth asking if she could borrow Pandy's dress for the audition, and Pandy having to come up with an excuse as to why she couldn't—had left her feeling slightly unhinged. As if she'd inadvertently stumbled onto the set of someone else's porn movie.

But maybe that was just an excuse for her own nerves.

At three o'clock, her phone bleated. It was Roger calling to let her know that SondraBeth had aced the audition, and that PP himself would be calling shortly. "She did great," Roger informed her. "She *was* Monica—or rather, PJ Wallis. It was uncanny. She was exactly like *you*."

Two long minutes passed before the phone rang again.

"PP for PJ Wallis, please," the hushed girl-woman voice said as PP himself came on the line.

"Congratulations," he said briskly, as if he barely had time for the call. "I'll see you and SondraBeth tomorrow for lunch. Jessica," he added to his assistant, "make the arrangements."

Pandy hung up and sank to her knees in triumph.

She had won.

☾

She and SondraBeth had a stiff, civilized lunch with PP on the terrace under the pink-and-white striped awnings at the Hotel Bel-Air. Pandy admired the swans, and everyone behaved like adults. Pandy limited herself to one glass of champagne, and SondraBeth didn't drink at all.

One month later, when SondraBeth Schnowzer moved to New York City, Pandy welcomed her real, live Monica with open arms.

Chapter Five

THAT FIRST summer, Pandy and SondraBeth were inseparable. *Monica* was in preproduction, and Pandy was consulted on locations and costumes and a variety of surprising details she'd never considered—but mostly she was tasked with instructing SondraBeth in the ways of becoming herself, and therefore Monica.

And so the transformation began: SondraBeth's hair was colored to match Pandy's by the very same stylist who did Pandy's hair; she was given replicas of Pandy's jewelry; she was even instructed to buy the exact same shoes that Pandy wore, in order to learn how to walk in them.

And because pink champagne was Pandy's, and therefore Monica's, favorite drink, it had to become SondraBeth's as well. Along with Pandy's social life. And so wherever Pandy went, SondraBeth went, too. This meant going to Joules almost every night, and to basically every other kind of social event imaginable, including the Polo in Bridgehampton, where SondraBeth eagerly stomped the divots and acquired a bevy of handsome new polo-player friends.

In general, SondraBeth was wonderfully game. She'd call Pandy into her room to solicit her opinion on what to wear, and would listen with great interest to Pandy's precise briefings on who would be at what event and how they fit into the social strata, as if they were colored data points on a graph.

Unlike Pandy herself, however, back then, SondraBeth never wanted to stay Monica for long.

"I'm a country girl," she'd say, scrubbing off her makeup with soap and changing into the loose, baggy clothing she favored when she didn't have to be "on." "I grew up helping the vet pull calves out of some cow's butt. I've seen it all, sista, and let me tell you, it's not all pretty." And then she'd give Pandy a shit-eating grin, and in a voice reminiscent of Glinda the Good Witch in *The Wizard of Oz*, she would add, "Not like here. Not like in *Monica Land*."

Pandy had to laugh. SondraBeth wasn't far wrong—and instead of the yellow brick road, they had miles of sidewalks, filled with glittering displays of the most glamorous life New York City had to offer.

Besides her hardscrabble background, Pandy discovered a few more things about her real-life Monica. Interestingly, these were the kinds of things that Monica herself never would have experienced firsthand.

Such as: SondraBeth had dated a heroin addict. Her most recent ex, she explained, was a well-known actor with a nasty habit on the side. "I thought he was the love of my life, but then I found out he loved his heroin more than he loved me. You know your life is pretty bad when you can't even compete with a bag of smack."

Pandy laughed appreciatively. Encouraged, SondraBeth continued. "He said, 'I love you, babe, but I love my horsie more.' That's what he called it: 'my horsie.' And even then, I didn't want to leave him. That's how stupid I was. But my agent and manager said I had to cut all ties." She shrugged; despite claiming she would never be a slave to the business, it seemed her agent and her manager wielded more power than most people's parents. "They told me to stay out of LA for a while. Take something in New York. That's why I was so desperate to play Monica."

"I thought you were desperate to play Monica because of me," Pandy replied, feeling surprisingly hurt.

"Of *course* I wanted to play Monica because of you," SondraBeth quickly countered, slinging her arm over Pandy's shoulder. "But you already know that, Peege. Monica is about you and me. Not some stupid guy."

This had made Pandy laugh. Because no matter how hard SondraBeth tried to ignore men, they simply could not tear their eyes away from her.

Pandy had had plenty of experience with the kind of electrical sexual attraction that women of great beauty exerted on men; a few of these great beauties were her closest friends. She had seen, all too often, how even the most accomplished and intelligent man could be easily reduced to his base animal desires when presented with a gorgeous woman—not to mention the self-serving fantasy that accompanied the prospect of sex. But even the seductive arts of a great beauty paled in comparison to what SondraBeth had. Her physical perfection was coupled with enormous charisma: she un-self-consciously managed to be wildly flirtatious while still remaining "one of the guys." Pandy figured it must be due to some kind of sur-vival mechanism. After all, unlike her own, the success or failure of SondraBeth's career rested in the hands of men like PP.

"Who needs a man, anyway?" SondraBeth had nevertheless de-clared. "It's not like we don't have plenty of fun without them."

This, Pandy did agree with. They *did* have plenty of fun. Too much fun in the eyes of some, as she would soon discover.

∞

"Hey, hey, hey." It was a Thursday afternoon in late July, hot as hell. Coming through the phone line, SondraBeth's husky voice sent prickles of electricity down Pandy's spine. "Whatcha doin', sista?"

"I'm bored as hell, sista," Pandy replied with giggle.

"Let's get out of Dodge."

"Yeah?"

"Yeah."

"How?" Pandy asked. "You wrangle some poor man's limo?"

"Betta, Peege." They'd spent enough time together to develop their own silly secret lingo. "I got wheels."

"Pick me up."

"You got it, baby."

Half an hour later, there was a terrific honking on the street outside Pandy's building. She leaned out the window to see SondraBeth getting out of a small, shiny black car, waving like a game show contestant.

Pandy grabbed her overnight bag and ran downstairs.

"What the hell?" she asked breathlessly, staring in awe at the brand-new car. It was only a Volkswagen Jetta, but to Pandy, who'd never owned a car, it might as well have been a Bentley.

"How'd you get it?"

SondraBeth tapped the palm of one hand with the back of the other. "Cold hard cash. I went to the dealership on Fifty-Seventh Street and bought this baby right off the floor. Thanks to *you*, baby." She pointed at Pandy. "I just got my first check."

"Nice."

"Get in." SondraBeth opened the passenger door for Pandy. "Inhale that new car smell." SondraBeth got behind the wheel, adjusting the mirrors.

"Where are we headed?" Pandy asked.

"I'm sick of the Hamptons. Too many goddamned journalists, even on the beach. How about Martha's Vineyard?"

"The Vineyard?" Pandy shrieked. "But it's a five-hour drive to the ferry."

"So?"

"Five hours in a *car*?"

"That's nothing. Back in Montana, you have to drive five hours to get to a supermarket." SondraBeth expertly steered the car into a tiny opening between a bus and a van. "Besides, it might be a good idea if we're not seen together in public for a couple of days."

"Are you breaking up with me?" Pandy chortled.

"Hardly." SondraBeth reached into the backseat and dropped the *New York Post* onto Pandy's lap. In the top corner was a blurry color photograph of Pandy, mouth wide open as she screamed into a mike. PANDABETH STRIKES AGAIN, read the caption.

"So?" Pandy said, pleased she'd made the cover.

"So read the story," SondraBeth said ominously. "PP certainly did."

"PP?" Pandy asked, aghast, as she quickly flipped the grimy pages to Page Six.

"The devilish duo known as PandaBeth caused Panda-monium at Joules on Tuesday night when they took to the stage to belt out their own rendition of 'I Kissed a Girl,'" Pandy read aloud. She scanned the rest of the story, emitted a short, unimpressed laugh, and tossed the paper onto the backseat. "That's nothing."

"Of course it's nothing. But..." SondraBeth frowned.

"What?" Pandy demanded.

SondraBeth shrugged. "It's just that I got a call from my agent. According to him, PP says you're in the papers too much. And not in a good way."

"Me?" Pandy laughed, outraged. "What about *you?*"

"I'm not as famous as you are, Peege. Anyway," she continued, honking her horn at a pedestrian trying to cross against the light, "don't get huffy. He's mad at me, too."

"About what?" Pandy said, outraged.

"About my sticky fingers."

"I see," Pandy replied knowingly as she leaned back and crossed her arms. She was all too familiar with SondraBeth's habit of picking up things that didn't belong to her, with the sort of careless impunity that implied she simply didn't know better.

"Come on, Peege," SondraBeth whined. "You know how it is. I borrowed from the wardrobe department a couple of times. I *have* to. Everyone expects me to look a certain way, but no one seems to understand that I can't actually *afford* to look that way. And, okay, maybe the clothes didn't come back perfect. But it's not my fault if I fall down every now and again. I've never had to walk in high heels on a goddamned sidewalk before." She swerved sharply to avoid hitting a taxi that had suddenly stopped to disgorge a passenger.

"Fuck PP. He's toast!" Pandy declared, slamming her hand on the dashboard for emphasis. "How dare a man who calls himself Pee-Pee tell *us* what to do?"

They laughed the whole way through the long, long drive up the coast, stopping for fried clams and Bloody Marys, screaming profanities out the windows at other drivers—"Asshat!" "Ass*wipe*!"—and even talking their way out of a speeding ticket.

They were drunk by the time they got on the ferry, and drunker and high when they got off. In the middle of the ferry ride, Sondra-Beth had pulled Pandy into the stinking stall in the ladies' room. SondraBeth shoved her hand down her bra and pulled out a small envelope of cocaine. "Stole it from Joules himself the other night," she said, handing Pandy the package and a set of keys. "It's melting...it's melting...," she opined, like the Wicked Witch of the West.

"It's your goddamned body heat," Pandy said, dipping the key into the powder and taking a hit. "You're just toooooooooo hot!"

"And don't I know it."

Full of themselves, they strolled through the packs of tourists in the lounge. It was their first time together away from the axis of LA and New York, and Pandy discovered yet another thing about SondraBeth: She had a disconcerting way of getting friendly with strangers. Which she immediately began doing the moment they entered the bar at the front of the ferry.

"Hello," she said brightly to the bartender as she plopped onto a stool. "What's your name?"

"Huh?" The bartender's head jerked up.

"I'm SondraBeth," she said, leaning over the counter. "And this," she added with a flourish, "is PJ Wallis."

The bartender, an old guy with a creased face who looked like he couldn't deal with one more drunk tourist, took a good look at SondraBeth. He wiped his hands on a cloth and suddenly beamed, causing the skin on his face to shatter into a million wrinkles.

"You don't say," he said, glancing quickly at Pandy and back to SondraBeth.

"PJ *Wallis*," SondraBeth repeated. When the bartender only cocked his head in inquiry, she hissed, "She's *famous*."

Before Pandy could intervene, SondraBeth was telling the bartender—along with several other passengers, all of whom were men—about how Pandy had "discovered" her in a hair salon in LA and had brought her to New York to be the star of the movie version of *Monica*.

∞

They got the last room at one of the big inns on the bay in Edgartown.

They spent the first night holed up in their room, sprawled on the king-sized bed, ordering vodka cranberries from the curious and yet seemingly amused staff. As the TV blared in the background, they snorted up the rest of the first gram, and then another that Sondra-Beth had hidden in her suitcase. "Did I ever tell you the story about the Little Chicken Ranch?" SondraBeth asked.

"No," Pandy said, laughing. She figured SondraBeth was talking nonsense.

"I'm serious. And you can't ever tell *anyone*. It could ruin my career."

"I promise," Pandy said.

"Well." SondraBeth took a deep breath, got off the bed, and pulled back the curtain. The view was of the Dumpsters behind the kitchen, which was why the room had been available. "Remember how I told you I grew up on a cattle ranch? Well, I *did*, but I ran away when I was sixteen."

"You did?" Pandy asked in awe. She'd never met anyone who had actually run away from home before.

"I *had* to," SondraBeth said, nodding as she tipped more powder onto the top of the shiny wooden bureau. "Once my boobs came in—well, let's just say those ranch hands got a little too grabby." She looked at the coke, then picked up a cigarette instead. "My father didn't do a thing—he'd always said he wished I'd been a boy—and my mother..." SondraBeth paused as she lit up the cigarette. "She was basically checked out." She inhaled deeply and passed the cigarette over to Pandy. "So I split," she said as she exhaled. "I'd heard about this place where they'd help you—but they were Jesus freaks, so I went and worked at this strip club called the Little Chicken Ranch instead."

"What? You ran away *and* you were a stripper?"

SondraBeth looked back at the line of coke. "Hello? That's what usually happens to runaway girls. They become strippers. Or worse."

"Oh, jeez," Pandy said as she picked up the straw, trying to digest this information. "I'm *sorry*," she added, wiping the sticky residue from beneath her nostrils.

"Best way to make money in a pinch," SondraBeth said, leaning over to take another line. "But it gave me an advantage, that's for sure. It made me realize how incredibly stupid men are. They're worse than animals—most animals have more respect for each other than most men have for women. But what the fuck, right? I didn't make the world; I just have to live in it. And then I got lucky—some guy saw me and said I should be a model. But the fact is, if I had to sell my body to survive, I would," she said fiercely, handing Pandy the straw.

And suddenly, Pandy understood. SondraBeth was an angry girl, too.

"That fucking sucks," she declared.

"Hey." SondraBeth shrugged. "I survived. So that was my childhood. What about yours?"

"Mine?" Pandy laughed. "It was terrible. My sister and I were the cootie queens of the school."

"You?" SondraBeth shook her head. "No way."

"We were pretty isolated. I never even went to see a movie in a movie theater until I was sixteen. Before that, I thought most movies were like those old black-and-white films on TV."

"Christ," SondraBeth said. "Where the hell did you grow up?"

"In Connecticut." Pandy smiled viciously. "In the smallest town on the planet. Called..." She hesitated. "Wallis."

SondraBeth's eyes bugged out of her head. "You've got a *town* named after you, sista?"

Pandy waved this away. "It's hardly a town. More of a village. My great-great-great-something founded it back in the early 1700s. And then they just stayed there."

"What about your parents?"

"They died in a car crash when I was twenty. So I'm kind of an orphan."

"What about your sister?"

Pandy hesitated. SondraBeth had just revealed one of her deepest secrets; for the first time in her life, Pandy was tempted to disclose her own.

Except it wasn't her secret to reveal. "She lives in Amsterdam," Pandy said quickly. "I haven't seen her for a while."

"Why on earth would anyone live in Amsterdam, except for the pot?"

"I guess she likes it there." Pandy's voice sounded unintentionally forlorn.

"Oh, Peege! I'm sorry," SondraBeth exclaimed. She got on her hands and knees and crawled across the bed toward Pandy. She flung her arms open and pulled Pandy's head to her chest, patting her on the back. "Don't be sad. From now on, *I'll* be your sister."

And she had been. For a while, anyway. But what SondraBeth didn't know was that even sisters didn't last forever.

CHAPTER SIX

Looking back on it, Pandy realized that she, too, should have known better. She should have understood the dangers of being so close with SondraBeth, and how the success of Monica would inevitably drive them apart. But she'd never suspected that a man—Doug Stone—would end up being the lever, inserting himself into their friendship like a wedge.

And she certainly should have known better about Doug.

But once again, when it came to romance, hope trumped common sense.

Three years had passed since that raucous party at the Chateau Marmont where SondraBeth claimed Pandy had made out with Doug in a drunken moment that Pandy still couldn't remember.

During those three years, Doug had been proclaimed the next big thing. Named one of *People* magazine's Sexiest Men Alive—which in turn landed him on the cover of *Vanity Fair*—he was now a genuine movie star. During a cold, blustery February, while Pandy was celebrating the success of another Monica book and the second Monica movie was in production, Doug Stone arrived in New York.

Pandy was seated at one of the coveted front tables at Joules when Doug came in with a posse that included a director and a womanizing television star. They were shown to the next table. Doug recognized Pandy; it wasn't long before one table joined the other and Pandy found herself next to Doug, reminiscing.

They laughed about the crazy party in her suite at the Chateau. Pandy admitted that she didn't remember kissing him, but would never forget how he'd ordered and eaten three breakfasts from room service. "I had the munchies," he said, pulling her chair closer.

He was even better-looking than she remembered.

Thanks to his success, Doug had mastered a star's ability to ingest the light in the room and reflect it outward, creating an irresistible magnetism. And yet he still maintained a semblance of what he must have been before he became an actor: the easygoing, beloved star quarterback of the high school football team, who assumed that life, having gone his way so far, would most likely continue on this track. Pandy wondered if his relaxed self-confidence came from knowing that he never had to work at attracting the opposite sex; never had to worry about being accepted or liked the way regular people did. His spectacular good looks granted him freedom from the concerns that most people deemed shallow but nevertheless had to deal with on a daily basis.

They had an immediate and easy intimacy that Pandy suspected he had with any woman on whom he focused his attentions. Nevertheless, that night, fate conspired against reason when a terrific clap of thunder followed by torrential rains trapped them inside the club. Joules locked the doors, turned up the music, and out came the pot and cocaine. At some point in the next twenty-four hours, Doug went home with her. Despite his condition, he made love in a passionate and expert fashion that was almost too good to be true. Pandy suspected that his performance was just that—a performance—and one he probably couldn't maintain.

But he did maintain it, for the next ten days, anyway. Ten days in which they blissfully hung out in Pandy's brand-new loft on Mercer Street, bought with her *Monica* earnings. It was mostly devoid of furniture, but that didn't matter. They drank, had all kinds of sex, ordered takeout, watched bad movies, and had more sex.

Conversation, Pandy had to admit, was minimal. Which was why she kept reminding herself that it was nothing more than a fling. But once again, as had happened so many times before, her entreaties to herself not to get too emotionally involved were useless against the power of her romantic fantasies. And so, unable to say no to what looked, smelled, and actually felt like love according to all those fairy tales, she allowed herself to fall in love with him—just a little bit, she cautioned herself, the same way most women promised themselves to have only one bite of chocolate.

But Pandy was never good with the one-bite theory, and before she knew it, she was sliding into that delicious time warp where everything is heightened, and everything the beloved says is brilliant, important, and meaningful.

Just like chocolate.

Or worse, she thought, recalling SondraBeth's old boyfriend, *like heroin.*

Then all of a sudden the ten days were gone, and Doug was scheduled to fly to Yugoslavia, where he would be shooting an action-adventure film. When he finally checked his schedule, he realized that he was already a day late.

There wasn't much that could be done about that, so Doug figured if he was going to be one day late, he might as well make it two or three.

This theory didn't technically make sense, but because Pandy wanted Doug to stay another night, she extolled the wisdom of his thinking.

With Doug's departure looming, they decided they should try to see SondraBeth Schnowzer before he left town.

Since the success of the first Monica movie, SondraBeth had become less and less available. There were times when she had to take a seven a.m. flight to LA, do a round of talk shows, and then take the red-eye back to New York, where she was driven straight to the set for another ten hours of shooting.

Due to her hectic schedule, SondraBeth hadn't been able to meet up with Pandy and Doug. But according to the location information that Pandy was sent every day, SondraBeth was back in the city and shooting *Monica*.

They decided to surprise her on the set.

The company was in Central Park, next to the sailboat pond. Half a dozen trailers were parked on a side street; inside the park were more trailers, the ubiquitous thick cables anchored to the ground with blue tape. A few dozen Monica fans were lurking, seeking autographs, some with their signature pink plastic champagne glasses strapped to their heads in honor of Monica.

Doug took her hand and squeezed it. "Just think, babe, all this is because of you. Because of something you *wrote*." Pandy squeezed his hand back. One of the things she'd learned about Doug was that he was in awe of her ability to write; he was genuinely impressed by a person who could conjure up stories from out of nowhere. It was nice to be with a man who at least had a passing familiarity with what she did.

She brushed off the compliment. "It takes a lot of people, really. I could never do what they do."

"They wouldn't *be* here if it wasn't for you," he insisted.

They discovered SondraBeth in "video village," located under a large black awning shielding a nest of directors' chairs and television monitors. She was seated in the least accessible chair at the end of the third row, staring perplexedly at a small pamphlet of "sides"—her scenes and dialogue for the day. Pandy squeezed past assorted producers and crew to get to her. "Hi!" she exclaimed.

"Ohmigod. *Hi!*" SondraBeth squealed. As soon as she saw Pandy, her demeanor changed; she became animated and gabby. Pandy jokingly called her "Talky Monica," thanks to her propensity to talk, talk, talk, going on and on about anything that was new and hot, like she was at a never-ending cocktail party. Pandy suspected she was modeling her behavior on Pandy herself, who was known about town as a real gadfly.

"Oh, Peege, I miss you," SondraBeth said, pulling her close for an embrace. Then, catching Doug's eye over the top of Pandy's head, she flung open her arms, and in a moment of Monica silliness, rushed Doug and jumped into his arms.

"Doug!" she screamed.

"Hey there." Doug laughed.

"Ohmigod. You guys look so cute together," SondraBeth said, bouncing out of his arms and smiling at the two of them. "I hope Peege is taking good care of you."

"Peege?" Doug cocked his head in confusion.

"Never mind," SondraBeth went on gaily. She slung her arm around Pandy's shoulder. "Peege rules this town. We both do. What do we say when things get bad?" She looked to Pandy. In unison, they pumped their arms and shouted, "PandaBeth!" Followed by the requisite bout of raucous laughter.

The script girl looked over, glared, and shushed them.

"Oops." SondraBeth put her finger to her lips. Lowering her voice, she said, "We've been so bad, the head of the studio, Peter Pepper, actually called me and told me to tone it down."

Doug crossed his arms and nodded. "That's impressive."

"Monica?" A woman holding powder and a makeup brush was suddenly in SondraBeth's face. "We're shooting in five."

SondraBeth obediently lifted her head to allow the woman to powder her face; when the woman held up a lipstick, she stretched open her mouth. And then, like the animals she'd grown up with, she was led away.

Pandy and Doug settled into two directors' chairs and leaned forward to watch SondraBeth on the monitor.

The director shouted, "Action," and then, after several seconds in which SondraBeth didn't appear, shouted, "Cut."

SondraBeth came storming back to video village, looked at Pandy and Doug snuggling next to each other, and with a grim expression, reached over to her chair and grabbed her sides.

"What's wrong?" Pandy asked, jumping up from her seat.

"It's this stupid line." SondraBeth thrust the pamphlet at Pandy and pointed to the offending sentence. "It just isn't something Monica would say. Would *you* ever say that?"

The line was funny, and was indeed the kind of thing Pandy might have said. But it was SondraBeth who had to speak the line, so she agreed. "You're right. It does sound awkward."

SondraBeth frowned. "And out of character."

"What are you going to do?" Pandy asked, as if the question were of dire importance.

"What *can* I do?" SondraBeth sighed dramatically, expressing a depth of sorrow that seemed better suited to the death of a child than a silly line in a movie comedy. "The director hates me," she hissed.

"No one could hate you," Pandy insisted, but SondraBeth shook her head. In a loud whisper, she informed Pandy that she'd worked with this director before and had had a "bad" experience; Pandy didn't press her for the particulars. "He refuses to listen to me," she added woefully. "But maybe you could talk to him?"

"Me?" Pandy said. "I wouldn't know what to say."

"Of course you do. You're a writer; knowing what to say is your job. And you're the author. He *has* to listen to you."

Pandy knew this wasn't true. As soon as the actual production had begun on the first Monica movie, the producers had made it clear they were no longer interested in Pandy's opinions. Pandy had greeted this fact with relief—there were too many personalities and nasty little high school–type conflicts on the set to make being involved appealing. But SondraBeth was staring at her with those sorrowful green eyes, and once again, Pandy found herself wanting to shield her from anything even mildly uncomfortable. "I'll see what I can do," she said fiercely.

She found the director talking about lighting with the first AD. It felt like a reasonable moment to bring up SondraBeth's concerns, but the director merely laughed.

"She sent you to do her bidding?"

"Of course not," Pandy said, as if the possibility were unthinkable.

The director wasn't buying it. "The line isn't going to change, and she knows it." He looked at Pandy kindly and smiled. "You haven't had much experience with actors, have you?"

"I've had my share."

"Then you know they're like six-year-olds," the director proclaimed matter-of-factly. "They always want to change their lines, and you have to tell them no. Give in, and before you know it, they want to change *every* line. And then the whole day is ruined.

"And, Pandy?" the director added. "Don't let her manipulate you. The moment she thinks she has the upper hand, she'll lose all respect for you."

Pandy gave him a curt nod and turned away, angered again on SondraBeth's behalf. SondraBeth wasn't a *child*, and neither was she.

She returned to find SondraBeth and Doug Stone in a surprisingly intimate tête-à-tête. Like a curtain, SondraBeth's hair had fallen across the side of her face, separating her and Doug from the rest of the crowd. Doug was nodding, as if SondraBeth had just imparted a fascinating piece of information. Pandy paused, trying to assess the significance of their conversation. And then came a jealous, irrational thought: *SondraBeth is trying to steal Doug!*

In the next second, they broke apart and SondraBeth beckoned to Pandy eagerly. "What did he say?"

Pandy made a disgusted face. "The director? You were right. He *is* an asshole. He said all actors were like six-year-olds."

SondraBeth blanched. Her demeanor suddenly changed and she became frosty. "Why did you even tell me that?"

"I'm sorry. I didn't think—" Pandy broke off as Doug stepped in.

"I'm sure she didn't mean it," he said. He and SondraBeth locked eyes and held each other's stare for several seconds; long enough for Pandy to wonder if they were engaging in some kind of *Star Trek* mind meld.

Pandy suddenly felt like she no longer existed.

SondraBeth blinked and once again, her mood inexplicably shifted. "Of course you didn't mean it, Peege," she said, her voice full of understanding. "How could you? I mean, how could you possibly know what it's like to be an actor?"

"She can't," Doug said fondly, reaching for Pandy's hand. "That's what's so great about her."

Pandy glanced up at Doug gratefully while SondraBeth looked on, a strange half smile frozen on her face.

"SondraBeth? They're ready for you." A PA appeared to lead SondraBeth away again.

"I love you. I'll call you," SondraBeth mouthed, raising her outstretched thumb to her ear.

Pandy blew a goodbye kiss, then fell back against Doug. "I didn't mean to make her upset. I swear."

"Forget about it," Doug said. "She's an actress. All actresses are unpredictable."

They were interrupted by one of the producers, who came over to say hello.

"You must be so thrilled about *Monica*. And the mayor," she gushed to Pandy.

Pandy shook her head and laughed, having no idea what the woman was talking about.

"The party the mayor's throwing in honor of *Monica?*"

Pandy's smile stiffened. "Oh, yes," she said quickly. "*That* party."

"What are you going to wear?"

Pandy's head was spinning. There was a party for *Monica?* Given by the mayor? And she hadn't been invited?

"Chanel is going to dress SondraBeth for the party. They should dress you, too," the woman continued blithely. "After all, you're the original Monica, right?"

Pandy's smile grew larger as she dipped her head in acquiescence.

"What the fuck?" she hissed to Doug as the woman walked off. "Let's go," she snapped.

"I don't get it," Doug drawled, dawdling behind her as she marched furiously ahead to the street. She looked back over her shoulder and sighed in annoyance. Reaching for her cell phone, she called Henry.

"Hello," Henry said brightly.

"Do you know anything about a party the mayor is throwing for *Monica?*"

Henry paused. "Actually, I don't," he said, sounding distracted.

"Well, apparently he is. And I haven't been invited!" Pandy's voice rose to a shriek.

"Why not?" Henry asked.

"You tell me," Pandy stormed. "Christ, Henry. This is the kind of thing you're supposed to know about."

"I thought parties were your department."

Pandy held her cell phone away from her ear; she was so enraged, she considered throwing the phone down and stomping on it. She took a deep breath. "Can you find out about it? Please? And call me back?"

"Hey," Doug said, catching up with her. "What's happening?"

"Nothing." Pandy turned on him, still angry. She willed herself to calm down. "I'm sorry. It has nothing to do with you. It's just that the mayor is throwing a party for *Monica*, and I haven't been invited."

"So?" Doug laughed.

His lack of understanding only fueled her anger.

"Forget about it," she snapped, wondering how this party was happening without her, and what it might possibly imply. "It's just that I created Monica. It's like you said; without me, there would be no Monica. But everyone seems to have conveniently forgotten this fact."

"How do you know they've forgotten?" Doug asked.

Pandy stopped and gaped at him. She inhaled sharply as the realization hit her. "They're trying to cut me out."

Doug raised his eyebrows. "You really think so?"

Pandy pounded her fist into her palm. "Of course they are. Because they think they don't need me anymore. They have Sondra-Beth Schnowzer. And she's the perfect Monica," she said sharply.

"Aw, come on," Doug said. "I'm sure it's not what you think."

"If it isn't, then why didn't SondraBeth tell me about it? A party with the mayor? It's not the kind of thing you forget about. And she tells me everything."

"I doubt that," Doug interjected.

"What do you mean?"

Doug shrugged. "She's an actress. I'm sure she doesn't tell *anyone* everything."

Pandy's eyes narrowed. "What were you talking about while I was off fighting with the director?"

Doug shrugged. "We were talking about Monica. And how much she loves playing her."

"Of course she does," Pandy hissed. She veered away and went to stand in front of a display of handbags in a designer shop window.

"Oh, I get it," Doug said, coming up behind her. "You're jealous."

Pandy grimaced and shook her head.

"You think she's taking away attention that belongs to you."

Pandy's phone rang: Henry. She hit ACCEPT and strode around the corner to take his call.

"Well?" she demanded.

"The party is for the film industry," Henry informed her.

"So?"

"It's for the film industry only. Some kind of celebration about Monica bringing the film industry to New York."

"But Monica didn't bring the film industry to New York," Pandy wailed in frustration. "And if it weren't for me—"

76

"Pigs would fly," Henry cut her off. "You need to stop behaving like this. It isn't attractive."

Pandy hung up. She saw Doug standing on the corner, watching her, his eyes going back and forth as if he was trying to make a decision.

She dropped her phone into her bag and strolled over. She sighed. "Henry says it's an industry party. For the film business."

Doug nodded.

"Well?" Pandy said.

"It's a fucky business, okay? A big fat fucky business. Where people get burned. Where people steal ideas and credit. Where they don't even pay you if they can get away with it."

"Okay. I get it," Pandy said miserably.

"Actually, I don't think you do." Doug looked bummed, as if Pandy had disappointed him. "This is the reason why I don't want to be with an actress. I don't want to deal with this shit day in and day out. You're a writer. I thought you were different."

Stunned, Pandy took a step back. Her chest felt swollen and achingly heavy, as if her heart were drowning in sorrow.

"I'm sorry, Doug. Please," she said plaintively. "I don't know what came over me."

She must have looked truly distressed, because Doug suddenly softened. "It's okay," he said, holding out his arms and pulling her close for a hug. "Let's forget about it, okay? I'm leaving soon anyway."

"Shhhh." Pandy put her finger to his lips.

Doug slung his arm over her shoulder. They strolled slowly down Fifth Avenue, shuffling their feet like the saddest old couple in the world.

They reached Rockefeller Center, where they stopped to watch the skaters.

"Want to go skating?" Doug asked.

"Sure," Pandy said with false enthusiasm.

She stared down at the awkward forms below. With a small sigh, she thought of how different they were from the perfect cast-iron figurines her family had placed under the Christmas tree when she was a kid. The skaters had been part of a traditional Christmas scene that included miniature houses and a church clustered around a reflective piece of old glass that formed a skating pond. She remembered how she and Hellenor had been fascinated by the "pond." The glass was more than a hundred years old and contained mercury, which their mother claimed could poison them if the mirror broke. Every year, she and Hellenor would hold their breath as their mother carefully unwrapped the ancient glass and gently placed it on its bed of white cotton batting under the tree.

Then they would all breathe a sigh of relief.

Hellenor said that if the mirror broke, they would have to use a speck of mercury to chase down the loose droplets. Mercury was magnetic; if they could herd the specks, they would miraculously join together, and then technically the mirror wouldn't be broken anymore.

Unlike what had happened to her family.

Pandy shuddered. She just couldn't lose SondraBeth, too.

∞

Doug left for Yugoslavia the next afternoon.

He promised to call, but as he stepped up into the white van waiting for him at the curb, Pandy sensed that he was beginning to morph into someone else—Doug Stone, movie star—and had already forgotten about her.

The van pulled away. Pandy walked beside it for a moment, willing Doug to catch her eye but getting only his profile. *I'm never going to see him again*, she thought as the van disappeared around the corner.

She went back up to her loft. The echoing space felt gray and cindery, as if she were trapped inside a cement block.

And at last, exhausted, frustrated, and miserably alone, she began to cry.

Two days later, when she was still dragging around in a funk—feeling "wounded," as she explained to Henry, who told her to buck up—she went out to buy the tabloids. There was a photograph of her and Doug in every one, taken by a sneaky paparazzo while they'd held hands strolling up Fifth Avenue.

They were smiling and laughing, staring into each other's eyes, entranced.

The photos must have been taken while they were on their way *to* the set. Back when they were still "happy."

DOUG STONE FINDS LOVE WITH THE CREATOR OF MONICA, read one caption, while another proclaimed they were "hot and heavy."

The words, all so untrue, were like shards of glass piercing her heart.

Pandy peered closely at the photographs, looking for clues to explain what had gone wrong, why the pictures and words showed one thing while the reality was so different. But no matter how hard she examined the photographs, she still felt like she was missing something.

Her own life, perhaps?

The next day, she called Henry. "I don't want to write another Monica book. I need to move on," she said bravely.

Henry told her to quit acting silly and reminded her that even without Pandy, Monica could go on for as long as she liked. Unless, he added jokingly, Pandy were to die. In which case, the rights would revert to Hellenor. And Hellenor, of course, was in Amsterdam.

∞

Two more weeks passed. Shooting for Monica wrapped, and Sondra-Beth went to Europe—"on business," she said, being uncharacteristically vague. Another month passed without a word from either her or Doug. Doug had mentioned stopping off in New York for a few days when he finished his movie, but when Pandy didn't hear from him, she figured he'd gone straight to LA. After all, it was only a fling. Why should she care?

And then SondraBeth called.

CHAPTER SEVEN

F<small>INALLY</small>, P<small>ANDY</small> thought, seeing SondraBeth's number at last. It was one of those blue Sunday evenings, one of those anxious nights in which the future looked inexplicably bleak, when it felt like nothing exciting or good would ever happen again.

"*Yarl?*" Pandy answered slowly, with one of their silly made-up expressions.

"Peege? It's *meeeeeeee*," SondraBeth squealed joyfully.

"Where have you been?" Pandy scolded, as if she couldn't live without her. "I've missed you."

"Me too. But now I'm back. How are *you*? You sound down."

"No. I'm just..." Pandy broke off. What was she? "Bored," she said.

"I am, too." SondraBeth spoke into the phone with a salty languor. "I'm so fucking bored."

"Where *are* you?" Pandy asked.

SondraBeth laughed, as if Pandy ought to know where she was. "I'm on 'the island.'"

"The island?" Pandy frowned. "What is that? Some kind of location?"

"Silly!" SondraBeth squealed. "I'm on a secret vacation. At that private island I told you about. In the Turks and Caicos? Where my ex-boyfriend and I used to rent a house?"

"Which one?" Pandy asked, rolling her eyes.

"You've got to come down and stay with me," SondraBeth insisted. Pandy could hear waves crashing in the background.

"Really?" Pandy got up and looked out the window. It was March, and the weather was depressing: blustery one minute, rainy the next. She didn't have anything on her schedule that couldn't be moved. The thought of that lusciously warm Caribbean air was suddenly irresistible—and so, too, was the prospect of seeing SondraBeth.

"I think I could come. But when?"

"Tomorrow! You don't have to stay long. Three days, maybe four."

"Tomorrow?" Pandy's heart sank. She looked around. "I can't get myself together by tomorrow."

"You don't understand," SondraBeth said, sounding like she was strangling a scream. "I can fly you back and forth by *private jet*."

"Are you *kidding*?" Pandy had to put her hand over her mouth to keep herself from screaming as well.

"No. I mean, yes. I'm serious. Gotta go. My assistant will call you in two seconds to make the arrangements."

Like clockwork, SondraBeth's new assistant, Molly, called right after SondraBeth hung up.

In a voice as natural and sweet as the hay in the heartland itself, Molly informed her that a car would be picking her up at nine the next morning to take her to Teterboro, New Jersey, where she would fly directly to the island by private jet. The whole trip, including the ride to the airport, would take a mere three hours. "You'll be there in time for lunch!" Molly exclaimed.

Bliss, Pandy thought, looking out at the rain.

She hung up the phone, happy again. *Thank God for Monica*, she thought. As she quickly began packing, she realized how foolish she'd been to get upset about that party. And how silly she was, telling Henry she wouldn't write another Monica book. What was she thinking? Monica *still* had her golden touch.

She could change rain into sunshine any old time.

∞

SondraBeth met Pandy's plane at the airstrip, waving madly from a golf cart while pointing to a colored drink in a plastic cup. "Cheers!" SondraBeth shouted over the noise of the jet's winding-down engines. She handed Pandy a cup. "The bartender here makes the best rum punch on the islands. It's a requirement!" She stomped on the gas and the cart took off with a jolt, spilling Pandy's drink down the front of her shirt.

"Oops!" SondraBeth screamed as they took off bouncing along a rutted dirt road.

Pandy laughed, guessing that this trip would probably end up like that crazy weekend in Martha's Vineyard.

The villa was right on the beach, on an isolated strip of land with views of the turquoise ocean stretching all the way to the horizon. A housekeeper took Pandy's bags to her room: king-sized bed, giant-screen TV, French doors leading out to her own private balcony. It was glorious.

SondraBeth hovered while Pandy unpacked, talking a mile a minute about how she'd gone to a spa in Switzerland and how Pandy should go, too. Pandy went into the bathroom to change into her bathing suit; when she came out, she found SondraBeth lounging by a small pool that was set into an incongruous patch of hardy green grass. SondraBeth had removed her blousy cover-up to reveal a string bikini. As Pandy went to lie down in the chaise next to her, she took a good look at SondraBeth and gasped.

"You've lost weight!" Pandy exclaimed.

"Can you tell?" SondraBeth asked proudly.

"You're so…skinny," Pandy said cautiously. She snuck another look at SondraBeth's slim physique and wondered if she'd

83

had something done to her thighs and stomach; liposuction perhaps.

"Come on, Peege," SondraBeth said lightly. "You'd weigh exactly the same if you were a couple of inches taller."

"You know that's not true—"

SondraBeth shot Pandy a warning look. "I have to be thin. To play Monica. It's part of the job. If I gain two pounds, the wardrobe people are all over me. They get really pissed off if they have to keep altering the clothes. They said I have to weigh myself every morning. If I gain a pound, it means I'm supposed to skip dinner."

"What?" Pandy screamed. "That's outrageous. This is Monica, not Dickens. Maybe I can call someone."

"Who?" SondraBeth grinned playfully. "PP? He's a man. All he cares about are the numbers. He's probably the one who came up with the idea."

"That's terrible, Squeege."

"That's the business." SondraBeth rolled onto her stomach, resting her chin on her hands. She turned her head and looked over at Pandy, her eyes a startling green. "Besides, it's not that bad. Not for me, anyhow. I'm like a racehorse; I like being in shape, and I like winning."

"Ha!" Pandy said.

"In any case, I'm not going to apologize for having a good body," SondraBeth continued, pulling herself forward and leaning over the edge of the chaise. She stared down into the turf. "People are always telling women to lose weight, and then when they do, other women attack them for it. It isn't fair."

SondraBeth picked at a short blade of grass. "This whole weight thing is like a conspiracy against women."

"Blah, blah, blah." Pandy made her fingers into a talking puppet shape, then made the puppet try to bite SondraBeth's nose.

SondraBeth swept this aside like an annoying fly. She rolled onto her back and gazed at a cloud. "Seriously, Peege. If every woman exercised, just a little, and ate healthy, there would be no need for diet products. And who do you think is getting rich from those diet products? *Men.*"

SondraBeth suddenly sat up. "Ohmigod. Did I tell you about *Doug Stone?*"

"What?" Pandy squeezed a tube of sunscreen too hard, causing a glob of lotion to shoot out and land on her thigh. "Did you see him? In Europe?"

"No. But somebody else did." SondraBeth's eyes narrowed. "You remember that girl? That *other* girl."

Pandy shook her head.

"You know, the actress? The one who wanted to play me? I mean, Monica. And then *I* got the part?"

"Lala Grinada?" Pandy gasped.

"That's the bitch. Well, she must really hate you, because guess who's been seen all over Paris with *Drug Stoner?*"

"Lala Grinada?"

"You got it, sista."

"Oh." Pandy listlessly rubbed the sun cream into her skin, trying to digest this information. She lay back and sighed. Doug had been too good to be true after all. "I guess that explains it, then. He's with Lala Grinada." She sighed dramatically and got up to pour herself another glass of rum punch from the pitcher in the refrigerator. "Meanwhile, I am once again alone. And fat. Because I was so upset when Drug Stoner dumped me, I ate ice cream with whipped cream five nights in a row. And that was after the pepperoni pizza!" she shouted through the kitchen island to SondraBeth.

"I hate her!" SondraBeth shouted back. "I hate her for what she's done to you."

"Her?" Pandy asked, strolling back outside. "What about *him?* He's the one who swore he'd never be with another actress again."

SondraBeth raised one eyebrow. "Obviously, he lied. Fucker." She held up her empty cup for a refill.

"Dickwad," Pandy seconded, taking the cup and returning to the kitchen for the pitcher. It felt good to swear; to be juvenile in the face of rejection. Indeed, it felt so good that she had to do it again. "Rotten rat bastard son of a pimp-nose!" she shouted.

"Ha! What is that?" SondraBeth called back.

"Joseph Heller. *Catch-22*. My sister and I memorized it when we were kids. I mean, come on!" Pandy poured more punch into SondraBeth's glass. She looked at the pitcher, thought, *Fuck it*, and brought the glass and the pitcher back to the terrace. "Lala Grinada? Pleeeeeze. She literally has three hairs on her head. And she's not even a good actress." Pandy put down the pitcher and took a sip of SondraBeth's drink before handing it over. "Even if she were okay, he still wouldn't respect her. He basically told me he couldn't stand to be around any actress."

"He said that?" SondraBeth's eyes widened as her expression froze.

"Oh, come on, Squeege. I'm sure he didn't mean *you*."

"I wouldn't care, except that you don't know what it's like. You really don't know."

"I'm sorry."

"You never even come to the set." SondraBeth sounded hurt. "I would think being the creator of Monica would be like being a parent. Going to the set would be like going to watch your kid's baseball game."

"Except that going to a baseball game isn't usually considered work."

"And writing is?" SondraBeth scoffed. "Of course, I understand that you have better things to do, but you never come at all."

"It makes me uncomfortable, okay?"

"But why?"

"It's all those people. 'People, touching other people. It's the creepiest thing in the world,'" Pandy sang out goofily.

SondraBeth pointed her finger. "Aha! I knew it! That's the

reason you never come to the set. You secretly want to be an actress."

"What?" Pandy laughed. Where the hell had SondraBeth gotten that idea?

"That little thing you just did. That is what people do when they think they can maybe act. They try it out."

"No," Pandy countered cautiously. "I only ever wanted to be a writer. I swear."

Even to her own ears, she didn't sound convincing, probably because SondraBeth was right: She *had* fantasized about acting when she was a kid. Who hadn't?

"I'll bet you practiced monologues. With your sister," SondraBeth posited cleverly.

"So?" Pandy said.

"So, I want to see. Show me your monologue."

"Now?"

SondraBeth parroted the island's pet refrain: "Do you have something better to do?"

Pandy scratched her arm. "You want me to perform? In front of you? I'd rather show you my vagina," she joked.

"Come on, Peege," SondraBeth wheedled.

Pandy sighed. SondraBeth knew her too well. Or at least knew her well enough to know that given the chance to show off, Pandy needed little encouragement.

"All right," Pandy said as she quickly cleared away some of the deck furniture to make a small stage.

Getting into the spirit of things, SondraBeth took a seat behind a table as if they were at an actual audition. "We'll pretend that you're the actress and I'm the writer." She cleared her throat and, squinting at an imaginary piece of paper, asked, "Pandemonia James Wallis?"

"I go by PJ," Pandy said.

"And what are you going to do for us today?" SondraBeth gave her the sort of fake smile Pandy had no doubt worn when she was auditioning actresses for Monica.

"Gwendolen's monologue from *The Importance of Being Earnest*," Pandy said.

SondraBeth shrieked with laughter. "That old thing? That's what every rookie chooses. Well, go ahead."

Pandy gave her a dirty look. She took a deep breath and began: "You have admired me? Yes, I am quite well aware of the fact. And I often wish that in public, at any rate, you had been more demonstrative. For me, you have always had an irresistible fascination—"

"Stop!" SondraBeth howled. "It's too awful. If you continue, I shall burst apart with laughter."

"I told you I couldn't act," Pandy grumbled good-naturedly.

"Oh, Peege." SondraBeth grinned. "You're hilarious. I've never seen anyone be so squishy and so elbow-y at the same time."

"And what, exactly, is that supposed to mean?"

"You keep wriggling around. Like a worm. Acting is all about being *still*."

Pandy awoke early the next morning to find that SondraBeth had already left the house. Pandy hadn't slept well, thanks to Doug Stone and Lala Grinada. She kept picturing them together, wondering what Lala had that she didn't.

Goddamned Squeege, she thought.

Wondering vaguely where SondraBeth had gone, Pandy made tea and perused a guidebook to the island's flora and fauna. There was a rare silver heron that could be found in one of the island's marshy coves just after sunrise.

Why not? Pandy thought, changing into a bathing suit. Why not chase down this elusive heron? After all, as SondraBeth kept pointing out last night before each shot of tequila, they didn't have anything better to do.

She winced slightly as she clapped a canvas safari hat onto her head. She picked up a towel from the floor, found her cell phone, and set off on the golf cart.

The air was warm but soothingly dry. The golf cart kicked up a small cloud of sparkly white dust on the pretty manicured roads made of ground shells. She passed several iguanas, the island's main residents, and a few wild chickens that had escaped from the workers who came to the island by small planes. The island felt blissfully deserted. This was twenty-first-century luxury, Pandy thought: no people.

She sped quietly past the airstrip and through a low, thick forest of scrub bushes and cacti, which she'd been cautioned not to attempt to cross on foot. The road curved along a point of land that sheltered a shallow inlet, where the rare heron could supposedly be found. Pandy parked the golf cart and made her way along a small path to the rocky beach. The vegetation was sparse, and she situated herself between two bushes to wait.

She heard a crisp snap, like laundry flapping in a breeze, and looked up to see two enormous herons navigating a landing in the shallow water in front of her. Pandy picked up her cell phone and took a few hasty shots. The birds stood stock-still in the water, their heads slightly cocked, waiting for the bonefish fry on which they survived. Finding the pickings slim, they began to move around the rocky point.

Determined to get a picture, Pandy crept along the path next to the shore. She peered through the tall grass and nearly gasped aloud. The herons weren't alone. Standing nude in the middle of the inlet, balanced on one leg, arms stretched overhead and palms together in a classic yoga pose, was SondraBeth. She was now so slim and her skin so white, Pandy at first mistook her for some kind of large, exotic bird and nearly dropped her phone in excitement. But birds didn't have mature female breasts.

Pandy let out a long, slow breath and began to creep closer.

SondraBeth continued to stare straight ahead, the pose rock-steady even as the herons began to approach. She was so still, the herons must have mistaken her for one of their own, for they hardly glanced in her direction. Moving one careful, silent inch at a time, Pandy slunk through the bushes until she was a mere twenty feet away.

Staring at SondraBeth, Pandy suddenly understood what her friend had meant when she said that acting was about being still. Pandy wondered how it must feel to be able to stand perfectly motionless like a statue; so much a part of nature that even nature took you for granted. She considered making her presence known, but then thought better of it. This was obviously one of SondraBeth's few private moments, and Pandy was encroaching. She'd back away slowly, and SondraBeth would never know she had been there. She'd file away the image as one of those unusual experiences that keep their power only when they remain secret.

She was about to sneak back to the golf cart when suddenly SondraBeth turned her head and stared straight at her. Embarrassed, Pandy froze. Had SondraBeth actually seen her, or had she merely sensed a presence?

"You look just like Margaret Mead," SondraBeth said.

Pandy stood up and laughed. "Did the hat give me away?"

SondraBeth dropped her pose and smiled. "Maybe." The herons, startled by the movement, raised their silvery wings and sped across the water like two small, shiny jets.

"Beautiful," Pandy murmured.

"Aren't they?" SondraBeth leaned over and splashed her face with water. She slicked back her hair and looked at Pandy. "Are you coming in? The water's fine."

"Sure," Pandy said in surprise. She removed her shorts and took a step toward the water. SondraBeth shook her head and laughed.

"You have to be naked, too. Otherwise it's not fair."

"Oh." Pandy considered her request. Normally, Pandy did not do naked, especially in front of other women. Even when she was a little girl, changing rooms had been a hurdle. She could never figure out how much nakedness was exhibitionist, and was torn between wanting to look around and wanting to act like it wasn't any big deal. She admired women who had mastered this issue, and longed to be like them, but an ingrained self-conscious embarrassment at her body's flaws always prevented her. SondraBeth was apparently free of such mundane concerns, but on the other hand, she actually did have a perfect body—or once had, anyway, before she became so thin. And she had certainly performed her share of sex scenes, albeit tasteful ones, in front of the camera. Pandy supposed that after a while you became desensitized, like all those topless sunbathers in France.

What the hell, she thought, unfastening her bikini top and sliding out of the bottom. She carefully folded the pieces into little squares and wrapped them and her phone in her shorts. A slight breeze tickled the fine hairs on her arms. Having made the decision to shed her clothing, she no longer had any reason not to own her nakedness. She strode confidently into the water.

The bottom was slightly squishy; she felt like she was walking in a bowl of oatmeal. Pandy laughed and raised her arms to balance. SondraBeth smiled approvingly. "Cool, isn't it?"

"Yes," Pandy said.

"You can walk for miles, and it doesn't get any deeper." She started splashing farther out.

"Amazing," Pandy murmured as she followed her.

"You're amazing, too," SondraBeth said. "Think about what you created. An entire world came out of your head. Think of all the people who benefited."

The sun and the warm air were like a dozy lullaby.

"I don't ever want you to think that I don't appreciate what you've done for me," SondraBeth said.

They were now so close that Pandy could imagine their breasts touching. She flushed at the thought. She took a step back, and

SondraBeth took a step forward. Pandy could feel SondraBeth's warm, salty breath on her lips. "Peege," she murmured softly, her eyes closing.

For one wild second, Pandy thought SondraBeth was going to kiss her. If she did...

But instead, SondraBeth's eyes popped open. A tiny reflection of the sun burned in each pupil, turning the irises iridescent green.

Then she blinked and laughed. "What in God's name are we going to do about *Doug Stone?*"

Chapter Eight

"Why do we have to *do anything* about Doug Stone?" Pandy grumbled a few minutes later, marching behind SondraBeth in the soft sand as they trooped back to the golf cart.

SondraBeth reached into the cart, felt for a bottle of water, and poured it down her throat. Scales of salt fell off her face as she tipped her head.

She wiped her mouth with the back of her hand. "Why shouldn't we?" she asked.

"I've been thinking about it," Pandy said, swinging into the driver's seat. "And I realized that I'm totally over Doug. While you were out there posing, I finally felt like I just didn't care."

SondraBeth paused to give Pandy a curious look. "Really?"

"Yeah." Pandy shrugged and turned on the ignition.

"That's too bad," SondraBeth said, sliding into the passenger seat. "I was thinking it might be fun to invite him to join us."

"Here?" Pandy gasped, looking over her shoulder as she backed the cart over a pile of broken shells.

"Why not? It might be fun."

"But I'm already having fun."

"You, PJ Wallis, are scared," SondraBeth said teasingly.

"Well, as you said, I am all squish and elbows," Pandy replied cheerfully.

The sun blazed through the windshield. "Whoa!" Pandy jerked the wheel to avoid an iguana the size of a large house cat.

"It's just too bad, is all. I'm sure if he knew you were interested—"

"He's with Lala Grinada, remember?"

"Oh, that. That means nothing." SondraBeth waved this away. "Besides, he might not still be with her."

Bouncing over the rutted track, Pandy remembered Doug braced above her. When she'd gripped his smooth, muscled arms, she'd noted, curiously, that his skin felt as soft as cashmere. In that moment, she'd told herself she must be the luckiest woman in the world. And in the next moment, she'd realized it couldn't last. It was just too perfect. Like a scene in a movie.

"Naw," Pandy said now, steering the cart up to the house. "I'm done." As she opened the door, the cold air-conditioning hit her like a slap. SondraBeth closed the door behind her. Pandy suddenly felt like she was being sealed inside a refrigerator. She walked across the polished living room floor to open the French doors. She inhaled the warm air and turned back into the room.

"The thing is, I had my fun with Doug," Pandy said. "I mean, I had sex with a movie star, right? That's not something that happens every day. On the other hand, it's never going to be my life. So why bother?"

"Oh, right." SondraBeth yawned pointedly. "I forgot that's all Doug is to you. An *actor*. A notch in your belt. He *is* a person, you know? But if you're really not interested..."

"It's not that. I mean, of course he's a person." Pandy sighed; she hoped SondraBeth wasn't going to get all huffy about being an actor again. She looked at her watch. "Do you think it's too early for a drink?"

"Probably," SondraBeth said. "I'm going to take a Jacuzzi." She went into her room and closed the door.

Pandy shook her head and went into her own room.

She sat on the bed and picked up the remote. Apparently it was siesta time, but Pandy wasn't tired. She got up, went out to the balcony, and looked at the ocean.

Suddenly bored, she marched across the living room and knocked on SondraBeth's door. "Squeege? Maybe you're right. Maybe we should call him. Just so we can make fun of the fact that he's with Lala."

SondraBeth yanked open the door and pulled Pandy into her room.

Frowning as if she were in some kind of agony, SondraBeth plopped down onto the bed. "I've been thinking, too. About this whole Doug Stone business. And I realized it's not really about him, or you. Or even you *and* him. It's about her, Lala Grinada. She's trying to fuck with me. She's trying to send me a message."

"She is?" Pandy asked.

"Yes. Don't you see it? She's sending me a message through you. And Doug."

"Hold on," Pandy said with a laugh. "How did I get involved in this? I don't know anything about a message."

"She hates you because you put the kibosh on her playing Monica. And now, she intends to get even. With both of us."

"By having sex with Doug?"

"She knows you and Doug were together. She knows you and I are best friends. And because of that, she knows that by hurting you, she's hurting me, too."

"I doubt she's smart enough to figure that out."

SondraBeth banged her hand on the pillow. "And by hurting us, she's hurting Monica."

"Oh, jeez." Pandy sighed. "Is this what you were thinking about when you were going all stork out there? Getting even with Lala Grinada? If that's the case, I'm definitely going to need that drink. Let's go to the club."

"Fine." SondraBeth swung her feet off the bed and wrapped a

sarong around her waist. "All I'm saying is that this isn't personal. It's *business*."

"Business." Pandy nodded dutifully.

SondraBeth lowered her gold Ray-Ban sunglasses, and giving Pandy her brilliant Monica smile, added, "*Monica* business."

∽

Arriving at the club, Pandy went directly to the bar, worried that the heat was somehow getting to SondraBeth. But as she took a seat and the bartender flipped a cocktail napkin in front of her, the world seemed to right itself on its axis.

"Hey," said the bartender.

"Hey, yourself," Pandy said.

"The usual? Rum punch?"

"Sure," Pandy said with a smile. She raised her glass. "To drinking your cares away," she added as the bartender replied with the island's mantra:

"You got something better to do?"

"Nope," Pandy said hopefully, glancing behind her for Sondra-Beth.

She saw several iguanas, but SondraBeth seemed to have disappeared. Perhaps she'd gone into the bathroom, Pandy thought with relief. "To the heat," Pandy said, raising her glass with one hand and wiping the back of her sweaty neck with the other.

She looked out at the view. The milky watercolor sea ran right into the sky. The bartender turned to gaze at the ocean as well. "That's what I call 'the womb of the sea.' It's where the sharks and stingrays lay their eggs. I've seen hundreds of baby sharks out there the size of your little finger. And you want to know the weirdest part?"

"Sure," Pandy said, sipping at the fruity cocktail.

"They're born with all their teeth. Rows and rows of teeth the size of pinheads."

"Incredible," Pandy said.

She yawned and, picking up her glass, walked out to the pool. Dropping her stuff onto a chaise, she waded slowly into the water. She curved her hands like a spout and dove under the surface. She pretended she was a baby shark, swimming happily underwater. When her breath ran out, she popped up to find SondraBeth standing at the edge of the pool, looming over her.

"I just remembered why I hate Lala Grinada so much."

"Really?" Pandy's mood sank. She had been hoping that Sondra-Beth had forgotten about Lala by now.

"I used to see her at auditions. I didn't remember it was the same girl until you said the thing about the three hairs. Her hair was dark back then, and she hadn't had her nose done. And she was such a snob. She acted like she was better than everyone else because she was English."

"So?" Pandy frowned, wondering why this particular fact would get SondraBeth so riled. She got out of the pool and dried herself off, following SondraBeth to an outside table at the restaurant.

"She was rich," SondraBeth said, sitting down. "You should have seen the way she used to look at me at auditions. Like I was a piece of lowly shit."

"Mm-hmm," Pandy said noncommittally, knowing what was coming next.

"She's just like those girls I went to high school with. The ones who called me a slut." SondraBeth picked up her knife and began tapping it on the table. "Lala needs to learn her lesson. And you need to be the one to teach her."

"Me?" Pandy squeaked so loudly, she flushed in embarrassment. She shook out her napkin and placed it on her lap. "Hey, kemosabe. I'm not part of this, remember?"

"Of course you're a part of it. How can you not be?"

The waiter came over. Pandy tried to divert SondraBeth away from the topic of Lala by engaging in a detailed discussion of the specials. Unfortunately, this didn't take long, as the "specials" were only two different types of fish.

When the waiter walked away, SondraBeth leaned across the table and banged her knife again. "Goddammit. Why can't you be there when I need you? When Monica needs you!"

Pandy laughed. "What does Monica have to do with it?"

"She's your child. And you're abandoning her."

"But—"

"If someone did something to *my* child, I would never let them get away with it. I would hunt them down to the ends of the earth. And then I would kill them."

"Are you suggesting we put out a hit on Lala?" Pandy smirked. "I suppose you're still in touch with those mob guys from Joules? Freddie the Rat? Maybe he could do it."

SondraBeth glared at her with disdain. She picked up Pandy's phone from the table and held it out to her. "I want you to call Doug Stone," she commanded.

"And say what?" Pandy balled up a piece of bread and tossed it to an iguana.

"Invite him to the island."

"No," Pandy said stubbornly. She was reminded of the incident with the director. Like that scenario, this one was bound to go wrong. And she'd be left feeling like an idiot.

"Why not?" SondraBeth asked.

"Because I don't want to look stupid."

SondraBeth sighed. She gazed out at the water. "I always have your back. Why can't you have mine?"

"I do," Pandy insisted. As soon as the words were out of her mouth, she knew there was no way out of the situation but to go along with it. "Fine." She picked up her phone. "It won't work, though. You said it yourself. I suck as an actress. I'll never pull it off."

SondraBeth raised one eyebrow. "You're a better actress than you think. If you call him, he'll come."

Pandy rolled her eyes and decided she might as well get this over with. Doug probably wouldn't answer anyway; if he did, she would pass the phone over to SondraBeth.

The phone rang and rang. Pandy was about to hang up when Doug answered breathlessly, as if he'd been searching for his device.

"Well, if it isn't PJ Wallis," he drawled smoothly, sounding like he'd been hoping she would call.

Shocked, Pandy giggled and said absurdly, "Paging Doug Stone."

"Paging you right back. Where are you?"

"I'm with SondraBeth Schnowzer. We're on a private island in the Turks and Caicos." She smiled at SondraBeth, who gave her a thumbs-up. Taking a breath, Pandy summoned her sexiest voice. "Want to come?" she asked.

"To the island? With you and SondraBeth?" Doug paused while Pandy found herself silently begging him to say yes. This, in spite of how she'd insisted she was so over him.

Ugh. She was being such a *girl*.

"When do you want me?" Doug asked.

Pandy's eyes widened as she realized that he might actually be joining them. She sat up straighter, and with a sly wink at Sondra-Beth, purred, "How about now?"

SondraBeth motioned wildly for Pandy to hand her the phone so she could give him instructions. And then, like two teenage girls who have just pulled a prank on a boy they both have a crush on, they collapsed onto the table in riotous laughter.

❧

Doug arrived early the next afternoon. He took a short hopper plane from the big island of Providenciales, arriving with two island staffers and several cartons of supplies. It was windy, and as Doug emerged, head tucked, from beneath the flap of the door, the plane began wobbling back and forth like a mechanical toy. Doug looked startled and then slightly afraid.

"Run, Doug, run!" Pandy shouted from the golf cart next to the runway, where she and SondraBeth were waiting to pick him up.

"Run, Doug, run!" SondraBeth seconded.

Doug was dressed in a flowing white shirt and camo pants, a canvas duffel bag slung over his shoulder. He came right up to Pandy and slid his hand under her hair, tilting her head back and giving her a showy kiss.

"I'm so glad to see you two lovebirds back together," SondraBeth said with a smirk.

"Enough." Pandy giggled and pushed Doug away.

"Hello, friend." SondraBeth smiled coolly at Doug and, taking on the persona of the grand lady, coyly tipped her head for a kiss on the cheek.

Pandy felt an unpleasant click and realized that she was jealous. This was not good. It had taken but one kiss to stir up all those scrambled feelings of being "in love" with Doug—feelings that she rationally knew weren't real, but which were capable of causing pain nonetheless.

And so, as she often did when faced with the chance of being hurt, Pandy became ridiculously silly instead.

"Run, Doug, run!" she said again.

Immediately this became the theme for the afternoon, with Pandy and SondraBeth shouting the phrase every time Doug went to refresh his drink, came out of the ocean, or even headed to the bathroom. "Run, Doug, run!" It never failed to spin them into gales of laughter.

Dinner was raucous; they behaved as if they were some kind of remarkable threesome. When SondraBeth got up to go to the bathroom, Doug ran his fingers down the back of Pandy's neck, a gesture that snapped her senses into overdrive.

"How is she?" Doug asked with sudden seriousness.

"Who?"

"SondraBeth," he hissed, as if she had some kind of fatal disease.

"I think she's okay," Pandy said sardonically, wondering at Doug's question. He'd spent the whole afternoon with them. Couldn't he see how well SondraBeth was doing?

Doug smiled. "I'm glad you two are still friends."

"Why wouldn't we be?"

Doug slowly drew the tip of his finger over the top of her hand. His touch was so light, her skin seemed to swoon. "It's hard for women to be friends in this business. There's a lot of competition and backstabbing."

"So I've heard. Like with SondraBeth and Lala Grinada." Pandy finished her glass of red wine while Doug reached for the bottle to pour her another. Thanks to the sun and the rum punches they'd consumed all afternoon, she knew another glass of wine was the last thing she needed, but she took it nonetheless.

"Speaking of which, what *is* the story with Lala?" Pandy demanded.

"Her?" Doug shrugged. "She's just a friend."

"Really?" Pandy asked with exaggerated curiosity. "That's not what SondraBeth said. She said you and Lala were seen together all over Paris."

"So?"

"She said Lala went after you. To get even with her, over Monica." Pandy shook her head as if the theory were too ridiculous to contemplate.

"That's because SondraBeth needs Monica." Playfully he tapped her on the nose. "More than you. More than anyone, really."

Pandy rolled her eyes. "Doug, that's crazy. Monica is a character. She's like a geometric object. Yes, she has sides—maybe she even has six, like a hexagon. But she's still an object. Objects have boundaries; they don't interact the way people do."

Doug looked at her in awe. "You're smart, Pandy. That's what I always say about you when people ask. 'That girl Pandy? She's smart.'"

"Doug, please." Pandy sighed. She suddenly saw that his flattery about her talents, which had once thrilled her, was merely another part of his act.

Nevertheless, when SondraBeth returned to the table, they ordered another bottle of red wine. By the time they left the restaurant, they'd all had too much to drink, and Doug had to carry Pandy out. As SondraBeth wove next to them, clutching Doug's arm, Pandy caught a surprising look of displeasure on her face—surprising because SondraBeth rarely disapproved of Pandy's bad behavior, no doubt figuring it made her look good in comparison. But when her expression turned from displeasure to pale anger, Pandy suddenly realized the truth: SondraBeth wanted Doug, too.

Of course she did. Pandy wondered what the hell she'd been thinking. She'd had this ridiculous idea that because of all her talk about teaching Lala Grinada a lesson, SondraBeth actually wanted Pandy and Doug to be together. Sickened, she saw now that this wasn't the case.

By the time they walked into the house, Pandy was silently and irrationally furious. SondraBeth, meanwhile, had recovered her equilibrium. She put on music, and she and Doug began to slow dance. Their focus on each other was so intense, it was like Pandy wasn't even there.

Defeated, Pandy went into her room and slammed the door. She crawled into bed, bunching the pillow into her face to silence her fury. Once again, "Monica" had made her feel like she didn't belong.

∞

It seemed just moments later when she was awakened by a weight on her bed. She was too confused to scream, wondering if she'd dreamed it, and then she felt the tickle of Doug's hair on her neck. "Pandy?" he whispered.

"Doug?"

He slipped under the covers next to her, holding a finger to his lips. "Shhhh," he said. "Can I come in?"

She sat up, knocking her head against his. "Ow!"

"Sorry." He giggled like they were two little kids under a tent.

"What happened to SondraBeth?" she hissed coldly.

"SondraBeth is sleeping."

"How do you know?"

"Because I just left her," he chortled.

"What?"

"Passed out cold. She was snoring."

"Did you just..." Pandy couldn't say the words.

Doug began running his hands down her torso. "She never has to know," he whispered. "If that's what you're worried about."

He slid down farther, pushing her legs apart. Pandy's body betrayed her; she groaned in pleasure.

"Doug, please," she moaned, tugging at his hair. "I don't think I can do this."

"Why not?" he murmured.

The question caught her off guard. *Why not indeed?* she wondered, temporarily mesmerized by the reaction of her own body. So what if she gave in and had sex with Doug? Was that so very wrong?

"Forget about SondraBeth," he murmured, crawling up her body to kiss her neck. "It was only a momentary thing. It lasted less than fifteen minutes."

Pandy suddenly came to her senses. Doug was going to double-dip? He was going to have sex with both Monicas? In one night? And she was going to be second?

Never!

"Get off me!" she cried, trying to wriggle out from beneath him. He laughed and grabbed her leg, pulling her back.

"I mean it!" She slapped at him wildly.

"Come on, Pandy," Doug crooned. "Don't be so uptight. No one's like that."

Pandy kicked him away. "Well, *I* am." She sat up and grabbed at the covers, clutching them to her chest.

Doug sat back on his heels. "You called me, remember? I thought this was what you wanted."

Pandy could only stare at him in shock.

Doug reached for her again. "What's the big deal? We're only playing. You know, like in a scene."

"A scene? You mean like acting?" Pandy gasped. "Is that all this is to you?"

"Of course," he said, grinning cluelessly. "What did you think it was?"

Pandy reached back, grabbed a pillow, and flung it at his head.

The pillow landed at the edge of the bed. Pandy couldn't take her eyes off it as it teetered for a moment, then slowly slid to the floor.

"Get out!" she hissed.

Doug put up his palms in surrender. "No problem. I get it. You're crazy. All you women are fucking crazy."

Pandy jumped out of bed and ran into the bathroom, locking the door behind her. She sat on the toilet seat, pressing her face into her hands until she heard Doug's footsteps cross the deck and go down the stairs. She went back to her bed and lay on her back, staring up at the darkened ceiling. *What the hell?* she thought. *What the hell?*

Pandy awoke at noon the next day. She felt ragged, torn, and feeble, like an old woman who was no longer in control of her world.

SondraBeth was on the deck, reading a script and nursing a Bloody Mary.

Pandy looked around. "Where's Doug?"

"He went bonefishing."

"Is that another one of your sick jokes?"

"My sick jokes?" SondraBeth asked, astounded.

"Doug came into my room last night."

"So?" SondraBeth stared at her as if she didn't understand. "You look like you need a Bloody Mary. Want me to make you one?"

"Doug came into my room last night," Pandy repeated. "After he was with *you*."

For a second, the aftermath of an emotion raced across Sondra-Beth's face—anger, surprise, consternation?—before she opened her mouth. "Oh," she said, and laughed.

"Oh?" Pandy demanded.

"Well." She shrugged.

"How sick is that?"

"I don't know." SondraBeth smiled queasily.

"You *don't know*?"

"Oh, Pandy." She sighed. "I told him to."

"You *what*?"

"I *told him to*," she repeated. "I sent him to you. Like a present?"

"A *present*?"

"Why not? Share and share alike." She went back to her screen-play. "I don't understand why you're so upset." She glanced up at Pandy again. "How was it?"

"You don't understand, do you?" Pandy said coldly. "I'm not that kind of girl. I don't need to be. I have standards. I don't want any-thing to do with this."

"But you have *everything* to do with this. You invited him to the island for Monica, remember?"

Pandy stormed out of the villa. She jumped into the golf cart and took off. She had no idea what she was doing, but halfway around the island, a tan, shirtless man leaped out of the brush and into her path. Pandy screamed and swerved into a cactus, the cart jouncing backward from the impact. The side of her head hit the roll bar.

She cried out in pain and anger as tears stung her eyes. "Jesus Christ, Doug! What the hell are you doing?"

"Why were you driving so fast?" Doug asked. He grabbed the side of the cart to keep it from rolling and leaned over her to turn off the key. He had the damp, grassy odor of fresh sweat and marijuana.

Pandy pushed past him and got out of the cart, rubbing the bump on her head. "I wasn't driving fast. What were you doing in the middle of the road?"

"I was looking for you," he said.

Pandy gave him a dirty look. "Why?"

She got back into the cart and began backing it up. Doug ran around to the other side, gripped the roll bar, and swung himself into the passenger seat.

"Would you like a ride?" Pandy sneered.

"Yes, please." He looked around the interior of the cart. "Got any water?"

"There." Pandy pointed to a half-empty bottle. He picked it up and drank, tipping his head back. Once again, Pandy found herself admiring his physique in spite of herself.

"Did SondraBeth talk to you?" he asked.

"Yep," Pandy said.

Doug suddenly looked uncomfortable. "What did she say?"

"What *didn't* she say?"

"Did she mention anything about..." He hesitated. "Last night?"

Pandy took her eyes off the road to give him a disdainful glare.

"As a matter of fact, she did." Pandy tore her eyes away to stare fiercely through the plastic windshield instead. "She said she told you to have sex with me. That you were a sort of gift. All in all, it was fairly insulting."

Doug let out a long groan. "It's not true, Pandy. She didn't ask me to have sex with you. She's lying."

"That makes it so much better," Pandy said sarcastically. "So you managed to think of it all on your own."

"Don't be mean, Pandy." He sounded oddly earnest. "I like you. I always have. You're the one who rejected *me*."

Pandy took a sharp left, heading back to the villa. "Doug." She sighed. "I honestly don't know what you're talking about. Your so-called interest in me has nothing to do with me at all. It's about *you*. You're playing at being interested in me so I'll pay attention to *you*.

And frankly, without the face and body, you're actually not very interesting at all. And neither is SondraBeth. In fact, you're both so terribly dull, you have to invent stupid little games that you think are daring but are merely pathetic, just to keep everyone around you from dying of boredom."

Doug laughed as if she were merely being funny again.

They arrived back at the villa. The door to SondraBeth's room was closed. Doug rolled a joint, lit it, and handed it to Pandy. Thinking the marijuana might calm her down, Pandy took a few hits. Doug strolled out to the pool and lay down on a chaise, where he promptly fell asleep.

Pandy went into the kitchen. "You're back," SondraBeth said, suddenly appearing in the doorway.

"It's a small island," Pandy said coldly.

"Come on, Peege," SondraBeth said soothingly. "Don't be angry. We're both Monica—so why would you mind sharing the same man?"

"You're kidding, right?"

"Why would I be kidding?" SondraBeth asked.

Pandy could only shake her head.

"What is *wrong* with you?" SondraBeth demanded.

"I'm not that kind of person. Unlike some people. 'Sista.'" Pandy pressed the button on the espresso machine, enjoying the racket of grinding coffee beans.

"Is that so?" SondraBeth narrowed her eyes.

"Sure looks that way." Pandy took a sip of her espresso and burned her mouth. "Goddammit!"

SondraBeth took a few menacing steps toward Pandy. "You think you're too good for this, don't you? You think you're too good for *me*. I thought you were *my friend*," she hissed.

"I thought so, too," Pandy snapped, throwing the hot coffee into the sink, where it landed with a dramatic splash. "But friends don't have sex with other friends' guys."

"Oh, I get it," SondraBeth snarled. "It's all because of that secret I told you."

"What secret?" Pandy scoffed.

"About the Little Chicken House. I knew it. I knew I never should have told you about that. I knew you'd use it against me someday."

"*That?*" Pandy said. "That has nothing to do with this."

And then due, no doubt, to the pot, Pandy looked at SondraBeth and had a terrible vision. SondraBeth's head split open and out shot a serpent, green and scaly, mouth open, teeth dripping spittle like something out of a cheesy horror movie. Up, up, up the serpent rose, until the tip of its snout nearly touched the ceiling. And then down it came, like an arrow, swooping toward Pandy; then—*pooft*—it disappeared back into the top of SondraBeth's head like it had never even happened.

The whole thing took less than a nanosecond. Pandy knew the vision wasn't real, but that didn't stop her from seeing it. Indeed, as she took a step back, she realized it was an image she could never forget. It was like a warning from the devil himself.

She took a deep breath and drew herself up. "So that's the kind of person you think I am? A person who would use someone's secret against them?" Pandy shook her head in disdain. "You, sista, are sick."

And with that, she marched off to her room and began packing.

SondraBeth tried to stop her, of course, but Pandy wouldn't hear of it. As she threw her bags into the golf cart, SondraBeth followed after her.

"Don't you dare leave, PJ Wallis!" SondraBeth shouted as Pandy jumped in the golf cart. "What about PandaBeth?"

"PandaBeth is dead!" Pandy roared over her shoulder as she spun out of the driveway.

Even then, she probably would have wound up staying and they probably would have made up—if it hadn't turned out that when

Pandy arrived at the airstrip, a small plane was about to leave for Providenciales.

Pandy got on it.

She was too angry to be deterred. When she reached the airport in Providenciales and the only ticket available was one-way first class, she bought it anyway, still determined to escape.

Sitting stiffly in her seat, she didn't think about the trip. She didn't think about Doug or SondraBeth. She didn't think about anything. When the flight attendant placed a Bloody Mary on her tray, she nearly threw up. She managed to get it down, nevertheless.

And then she must have slept, because when she woke up, the plane was making its descent. Outside, it was raining, the water creating rivulets like endless tears. Pandy put her hand on the window. *Run, Doug, run*, she thought sadly.

And then: *PandaBeth*. Ugh. She hoped she'd never see SondraBeth Schnowzer or Doug Stone ever again.

∞

One month after that terrible incident on the island, it was announced in the tabloids that Doug Stone and SondraBeth Schnowzer had fallen in love and were now soul mates.

As if in confirmation of this fact, three months later, SondraBeth threw an over-the-top birthday party for him at a venue specially constructed on the Hudson River piers. It was so excessive, Pandy figured the studio must have paid for it. A barge shot off a volley of fireworks, including a heart-shaped display that contained the initials of the happy couple. The West Side Highway was shut down for three hours in order to give them and two hundred of their closest A-list friends "privacy." Nevertheless, a dozen helicopters hovered overhead, and long-lens cameras were pointed at the event from every angle, including New Jersey.

Both the press and the fans were thrilled. It was all so very *Monica*.

No one seemed to notice that the actual creator of Monica—the *real* Monica, PJ Wallis—was not invited.

Pandy told herself that it didn't matter. By that point, she was too deeply involved with Jonny Balaga to let it bother her.

A short time after the birthday party, Pandy ran into Doug at a charity dinner for a theater group. She was seated at his table, and he moved the place cards to sit next to her. His hair was long and unkempt, his beard was scruffy, and he had that telltale whiff of perspiration that suggested he'd spent a couple of days partying. This was confirmed by his candid volubility.

"I wanted to invite you to my birthday party," he confided. "But I couldn't."

Pandy smiled at him reassuringly. She'd already vowed not to react to anything he—or anyone else—might say about him and SondraBeth. She shrugged. "I didn't think I'd be invited anyway."

He shook his head vehemently, as if refusing to take her at her word. "I wanted you to be there. I mean, I consider you a friend, right?"

"Sure," Pandy agreed, although she couldn't understand how he could possibly make this declaration, given the fact that she hadn't seen or heard from him since that awful trip. It must be the actor's way, she decided, to make statements simply because they vaguely suited the occasion.

"But I couldn't, you see?" he said.

"Couldn't what?"

"*Invite* you," he hissed.

"Doug," she said. "I honestly *don't care*."

"But *I* do. Because..." He paused and glanced around to make sure there were no eavesdroppers. "Because of SondraBeth."

"It's okay," Pandy said patiently.

He shook his head. "It's not. Because SondraBeth really believes she *is* Monica."

Pandy laughed. "Well, she does play her."

"You're not hearing me," he said. "That's the whole point. She doesn't think she's *playing* her. She thinks she *is* her. She thinks she actually is Monica. *In real life.*"

"Oh," Pandy said. She wasn't quite sure what she was supposed to do with this information. After all, there were plenty of stories about actors who insisted on staying in character for the length of a shoot, much to the annoyance and consternation of the other actors. "Monica is pretty appealing. Maybe she's simply enjoying herself."

"That's just it," Doug exclaimed. "She's enjoying herself too much. I can't get through to her. And I couldn't invite you to the party because she would have freaked out. How can she be Monica when the real Monica—*you*—is there?"

"Maybe it's just a phase," Pandy said. "Maybe it's—I don't know…" She hesitated, grasping at straws. "Maybe you two will get married, have a baby, and she'll grow out of it."

Doug leaned back in his chair and guffawed, startling Pandy with his incomprehensible reaction.

"She'll never have a baby." He brought his chair down with a thump. "Not while she's Monica, anyway. A baby would ruin her schedule."

Doug sounded unaccountably bitter. "The other day she asked me to meet her in a shop in Soho, and I walk in and find out she's in the middle of another fucking photo shoot."

"It's part of her job," Pandy said, narrowing her eyes.

"No, it's not. Not when you say yes to everything because you're afraid it's all going to go away."

"So she's scared." Pandy shrugged. "Maybe you need to reassure her."

"All I do is reassure her!" Doug snorted. "Every day, it's 'Am I pretty enough? Thin enough? What about my hair?' It's, like, *twenty-four hours a day.*"

Pandy smiled coldly. "She's an actress, remember?" This whole conversation, she realized, was merely another scene to him. "I'm sorry. But your relationship isn't really my concern."

"But SondraBeth is."

"I never even see SondraBeth anymore. Except at the occasional *Monica* event." Where, Pandy now recalled, SondraBeth always cleverly managed to avoid being photographed next to Pandy. Pandy had suspected it was deliberate, but she had dismissed the thought as her own paranoia.

"I don't think you get what I'm saying," Doug said, looking meaningfully into her eyes. For a moment, Pandy wondered if he was actually flirting with her, thinking he might get her into bed for another meaningless fling. Even if she weren't with Jonny, Pandy would never have stooped so low.

"What are you trying to say?" she demanded curtly.

"Only that you need to watch out. Look." Doug brought his face close to hers. "I live with the woman, okay? She hates you."

Pandy drew back in surprise. And then, recalling her last moment with SondraBeth, she became angry. "She has no reason to hate me. I've never done anything to her. Never said a bad word about her. Raved about her in the press. What could she possibly have against me?"

"Don't you understand?" Doug asked. "Without Monica, who is she? Who is SondraBeth Schnowzer? Nobody cares about Sondra-Beth Schnowzer. They care about *Monica*. Without Monica, she'd have no life. *She* doesn't exist. That's why she hates you."

Pandy looked around the room and suddenly realized that maybe SondraBeth had been right—she didn't understand actors. And she didn't belong here.

"You know what, Doug?" she said, gathering her things. "Sondra-Beth can have her. She can have Monica *all to herself* if she needs her that badly."

And for a moment, as she stormed off, she felt good. But as each block clicked by on the taxi meter, the metronome of sadness in her heart also gave another tick.

Pandy looked out the window at the still-bright storefronts and sighed. Ever since she'd met Jonny, she'd been secretly hoping that she and SondraBeth could get over their stupid rift and become friends again. Maybe even revive PandaBeth.

Doug, however, had made it patently clear this was never going to happen.

And two weeks later, when Pandy ran into SondraBeth in the bathroom at that black-tie event, SondraBeth did as well.

∞

The incident occurred at a benefit hosted by Peter Pepper—*PP*, she thought in disgust, remembering what SondraBeth had said about how he didn't approve of their friendship. *He needn't have worried*, she thought ironically when she spotted four bodyguards holding back a crowd that threatened to engulf the head table. The focus of all the attention was, naturally, SondraBeth Schnowzer, who, thanks to the success of *Monica*, couldn't go anywhere without being mobbed by fans.

With a sharp ache that nearly made her cry out in pain, Pandy remembered how much she'd loved SondraBeth, and how much she missed her. But then she recalled what Doug had said about SondraBeth hating her. Was it really true? For a second, Pandy considered approaching her, but the prospect of being turned away by the bodyguards was too embarrassing to consider, especially since she was with Jonny.

Halfway through the evening, Pandy snuck off to the ladies' room. She was touching up her lipstick when there was a knock on the door; in the next second, a bodyguard pushed open the door.

"Excuse me?" Pandy demanded.

"I'm sorry, ma'am, but I need you to vacate this space."

"Why? Has something happened? Is there a fire?"

And then she heard SondraBeth's voice coming from behind him. "Really, Julio. This isn't necessary."

The bodyguard stepped back to let her pass. Before Pandy had time to figure out how to react, there was Monica herself, less than five feet away.

Her hair was teased up into a gorgeous golden puff with the shine of a glazed donut. A scattering of rhinestones were arranged like stars across the dark navy mesh of her bodice. The shock of seeing SondraBeth—Monica—a mere three feet away was so intense, it was like being in a car accident. It took Pandy a couple of seconds to comprehend that the situation was real; the subsequent rush of adrenaline caused her hands to shake as she tried to nonchalantly replace the cap on her lipstick and drop it into her bag. For a moment she was sure SondraBeth was equally distressed, but then her face relaxed into that impenetrable mask of eternal happiness.

"How are you?" SondraBeth asked pleasantly, as if she and Pandy were casual acquaintances who had run into each other at a party.

"I'm doing *great*," Pandy said firmly, with a touch too much enthusiasm to sound convincing. Not knowing how to proceed, she added quickly, "I'm finally seeing a guy I really, really like."

SondraBeth's smile stiffened. "I heard. Jonny Balaga, right?"

"That's right." Pandy nodded awkwardly.

"Are you..." SondraBeth unexpectedly faltered. "Is it *serious?*"

Pandy raised her eyebrows and tried to laugh. "I certainly hope so."

"Oh."

"Why?" Pandy stared at SondraBeth in confusion. Then she thought she understood. "Don't tell me you want him, too?" she snapped.

SondraBeth suddenly looked stricken. By guilt, Pandy guessed. As if Pandy had actually hurt her, she cried out, "Why on earth would you say that?"

Pandy stared at her in confusion as all of her complicated feelings toward SondraBeth swirled around her brain like detritus in a hurricane. She wanted to scream, "Squeege, it's *me*, remember? We're *best friends!*" but she was overwhelmed by the fear of SondraBeth's rejecting her; the mermaid fishtail of her tulle and sequined gown trailing over Pandy's shoes as she swished by...

"Pandy?" she heard SondraBeth say. "Are you all right?"

The guard rapped on the door. "SondraBeth?"

SondraBeth's eyes shot from the door back to Pandy in panic. "You've got to listen to me," she said urgently. "Jonny Balaga is a bad guy. I know some people who were going to do business with him, and—"

"SondraBeth!" The voice was more impatient and threatening this time. SondraBeth quickly gathered up her skirts. "Hate me as much as you like," she hissed, "but don't ever say I didn't warn you."

A thick arm in a black suit jacket swung the door open, and in the next second she was gone, leaving Pandy staring at the door. "Sondra*Bitch*," she swore.

Of course she didn't listen. Why would she? And besides, it was already too late. One month later, she and Jonny were married.

CHAPTER NINE

JONNY *BELUGA*, Pandy originally dubbed him.

Her first encounter with Jonny Balaga took place at the newsstand, where Jonny was staring out smugly from the cover of *New York* magazine, above a headline that read: "Is This Man the Messiah of French Food?"

The man in question was young, hot, and brandishing a knife.

Pandy hated him immediately. Unable to tear her eyes away, she'd picked up the magazine for a closer look.

His hair appeared to be some kind of statement in itself. It was his best feature—long, dark curls that you wanted to run your hands through, rippling from a center part. Pandy surmised that he'd carefully chosen this particular hairstyle to frame the sharp cut of his jaw while deflecting attention away from his nose. It started off fine but then went to the left, as if it had been smashed with a baseball bat and the doctor had tried to smoosh it back into place. (Pandy would later discover that this was indeed true.) His curved lips formed what was probably an unintentional sneer; his ink-dark eyes shone with the knowledge that he was someone special—and he hadn't landed the cover of *New York* magazine at the ripe old age of thirty-two by accident.

Pandy was broke, but she bought the magazine anyway, mostly out of envy.

This was back when she was penniless and struggling, before SondraBeth Schnowzer and Doug Stone, before *Monica*, even. In those days, there was nothing that raised her ire more than a contemporary who was actually "making it"—in comparison to her own diminished circumstances.

Asshat, Pandy thought as she turned the pages to the story.

Jonny Beluga was no doubt extremely lucky and completely undeserving of his success. At the very least, he must be hopelessly shallow.

"A culinary wunderkind," proclaimed the magazine, with its usual irritating and demoralizing hubris. Pandy went on to read that Jonny had grown up on Second Avenue; his mother had been only seventeen when he was born and had raised him as a single parent. The man who had supposedly been Jonny's father had died of a drug overdose before Jonny was born. In his youth, Jonny had been part of a gang, which Pandy decided must be yet another self-serving aggrandizement—who could believe there were gangs on Second Avenue?

According to the article, after being in and out of trouble, including a short stint at "juvie," as Jonny laughingly referred to it in the piece, he had lied about his age, claiming to be sixteen when he was only fourteen, and taken a job as a busboy at an upscale pickup joint called Peartrees. By eighteen, the magazine claimed, Jonny was practically running the place.

And then he'd taken all the money he'd made in tips and gone to culinary school in France.

This was followed by the usual: He returned to his beloved city determined to create an exciting new version of French food for the New York lifestyle—*Whatever the hell that means*, Pandy thought with a snicker. While working as a head chef for various establishments, he raised money to open his own restaurant. Apparently it had been one of New York's "best-kept secrets"—perhaps too well kept. It had failed, along with his second attempt. Jonny, seized by the spirit of the great American entrepreneur, declared his failures mere learning experiences that had allowed him to open his dream "eatery," Pétanque. Pandy recognized the name—it was a game played by old men in the South of France. She rolled her eyes. Beluga, she decided, wasn't quite as clever as he thought.

She tossed the magazine in disgust, and forgot all about Jonny.

In the next few years, Pandy would hear his name bandied about, and while he was often in the gossip columns, she skimmed over his mentions. He didn't come back into focus until Pandy's friend Meghan had an affair with him. She met him—where else?—at the bar at Pétanque. They started talking and the next thing she knew, she was going home with him to the same white brick apartment building he'd grown up in on Second Avenue. Then he asked her to go away with him to Atlantic City.

There was a great deal of excitement around this event. With the success of his restaurant and some new cooking show that Pandy had never watched, nor cared to, Jonny had become quite the man-about-town, a regular on everyone's list of the city's most eligible bachelors. Meghan was nevertheless determined to hook him, despite Suzette's warning that Jonny took every woman to Atlantic City. Pandy suggested that this seduction strategy would also make Jonny the perfect serial killer. He lured women to his hotel suite, stabbed them with his enormous butcher knife, cut up the bodies, and then cooked them in a stew.

Meghan had been furious at the suggestion.

But looking back on it, Pandy wondered if it was purely coincidence that before she'd even met him, she'd associated Jonny with death and destruction.

⌘

When Meghan returned from her weekend, Pandy and Suzette heard all about it: the endless sex, including sex standing up, which Suzette declared she'd heard was his trademark move. They were also informed of the usual excuses as to why Jonny Balaga couldn't get serious: No woman, he'd claimed to Meghan, could tolerate his schedule, and he wouldn't want to put any woman to the test. His restaurants didn't close until midnight, and then there was still work to be done, meaning he often didn't get home until four in the morning.

Pandy had roared with laughter when she heard that one. "Come on, Meghan, you know better than that. He's out partying."

True to form, after two weeks of this whirlwind romance, Jonny stopped responding to Meghan's texts. When Meghan went to Pétanque to confront him, he acted like he hardly knew her.

This made Pandy hate him even more.

∞

And then Pandy began running into him. Every time she went to Pétanque, which seemed to be everyone's favorite place for first dates, whatever man she was with at the time always made a big show of "knowing" Jonny when he came out of the kitchen in his chef's cap and tightly wrapped bloodstained apron. The man would be effusive in his praise, while Pandy tried to say as little as possible, doing her best to ignore him.

This wasn't easy.

Jonny had presence. Pandy herself had to admit that he possessed that indefinable "it" factor. He was one of that rare type of man to whom women couldn't help but be attracted in spite of themselves. Like Bill Clinton and Bobby Kennedy Jr., they oozed sex appeal like musk aftershave. You might not like them, you might even despise their politics and their double-dealing attitudes toward women and cheating, and yet when you were near them, you couldn't help imagining what it would be like to be one of those cheatees yourself.

This, coupled with Jonny's unapologetic arrogance, was enough reason to stay away. Why, Pandy wondered, must the Beluga come rolling out after every meal, stopping to greet every patron so they could congratulate him and tell him how wonderful he was? This sort of patronizing strutting was the sort of thing only men could get away with, and it just made Pandy resent Jonny more. He was like an actor standing around the exit of the theater after a play, begging for compliments from the departing crowd.

And then, as often happens in New York, Pandy's orbit changed. Five years would pass before she would encounter Jonny Balaga again. Five years in which she herself changed: from struggling writer to the creator of Monica and the toast of the town.

Returning to New York from that disastrous trip to the island with SondraBeth Schnowzer and Doug Stone, Pandy had vowed never again to allow herself to be drawn into such moral debauchery. Despite having seen just about everything, she was proud to fall back on her prudish side, which, she believed, allowed her to run to the edge of the cliff and watch everyone else jump off while she remained on terra firma. She chastised herself for having momentarily gone against her better values, and for thinking she could escape from life's vicissitudes by scooting behind the curtain of movie-star glamour. She vowed to get back to real life; like Odysseus, she would stuff her ears to resist the siren's call to land on that treacherous rock called showbiz, where, as her literary friends had warned her, no self-respecting novelist belonged.

She tried politics instead.

Enter the Senator. Twenty years older and twice divorced, at least he spent his time trying to make the world a better place.

He was nearly sixty. Almost old enough to be her father. This he informed her of within ten minutes of making her acquaintance at Joules. Within the next hour, he sadly revealed that he'd had prostate cancer. And he was still in love with his first wife, who had died of cancer. So she shouldn't get her hopes up.

Pandy promised that she wouldn't.

Other than that, he explained, his life wasn't bad. He dined at only the best restaurants, where he was often comped. He lived in the most exclusive building on Park Avenue and named several billionaires as his closest friends. Indeed, he pointed out that while most people associated the Republican Party with billionaires, the Democrats actually had more billionaire supporters. This, Pandy said, was no doubt due to the fact that if a man was smart enough to make a billion dollars, he must possess the intelligence to be a Democrat.

The Senator agreed, and invited Pandy to accompany him to Palm Beach for the weekend, where they would be hosted by his billionaire friend and supporter Steven Finiper and Steven's wife, Edith, a Harvard Law School graduate.

"I think you'll like Edith," the Senator said. "When she found out I knew you, she wouldn't stop bothering me. Monica is her favorite character, and you, my dear, are her favorite writer."

"I'd love to come," Pandy said, flattered.

∞

They took a commercial flight from LaGuardia to Palm Beach. Walking through the airport with the Senator, Pandy was astounded by how popular he was. Every few feet, someone would come up and gush about how grateful they were to him and how he'd made such a difference in their lives.

"Wow," Pandy said as they took their seats in first class. "Now that is something that's never going to happen to me."

"What, my dear?" the Senator asked, cocking his head. He was a little hard of hearing.

"People coming up to me, telling me how much I've meant in their lives." Pandy raised her voice and realized how foolish she sounded.

The Senator smiled and patted her knee. "Oh, it will happen, my dear. Especially when you become a grandmother."

Pandy smiled and rolled her eyes.

When they landed in Palm Beach, Pandy's phone began beeping. She checked her messages: Page Six had called three times. During the two-hour flight, word had gotten out that she and the Senator were traveling together; now everyone was wondering if they were dating.

Pandy laughed and deleted the messages.

∞

The Finipers' Palm Beach home was a monstrosity of contemporary architecture: an enormous glass-and-brick rectangle with a helicopter landing pad made of the traditional coral and cement mixture.

Pandy wondered how long the structure would last. The house clearly didn't belong there, but, given the scrub and the mangrove swamps, what did?

Pandy and the Senator were given separate rooms across the hall from each other. Showing Pandy her room, Edith informed her that the house had ten bedrooms, each with its own bath. Pandy noted the fancy monogrammed hotel-quality sheets and towels, the assortment of travel-sized toiletries in a basket on top of the commode, the generic furniture comprised of dark wood and beige linen. There was always something impersonal about these billionaire houses, as if they were merely comfortable resting places for the enormous amounts of money they cost. Perhaps the owners assumed that, like Monopoly buildings, these houses would soon be bought by yet another billionaire.

In the meantime, Pandy planned to enjoy herself.

The first evening passed without incident. The Senator and Steven had serious business, and so, it seemed, did she and Edith. "I'm such an admirer of yours," Edith said, hugging Pandy as she came downstairs. "I just love Monica. You've changed how people see women."

"Why, thank you," Pandy said. Edith had a good, solid view of the world and a healthy dose of cynicism, especially when it came to men. She and Pandy discussed why there weren't more women CEOs while the men talked Super PACs.

On Saturday morning, Pandy came down to breakfast to discover they'd been invited to tennis and lunch at the home of another billionaire couple: Pope and Lindsay Mallachant.

"Do you play?" Edith asked.

"Tennis?" Pandy said, helping herself to several pieces of bacon from the breakfast buffet. She hesitated and then gave her usual answer: "I learned when I was four, and never got any better." This was not the complete truth. Having grown up with a crumbling tennis court in her own backyard, Pandy was a natural.

She knew better than to boast about her skills, however. For her, tennis was a purely social event. As teens, she and Hellenor had viewed it as a pleasant enough way to lure friends to the house, the deal made sweeter when accompanied by contraband: namely, cigarettes and airplane bottles of alcohol stolen from parents. If forced, she would play an actual game, but she could rarely be bothered to muster up the enthusiasm needed to win.

"Don't worry about me," she said to Edith. "I'm happy not to play. I'm much better on the sidelines, I promise you."

Edith cleared her throat. "I don't love it myself, but I'm afraid we have to play. Lindsay and Pope are crazy about tennis, but the Senator doesn't play, so they've invited Jonny Balaga to take his place."

Pandy nearly dropped her piece of bacon.

"But I'm not very good," Pandy protested. "Pope will only get annoyed with me."

Edith smiled encouragingly as she helped herself to a tablespoon of scrambled eggs. "The worse you are, the better. Pope gets furious if he doesn't win."

"Fantastic," Pandy said. Pope Mallachant was some kind of legendary investment banker. He was in his early seventies and was considered a "billionaire's billionaire." Lindsay, his third and much younger wife, was highly admired for having landed him.

Jonny Balaga was the last person Pandy would have expected to be friends with them.

"You must know Jonny Balaga?" Edith prompted. When Pandy shook her head, Edith added, "He's down here looking for money for his new restaurant." She dropped her voice; in an aside meant for Pandy's ears only, she hissed, "He and Lindsay have become 'very good friends.'"

"This sounds like a disaster," Pandy chortled.

"Personally, I can't stand her," Edith said. "I would cancel if I could. But the Senator wanted to put Pope and Steven together. So I tell myself I'm doing it for the sake of the Democratic Party."

The Mallachant house was the opposite of the Finipers': a classic Palm Beach mansion built in the 1930s. Constructed of yellow stucco with ornate white moldings, it resembled an enormous wedding cake. *And there's the bride*, Pandy thought as Lindsay, dressed in pristine tennis whites, greeted them at the door.

They followed her to the back of the house, where a table was laid with crystal, silver, and black-and-yellow enamel bees, place cards grasped between their filigreed wings.

The terrace overlooked formal gardens, a very blue pool, and a very green tennis court, complete with bleachers and those eerie salty-white stadium lights. Pandy groaned inwardly.

At least Jonny was going to be late.

This Lindsay informed them of immediately, asking them to please sit down. Jonny would join them in time for the matches.

Two white-gloved servers in gray uniforms attended to the table. The lunch consisted of three small courses: a salad of radish and orange slices sprinkled with chives; a ceviche of lobster and shrimp; followed by an espresso, which Pandy refused, and a crème brûlée, which she did not. Pope Mallachant, a tall, stooped man with hooded eyes and unnaturally black hair, explained that by restricting his calories, he was extending his life. He asked Pandy if she restricted her calories. Pandy said she didn't. Pope Mallachant suggested she try it, pointing to himself as an example of the efficacy of his diet. He was seventy-three, he boasted, and was free of both cancer and heart disease. "The only way I'm going to die is if someone kills me," he said.

Pandy laughed. She could never take these people too seriously. But then again, she didn't have to. All she needed to do was be polite.

"How's your tennis?" Pope asked.

"Terrible," Pandy declared. And just to prove how hopeless it was, she asked for another glass of champagne.

Her champagne arrived, followed immediately by Jonny.

He may have merely walked through the French doors, but to Pandy, it felt like he had suddenly burst onto the terrace like a small, fiery sun. The atmosphere immediately changed and became lively; the women laughed and the men's voices became lower and more knowing. Jonny went around the table, tucking his still-long hair behind his ears as he lowered his head to greet the women with kisses and the men with handshakes and pats on the back. Compared to Jonny, who was slightly tanned and slimly muscular, everyone else at the table seemed ancient.

Impatient to get to his tennis, Pope stood up before Jonny could reach Pandy. The rest of the table followed suit. Pandy wondered if Jonny had even noticed her.

As Pope led Jonny down the stairs to the court, she heard Jonny ask him whom he was playing with. Pope glanced around for Pandy, then motioned her over. "Meet your partner," he said to Pandy. "Jonny Balaga…" He hesitated. He'd clearly forgotten Pandy's name.

"PJ Wallis," Pandy said quickly, extending her hand. Jonny looked at her hand, shook his head, and laughed, leaning over to give her the requisite kiss on the cheek. "We already know each other. But maybe you don't remember." He laughed again and strode off while Pandy hurried to the changing rooms, the skin on her neck still tingling where Jonny's hair had brushed against it.

His hair was just as soft as she'd imagined it would be.

Her heart was still pounding as she entered the cabana. It was fitted out like a luxurious spa, with showers and a steam room, folded white towels, and the ubiquitous basket of toiletries. Arranged in one plastic tub were brand-new tennis whites still in their cellophane wrappers; in another were an assortment of new to barely worn sneakers. Pandy selected a short white tennis dress and bloomers and looked over the sneakers, flexing them back and forth to find the pair with the most give.

She changed her clothes and stood in front of the mirror. She reminded herself that just because "Beluga" was playing and they were teamed up together, there was no reason to get all churned up. She must play exactly as she would have if Jonny weren't there.

She extracted a headband from a plastic wrapper and jauntily stuck it behind her ears. She looked in the mirror and wished she had something to put in the headband. Like a feather, perhaps.

She took a deep breath.

Let the games begin, she thought with a sigh. She wished she really did have a feather. Something to show everyone how silly she was, which would no doubt get her quickly kicked out of the game. But there was nothing. Not even a speck of dust.

She joined the rest of the group.

Edith was correct: Pope did take his tennis seriously. He was standing on the court holding his racket over his head, doing deep knee bends. Jonny was laughing with Lindsay as he downed a glass of iced tea. The Senator and the rest of the guests were gathered at a table under an umbrella. Jonny spotted her and called out, "Hey, partner. You ready to win?"

Lindsay explained the rules. She and Pope would play Steven and Edith, then Pandy and Jonny would play the winner. From the way she glanced at Pope when she said "winner," it was patently clear whom that winner was meant to be.

The first match began. Steven was portly but aggressive. Edith played a decent game of country club tennis, meaning she'd had a lot of lessons but possessed no real feel for the game. Pope and Lindsay were a different story. Despite his age and his inability to run as fast as Steven, Pope had real skills. He was precise and, like a lot of old men who have been playing all their lives, made up for what he lacked in speed with the placement of the ball.

Lindsay was the opposite. Pandy knew the type: Lindsay had probably played on her high school team, and she was used to people telling her how great she was. This made her think she was a better tennis player than she actually was. On the other hand, she really did like to win, and that counted for a lot.

Steven and Edith were dispatched handily.

It was Pandy and Jonny's turn.

"You want to hit a few? To warm up?" Jonny asked.

Pandy shook her head. "It won't make any difference. I'll still be bad."

"If you talk like that, you will be," Jonny said.

Pandy shrugged and gave him a sharp smile. "Just being honest."

Pandy served first to Lindsay. She delivered her usual puffball, which landed just inside the line. It was an easy shot and Lindsay smacked it, sending the ball to Jonny's feet. Jonny leaped back, swung, and missed. Lindsay and Pope exchanged a look. Jonny picked up the ball and tossed it to Pandy.

"Sorry," Pandy said, catching the ball on her open racket.

"Doesn't matter," Jonny murmured, moving toward the net. He bent over, swaying back and forth. Pandy looked at his ass and decided he must work out a lot.

Taking a breath, she tossed the ball and swung.

Another puffball, but this one was more deceptive. The ball bounced high, and then quickly lost momentum. Thinking, as Pandy knew he would, that it was an easy shot, Pope ended up smashing the ball into the net. As Pandy turned away, she smiled. Jonny caught her tiny expression of triumph and raised his palm for a high five. "All right, partner," he declared.

Pandy gave him a dirty look.

Lindsay and Pope mis-hit Pandy's next three serves, giving her and Jonny the game. He leaned over her shoulder and whispered, "We're going to win."

"No," Pandy hissed back. "We're not."

Jonny gestured at his chest with his thumbs. "Watch me."

Pandy glared and stomped to her position at the net. *Fuck*, she thought. This was all she needed. Pope played every day, and while Jonny was at least thirty years younger, he was also determined to win. Which meant the match would go on forever. One game would have twenty or thirty points. Then there would be a tiebreaker. The sun would grow higher and the heat would increase. Tempers would flare.

Pope launched his serve at Jonny. It was fast, low, and clean.

Jonny hopped back into position, swung, and hit hard to Lindsay.

So Jonny had a mean streak, Pandy thought. This was another strategy in mixed doubles: Take out the easiest opponent, namely, a woman.

Lindsay, however, was expecting his shot. She passed the ball neatly back to him.

They rallied back and forth several times. Clearly, they had played before. This wasn't surprising, considering what Edith had hinted about Lindsay and Jonny having an affair. Jonny must have gotten nervous, though, because he mis-hit. On the other side of the net, Pope scooped up the shot and lofted the ball toward Pandy.

It was the kind of ball Pandy wouldn't normally bother to hit. From the corner of her eye, she saw Jonny looking at her curiously. On the other side of the net, Lindsay was already turning away, thinking they had the point.

Assholes, Pandy thought. She stepped forward, winged her racket back, and before anyone knew what had happened, hit a backhand slice that landed on the white line two feet from the net.

As the ball bounced and whizzed into the chain-link fence, everyone on the court turned and stared at her in shock.

"I knew it," Lindsay said loudly. In a voice full of disdain, she added, "Pandy is one of those women who say they can't play, and then you find out they were a national champion."

"I thought you said you sucked," Jonny said gleefully. He swung his racket, playfully tapping her behind, stoked by the prospect of winning.

"I guess you're not the only one with secrets," Pandy said.

∞

An hour and a half and three sets later, they were still playing the tiebreaker for the win. As Pandy had predicted, the game had gotten ugly. Pope and Lindsay weren't speaking, while Jonny, on the other hand, couldn't stop talking. He kept up a running commentary until Pandy was forced to set him straight.

"We need to let Pope win," Pandy hissed as they changed sides yet again.

"Yeah, right." Jonny's eyes crinkled in amusement; he thought she was joking.

"I'm serious."

Jonny wiped the sweat from his forehead. "So am I."

Pandy decided to take matters into her own hands.

"Add in," Lindsay declared, bouncing the ball under her racket.

She served to Pandy. Pandy sent an easy lob back to Pope. She figured he would place it right on the baseline, in between her and Jonny, where neither one of them could get to it.

Which was exactly what he did, save for the fact that the ball landed just outside the line.

"In!" Pandy shouted firmly. "That's game, set, and match." She lowered her racket. "Amazing shot, Pope. Well done."

Jonny strode to the net and angrily tapped his racket on the tape. "That ball was out." He turned accusingly to Pandy. "It was out, right?"

Pandy shrugged. "I thought it was in."

"It was definitely out," Lindsay said. "I saw it."

"Do-over," Jonny declared, giving Pandy a dirty look.

"Jerk," Pandy said under her breath.

Pope had used up his last reserves of adrenaline on what he thought would be the winning shot. He fluffed the next two balls, and Pandy and Jonny won.

Pope stalked off the court. Lindsay shrugged and looked at Jonny. Pandy smiled to herself. She guessed that Jonny and Lindsay wouldn't be hanging around together much longer.

And then Jonny made a pass at her in the changing rooms. Or what apparently passed for a pass in his world.

She looked up from where she was untying her sneaker to see Jonny, naked from the waist up, crowding the door. The sun was behind him. Her pulse pounded in the hollow of her throat. Her body was suddenly awash with desire.

"Whaddya say, Wallis? You and me. Right now. Standing up in the shower," he said.

Pandy remembered the sensation of his hair on her cheek and was shocked to find herself considering the offer. Then she remembered Pope and Lindsay, and the Senator, and came back to her senses.

"Are you insane? Do you think I would have sex with a guy who has absolutely no manners?"

Jonny chortled. "I certainly hope so. Manners and sex don't usually go together."

"Well, manners and tennis certainly do." Pandy removed her sneakers and flung them into the bin. "You should have let Pope win."

"Are you kidding?" Jonny took a step forward. He frowned as

if he truly didn't understand. "Why would I let Pope Mallachant beat *me*?"

He sounded so befuddled by the prospect that Pandy had to laugh at his ignorance. "Because he's our host. This is his house. His tennis court. And he's old."

When Jonny continued to look confused, she said, "It's just good manners. What difference does it make if he wins? It's only a stupid game."

Jonny's eyes widened. "Lemme tell you something. If you think I'm ever going to let a guy like Pope Mallachant win, you're crazy. He didn't get to be a fucking billionaire by accident. He's a fucking killer, okay? I can promise you that showing mercy to his opponents is not one of his strong suits. And it's not just a game. *Nothing* is a game with these people."

He took a breath. "I thought you were supposed to be smart. I mean, you write about these people, don't you? I would think *you* would know better."

"Hey!" Pandy said as Jonny shook his head in disgust and turned to leave.

"Hey!" Pandy repeated.

"What?" Jonny turned back.

Pandy sighed. "Nothing."

∞

She changed quickly and hurried back to the house. The billionaires were saying their goodbyes. Pandy asked Lindsay for the bathroom, and when Lindsay said the Senator was using the downstairs powder room, Pandy slipped upstairs. She went into the first bathroom she could find, which was in Lindsay's room. There, she checked the medicine cabinet for pills just for the hell of it, noting that Lindsay had quite a bit of Vicodin and several packages of hormone shots. Pandy quickly shut the cabinet, opened the French doors, and stepped out onto the balcony.

She immediately spotted Jonny, in designer swim trunks, walking toward the pool with the purpose of an athlete. He reached the edge of the water and stared down into the depths as if transfixed.

It took Pandy a second to realize he was looking at himself.

Narcissus, she thought.

Jonny pulled himself away from his own image and raised his arms in triumph, running down the steps into the water.

When the water reached his waist, he stopped. Closing his eyes, he ducked straight under, emerging a second later. He took a breath as the water sluiced off the smooth surface of his body.

His chest rose as he raised his palms to his face and tilted his visage. His profile was poised against the deep blue water. Dark. Unknowable. And just out of reach.

Pandy wondered if he knew she was watching him.

As if sensing her presence, he opened his eyes and jerked his head in her direction.

His eyes widened slightly.

And then he smiled at her knowingly, as if they shared a secret.

Pandy slipped back behind the French door.

ꝏ

On the car ride home, Edith couldn't stop talking about how furious Pope was at Jonny. Pandy, who was feeling no pain, laughed giddily. Edith asked Pandy if she found Jonny attractive, convinced that Jonny was interested in her. The Senator chimed in. "If you want him, take him," he exhorted to Pandy, referring to Jonny as if he were a stuffed animal. The Senator then held up his hand and balled it into a fist. "But if you get him, don't stop."

"Don't stop what?" Pandy asked.

The Senator shook his fist in front of Pandy's face. "Squeezing," he said. When Pandy continued to look confused, he flexed his fingers. "His balls," the Senator said. "Don't ever stop squeezing his balls."

Pandy woke up on Monday morning to discover that Page Six had run with the item about how she and the Senator had been spotted together in Palm Beach and were rumored to be dating. Pandy shook her head; it was the kind of thing that would be quickly forgotten. Then her phone rang.

"Are you really seeing that guy?" a male voice demanded. Pandy felt a rush of heat.

"Who is this?" she asked sharply, despite knowing it was Jonny.

"Who do you think it is?"

Pandy hesitated as she tried to come up with a clever riposte.

"Well?" Jonny insisted.

"Of course I'm not dating him." Pandy leaned back in her chair and put her feet up on her desk. She yawned. "On the other hand, maybe I *am* dating him."

"Then stop. Unless you want to be labeled a cheater."

Pandy dropped her feet to the floor with a thump. "Excuse me?"

"I'm inviting you to the preview of my new restaurant."

"Is that so?" Pandy was glad Jonny wasn't there to see her. She could feel herself flushing. "How did you get my number?" she asked, stalling her answer.

"Come on, Wallis. Can't you give me more credit than that? Thursday. Eight o'clock. The name of the restaurant is—"

"Let me guess," Pandy said, cutting him off. "Chou Chou."

Jonny sniffed in surprise. "How did you know?"

"Because all your restaurants are named after French games, and Bilboquet is already taken."

"Clever," Jonny purred in approval. "Most of the women I date wouldn't know to put that together."

"That's because most of the women you date have their mouths too stuffed with your foie gras to speak."

Jonny broke up in laughter. "You're right. My skills are legendary. And the best thing about it?" he added.

"What?" Pandy said.

"I've yet to have a dissatisfied customer."

Pandy couldn't help it; she laughed. And the next thing she knew, she was agreeing to go.

As she hung up the phone, she recalled all those rumors she'd heard about Jonny.

But then Henry called. He had good news.

Chapter Ten

I T WOULD turn out to be one of those rare weeks when the universe conspired in her favor. Two different women's groups wanted to give her awards, and she was invited to sit at the head table at the Woman Warrior of the Year Awards. Those awards were given to five women for fierce, daring, and breakthrough work in the world of entertainment, and Pandy hoped to someday receive one herself. But most incredibly of all, Henry had gotten her publisher to agree to a million-dollar advance on the third Monica book. It was her first-ever million-dollar contract. As if in alignment with this event, American Express suddenly informed her that she was eligible for a Black Card.

You've finally made it, the letter said. *We now invite you to join the most exclusive club in the world.*

"And it's all because of the million dollars," Pandy exclaimed breathlessly to Henry. Henry's call about the contract had caused her to shoot out of her apartment with the urgency of someone running from a fire, although it didn't prevent her from pausing to carefully consider what she should wear. She pictured this "million-dollar moment" as very *Breakfast at Tiffany's*, meaning it required some type of headgear. Rifling through her closet, she found an old hatbox with a black straw Philip Treacy boater.

She'd had to take the hat off during the twenty-block speed-walk to Henry's office—straw hats were simply not practical anymore, under any conditions—but she put it back on the moment she walked into the building.

Henry now glanced curiously at the hat.

"A million dollars!" Pandy exclaimed again. "I know a million isn't what it used to be, but still. This is big," she said, pacing in front of Henry's desk. The pacing was slow and measured, due to the necessity of balancing the hat on her head.

"Remember, you don't get it all at once. It's broken up into four payments. Over at least two years," Henry admonished her.

"Oh, I know what you're going to say: 'When it comes to money, prudence is a virtue.' To which I will counter with a quote from Blake: 'Prudence is a rich ugly old maid courted by Incapacity.' Which might be a more apt description of myself than I would like to admit," Pandy said. "But either way, it's a hell of a lot better than a kick in the teeth. And God knows, we've had enough of those."

"It hasn't been quite that bad," Henry demurred.

"I can only imagine what Father would have said: 'A million dollars. That's one thousand thousands.'"

"'Or one million ones,'" Henry added, finishing the thought for her. "Nevertheless," he continued, "the income is two hundred and fifty thousand a year. After taxes, that's a hundred and twenty thousand. Giving you an extra ten thousand a month."

"A fortune!" Pandy crowed.

"Don't go buying a private plane, okay?" Henry said with his usual sarcasm.

His phone rang. "Yes?" he said. He smiled wickedly. "Hold on, I'll find out."

"Well?" Pandy asked expectantly.

"A young lady from the press. She wants to interview you."

"About the million dollars?" Pandy gasped.

"About your upcoming fortieth birthday."

"But that's not for four months!"

"Shall I tell her to call back in four months, then? When you're crying into your champagne?" Henry asked teasingly.

"Nah. I'll take it," Pandy replied. "I just made a million bucks. I've got nothing to be afraid of—and certainly not age." She took the receiver from Henry. "Hello?"

"Oh, yes. Hi," she said broadly, tossing her hat onto Henry's Le Corbusier chaise. She fluffed her hair. "Yes, it certainly *is* a milestone. I don't mind talking about it at all, but it's not for four months." Pandy winked at Henry and motioned for him to pass her a pen. Snatching a piece of paper from one of his manuscripts, she wrote: *Milestone. One syllable away from both gravestone and millstone—significance?* She passed the missive to Henry, who smiled.

Pandy nodded her head. "Well, sure. I understand. Your boss wants it now. God knows, I've been in that position myself. How can I help you?"

She smiled at Henry. "Well, you're right. I have never been married, and I do not have children. And I'm about to hit forty. Do I regret not having children? Certainly not." She looked at Henry, who gave her a sharp frown and a quick shake of his head.

Pandy changed her tone. "I mean, of course children are wonderful. Who wouldn't love having an adorable mini version of oneself under one's feet all the time? But I really believe that if children are meant to be, they will be. I've accepted that having children may not be part of my fate. On the other hand, I'm not quite ready for the glue factory yet." Clutching the phone to her ear, she made a foot-clomping motion in front of Henry.

"Of course, it reminds me of how lucky I am to have my career. Because I think of my career as a relationship I have with myself."

She paused, glanced over at Henry, who was nodding, and suddenly remembered the million dollars. "In fact, I've just signed an enormous contract for my new Monica book."

Pandy held the phone away from her ear so Henry, too, could hear the young woman's squeal of joy. "I know. Isn't it wonderful?

I'm so excited that Monica is going to have all kinds of new adventures. Excuse me?" Pandy hesitated and then laughed naughtily. "I'm afraid my agent would kill me," she said with a glance back at Henry, who was indeed looking displeased. "In fact, I *know* he would kill me if I ever revealed the amount of the advance. But let me just put it this way: It's more than six inches." She dropped her voice on the last word, hoping the journalist would understand that "inches" was a euphemism for "figures."

∞

PJ WALLIS SAYS MONEY IS BETTER THAN A MAN, screamed the blog later that afternoon.

"What the hell is this? 'Money is better than a man,'" Suzette scoffed loudly over the phone. "Say it ain't so."

Pandy had returned to her apartment and was trying to work, but the thought of the million dollars had made her too overwhelmed to concentrate.

"Aw, forget the headline," Pandy said excitedly. "I was just going to call you. Something's happened." She paused dramatically. "I'm *rich*."

"Oh, honey. I'm so happy for you. How?" Suzette asked politely.

"Well, Henry went back to my publishers and renegotiated, and now I've got a million-dollar contract."

"Good for you!" Suzette said. "Now tell me. What are you going to wear on this date with Jonny Balaga? And how did this happen, anyway?"

"Jonny Balaga? Who cares about him?" Pandy snorted. She lowered her voice. "But in the meantime, American Express just offered me the Black Card. How do they know when someone signs a million-dollar contract? It makes you wonder if there are spies everywhere, or if it's all just coincidence. You know—something good happens to you, and you let off a different energy that attracts other good things."

138

"Like Jonny," Suzette said.

"Jonny is just a side thing. Nothing is going to happen with Jonny," Pandy scoffed. Thinking again of her good fortune, she added, "I'm also getting two awards. Will you come, please?"

"I'll come over and help you choose something to wear for your date with Jonny. Oh, by the way, I told Angie, Portia, and Meghan about Jonny. I thought it was best that way. I didn't want Meghan to get upset and think the wrong thing."

"Ugh," Pandy groaned. She'd forgotten about Meghan in her brief excitement over Jonny. "See? This is why I'm thinking I shouldn't even go on this stupid date. If Meghan is upset, it's not worth it."

"She's not upset," Suzette broke in. "In fact, she's just the opposite. In *fact*," she repeated, "we all agree that you and Jonny might not be a terrible thing. Meghan wanted me to be sure to tell you that while Jonny wasn't right for her, it doesn't mean he isn't right for *someone*. And why shouldn't that someone be you?"

The question startled Pandy, enough so that it caused her to pause for several seconds while she considered which version of "Who cares?" Suzette might understand. The pause gave Suzette an opening; she blurted out: "We're coming over right now to discuss it."

She hung up before Pandy could object.

∞

Forty-five minutes later, Pandy opened the door to find Suzette, Portia, and Meghan standing there, each clutching a bottle of white wine.

From the looks of them, Pandy guessed they'd been at one of those Upper East Side bistros when Suzette had called.

"Hello, my darlings," Pandy said. "Please tell me someone has brought cigarettes."

"Only five," Meghan said.

"Give me one," Pandy said quickly. "I'm celebrating."

"What are you going to wear?" Portia asked breathlessly.

"I'm going to wear sleeveless white wool and put my hair up into a bun. For shoes, I'm thinking an off-white textured kitten heel. Simple jewelry."

"Sleeveless white wool? On a date? That's not very sexy," Portia said.

"Oh, I'm not talking about the date," Pandy continued blithely. "Didn't Suzette tell you about my contract? It's a huge deal, so I'm heading up to Henry's office first. He's going to take photographs of me signing the papers. I'll meet Jonny afterward."

She went into the kitchen to pour them each a nice tall glass of white wine.

Why was everyone so excited about Jonny and not her good fortune, she wondered, removing four slightly warm glasses from the dishwasher. They all knew how important her career was to her; they were also well acquainted with Jonny's questionable reputation. An image of the million dollars—two big gold dollar signs flashing in Monica's pupils—came to mind, and she smiled. In the shadow of the money, Jonny's allure had faded and now seemed slightly tarnished.

Lining up the glasses, she wondered why she was even bothering to meet Jonny at all. Exiting the kitchen, she handed each of her friends a drink.

"Listen," she began. "Now that I've—" She considered bringing up the million dollars again, but thought better of it. "Now that I've had a bit of success, I'm suddenly realizing that I really don't need a man. In fact, you could say that my career *is* my husband. Although unlike a man, it's always there for me."

"Oh my lord. Don't you ever say *that*. Especially to a man," Meghan scolded, as if Pandy were a child.

"Now, listen," Portia said gently, looking at Suzette and Meghan, who both nodded. "You haven't had a proper boyfriend for three years. You're beginning to look—"

"What?"

"Desperate." Meghan sighed grimly.

"Oh, no." Pandy groaned playfully. "Are we really having this conversation? Again? I had to have it ten years ago. Am I going to have to have it every ten years? I get it, okay? Maybe I never will be with a man again. But maybe I don't *want* to be."

"Oh, pish," Suzette said. "Of course you do."

"Please." Pandy put down her glass. "I appreciate your concerns, but I don't want you to be disappointed. Look at Jonny's record: He's slept with at least a hundred women, but hasn't stayed with anyone for longer than two weeks. Not surprisingly, he has never managed to get married, although he, too, is nearly forty.

"Now me. I've had several serious boyfriends, all lasting two to three years. I've practically lived with some of them. And after two years, what happens? I get bored. Not with *them*, but with the sex. I'm sorry, but after you've had sex with the same man hundreds of times—"

"You know most women don't feel that way, right?" Portia said nervously.

"I have to agree with Pandy," Meghan said. "It does get boring."

"It doesn't if you're really in love," Suzette said. "And that, I'm afraid, is your problem," she said victoriously to Pandy. "You've never been in love!"

"You're a love virgin," Portia said. "You're nearly forty years old, and you've never really been in love."

"But that's not true!" Pandy exploded theatrically. "I was in love with every single one of those men I dated. Don't you understand? That's the problem. I think I'm in love with them and then all of a sudden, that 'in love' feeling goes away, and there's no getting it back. Not to mention that I'm perfectly happy with my life right now. I don't need the complications of a Jonny Balaga. Or any other man, for that matter."

"You see? *There's* the problem," Portia said triumphantly. "You're not vulnerable. With men, you need to show your vulnerable side. That's why no one's ever asked you to get married. When you don't show vulnerability, it makes men think you don't need them."

"But I *don't* need them," Pandy insisted, thinking of her million dollars.

"Every woman needs love," insisted Suzette.

"No, what every woman needs is a million dollars cash in her savings account. That she earned through her own hard work," Pandy declared.

∽

"Is it human nature or just female nature to keep hoping for love, beyond any evidence that such a thing is possible?" she groaned to Henry on the phone when the girls finally left at eleven.

She hung up, fluffed her pillow, and leaned back against it with a mighty sigh.

How she wished she could make her friends understand that not being married and not having children was a small price to pay—if, indeed, it even *was* a price—for the deep self-esteem and self-confidence gained by being a self-made woman.

Society celebrated the self-made man, but the concept of the self-made woman hardly even existed. Probably because what society insisted defined a woman were her relationships to other people.

The next morning, she was still riled. "Henry," she said on the phone, "doesn't anyone realize that for men, marriage and children aren't considered achievements? Or even accomplishments? For men, marriage and children are a *lifestyle*. And that isn't right!"

Henry laughed. "And yet I'm assuming that none of this feminist talk is going to prevent you from going on that date with Jonny Balaga."

"You're right," Pandy conceded, rolling out of bed and pulling up the shade. "I'm a complete hypocrite. And I hate myself for it."

"Life makes hypocrites of us all, my dear," Henry said kindly.

"Oh, Henry." Pandy plopped back onto the bed and sighed. "When it comes to love, I'm a lousy human being. I'm like Romeo. I'm in love with being in love."

"'Alas, that love, so gentle in his view, should be so tyrannous and rough in proof!'" Henry quipped, quoting Shakespeare.

"In other words, I'm doomed," Pandy said.

⬠

By the time she was in the taxi heading for Jonny's new restaurant, Pandy had recovered her equilibrium. The seesaw had tilted in the opposite direction, and she was now on top. As she'd signed her name to the contract and then smartly replaced the cap on the sterling silver pen she saved for these rare occasions, she felt quite sure that a new phase in her life had begun. How could it not? She was a woman in her prime: no longer young and foolish enough to put her career aside in hopes of securing a man; and after twenty years in her profession, experienced enough to finally be taken seriously. But mostly, she still had time. Time to truly make her mark in the world.

But not enough time, she thought, glancing at her watch in annoyance, to sit in ridiculous theater traffic.

Irritated, she called Suzette. "I don't care what you guys say. I am not yet desperate enough to sit in traffic for forty-five minutes for a man. I haven't even gotten there, and I already hate Jonny Balaga and his stupid restaurant."

Suzette laughed. "Stop complaining. I've heard it's going to be the hottest place in town."

The taxi turned the corner. Once again, thanks to Jonny's opening, the traffic was stopped.

"Gotta go," Pandy said, glaring at the huge crowd standing out in front.

Apparently, Suzette was right. About the restaurant, anyway. The paparazzi were massed five-deep on either side of the red carpet. Pandy stopped and posed dutifully, meaning she stood stiffly with her hands at her sides and stretched her lips into her widest smile. SondraBeth had always been after her to work on her posing skills, but Pandy hadn't listened.

Two uniformed doormen swung open the doors to the restaurant and Pandy stepped inside.

She gasped. It was like walking into a mouth.

The walls were red lacquer. There were gilt mirrors and booths behind red-velvet curtains. Dark oak chairs with shiny silk cushions.

It was, she realized, the ultimate expression of Jonny's aesthetic: a plush French bordello.

Pandy joined the crush at the bar. It didn't take but a minute for her to start having a good time, as she immediately saw four people she knew. It wasn't until half an hour had passed that she remembered Jonny. Ought she to go look for him? On the other hand, he should be the one looking for *her*. In any case, there was no rush; she was bound to see him eventually. In the meantime, she would use the bathroom.

Turning the corner into the darkened hallway that led to the toilets, she nearly ran straight into him.

"Hey!" he exclaimed. And with a proprietary intimacy, as if they were already a couple, he pulled her into him and squeezed her hard against him. Pandy felt an intense, girlish rush of joy.

"I'm so sorry," he exclaimed.

"For what?" she asked, feeling a little tremble at the base of her throat.

"For not finding you right away. I kept looking for you, and then someone told me they'd seen you go in this direction."

They stood for a second, smiling, staring into each other's eyes.

"Come on," he said, taking Pandy by the hand. "I want you to meet my mother."

Jonny squeezed her palm. Pandy noted that the crowd parted as he guided her through them, their expressions lit up as if they were pleased by this potential coupling.

And then he was escorting her across the floor to the head table. There, squatting behind two swags of red velvet like a gypsy in a fortune-teller's booth, was Jonny's mother.

Pandy slid in next to her. It was one of those booths that once you got into, you couldn't get out of easily.

Jonny leaned over the table. "MJ, meet PJ," he said loudly and with great affection. He gave Pandy a grateful smile. "She's been pestering me all night to introduce you."

"How wonderful," Pandy exclaimed. She turned her head to look directly at Jonny's mother. This required some courage. Her first impression of MJ had been of bad face work topped by a blue silk turban coupled with enough bright gold jewelry to rival the Franklin Mint.

Pandy forced herself to look beyond all that and right into MJ's eyes. It was like looking into chocolate kisses, Pandy realized with a start. She was sure she saw kindness, along with something else—a mesmerizing dash of Jonny's intangible allure.

So that's where he got it from, Pandy thought. She tore her eyes away and smiled up at Jonny.

"Now listen," MJ said, commanding Pandy's attention again. "I've read everything you've written, and I've watched both the movies. I'm your biggest fan."

"Now, MJ," Jonny said warningly.

MJ turned back to Pandy and spoke conspiratorially. "He told me I wasn't supposed to embarrass you." She glanced at Jonny and inhaled sharply. "But I told him I don't care who knows, and I'm not ashamed to say it.

"I absolutely *love* Monica."

Two hours later, Pandy and MJ were still talking.

"How come a girl like you isn't married?" MJ asked.

"There are a million girls like me who aren't married," Pandy said.

"But smart women usually can get married if they want to," MJ countered. "When I see a smart woman who isn't married, I think to myself, there's someone who doesn't *want* to get married."

Pandy leaned back in the booth, staring at MJ in awe. She could hardly believe it. Here was someone who might finally understand her own feelings about marriage.

"Why did *you* never marry?" she asked MJ cautiously.

"Because I've already got my man. *Jonny*," she said. "He came into my life and saved my life. And I don't want to be greedy. If a woman gets one good man in her life, she's lucky. She should be happy. Asking for two good men is tempting fate."

Pandy agreed with spirited enthusiasm. Henry, she thought, was *her* good man. On the other hand, Henry was her agent, and probably not exactly the sort of man MJ was talking about.

The name Henry, however, reminded her of the million bucks.

"Well, I, for one, am perfectly happy by myself," Pandy said. She leaned toward MJ and hissed quickly, "I just made a million dollars."

MJ looked at Pandy in astonishment, and then, in a motherly gesture, clapped her hands on either side of Pandy's cheeks and squeezed affectionately.

"Now that's my kind of girl," she said in a comforting baby voice. "Money," MJ confirmed, nodding her turbaned head. "That's what life is about. You know how they say that if you don't have your health, you don't have anything? Well, I say that if you don't have *your money*, you don't have anything."

"I couldn't agree more," Pandy said. MJ, she decided, was a true feminist. It was shocking that Jonny had turned out to be the enemy of feminists everywhere—but perhaps this wasn't MJ's fault.

"Tell me the truth," MJ said in a kindly tone of voice. "Why *haven't* you been married?"

"Just haven't met the right guy, I guess." Pandy shrugged.

MJ peered at her closely, and then, like a soothsayer, said, "I'm a bit of a psychic. I sense things. And what I'm sensing is that this doesn't have anything to do with a man. It has something to do with a woman. A woman you were very close to, but"—she sniffed the air, as if sensing an unpleasant odor—"there's something sad there. You lost someone you were close to?"

"My mother," Pandy gasped.

"Is she alive?"

Pandy shook her head. She usually tried to brush off the lingering sadness of the tragedy that had happened twenty years ago, but with MJ, she suddenly felt like she didn't need to pretend.

"She and my father died in a car accident. When I was twenty and my sister was eighteen. For a while, when I was in my twenties and some of my friends started getting married, I thought maybe I might get married, too. But every time I tried to imagine my wedding, I couldn't. Can you imagine a woman who can't even picture her own wedding? And then I realized it's because weddings are about family. And tradition. You need your mother. How could I pick out the china pattern? Or the dress? Or remember the traditions? And on top of it, I didn't even have my father to walk me down the aisle. Because he's dead, too—"

Pandy sat back, stunned at this revelation. She couldn't believe how quickly she'd revealed feelings to MJ that she wouldn't even admit to herself. Feelings she'd never even known she'd had until MJ had drawn them out of her.

"This is good," MJ said approvingly. "You've acknowledged your fears. Perhaps your parents' deaths make you feel like you don't deserve happiness in love."

"Perhaps you're right," Pandy said in wide-eyed wonder.

She smiled. And for some mysterious reason, she felt happy.

Chapter Eleven

Pandy was still unaccountably happy the next morning when she awoke.

Indeed, for the first time in a long time, the usual nagging voice in her head was quiet.

You should be doing more. You should be doing better. Look at you! You're a loser! the voice would exhort, and she'd want to pull the covers over her head.

But on this particular day, the nasty voice appeared to have taken a vacation.

At first, all she noticed was the silence. But then she observed a heaviness to the silence; a blanket of white noise muffling the usual sounds of the day.

Snow!

She hopped out of bed, rushed to the window, and yanked up the blind like a pirate ratcheting up a black flag. Snowflakes the size of daisies were steadily falling. The street outside her window had yet to be plowed; there were tire indentations swerving from one side of the road to the other, ending in a snow-covered lump where it appeared someone had abandoned their car.

A snow day! she thought ecstatically.

She clicked on the television. There it was: Manhattan as snow globe, engulfed in a rare spring'easter. Everyone was totally freaking out.

She called Henry. "Hello?" he said briskly.

"Do you know about this?" she demanded. She glanced back at the TV. "This spring'easter?"

"Ah, yes. This recent snowstorm caused by global warming. A nor'easter that comes in April. Around Easter."

"So what are you going to do today?" Pandy asked.

"I'm going to lounge around in my velvet smoking jacket reading manuscripts like an old-fashioned person," Henry said with his usual sarcasm. "I could really use the time to catch up," he added firmly.

"Oh, me too," Pandy said. "I'm just going to stay in my house and work on the next Monica book."

"Good idea," Henry said. "Oh, by the way, how was Jonny?"

Jonny?

Pandy had to suddenly sit back down on the bed. The sound of Jonny's name caused an uncontrollable physical reaction. A sort of melting sensation between her legs, as if the next time she saw Jonny, she wouldn't be able to walk.

She'd be like ice cream puddled in his hands.

"Hello? Are you there?" Henry cracked.

Pandy coughed. "He was fine. It was nothing."

"Good," Henry said. "Check me later."

"You too, bro," Pandy replied casually.

After she hung up, she ran back to the window and looked out. It was bad out there, but not terrible. Not bad enough to deter someone like her. Growing up in Wallis, she'd been through huge snowstorms. She knew how to navigate difficult weather.

And maybe even difficult men, she thought dreamily, thinking of Jonny. And that's when she decided: Somewhere, somehow, on this magical snow day, she was going to see Jonny.

∞

She made a large pot of coffee and turned back to the TV.

The mayor was speaking at an emergency press conference,

exhorting everyone who was not emergency personnel to remain inside.

Then the storm expert spoke. The snow would continue for the next hour, followed by a brief moment of calm, when the eye of the storm would reach the city. Residents shouldn't be fooled: When the eye passed over, the winds would pick up another blast of cold air, and—*blah, blah, blah*, Pandy thought dismissively. The expert described what would come next as a storm of biblical proportions: ice, sleeting rain, snowballs the size of baseballs—perhaps even a plague of frozen locusts—but Pandy wasn't concerned.

Nor was she worried about the mayor's insistence that residents stay inside. Those kinds of warnings were only for people who hadn't grown up with nor'easters.

A satellite map came up on the TV screen. The eye of the storm, shown in pink, was inching straight for the center of Manhattan like a large frosted cupcake.

Pandy became efficient. She did some calculations and checked her watch. The eye would reach Manhattan in fifty-two minutes. After that, everyone would have another fifteen minutes to get where they were going before the next blast hit.

She would need to be inside by then. Someplace safe where she could wait out the storm.

Like Jonny's house, she thought wickedly, recalling how he'd mentioned that he still lived in the same apartment building he'd grown up in on Second Avenue.

She would have to come up with a very good reason for showing up at his door, but no doubt she'd think of something along the way.

She quickly got dressed in several layers, including stretchy high-tech long underwear, an eight-ply cashmere sweater, bright orange ski pants with zippered pockets, and then the pièce de résistance: a hooded Bogner ski coat with an embroidered dragon on the back. Admiring the coat, she was reminded of how her interest in fashion was merely an outgrowth of her love of sports gear. She had grown up in it: horse gear, skiing gear, skating gear, fishing gear, hunting gear—just about any activity that required its own special outfit.

It was twenty-two degrees outside, but Pandy figured she was wearing enough high-tech snow gear to cross an ice floe.

She got into the elevator, pressed the button for the ground floor, and smiled, thinking of Jonny.

After giving each other goo-goo eyes all night, she and Jonny had finally gotten a moment alone. They were about to have their first kiss when the manager appeared, breathless and worried.

"I think you'd better take MJ home," he'd insisted to Jonny.

MJ did indeed look quite green around the gills. Her turban had come loose from its moorings and was hanging by an elastic strap, resting on the side of her face like a deflating balloon.

Poor MJ! Jonny said she had recurrent Lyme disease.

MJ was so different from the other mothers Pandy had known. And when you had a mother like MJ . . .

You get a son like Jonny, Pandy thought as a silly grin froze on her face.

Still fixated on Jonny, she pulled open the door and stepped into a winter wonderland.

The snowflakes on her cheeks were like little kisses. Pandy laughed aloud and began running. She ran the block and a half to Houston Street, where she stopped, panting. The run had raised her temperature and she no longer felt cold.

The snow, on the other hand, was deceptive. It was heavier than it looked. It was the kind of snow that caused heart attacks when men tried to shovel their driveways.

The light changed, and she walked briskly across the six lanes of Houston Street. At least the power was still on. Reaching the other side, Pandy realized that she should call Henry, who lived only a few blocks away. She ought to at least inform him that she was heading uptown in the storm. She might be adventurous, but she wasn't stupid.

Taking off one glove, she tried to call him. The phone wasn't dead, but she couldn't get a signal. The satellite must have just gone out. She zipped the phone back into her pocket and plowed up MacDougal Street in the direction of Henry's apartment until she was forced to stop and catch her breath. With a laugh, she realized she was standing in front of a psychic shop—which reminded her of MJ, which naturally reminded her of Jonny. Pandy peered into the shop. It was empty, save for the smattering of tarot cards taped to the window.

The dark handsome man in the middle—he was the Sword Prince, and therefore, Jonny, Pandy decided. Above Jonny was a Coins card. Pandy smiled; that would be the million dollars. Jonny's mother would be the High Priestess. And the Empress, that beguiling woman in white who represented sex, would be SondraBeth Schnowzer, Pandy thought with a start.

Pandy stomped her feet to knock the snow off her boots. Why should she care about SondraBeth Schnowzer? She didn't need SondraBeth or Doug—whom the tabloids were declaring "soul mates."

Not only did she have a huge contract for a new book, but she potentially had one of New York's most eligible bachelors on the line. "Take that, my little friend!" Pandy said aloud in a witchy voice, wiggling her gloved fingers at the card. She was becoming giddy. She remembered how she and Hellenor used to warn each other of the dangers of too much time spent in a snowstorm: You started laughing, and then you lay down and went to sleep.

And then you froze to death.

A gust of wind whipped around the corner, sending shards of ice into her face. Pandy came to her senses with a start. What the hell was she doing? She looked up MacDougal. It was a picture-perfect snow scene, save for one thing that was missing: people. Was she truly the only person in Manhattan who was crazy enough to be out in this storm? And for what? Jonny Balaga?

No, she thought, grabbing on to the nearest lamppost to steady herself against another gust. She could not be the woman who went out in a blizzard to stalk Jonny. What if something actually *did* happen? What if she broke her leg? She'd be all over the news. People would claim she was crazy.

On the other hand, what would really happen next was so predictable: She would go to Henry's, and she wouldn't see Jonny after all. By the time the storm had passed and the city was up and running, she and Jonny would be swallowed by the demands of their regular lives. They might remember to call each other, but wouldn't find the time to get together, and then years would pass. Someday they would run into each other and laugh about how they had almost kissed one night.

But it isn't just that, she realized, bending her head against the snow and pulling the hood closed in front of her face. *It's about not having the courage to have a relationship anymore.*

She battled forward into the storm, feeling inexplicably sad.

And then she turned the corner and gasped. Life might disappoint, but nature did not, she thought as she stared at Washington Square Park in awe.

The brownstones on the north side of the park were like gingerbread houses with peaked roofs of snowy meringue. Bowing down beneath a heavy frosting of snow, the trees created an entrance into what could be the magical village scene under her childhood Christmas tree.

Pandy rushed forward joyously into the snow, picturing herself on skates, whirling around until she fell down, dizzy. She raised her head and looked at the fountain. The snow was coming down so hard that it appeared to be engulfed in sparkly white champagne bubbles.

And then she couldn't see anything at all.

She was in the middle of a whiteout.

∞

Luckily the whiteout only lasted half a minute, but still, it was a harbinger of the far worse weather to come.

Forget Jonny, she thought, struggling to her feet. She might be a hopeless romantic, but she wasn't brain-dead. At least, not brain-dead enough to waste another minute outside. Brushing the snow off her clothes, she realized that the tips of her fingers were numb and her nose was no doubt as red as Rudolph's.

She needed to get to Henry's house, and fast. She knew he wouldn't have anything to eat; he was awful about stocking up on supplies. But she could warm up for a few minutes and then convince Henry to come home with her, since her own fridge was full.

But as quickly as her romantic fantasy about Jonny retreated, the real-life Jonny stepped in.

She looked up and saw him trudging through the snow.

She blinked.

Her first thought was that this wasn't possible. She hadn't passed another person yet; it must only be someone who *looked* like Jonny.

And yet it *was* Jonny. She recognized his movements.

He was leaning into the snow bareheaded, the silly goose. He wasn't even wearing a parka, but a canvas-type hunting jacket. And he was carrying groceries. Three bags in each hand.

"Jonny!" she screamed, jumping up and down.

Jonny lifted his head and stopped in his tracks. The smile that spread across his face made Pandy gasp. It was, she realized, the smile of a man who wanted to marry her.

Ridiculous, she told herself. Nevertheless, she became childlike with the pure ecstasy of the moment, skidding clownishly across the snow to him. Jonny shook his head at her silliness, as if enchanted.

He held up his bags. "I was just headed to your place. Thought you might be getting hungry."

"Oh, yes." She nodded eagerly, her words blown away by the wind. Jonny dropped the bags, and then they were kissing. Pandy forgot about the snow and the wind and the cold, her entire being embodied in this ancient exchange. Soul recognized soul, and for a moment, she was sure she knew everything about him.

The kiss might have gone on forever, if not for the wind. The air screamed as it roared down Fifth Avenue gathering energy, and then hit the open space of the park like a giant wave.

"Fuck!" Jonny said as the wind tore them apart and sent them spinning backward.

"Get down!" Pandy shouted, tugging him to his knees. "Put your back to it with your hands over your head."

There was another terrible blast, and then the air suddenly went still.

Pandy and Jonny rose to their feet, staring up at the sky in astonishment. The sun was flickering behind a heavy black cloud, turning it shades of an eerily beautiful iridescent green.

"Whoa!" Jonny said.

"Incredible, isn't it?"

Their eyes widened as they took in each other's appearance. They were both mortared in snow, covered head to toe like two plaster-of-Paris models.

Pandy began laughing. In the next second, Jonny was laughing, too; once they started, they couldn't stop.

And then they both took a deep breath and came back to their senses.

Exhaling a reassuring cloud of steam, Jonny began picking up his bags of groceries. "Let's go, Wallis," he exhorted, tossing her one of the bags. Pandy caught it in her arms like a baby. It was heavy; possibly a ham. Or even a whole prosciutto.

Pandy smiled at the thought of the paper-thin pink flesh with its frosting of creamy fat. Jonny was a famous chef; he probably had whole prosciuttos lying around all over the place.

"You got anyone else I need to feed besides you?" Jonny called out.

"Henry," Pandy said. "He probably doesn't have a thing in his house." Carefully she tucked the prosciutto—for it *was* a whole prosciutto after all—under her arm like a linebacker with a ball.

"He's on Gay Street. Let's pick him up and then go back to my place." She hurried to catch up with Jonny, leading him past a red-brick wall that led to a tiny, curved street.

The snow was nearly to Pandy's knees. Her feet felt the way up the small stoop of a three-story brick house with a shiny black door. She lifted the heavy brass knocker and banged three times.

Henry opened the door. He hadn't been lying about the smoking jacket, Pandy noted, suddenly annoyed.

"Can I help you?" he asked drolly, eyeing Jonny, who was heaving behind her.

"Oh, come on, Henry. Move aside," Pandy said. She pushed past him into the tiny kitchen. "The internet's gone out. And Jonny has a prosciutto."

"And lots of other food as well. We were going to go to Pandy's place and I was going to cook. We came to pick you up," Jonny said, in a voice that displayed his willingness to please.

"We didn't want you to be alone," Pandy added coyly.

"No. You didn't want *you* to be alone." Henry gave Jonny a strange look, as if he couldn't quite believe what he was seeing.

"Come on, Henry," Pandy said, grabbing Henry's cashmere coat off the hook and handing it to him. "And you, too, Jonny. You need something on your head."

"I insist," Henry said, handing Jonny an old wool cap. "I refuse to be the only man wearing a hat," he added.

Back at Pandy's loft, they had a magnificent meal involving figs, tiny langoustines, and an herb-infused cheese soufflé that was so good, Pandy made Jonny promise to make it for her again.

And after more wine, they began playing cards. Poker, Jonny's favorite game. He took a hundred dollars off Henry, but graciously returned it. Henry, however, wouldn't think of taking it back.

The storm blew out to sea around midnight. Henry was still try-ing to clean up when Pandy was finally able to shoo him out.

Pandy could tell that Henry wasn't as enamored of Jonny as she was. And vice versa: At one point during the evening, Jonny had pulled her aside and confessed that Henry was the strangest man he'd ever met. "It's like he's from another era," he said. "Like he learned how to be a man from watching old black-and-white movies."

Pandy had laughed.

"You know what your problem is?" Jonny whispered in her ear as the door closed behind Henry.

"What?"

"You like everyone."

"Oh, Jonny," Pandy said. She had a feeling he was referring to Henry, but she brushed it off. Besides, what Jonny said was true. She liked most kinds of people, although she didn't often admit it. Jonny, she realized, was already making her see her best self.

She had been wrong about him, she thought as he laid her down on the old leather couch and began removing her clothing. He was not an evil scumbag intent on hurting women. He was the opposite: a worshipper of women who lived only for the woman's pleasure.

And then she found out what that "never having a dissatisfied customer" comment was all about.

It wasn't about Jonny's penis, which was perfectly adequate. It was about the vagina. And how Jonny knew exactly what to do with one.

When he stuck his tongue inside her, it felt like her soul had flown straight up into the universe.

And after that, like a little slave girl, she'd willingly done what-ever he requested.

❧

Jonny spent the night, and basically never left.

On their fourth evening, Pandy convinced him to skip out of Chou Chou early so she could make dinner for him.

"Should I have brought a doggie bag?" he asked jokingly, eyeing the ingredients she'd put out on the counter.

"Not unless you consider yourself a dog," she replied, breaking the tips off a pile of French green beans.

"What am I having? Besides you?" he asked, coming up behind her to wriggle his hands down the front of her jeans.

She leaned back into him. "Lamb chops," she moaned. "With mushrooms. In a heavy cream sauce."

"Sounds French," he murmured into her ear, turning her around to face him.

"It is. I learned it from my French roommate."

"When did you have a French roommate?" he asked in between kisses.

"When I was in school. In Paris," she added, as if somehow he should have known this.

"You went to school in Paris?" Jonny sounded impressed.

"Only for a couple of months," she said, pulling his shirt over his head. "My sister was in Amsterdam, so I went to France to be near her. I learned one recipe while I was there—"

Jonny lifted her onto the counter and pushed her legs apart. Pandy fell back like a rag doll.

Fifteen minutes later, legs still slightly shaky, Pandy went back to her cooking. She browned the lamb chops, then added butter and sliced fresh mushrooms to the juices in the pan. When the mushrooms were browned, she poured in half a cup of heavy cream. She stirred briskly and poured the mushroom cream sauce over the lamb chops.

The meal was, as her Parisian roommate had guaranteed, what was known in France as "le closure." Meaning it was the meal that closed the deal between you and your potential husband.

Sure enough, the next morning Jonny shook Pandy awake.

"What?" Pandy gasped, suddenly afraid. Jonny was glaring at her as if she'd committed some heinous crime.

"I can't keep doing this," Jonny said, with real irritation or fake, Pandy couldn't remember. Because all she *could* remember was what he said next: "I think I'm in love with you. We're too old to live together, so we're going to have to get married."

"My son is marrying Monica!" MJ proclaimed to everyone and anyone who would listen.

⌒

The next few months were a whirlwind of bliss.

For once, the man in her life was saying and doing exactly the right things. Without her having to prompt him! It was a miracle, Pandy exclaimed.

Indeed, she never tired of reminding people of the wondrous fact of Jonny. "I was convinced that since I'd been so lucky in my career, I didn't deserve true love as well. I never dared to hope that I could have both; that true love could actually happen to *me*." And on and on she went, proclaiming herself one of the converted. Love did conquer all, after all.

Once again, Pandy was the toast of the town. And so, too, was Monica. "Monica" was finally getting married.

There was only one person, it seemed, who disapproved. Henry was being a real Eeyore about the whole marriage, insisting that she and Jonny were sure to end up like Elizabeth Taylor and Richard Burton in *Who's Afraid of Virginia Woolf?*

Pandy brushed this away, reminded of Jonny's comment regarding Henry's being old-fashioned.

And so, at ten o'clock on a cloudless morning in late September, Pandy and Jonny got married. The mayor performed the ceremony. Pandy wore a chic white lace suit with three-quarter-length sleeves and gorgeous white patent leather Mary Jane shoes. Then they all had a long, boozy lunch at Chou Chou.

Only sixty people were invited.

The wedding was exactly what MJ had promised it would be: small, discreet, intimate, and very meaningful.

Chapter Twelve

People always said the first year of marriage was the hardest, but for Pandy and Jonny, the opposite was true.

There was the sex, of course. A wink, a stare, a nod of the head, and off they'd be, in the bathroom at a party or in the alley behind the restaurant. Once, they did it in the back of some billionaire's car.

Sometimes it was shameful and downright tawdry. Like when the taxi driver made them get out of the cab. Afterward, they'd gone home and made love contritely, unable to look each other in the eye.

It was, as Pandy explained sheepishly to her friends, "One of those things. You try to stop, of course, because it's so embarrassing. But then you can't."

"Is it unseemly?" she'd ask Jonny.

"Babe," Jonny would reassure her, "they're just jealous. We've got something they never will."

This went on for weeks. Once again, Henry was not a fan. "You're not writing," he reminded her sharply. "You've written no new Monica pages since you got married."

This was true, and Pandy didn't know how to justify it. Jonny seemed to think he actually *had* married Monica, at least in the sense that he expected Pandy to stay out late with him several nights a week. He had yet to comprehend that in real life, "Monica" had to work. But it was too early in their marriage to disappoint him.

So she disappointed Henry instead.

"Monica, Monica, Monica," she'd say with a sigh. "I'm so sick of Monica. Can't I live my life as *me* for a moment?"

"Just give me twenty pages of Monica. Please," Henry would beg.

And, feeling guilty, Pandy would promise to deliver pages by the end of the week.

But then her love for Jonny would once again get in the way, and forgetting about her promises to Henry, she'd put her energies into her husband instead.

For at last, just like in a fairy tale, after all those long years of uncertainty about marriage, career, and money, it seemed her life had actually worked out. Gone were the nights when she would wake at four a.m., tossing and turning and fretting about her future. Now, if she awoke at all, she'd feel the glorious heat from Jonny's naked body and remember that all was well.

Indeed, even when they weren't together, Jonny was like Peter Pan's shadow, sewn onto her shoe by Wendy. She couldn't shake him; at times it felt as if she had truly absorbed some of his molecules. She couldn't pick up a lemon in the supermarket without wondering what Jonny would think of it; couldn't pass a cute puppy on the street without wishing Jonny were there to admire it with her.

Of course, it wasn't completely perfect.

There were some things they'd never be able to do together— like swim in the ocean. Jonny, it turned out, had never learned to swim, which seemed inexplicable to Pandy but perfectly reasonable to him. Lots of the kids he'd grown up with couldn't swim— he hadn't even seen a real pool until he was sixteen, when a hot older waitress had invited him for the weekend to her house in Hampton Bays.

Nor did they share similar tastes.

Jonny had come with a storage locker full of contemporary furniture, along with twenty or so plastic containers of his junk. The furniture was the kind of cheapish high-end box store stuff that a bachelor would buy, perhaps anticipating that when he married, he would get rid of it in deference to his wife's tastes.

But Jonny didn't want to part with one piece of it, and when Pandy asked him to and he refused, she realized she was already beginning to take on the dreaded "nagging wife" role. Vowing not to become a fishwife, she turned a blind eye to the furniture.

Unfortunately, what couldn't be ignored were some of the matters of basic housekeeping. It turned out that along with his other masculine qualities, Jonny possessed that male propensity to completely overlook his own mess. You'd think with all the space in her loft, Jonny could have chosen one corner in which to dump his dirty laundry. But he couldn't. Instead, he spread it all around like a dog marking his territory.

She'd tried scolding him, and once even picked up all his laundry and dumped it on his side of the bed. But Jonny feigned ignorance and lay down on top of it, making her feel that she was being petty. And so, instead of complaining, she reminded herself that love was about how you framed your partner in words. She decided that the words "Jonny" and "flaw" would never appear in the same sentence—even if that sentence was only in her mind. And so, when married friends expressed dismay with their husbands, Pandy affected a sort of astonishment, followed by the sentiment that she must be incredibly lucky, because Jonny was not like that *at all*.

This didn't stop her from complaining to Henry, however.

"Does that dirty sock stuff still go on in marriages?" Henry asked over the phone. "How incredibly dull. How's Monica coming?"

"I'm feeling a little boxed in," Pandy said, eyeing a stack of plastic containers.

"Boxed in? How is that possible? You have nothing but space in that loft."

"You know how men are. They come with *stuff*," Pandy whined.

"Perhaps you should have considered that before you married him," Henry said sharply.

"That's not how a woman thinks when a man—a man like Jonny, by the way—says he's in love with her and wants to get married," Pandy replied.

Henry laughed. "My god, girl. What has happened to your brain?"

Little did Pandy know that she would soon be asking herself this very question.

⁂

Jonny wanted a restaurant-quality kitchen in the apartment, and Pandy agreed. She wanted him to be happy; after all, he was Jonny Balaga, the world-famous chef. Of *course* they must have one.

She assumed that the term meant high-end appliances. Only when the plans were drawn did she understand that for Jonny, "restaurant-quality kitchen" meant the kind of kitchen you would find in an actual restaurant.

The kind of kitchen that cost four hundred thousand dollars.

"But so what?" Pandy said to Henry when she stopped by his office to sign some papers. "What's money, when it comes to love?"

"And is *Jonny* paying for his kitchen?" Henry asked.

Pandy blushed. "Jonny is paying for half. I'm paying the other half. I mean, really, Henry," she said, reacting to his horrified expression. "It *is* my loft."

"That's exactly the point. Jonny moved into a space you've already paid for. Therefore, he should be paying for the renovations."

"Everyone says the biggest mistake in marriage is keeping track. It's not going to be fifty-fifty all the time," Pandy admonished him.

"That's exactly what worries me. Please tell me you had him sign a prenup."

"Of course I did!" Pandy exclaimed.

She had never lied to Henry before. And certainly not about something so important. On the other hand, it wasn't Henry's business. And if she ever, for one minute, believed that Jonny would screw her over financially—well, she never would have married him!

Besides, Jonny's career was booming. Some men from Vegas had contacted him, and wanted to meet him in LA the next month.

"Wouldn't it make more sense to go to Vegas?" Pandy had asked.

"That's not how these things work." Jonny smiled at her like she was an adorable nitwit.

"How's the book coming?" Henry asked again two weeks later.

"I'm thinking a change of scenery might help," Pandy said, feeling guilty.

"Good idea. Why don't you go to Wallis? Work undisturbed for a bit," Henry said. Her childhood home was completely isolated.

"But then I couldn't see Jonny every day!" she protested. "I was thinking more of LA. What do they call those pointy trees that are everywhere?"

"Cypress trees?"

"Yes. The cypress trees. I find them very inspiring. They always remind me of Joan Didion."

Closing her ears to Henry's protests, she flew off to LA with Jonny. They stayed at the Chateau Marmont, "in Monica's new favorite room," the desk clerk said, waving the key on its scarlet tassel as he led them down the brown-carpeted hallway to number 29. It held a white baby grand piano, and Jonny turned out to be a man who could play a little.

They had a ball, with Pandy staging intimate champagne evenings with her Hollywood pals during which Jonny played show tunes and everyone else sang.

And then, having heard they were in town, Peter Pepper himself called.

Pandy was shocked, but then pleasantly surprised when it turned out that PP was a huge fan of Jonny's. A dinner for four was arranged on the terrace at the Chateau; PP was bringing his girlfriend. What was decidedly less pleasant was her identity: Lala Grinada.

Pandy couldn't believe it. Lala, the very same actress who'd tried to steal Doug Stone to get even.

This, Pandy decided, was going to be interesting.

Naturally, Jonny and PP—who knew nothing of this history and would have dismissed it as stupid girl stuff if they had—got on like a house on fire. They had tennis, golf, and cigars in common. They had other men in common, guys with names like Sonny Bats and Tony Hammer. Pandy and Lala, meanwhile, had both nothing and too much in common.

SondraBeth was right about one thing, though: Lala was a snob. She and Pandy managed to studiously ignore each other throughout the entire dinner. It was an old British girls' boarding school trick, and Pandy knew it well. Indeed, she might have managed to avoid talking to Lala at all if Jonny hadn't gotten up to go to the bathroom, leaving her alone with the other two.

Since PP couldn't be bothered to make conversation, he nudged Lala to speak. Lala wobbled her head on the stalk of her neck and said, "I've always thought Jonny was just *gorgeous*," which meant something entirely different in British than it did in American.

Pandy smiled coldly. "Have you?"

And then, of course, she and Jonny ended up having their first fight.

Over Lala, naturally. Pandy was sure he'd begun flirting with Lala when he'd returned to the table. In the elevator going back to their room, she passionately informed him that if she ever saw him flirting with another woman again—well, he'd better watch out.

Then Jonny apologized and they had mind-blowing sex on the terrace, where it was just possible that other guests might have caught a peek.

And if they had? They would have been "envious," Jonny said.

Afterward, back in bed and cuddled into the down pillows, Jonny kissed the top of her head. "We don't ever have to see PP and Lala again if you don't want to." He yawned and rolled over. "They're silly people anyway. They're not real. Not like we are, babe."

"No, they're not," she agreed, curving herself behind him and stroking the striated muscles of his shoulder.

She loved him so much then.

∞

They returned to New York and got back to work. And this time, it really felt like they were partners on the same track. By nine a.m., they were both up and ready to go. She with her Earl Grey tea with lemon, seated in front of the computer, ready to begin another day with Monica; he with his protein drink and Nike warm-up pants, preparing to head to the gym.

Monica was rolling along at last. Nevertheless, Pandy felt a vague frustration. Marriage, she believed, had grounded and deepened her, and she wanted her work to reflect this as well.

"Of course I want this to be the best Monica book ever. But there's so much else I can write," she said one night when they were in the kitchen and Jonny was cooking.

"Is there?" Jonny asked as he rinsed some asparagus.

She explained how she'd always wanted to be taken seriously, to be considered a "literary writer."

"Then do it," Jonny said fervently. "Be literary. Be whatever you want, babe."

"It means taking a chance," she said. "It means I'll probably make less money."

Jonny dismissed this. "If you want something, you've got to take it."

"Huh?" Pandy said.

"You don't *ask* for it. You *take* it. How do you think I got to be the manager of the hottest restaurant in the city when I was just a kid? Eighteen years old, and I've got every pretty woman begging me to take her number."

"Jonny," Pandy said, laughing, "this isn't about sex."

"You want people to think you're literary? Then *be* literary," Jonny said, as if the answer were just that simple.

"It doesn't work that way," Pandy tried to explain. "You can't just demand things and expect to get them. You have to earn your status."

Jonny laughed. "Earn your status? You have to *take* your status. Listen, babe," he said, motioning for her to sit. "Do you think I really give a rat's ass about French food? The only reason I ended up going to France was because I needed to get out of town, and one of my buddies had a house in Saint-Tropez. When I saw what a big deal all the women were making out of the food..." Jonny shrugged.

Pandy nodded, thinking she understood. The next day, they both went back to work, like two little trains chugging around and around a track.

∞

And then, after four months of labor, Jonny brought home a magnum of expensive red wine and said they were celebrating.

"That's amazing!" Pandy declared, after Jonny told her all about the restaurant deal in Vegas and how it was finally coming through.

PP, it seemed, had put Jonny in touch with his pal Tony Hammer, who was some kind of Hollywood "guy" who had access to a celebrity clientele that liked to invest in restaurants. That made the Vegas guys happy, and in any case, the long and short of it was that Jonny was going to be opening a restaurant in Las Vegas.

Pandy was outwardly thrilled. But secretly, she was nervous. For she'd learned another thing about Jonny: He had far less money than she'd imagined. He had to take the money he earned and put it back into his restaurants. Adding another money-gobbling venture to what was already in the red didn't seem like a good idea. But what did she know?

Instead of confronting him directly about it, she found herself pouting and then claiming to be angry that he'd "lied," at least about PP. Hadn't he sworn he was never going to talk to PP again?

Jonny pointed out that he'd never said *he* would never talk to PP again. He'd said Pandy didn't have to if *she* didn't want to. And there she went, being all emotional about business again. Which was the very reason he hadn't told her about the one or two occasions when PP had been in New York and he and Jonny had gotten together.

While it disturbed her that her husband was having secret meetings with the head of the studio that produced Monica, she couldn't exactly object. Especially when Jonny reminded her that she was the one who had introduced Jonny to PP in the first place.

On another night, a couple of weeks later, when they were again enjoying their enormous new kitchen, she once again tried to explain. "It's just that..." She faltered, trying to find a way to express her feelings of dismay. "I guess I'm a little hurt. I thought we were a team. I thought we were supposed to be doing things together."

"But we are!" Jonny beamed. He swung a stool around and motioned for her to sit. He took her hand. "I *want* you as my partner," he exclaimed, as if they'd discussed this before.

"Your partner?" Pandy was confused.

"In the restaurant!" Jonny crowed proudly. "You've been a great partner in marriage, so I want to make you a partner in the business as well."

"Really?" Pandy sat back, knowing Jonny expected her to be excited, but unable to push down a slight feeling of dread. "What does that even mean? What would I have to *do?*" At that point, she was up against her Monica deadline and desperately needed to finish. She didn't have time to get involved in some restaurant in Vegas.

"That's the beauty of it," Jonny said, smiling. "You don't have to do anything. All you have to do is write a check."

"But—"

"You and I will be fifty-fifty partners. Together, we'll own thirty percent. I have four other investors lined up for the other seventy percent; guys in Vegas that the LA guy hooked me up with. But you and I will be the majority. We'll each get fifteen percent of the profits. Look," he said, scribbling numbers on a piece of paper.

Pandy put her hand over his to stop him.

"It's okay. I understand the numbers," she said.

∞

For days, she was horribly uneasy. She'd always had an anxious rela-
tionship with money. She loved beautiful things, but felt guilty every
time she splurged, so she didn't splurge often. When she was growing
up in Wallis, money wasn't mentioned, except in the negative and
oft-repeated phrase, "We can't afford it." And the reality was, they
couldn't. So when money did happen to come along, it was supposed
to be saved for the proverbial rainy day.

She wished she could have talked to Henry about her dilemma,
but she already knew what he would say: Don't do it.

But if she *didn't* do it, what would Jonny do? Would he leave her?

She decided to put off her decision until she'd at least gone with
Jonny to Vegas to look at the space.

And so, despite her Monica deadline, and without telling Henry,
she snuck off with Jonny to Vegas three days later. The potential
restaurant space was located in a major casino, where she and Jonny
stayed in the Joker Suite, which contained a fountain that could be
turned into a Jacuzzi. They met up with a couple of pasty-faced men
in gray suits, one of whom had known Jonny for years.

This man revealed to Pandy that before he'd gotten married,
Jonny had been known as a bit of a gambler.

Please, no, Pandy thought. Gambling made her want to cry.

She wanted to cry when she saw the same sad, chain-smoking
women at the slot machines at midnight and then again at eight the
next morning. The glitz and glamour and the celebrities were great,
but it was on the backs of women like these that Vegas wealth was
built. It was all those little dollars from those little old ladies who
should have known better. And while Pandy would remind herself
that every vice, including gambling, was considered a choice, it still
somehow didn't seem fair.

And it would turn out that, like those little old ladies at the slot machines, she, too, "should have known better."

Instead, she wrote out a check for two hundred thousand dollars. Nevertheless, before she handed it to Jonny, she did scold him about how, at this rate, her advance would be gone before she'd even finished the third Monica book. This was a one-time thing, she insisted, and she wouldn't be able to do it again. After all, she had only been paid a quarter of her advance so far, and wouldn't get another quarter until she completed the book.

Jonny laughed this off, but pointedly tiptoed around her for the next three weeks so she could finish the manuscript.

Which she did. Receiving the check two weeks later.

And once again, Jonny was the loving, affectionate, caring man she thought she'd married, surprising her with a pair of one-carat diamond earrings to celebrate, along with a piece of astounding news: *Architectural Digest* wanted to photograph their loft. They wanted to do a ten-page spread, featuring Pandy and Jonny as the perfect example of a modern New York couple. The issue would come out on Valentine's Day.

It was all so very Monica again, especially as the other Monica—SondraBeth Schnowzer—and the so-called love of her life, Doug Stone, had managed to become first engaged and then disengaged in the past nine months.

Pandy had barely noticed.

The shoot took two days. The photographer got playful photos of her and Jonny feeding each other in the kitchen, and even an adorable shot of the two of them in bed, peeking over the covers at each other. "When I first heard about you guys getting married, I didn't believe it was real," the photographer remarked. "But now that I've seen you together, it's obvious you really *are* in love."

"Yes," Jonny said. And turning to Pandy, he gave her that special look.

"We're lucky," Pandy said with a confident sigh.

But she didn't feel so lucky a few days later when her editor called with the corrections on *Monica*. Her editor suggested that since Pandy was married, maybe it was time for Monica to get married as well.

Pandy lost it.

"No. I will not allow Monica to get married!" she told her editor over the phone. "It makes Monica seem weak. Like she has to do what every other woman does. Like she *has* to give in to convention."

Undeterred, her editor pointed out that *she* was now married.

"Yes, I suppose I am," Pandy grumbled. "But Monica doesn't have to do everything I do. *Monica is not me*. She's a beacon of singlehood for all the women out there who will always be single, and who have fought honorably for their single lives. Meaning they have the right to be accepted and left alone, instead of being constantly hunted down and tortured with all this marriage crap." She hung up in disgust to find Jonny standing behind her.

He was beaming.

"Well?" she demanded, so riled that she wanted to tell him to wipe that silly grin off his face.

"That was my idea, babe. Monica. Getting married. I told PP that since you and I were married, maybe Monica ought to get married, too. And he agreed."

Pandy's knees buckled. Overcome with a case of the dry heaves, she had to run into the bathroom.

When she came out, she tore into him like a madwoman.

Why was he doing this? Why was he messing with her career? Did he think she didn't know what she was doing? Her tantrum ended with her screaming red-faced at the top of her lungs, "Keep your dirty mitts off Monica!"

The last thing she remembered before he walked out was the look on his face. It was blank, as if he no longer wished to know her.

He said: "No one ever speaks to me like that and gets away with it."

Pandy called Henry in tears.

"I don't understand what you're so upset about," Henry said sarcastically. "Just agree that Monica might get married in the next book. And when the next book comes along, you'll see. *You* might not even be married by then. And then Monica can get divorced!"

She knew that Henry was only trying to make her feel better by making her laugh, but she was too angry to see the humor. "Actually, I don't need to worry about it. Because there isn't going to be another Monica book. This is the last one. When this one is finished, I'm going to write that literary novel I've always been talking about."

She managed to spend another hour alone before she called Jonny twelve times on his cell phone. He finally answered, revealing that he was with one of his "buddies." Pandy convinced him to come home and apologized profusely.

It took him three days to defrost. But he finally did, when she showed up at his restaurant with a peace offering: an ornate antique silver bottle stopper. He held it up briefly before returning it to its box, although not before catching the eye of the waitress who was passing by, and Pandy realized that she had miscalculated again. The silver stopper was the kind of thing she loved, but he had no use for. And even as she was buying it, she had recalled how he'd told her he hated old things; how antiques reminded him of the decrepit old people who'd surrounded him in the building he'd grown up in with his mother and grandmother—but she'd dismissed this and bought it anyway. It seemed to be some kind of metaphor for their relationship: In giving him the antique *objet*, she was trying to get him to accept a piece of her true self.

Or maybe the part of her he just didn't seem to want to see.

And all of a sudden, that revolving top of fear was back, spinning in her head and keeping her awake at night. Her thoughts were a tsunami of *what-ifs*: What if Jonny had only married her for her money? What if Jonny kept asking for money? What if Jonny lost all their money, and they had to sell the loft? What if Jonny took all her money and left her for another woman?

She'd be ruined. Emotionally and financially. And there wouldn't be a damn thing she could do about it, because she hadn't made him sign a prenup. Not only had she *not* insisted on his signing this now very valuable-seeming piece of paper—she was too ashamed of her stupidity to tell anyone.

So she continued to tell herself that somehow, it would all be okay.

And for the next year, it was. On the surface, anyway. They still did the same things and saw the same people, but they seemed to see each other less and less. She didn't wait up for him to come home anymore, and there would be days when they only saw each other for half an hour in the morning.

Jonny began spending more time in Vegas.

He came back for the holidays, though, and for some reason, he was in a terrific mood. He was convinced that the restaurant would be open soon. Pandy didn't dare ask too many questions, not wanting to destroy what had now become a tenuous happiness that, like the old mirrored skating pond under her childhood Christmas tree, felt like it could fracture at any moment.

New Year's passed. Pandy's accountant called, mystified by how she'd been running through her money. She wasn't exactly broke—after all, she still had her apartment—but she certainly didn't have enough to take a chance on writing a literary book that might not sell.

She finished the edits on her third Monica book, and agreed to write a fourth. In a daze, she even agreed that Monica would get married in it.

"Well? Aren't you happy?" Jonny demanded. "You've got another contract. And for even more money this time." When she could only shrug sadly, he began scolding her: "You were certainly happy the last time. What is wrong with you?" And then he suggested she give him a blow job, reminding her that they hadn't had sex for a while.

This was true. She discovered that now when he touched her, she froze. She could feel her vagina shut up tight, like the door of a safe slamming closed.

Jonny had finally managed to render her impotent over her own life. And being involved with Jonny meant that she had no control over her future.

⁂

The restaurant still hadn't opened four months later, when Jonny began to be gone for two weeks at a time. To Vegas, he said. When Pandy found a plane ticket that showed he'd actually gone to LA instead, he laughed it off. "What's the difference? I go to LA for meetings, and then I take a private plane to Vegas."

"Whose plane?" Pandy asked, unable to believe that while he was jetting back and forth, she was stuck in the loft, trying to crank out a book in which she had absolutely no belief. To her, Monica's getting married was a lie—just like her own marriage was a lie. And one to which she couldn't seem to admit. When friends asked how things were going with Jonny, Pandy still told them they were going "great."

Jonny asked for another hundred thousand dollars to finish construction.

Pandy told him that she couldn't even think about it until she finished the fourth Monica book.

And then they had a terrible fight that ended with Jonny shouting, "The difference between you and me, babe, is that I'm a man. I don't need anyone to hold my hand!" He stormed out to stay with another one of his seemingly endless string of "buddies"—who Pandy now suspected were other women.

It wasn't until the week before Pandy's birthday, when Jonny carelessly informed her that he'd be in Vegas, that she finally broke down and called Suzette.

Suzette told Pandy to get Jonny to a marriage counselor ASAP, and gave her a number.

⚭

Pandy agreed to give the shrink a try, but she had to admit she was terrified. She hated confrontation, especially when it meant she might be told a truth she wasn't going to like. She was pretty sure if she asked Jonny to go to a counselor, he would ask for a divorce.

The thought made her feel sick. It was like the mirror under the Christmas tree had finally broken. And now it was in her stomach, the shards stabbing her insides like tiny butcher knives.

Jonny came home two days later from another trip to Vegas. Pandy tried to pretend that everything was the same: greeting him with enthusiasm, opening a bottle of wine and pouring out glasses. She tried not to react when, as usual, Jonny kissed her absentmindedly on the forehead. Mumbling something about work, he sat down in front of the TV with his laptop on his thighs. It wasn't long before he got the inevitable phone call, the one that he always took in the bathroom because it was "business."

Pandy realized Suzette was right: She couldn't go on like this. "Jonny?" she asked, knocking on the bathroom door, and then angrily trying the knob when she heard him laughing inside. The door was locked; she pounded on it until he blithely opened it, still wearing a smile for whoever it was on the other end of the phone. Then his eyes focused on her, and his face twisted into that old puppy-dog expression that now made her sick. As he closed the door again, Pandy heard him hiss, "I don't have much time."

She stood there for a second, feeling too insulted to knock again.

Instead, she went into the kitchen and opened one of Jonny's most expensive bottles of white wine. She tipped the bottle and poured herself a big, tall glass. She planned to sip in style while she girded herself for the inevitable confrontation. For surely it was coming. Just like that big fat pink cupcake of a storm that had brought them together in the first place.

That was only four years ago. And it was all so perfect at the beginning. Why had Jonny ruined it?

She took a gulp of wine, and hearing Jonny's footsteps in the hall, braced herself.

He came around the corner and gave her what was now his usual look, the one she hated—a tight grimace of annoyance and incomprehension. Pandy had a nearly uncontrollable urge to throw her glass of wine in his face. Only some ancient code of propriety prevented her.

"I've had it!" she shouted. Taking a threatening step toward him, she spat, "Listen, buddy. I'm giving you one last chance. You agree to go to a marriage counselor, or else."

Jonny was so arrogant, he actually hadn't been expecting this. It was as if he had no idea she'd ever been unhappy. This was the only way she could explain his stunned expression. Which went on for several seconds, as if he were seeing his life pass before his eyes. He was such a narcissist, Pandy thought.

And picking up her purse and slinging it over her shoulder, she realized she couldn't even be bothered to hear his answer. Yanking open the door, she shouted angrily that she was going to go stay with one of *her* "buddies" while he thought about it.

She hadn't gotten more than two blocks before Jonny called. And trying to laugh it all off, he convinced her to come home.

Where, sipping the wine she had poured him earlier, he contritely agreed to see a therapist. Pandy was so floored, she barely registered Jonny going back into the bathroom to make another call. Then she realized that she needed to make a call as well. Grateful that Jonny was in the bathroom, she went into the bedroom and, in hushed tones, explained every detail to Suzette.

"This is *amazing*," Suzette shrieked. "Your marriage can *still be saved*."

And once again, because there was still some stubborn piece of that stupid fairy tale hidden away inside her—like a gold crown secreted inside a piece of Mardi Gras king cake—Pandy convinced herself it was going to be all right.

And then the dam broke and relief flooded in when she realized that the fact that she and Jonny were seeing a marriage counselor gave her an excuse to tell her friends the truth about her marriage: It wasn't perfect after all.

In fact, at times it wasn't even that great. But the good news was that while she and Jonny had grown apart, they'd realized it just in time and were going to fix things. Once again, all her friends were thrilled for her. All except Henry.

"I don't like it," he'd said warningly.

"Well, everyone else does," Pandy said, not having the patience for a naysayer at the moment.

"My guess is that he's placating you."

"Men hate shrinks. And if there's anything Jonny is, it's a man. I promise you, he really wants to make this marriage work."

"I'm sure he does. After all, it's worked very well for him so far, hasn't it?" Henry drawled ominously. "He has everything *he* wants. Technically, he's married, and yet he conducts his affairs like a single man."

"That isn't true," Pandy snapped. Angered by Henry's unhelpful perspective, she recalled what Jonny had said about Henry being like a character in an old black-and-white movie.

∖ ℂℂ

The shrink asked: "Why did you fall in love with Jonny?"

The question reminded Pandy of all those meetings with editors and studio executives when they talked about male characters. The biggest question in the room was always: "Why did she fall in love with him if he turns out to be so awful in the end?"

And despite hours spent debating the topic, there was only one answer: He wasn't like that when she fell in love with him.

Or was he, and she just didn't know it yet?

But she was there to save her marriage, not ruin it. So she told the truth: "I thought he was the love of my life."

"And why was that?" the shrink asked.

"We seemed to understand each other. I mean, it was like all I had to do was *think* about him and he'd be there. Like one time, there was this snowstorm, and Jonny showed up. With a prosciutto—"

"So it was the prosciutto that did the trick?" the shrink asked, in an attempt at levity.

"It's always the prosciutto, Doc," Jonny quipped.

And right on cue, the shrink laughed.

And then Pandy laughed. And since Jonny was already laughing, for the first time in a very long time, they were laughing together.

They talked a little more, and then the shrink put forth his theory. Here were two people who were used to admiration and respect. They were used to being known. Neither one of them considered themselves ordinary, but this was nothing exceptional because *every* person considers himself extraordinary. They believed in the fate of their own good luck, and that they deserved good fortune.

But then, real life intervened. After a while, the excitement about the marriage calmed down. It no longer caused so much attention, and then she and Jonny went back to doing what they did best: their careers.

And this was the problem. For a lot of couples, ambition and love didn't go together.

The shrink told them to go home and talk about it.

Unfortunately, that conversation never happened, because Jonny had squeezed in the shrink appointment right before his flight back to Vegas. Pandy told him she didn't mind, and gave him a long kiss goodbye. As she went into the loft, she looked around at the beautiful furnishings, at the kitchen, at all the things they'd managed to create together. She was suddenly convinced that she wanted her marriage to work. She would do anything to make it happen.

And then, after she and Jonny had a couple of long chats on the phone, she felt that there was really nothing wrong with their relationship that a little communication couldn't fix. Perhaps they didn't even need the shrink after all.

When Jonny returned home, it was he who insisted they go back. In their new spirit of communication, he said, "See? This is the problem I have with you. You say you're going to do something for our marriage, and then you don't."

Pandy looked at him with tempered surprise, determined to make an effort to keep her excessive emotions in check, as the shrink had also suggested. "*Everything* I do is for our marriage," she said quietly. While Jonny's comment naturally reminded her of all the money she'd given him, she managed to stay calm.

Jonny did too. "I don't care either way." He shrugged and gave her a deliberate smile. "I'm only going along to support you. I know you want to fix yourself, and you need me there."

Pandy was startled by his incomprehension. During their second shrink appointment, she brought up the fact that Jonny thought *she* was the one who needed "fixing."

The shrink turned to Jonny. "Do you agree that this is the essence of your problem?"

"Well," Jonny said, sitting back on the couch and jokingly stroking his chin. "I do think I was cheated. I thought I was marrying Monica. But I got *her* instead."

Once again, they laughed. And once again, Jonny went back to Vegas.

But this time, Pandy was crying on the inside. What she wanted to say was, *You thought you were marrying Monica. But instead, you married someone who ended up supporting your dream while losing her own.*

Once again, she kept these thoughts to herself. She even reminded herself that if she wanted her marriage to survive, she was going to have to stop thinking about herself all the time.

∞

Jonny returned to New York for a third session. This time, because they were doing so much better, the shrink gave them an exercise. They were to get to know each other better by exploring each other's pasts. "You will go to each other's hometowns. Like on *The Bachelor*," the shrink explained.

Pandy and Jonny looked at each other. "New York City *is* his hometown," she said.

"But what about Pandy's hometown?" the shrink asked.

And suddenly, Pandy realized this was real.

And then she felt anxious.

Jonny would hate where she grew up. The house was filled with antiques. But that wasn't the worst of it. Jonny would take one look at the place and assume she was rich. And then he'd ask for more money for his restaurant.

Which may have secretly been one of the reasons she'd avoided taking him there in the first place. In fact, during their marriage, she'd barely mentioned Wallis. It had come up a couple of times, but Pandy mentioned that there was no Wi-Fi or cell service. What Jonny didn't know couldn't hurt him, she'd thought.

"Well?" the shrink asked, looking at her expectantly.

"Sounds like a great idea, Doc," Jonny said. He grabbed Pandy's hand and gave it a good, hard squeeze, like the two of them were teammates.

And that was how they ended up in Wallis, on the trip that Henry would later dub "Helter-Skelter." As in, "That Helter-Skelter weekend when you tried to kill Jonny."

"I did not try to kill Jonny!" Pandy exploded.

But oh, how she would come to wish she had.

CHAPTER THIRTEEN

THE NIGHT before the trip to Wallis, Jonny returned from Vegas in a bad mood.

He was still in a bad mood the next morning, complaining that his back hurt. During the two-hour drive, he kept shifting in his seat. When Pandy asked if he wanted her to drive instead, he snapped, "Do you want to take that over, too?"

She kept her mouth shut and prayed the weekend wouldn't be a disaster. And it wasn't just because of Jonny. It was nerve-racking for her to bring *anyone* to Wallis. As Henry always pointed out, "Wallis House makes people act strange." Henry was her only frequent guest.

Wallis House was "complicated."

Indeed, it wasn't a house at all, but a mansion. A rare, once-famous Italianate Victorian built on the top of a two-hundred-acre mountain. It featured a clay tennis court, a stream-fed marble pool, a carriage house big enough to hold a basketball court, and—because Old Jay, the ancestor who had built the house, had also been eccentric—an actual Victorian theater where he and his New York friends had staged plays.

According to the photos, from 1882, when the mansion was completed, to 1929, when the stock market crashed, the house had been a real showplace. Unfortunately, it had gone steadily downhill from there. Passed from one generation to another, with each descendant wanting it less and less. It was what was known as a white elephant: too costly to maintain, too expensive to renovate; located in an area too remote and inconvenient to entice a buyer. When she and Hellenor were growing up, it had been an embarrassing wreck, with peeling paint, doors that barely opened, and missing floorboards. The plumbing clogged on a regular basis, the electricity was unreliable at best, and the house was filled with a million dusty family heirlooms.

When Pandy was living there people insisted the place was haunted, and the family who lived there was suspect. The two Wallis girls were teased and bullied mercilessly, partly due to the house and partly due to the fact that they were weird kids who didn't fit in. Someone once took Hellenor's clothes from her gym locker and tried to flush them down the toilet because they were "ugly." Pandy's moniker was "Devil Spawn." Together, the two Wallis girls were known as "the Cootie Kids." Unlike some of the other taunts, this was usually said to their faces.

"'*Cootie*. A slang word of indeterminate origin believed to have originated with soldiers. Also, referring to lice,'" Hellenor had read from the dictionary.

When their parents had died, Pandy and Hellenor had inherited the house. Like generations of Wallises before her, Hellenor hadn't wanted it, and she had run off to Amsterdam.

The mansion had continued to languish and decay, until Monica came along. And then, with Henry's guidance—Henry having a deep love for storied historic homes—Pandy had begun to fix up the place. The result was a perfect rendition of what the house had been more than a hundred years ago—replete with the same lousy plumbing and electricity, and a million other inconveniences unimaginable to guests of today. Such as the fact that there was only enough hot water to fill one bathtub. Per *day*. And yet, from the outside, it appeared cosmetically perfect.

Sort of like Monica, Pandy now thought. People looked at the house and assumed she was amazingly rich, when the reality was that when she had actually *lived* there, she'd been pathetically poor.

And so, while *she* remained the same, when people saw the house now, they reacted a heck of a lot differently than they had when she and Hellenor were kids.

It was just this sort of reaction that she was worried about with Jonny.

☙

"You're kidding me, right?" he asked, annoyed, when they finally reached the "town" of Wallis, Connecticut—consisting of a gas station, a general store, and three churches.

When he was forced to maneuver the car up the rutted dirt track known as Wallis Road, Pandy suspected he was on the verge of killing her.

But Jonny's mood began to change as they proceeded up the mile-long driveway that ran under the linked branches of ancient maple trees. Seeing his eyes widen as they passed the old stables and the carriage house, Pandy felt that familiar sense of trepidation. She should have brought him here sooner. Or at least explained the situation to him. But she'd been so caught up in being married to him, she'd "forgotten" about her past.

It hadn't seemed relevant. Or rather, it hadn't seemed relevant because she was afraid that Jonny wouldn't understand.

The driveway wound past the lovely filigreed boathouse perched on the edge of the lake—and there it was, rising up from the top of the green mountain like a white castle in a child's picture book: Wallis House.

Jonny stomped the brake so hard, Pandy nearly hit the dashboard. He turned and stared at her accusingly, as if to say, *Why didn't you tell me you were rich?*

Pandy had seen it happen a million times. She cautioned him the same way she warned everyone who came to Wallis House: "It's not what it seems."

Pandy got out of the car and went into the house.

And then, momentarily forgetting about Jonny, Pandy did what she always did when she entered: She walked across the black-and-white checkerboard marble floor, passed underneath a crystal chandelier the size of a small planet, and strode between the flaring flanks of the grand staircase to the grandfather clock. She opened the cabinet and wound the key.

There was the faintest whirring as the mechanism went round and round. The middle doors opened, revealing a carousel of lords and ladies going up and down on their brightly colored hobbyhorses. Several went by, until the twelfth lady passed on her miniature steed. Then the top doors flew open, and out sprang the wooden bird himself, two mechanical wings unfolding as he called out that familiar refrain: *cuckoo, cuckoo, cuckoo.*

"Jesus fucking Christ," she heard Jonny swear behind her. "Did you really grow up here? It's like a fucking museum."

Pandy decided she'd better take him straight to the kitchen.

Inhaling deeply, as if he were literally absorbing the enormous bare space into his body, he then released a howl of agony. "How the *hell* am I supposed to *cook*"—he paused clownishly—"in *here?*"

"What do you mean?" Pandy asked nervously. She knew the counters were bare and the appliances dated. When she and Henry were there, they ate simply: fried eggs and bacon, or heated-up cream of mushroom soup. On the other hand, you could roller-skate across the linoleum floors, which was something Pandy and Hellenor had done as children.

"Where's the garlic press? The meat grinder? The double waffle press?" Jonny demanded, determined to play out his charade. Taking in her expression, he swatted her on the butt. "Come on, babe, I'm just kidding."

Pandy gasped out a laugh of relief. Of course he was kidding. For a moment, all she'd been able to think was that her worst fear was about to come true: Jonny was going to try to do the same thing to Wallis House that he'd done to her loft; turn it into Jonny House. But of course that was impossible. "Jonny," she began.

But Jonny had moved on. He was circling the kitchen, holding his cell phone aloft as he searched for a signal.

"Oops," Pandy said apologetically. "There's no service here. Except by the boathouse. Sometimes you can get a bar or two there."

Ugh. She hated having this conversation with guests. Some people couldn't tolerate the lack of service and headed back to New York early, while others spent the entire weekend trooping back and forth to the boathouse. Pandy hoped that this weekend, possibly one of the most important of her life, wasn't going to end up being one of *those* weekends.

"Come on, Jonny. You're supposed to be seeing my history," she said firmly. At the very least, she was determined to do what the shrink had suggested.

She led him past the smoking room, through the music room, and into her favorite place in the house: the library.

Pandy smiled proudly as she began the grand tour, pointing out the first editions, adding that the library also included signed books by Walt Whitman and F. Scott Fitzgerald, both of whom had been guests at the house.

With the flair of a teenage tour guide, she explained that the marble fireplace was made from local stone that had been sent to Italy, where special craftsmen had done the ornate carvings. And recalling again how the shrink had encouraged her to tell Jonny about the most important people in her life, she attempted to speak to Jonny about the woman who had been her inspiration growing up.

But Jonny was no longer with her. Jonny was by the bar cart in the opposite corner of the room, examining bottles.

"Yeah?" Jonny asked, looking up.

"There's something I want to show you."

"Sure." With a reluctant glance back at the cart, Jonny ambled across the forty-foot Aubusson carpet to join her in front of a large oil painting. "This is a portrait by Gainsborough of Lady Wallis Wallis, painted in 1775, when she was sixteen." Pandy gazed reverently up at the painting of a young woman dressed in a period riding costume. The cloth of her habit—a powdery grayish-blue—was cut in a military style. The girl's skin was very white; on her cheeks were perfectly shaped pink circles. Her powdered hair, decorated with tiny flowers and silk butterflies, rose a foot and a half above her forehead.

"Weird hairstyle," Jonny remarked.

"She was considered not only the most beautiful woman in the Colonies, but one of the best educated," Pandy continued in a slightly schoolmarmish tone. "She was a spy for the Patriots during the American Revolution—"

"Seventeen seventy-six," Jonny said by rote. He smirked.

Pandy suddenly felt foolish. "Well, she's my great-great-great-something-grandmother. And she was supposedly a writer—maybe the first female novelist in the Colonies. When I was a kid..." On the verge of explaining how she used to stare up at this portrait of Lady Wallis Wallis, wishing she could magically be her instead of herself, she realized that Jonny was no longer by her side.

He was back at the drinks cart, uncorking one of the ancient bottles of alcohol.

Pandy stared in shock. No one had ever opened one of those bottles. She'd kept them for authenticity only; at close to a hundred years old, the contents must be suspect. Pandy took a step forward to stop him, but it was too late.

"Check this out," Jonny said. He stuck his nose into the top of the bottle and took a deep sniff. His head drew back with a snap as if he'd inhaled something sharp and potent, then he cautiously took another sniff.

"It's gin," he said, with a sudden air of authority. At last, here was something he understood. "Possibly genuine bathtub gin." He poured the liquid into a tumbler and took a sip, pressing his lips together to test the flavor. "Yep," he said, with the confidence of an expert. "That's pure 1920s bathtub gin. Maybe even made in one of the bathtubs in this place, huh?"

He took another sip and jerked his head at the painting. "Who did you say that was?"

"My inspiration. Lady Wallis Wallis."

"Not her. The *painter*."

"Gainsborough," Pandy replied.

"What's something like that worth?"

Pandy looked at him, sipping one ancestor's gin while leering at another, and snapped, "I don't know. What's *your* inspiration worth?" as she walked out of the room.

Jonny caught up with her in the gallery that she and Hellenor had dubbed "the Hall of Ghouls," due to the hundreds of portraits and photographs of the Wallis clan dating back to the early 1700s. "Pandy," he said, coming to stand beside her. "I didn't mean it, okay?"

"Sure," Pandy said, accepting his apology, as the shrink had advised, while noting that Jonny had brought the tumbler of bathtub gin along with him. "Forget it. It's not a big deal."

"But it is. I said I'd do this for you, and I will. Just like the shrink said. So who are all these people?"

"Well," she began, but Jonny wasn't listening.

Leaning forward to peer at a photograph, he laughed like a frat boy and remarked cleverly, "Must be nice to have ancestors. I've only got assholes in my family."

"Oh, Jonny." She shook her head at his silliness. "Look," she said, pointing to an ancient black-and-white photograph of two dozen people lined up in front of the house. "All those people. All those lives. And this is all that's left of them."

"So?" Jonny chortled, taking another swig.

"Henry says I should turn the place into a museum when I die."

"Great," Jonny exclaimed sarcastically. "Another one of Henry's 'brilliant' ideas."

Pandy did her best to ignore him as she considered what to show him next. The schoolroom with the window-seat nook where she had loved to read as a child? The conservatory, with its collection of rare butterflies? *Old Jay's bedroom*, she thought suddenly; that always impressed men.

Indeed, you couldn't get more manly than Old Jay's bedroom. The entire suite—bathroom, dressing room, smoking room, and the bedroom itself—was paneled in dark mahogany. The enormous four-poster bed sat squarely in the middle of the room; Old Jay had apparently liked to sit in his bed in the mornings and watch the comings and goings from the French windows that faced out in three directions. Besides being somewhat of a busybody, Old Jay had also been a great traveler. His room was filled with astonishing souvenirs from his trips, like a Zulu spear and what was supposedly an actual shrunken head from a real, once-living human.

But Jonny wasn't interested in any of that.

He strode into the room, took a spin around the bed, and then, as if he'd already decided to take possession of the space, went into the bathroom. He shut the door with a proprietary click; when it remained shut for several minutes, Pandy began to fret. That particular toilet hadn't been flushed for years; it was highly likely to clog. No one, including Henry, had even *stayed* in Old Jay's bedroom. No one slept in his bed, much less took advantage of the facilities.

Jonny using Old Jay's bathroom? Pandy couldn't even think about it. She reminded herself that she must never tell Henry, either.

Henry would be mortified.

When he came out of the bathroom, drying his hands on Old Jay's black monogrammed hand towel and then dropping it to the floor, she'd had enough. She reached her hand out to take his. "Come on. I want to show you *my* room."

Tugging him across the hall, she pushed open the door. And there it was: Her room! With its tall French windows and heavy lined drapes. And her bed! With the tattered pink silk canopy. It had been ages since she'd been there—not since before she'd married Jonny. She ran across the room and threw herself onto the bed, hitting the old feather mattress with a thump and rolling into the dip in the middle. The same dip that had held generations of little girls. You lay down, and the feathers embraced you. And you slept without tossing or turning, and woke up refreshed.

She suddenly remembered Jonny and sat straight up. She'd forgotten about him for a second, and, as with a baby, that probably wasn't a good idea.

Sure enough, he was standing in front of her desk, tapping absentmindedly on one of the keys of the large metal Smith Corona typewriter.

Pandy cleared her throat, hoping to get his attention. Not only was that the desk where Monica was born, but scattered around the typewriter were more of her youthful "creative works." There were drawings and bits of short stories, little-girl diaries with latches and tiny keys, and the black leather journals with unlined pages that she'd asked for every year at Christmas. But mostly, there were dozens and dozens of school notebooks—the type with that blank space on the front where you were supposed to write in the subject.

Jonny picked one up and read the label. "Monica?" he asked.

Pandy leaped off the bed and snatched it out of his hand. "That's private."

"If it's private, why do you leave it lying around where everyone can see it?"

Jonny picked up another Monica book and pointedly put it back down. "Why do you keep these, anyway?"

Pandy shrugged, carefully straightening the notebooks. She laughed, trying to make a joke of it. "Henry always tells me I can put them in my museum—"

Pandy broke off, embarrassed again. She was being juvenile, and

Jonny didn't like it. "That little-girl stuff is not sexy," he'd once said dismissively when she'd accidentally squealed about something she was excited about. This time, she needn't have worried. Jonny had just finished off his gin and, carefully putting down the glass, he began swaying his hips slightly from side to side. Then he put his arms around her. He turned her around and ground his pelvis into her bottom. He lowered his head and began kissing her neck.

Pandy tried to stifle her instinct to swat him away, as one would an annoying insect.

"Jonny." Smiling, she disentangled herself, knowing, nonetheless, that she was going to have to have sex with him. If only because she had promised herself she would, knowing it was the only way she and Jonny could ever truly get back together. Indeed, she'd even considered bringing a piece or two of the sexy lingerie she used to wear for him. But when she'd found the garments in the back of her drawer, they'd looked like something a cheap hooker would wear.

Jonny had his pants around his ankles and was hopping up and down, trying to get out of them. With a sigh, Pandy went to her bureau, opened the top drawer, and grabbed a vintage silk negligee.

Jonny got out of his pants. He saw the piece of old silk in her hand and pulled it away, waving it over his head. "I've got a better idea. Let's do it in Old Jay's bed," he leered.

Pandy shrieked. "What?" She snatched back the negligee. "Old Jay's bed has an old horsehair mattress. It's infested. With *bugs*."

She hurried to the bathroom door and then turned to Jonny. "I'll be right back," she said, watching him until he shuffled over to her bed. When she finally closed the door, she was quite sure he was on top of it.

When she opened the door, he wasn't.

She stepped into the room to look for him, but Jonny had vanished. And Pandy had a very good idea where.

"Why can't we do it in the old man's room? I want to do it in *his* bed," Jonny whined, standing in front of the massive wooden structure.

191

"No," Pandy said firmly, her voice once again taking on the cast of the reluctant schoolmarm. "I'm not going to 'do it' in Old Jay's bed. It isn't *proper*."

"You think I'm not good enough!" Jonny shouted.

"Don't be ridiculous." She reached out for him, but he slapped her hand away.

Then he put his hands over his head. Swaying back and forth with his head tucked under his arms like a petulant child, he said, "Listen, babe. I fucked up."

Pandy froze.

And suddenly, it all somehow made sense: He was going to ask her for a divorce. That's why he'd agreed to go to the shrink; why he'd agreed to come to Wallis House. To tell her in a place where no one was around, so if she freaked out, she wouldn't embarrass him. Because that was what men like Jonny and PP did.

PP. And then she had a far worse thought.

"You lost all the money," Pandy said.

"The money?" Jonny waved this away. "That was gone long ago. But the restaurant..."

"You lost the *restaurant*? You lost *all* our money?" Pandy's heart was so constricted that her voice came out in a high, glass-breaking shriek.

For a second, they locked eyes. Pandy sensed a change in the atmosphere, as if Jonny was suddenly sizing her up as an opponent.

The hatred she felt for him at that moment was so intense, she felt as if she had turned to stone.

"Come on, babe." He strutted toward her. "This is why I so don't want to talk to you about business. I don't want you all over my fucking back. Let me take care of the money stuff," he pleaded, rocking from side to side. "You've got this beautiful house. We could do something amazing with the place... Remember *Architectural Digest*? It could be just like that."

"Jonny—"

"I'm going to convince you. Just the way I always do," he said playfully, lifting one finger in the air for emphasis as he took another step forward.

Pandy found she was unable to move. Jonny took another step and fell on top of her, pinning her to the bed.

He lifted his head, looked around, and then looked down into her face. This time his eyes were unfocused. In that same silly, faux-warning voice, he repeated, "I'm gonna convince you…"

And then he blacked out. Too much ancient gin.

Pandy put her hands under Jonny's chest and shoved him off. He rolled to the edge of the bed.

Pandy got up and doubled over, trying to push down what the convulsions from her stomach were trying to push up.

Jonny belched. He opened his eyes and stared at her, still on his stomach. He smiled. "I'm so happy we worked everything out," he slurred. His mouth involuntarily pursed, and he raised his palm to cover it. "Oh, and by the way?" He swallowed like a guilty child and sat up. "I don't know if your friends have mentioned it, but people think Lala and I are having an affair. We're *not*. I did have sex with her, but only twice. I'm sorry, babe," he said with a wave as he slowly fell backward. "It won't happen again. She respects you too much for that. And don't worry, she's *discreet*."

Sometime later, Pandy stood in the Hall of Ghouls, scratching her head as she peered at a photograph of a dark-haired man with a large handlebar mustache: Captain Rarebit Welsh. He had supposedly tried to extort money from his wife, but the Wallis men had soon set him straight.

Pandy shook her head with a laugh. Unfortunately, there were no Wallis men left to help her. But there, on the walls, were plenty of women. Generations of them.

It was said that Wallis women stood up straight and would talk back to any person. Meaning a *man*, of course. She thought briefly of Jonny, asleep and snoring off Old Jay's gin in Old Jay's bed. She had trusted him with both her love and her money, and he'd casually frittered both away.

So much for so-called male *authority*.

On a strange sort of autopilot, as if Jonny had never come to the house at all, Pandy poked her head into the kitchen. The large clock on the wall indicated that it was two p.m.; traditionally an ideal time for a swim in the marble pool. The sun would be high overhead, and the pool would be at its warmest point of the day.

She grabbed a long striped towel from the mudroom and slung it around her neck. The fabric, softened by years of washing, was like a pashmina. Stepping outside, Pandy draped the towel over her head.

She set off along a path of cedar wood chips that rose gently into the pines. Under the trees were thick beds of pine needles where you could lie down and make a bed, the way the deer sometimes did.

Heading down into the private hollow where the pool was located, she removed her negligee, tossing it onto a piece of statuary. Then she stood naked at the side of the pool, staring into the mirrored surface. The stream running through the pool would be about fifty-eight degrees. The water in the pool, heated by the reflections of the sun's rays against the black marble, would be about sixty-eight degrees. Not a completely unreasonable temperature, but for the uninitiated, shocking.

She dove in.

The smack of the cold water was like an electric jolt. Every circuit in her body lit up like a Christmas tree. She swam underwater until she could feel her body screaming for oxygen. Pressing the last bit of air out of her lungs, she popped up out of the water, heart thumping with adrenaline, giddy with relief, her mind clear and her heart restored.

Striding out of the pool and up the marble steps, she stared straight into the western sun and knew what she needed to do.

And then she blinked, suddenly aware of a cartoonish blot in the periphery of her vision. The blot grew arms and legs, and appeared to be engaged in the sort of frenetic dance practiced by the Romans at a bacchanal.

In the next second, the reveler burst toward her in full living color: Jonny, naked and screaming, scratching at his groin so fiercely that Pandy was afraid he would rip his cock off.

Chiggers.

While Jonny lay sleeping on Old Jay's mattress, the heat of his body had warmed the dormant chigger larvae. They had awakened from their long nap and had begun doing exactly what Mother Nature intended: They began feeding.

Chiggers had exceptionally small mouths, and were only able to bite through the body's more delicate skin. Specifically, the crotch, the armpits, the ankles, the groin, and behind the knees.

"Help me!" Jonny screamed.

Pandy took one look at him and thought, *I told him not to sleep in Old Jay's bed.* Then she did what she had been taught to do in just this sort of emergency:

She pushed him in.

The cold water would immediately kill the chiggers, and act as a sort of ice pack on the bitten areas.

Jonny landed safely in the four-foot shallow end, and flailing like a monkey, he began screaming again, scratching at his underarms as he plowed through the water to the steps. He pushed Pandy aside, collapsed onto the grass, and curled up in the fetal position.

He felt Pandy's shadow looming over him and stared at her accusingly, his eyes full of black hatred.

"You pushed me in!" he screamed.

"I had to." Pandy shrugged.

"I nearly drowned."

"Oh, stop," Pandy said. "The top of your hair is barely wet."

Hauling himself to his feet, Jonny took a few threatening steps toward her. "Don't you know *I can't swim?*"

"Yes, Jonny. I do." Pandy nodded sharply. "You told me, remember?" And before he could begin shouting again, she said quickly, "I want a divorce."

Fifteen minutes later, Jonny was dressed and at the car. Hauling open the trunk, he threw his overnight bag inside. "I'll never forgive you. You tried to drown me!" He slammed the trunk, spun on his heel, and pointed his finger. "You're going to pay for this, baby. Boy, are you going to pay."

"Fine!" Pandy spat as he stomped around the side of the car. "I'd do *anything* to get rid of *you.*"

"And you want to know something else?" He yanked open the door, got in, closed it, and stuck his head out the window. "I only went out in that fucking snowstorm because my mother thought you would be good for my *career.*"

"I knew it!" Pandy screamed. "You *are* a fucking mama's boy. Henry warned me—"

"Henry? *Henry?*" he spat, tilting his head back and laughing maniacally. "As if *Henry* knows anything about being a *man.*"

"He knows a lot more than you do, Diaper Boy."

"You frigid cunt. Hasta la vista, baby. Nice knowing you." Jonny started the car and stepped on the gas, flipping her the bird out the open window.

"Fuck you!" Pandy screamed. "Fuuuuck youuuu!" She ran down the drive after him, continuing to yell until his car disappeared around the corner.

Jesus H. Christ, she thought, marching back up the driveway barefoot. What a way to end a marriage. With a "fuck you."

How incredibly...unoriginal.

She went into the house, slammed the door behind her, and marched into the library.

She didn't care. There was only one thing that mattered now.

She knew exactly what her next book was going to be about, and it wasn't Monica.

∞

And so, as she danced to the music of her own imagination, dreaming of great triumphs, the divorce cyclone out in the real world began to whirl. First it picked up people—lawyers, private investigators, process servers—a whole Dickensian underworld of characters, each with his or her hand out.

Then it picked up the press: ANOTHER CELEBRITY MARRIAGE ON THE ROCKS!

And then it picked up paper: endless requests for bank statements, contracts, emails, and texts. And on and on, and back and forth about what was or was not relevant, and who'd said what to whom. She had managed to live through it only by escaping from it as often as possible. Specifically, into the eighteenth century and the mind of Lady Wallis Wallis when she arrived in New York City, circa 1775.

At the time, Pandy didn't know if what she was writing was literary or historical. It might have been YA. All she knew was that trying to tell Lady Wallis's story was what had given her courage.

What she'd never imagined was that it could fail.

Now, Pandy looked out the window of the town car Henry had arranged to drive her from the Pool Club and saw that she was nearly *back* in Wallis. Where she'd been only once since that long, awful day when she had told Jonny she wanted a divorce.

Through the endless dealings with Jonny's lawyers and demands for money, Pandy had assumed that Lady Wallis would make it all okay in the end.

Except she hadn't.

The driver hit the brakes. "Which way?"

"That way," Pandy said, pointing to the narrow rutted track that was Wallis Road.

And right there, at the last outpost of cell phone service, her phone began fluttering those happy notes from Monica's theme song.

Pandy picked it up.

CHAPTER FOURTEEN

H ENRY?"
Her voice came out thickly, like she was speaking through clotted cream. She had to take a sip of water before she could continue. "Please tell me what I think happened two hours ago back at the Pool Club didn't happen?"

"I wish I could, my dear," Henry said with firm sympathy.

"You mean, it *did* happen?"

"Yes."

"Are you sure?" Pandy began to protest as she became aware of a terrible poisoned feeling. Her body felt stuck between a blackout and a terrific hangover, in a sort of alcoholic purgatory.

It was all that champagne she'd drunk. At the Pool Club. With her friends.

She shook her head, trying not to remember too much. If she did, she might very well become sick. In fact, she probably *would* be sick.

And yet, there was something in Pandy that still wanted to resist reality, especially when it was this bad. She took another gulp of water. "Are you absolutely and completely sure about the book?" she asked.

"Yes. They rejected it," Henry said.

"Lady Wallis?" Pandy sat back in her seat, still reluctant to

199

embrace the truth. "Are you sure you sent them the right manuscript?" she asked desperately.

"Was there another one?" Henry asked drily.

"But why?" Pandy moaned softly, like an animal in pain.

"They didn't like it," Henry said simply. "They said the book didn't *sound* like you. They said it wasn't a, quote, 'PJ Wallis book.'"

"And what did *you* say?"

"I said, 'Of course it's a PJ Wallis book. How can a book written by PJ Wallis not be?' And then they said, 'But PJ Wallis doesn't write *historical* fiction. So people who are looking for a PJ Wallis book will be angry. *Disappointed*.' I said that begged the question as to their publishing it under another name. Which they'd likely do, but not with your current advance. So if you want to *keep* the advance, you'll have to give them their PJ Wallis book. And they want it to be about Monica. They suggested that Monica get divorced. Try *online dating*. The thought, I agree, is terrifying. I told them, 'We'll see.'"

He paused. He must have realized that Pandy hadn't interrupted him. "Pandy?" he asked. "Are you there?"

Pandy looked out the window. They were just starting up the driveway.

"What happens if I refuse to write another Monica book?" she asked.

"Let's not worry about that now," Henry said firmly. "Right now, I want you to take a deep breath and relax. Go for a walk through the pine forest. Take a swim in the pool. Or better yet, canoe around the lake. And then have a nice hot bath. Get a good night's sleep, and call me in the morning."

"So this means I won't get the money."

"You *will* get the money. When you deliver the next Monica book. If you work really hard, I'm sure you can knock one off in six months. After all, you do know all about ugly divorces now."

"Thanks, Henry," she sniped.

Henry sighed. "I *did* warn you about historical fiction. Most editors won't go near it these days. It's not *popular*."

She lost Henry when the driver slammed on the brake and her phone dropped to the floor. They had reached the final switchback to the house, and the driver turned around to gape at her. Then he slowly turned his head and looked back at the house, as if trying to put two and two together.

"You *live* here?" he asked.

Pandy sighed, gathering her things. "It's not what it seems."

She got out of the car and started briskly up the path to the house, pausing for a moment to admire the rose garden. The *S. Pandemonia* and *S. Hellenor*, the two roses for which she and Hellenor were named, were in full bloom.

This situation—the looming divorce settlement and the book's being rejected—was going to be a huge problem, she realized as she went hurriedly up the stairs and into the house. Without pausing to wind the clock, she went right into the kitchen.

She placed her sack of groceries on the counter, opened the refrigerator, took out the container of milk, and threw it in the trash.

The milk was from the one and only time she'd been back to Wallis House since that terrible scene with Jonny. It had been nearly a year since the night when she'd secretly moved all her papers to Wallis House.

All the files and contracts; the tax returns, the old phone bills, drafts of manuscripts and *Monica* scripts; a copy of the will she'd just signed that left everything to Hellenor—including the rights to Monica—on the off chance she might have something to leave behind when Jonny's lawyers got through with her. In short, anything and everything that Jonny might get his hands on and could then use against her.

He'd already tried to claim that Pandy had attempted to murder him when she'd pushed him into the pool.

Pandy sighed and began unpacking the groceries Henry had shoved into the back of the car at the last second. If she'd known then what she knew now about Jonny, would she have let him slide under the water, watching those last air bubbles rise to the surface— a series of small ones, then a pause, and at last that final balloon-shaped burst of air as the water rushed in and forced out the last molecules of oxygen?

She would have only had to wait fifteen minutes for Jonny to be brain-dead and dead-dead. And then, for the sake of authenticity, she would have retraced her steps, hurrying down the path as if she'd just discovered he wasn't in the house. When she spotted him float-ing in the pool, she would have splashed in, lifting him under the arms and laying him flat in the grass. She would have pulled back his head and pinched his nose.

She would then have performed textbook-perfect CPR. After ten minutes, she would have given up. She would have run back to the house, called 911, and waited the thirty minutes it would have taken for the volunteer fire department to arrive.

And by then, it would have been far too late.

Jonny would be dead—an accident! He had taken a nap in Old Jay's bed, been attacked by chiggers, and had run into the pool to es-cape them, where, unfortunately, he had drowned.

And what a happy widow she would have been! Free of Jonny without the bummer of becoming another middle-aged divorcée in New York. Instead, her reputation would have grown as that of a tragic figure.

She would have had what her English friends called "the black wedding." The black wedding was what you wished for ten years af-ter you'd had the white wedding. After you'd produced a couple of children and had had enough time to realize that yes, indeed, your husband *was* totally useless. You wished for the black wedding—your husband's funeral. You'd get the money and the lifestyle and the chil-dren, without the hassle of the man.

Of course, when it came to marriage, the English had always been far more practical than the Americans.

Fuck, she thought, extracting a package of Cheddar cheese.

The pathetic fact was, Jonny had managed to get so much money out of her during their marriage that when it came time to talk about a settlement, she'd had no cash left.

Neither, unsurprisingly, did Jonny. In fact, it turned out that technically, Jonny didn't own anything at all.

As a matter of fact, Jonny *owed* money. And that meant *she* owed money, too. This, at least, was the gist of it. This, and the fact that Jonny did, indeed, own something, after all: half of everything *she* owned.

She'd had to promise to pay him her entire advance—the very same advance she'd been expecting her publishers to pay her when she delivered the book.

And now, because her publishers had rejected her book, she would have no money to pay Jonny after all.

She wandered into the library, looked up at the portrait of Lady Wallis Wallis, and cringed.

On the other hand, it would be easy enough to pay Jonny off. All she had to do was sell the portrait. It was probably worth millions.

Pandy emitted a harsh laugh. Forced to sell a painting that had been in her family for three hundred years to pay off Jonny Balaga? Never. What would Lady Wallis say?

Disgusted with herself, Pandy went upstairs to her room. There, she sat down at her desk and looked at her pile of old Monica notebooks. Of course she didn't have to sell Lady Wallis Wallis. Not when she still had Monica.

And people still *wanted* Monica.

Which meant there was absolutely no excuse for her *not* to write another Monica book. She would agree to it, and her lawyers would make some kind of arrangement with Jonny's lawyers as to a payment schedule. Nevertheless, Jonny's settlement would be delayed; to compensate, Jonny's lawyers would attempt to up the amount. And then, it wouldn't be just one more Monica book that she needed to write, but two or three.

If, indeed, Monica even lasted that long. Eventually, people would grow tired of Monica. And then Monica and PJ Wallis would end up back here. Back where they started. And eventually the cats would come…

Pandy picked up one of the notebooks.

It was the first Monica story, entitled "Monica: A Girl's Guide to Being a Girl." She'd created the perfect imaginary little girl—Monica—who knew everything about being a girl, for the instruction of Hellenor. By seven, Hellenor was becoming what her teachers deemed "a problem child." She refused her mother's and then Pandy's entreaties to dress like a girl, act like a girl, *be* a girl, and so Pandy had created Monica and the Girl's Guide to help her. She had used the *Girl Scout Handbook* as her inspiration.

Pandy picked up another notebook. Dated 198–, it was the last installment of Monica. She flipped to the back page. It was blank, save for the small lettering written in Hellenor's hand. Pandy held the page away to read the tiny block letters painstakingly formed in red ink:

KILL MONICA. PLEASE.

And for a brief moment, Pandy laughed. Hellenor had always hated Monica.

Until she hadn't. Once Monica started making money…

She snapped the book shut and replaced it on the pile.

She should have put her foot down after the second Monica book. She should have said, "No more." But how was she to know what the future would hold? When she'd reinvented Monica ten years ago, she'd made her a more perfect version of herself. Bad things might happen to PJ Wallis, but only good things happened to Monica. In Monica's world, everything always worked out.

And then, some of Monica's stardust rubbed off on Pandy herself, because suddenly good things were happening to Pandy as well. And for a while there, it seemed she really *was* Monica…

Until she wasn't. Because the bad things that were now happening to PJ Wallis were not the kinds of things that were supposed to happen to Monica.

The audience wouldn't like Monica if she were the way Pandy was now: destitute, on the verge of a breakdown; a pathetic woman who'd dared to believe in herself and had lost everything.

And it wasn't just about the money! Indeed, it wasn't really about the money at all, but the fact that in taking her money, Jonny had robbed her of her creative freedom. He'd stolen her opportunity to take a chance on herself, and in doing so, had enslaved a piece of her soul.

Collapsing onto the typewriter, she sobbed and sobbed. What was the point? She might as well destroy Monica, and she would start by burning the original notebooks. Wiping her cheeks with the backs of her hands, she picked up the last notebook and once again examined the page where Hellenor had written KILL MONICA.

And then, like a drunk who instantly feels sober when faced with a crisis, Pandy felt her tears dry up. Without the advance, Jonny would certainly take her loft, but it wouldn't be enough. And then he'd try to go after something else: either Monica or Wallis House—most likely both. He probably couldn't get them, but he was nevertheless free to make her life miserable by trying. He could file suit after suit. Because, as her lawyers had explained again and again, she'd never signed a prenup, and was therefore "vulnerable."

Which meant that in order to prevent Jonny from attempting to take Wallis House, she might have to produce the one person who stood in his way: Hellenor.

And that would not be good.

Once they started looking, who knew what they might find out?

Fucking Hellenor, Pandy thought with a start. Now she had to tell Henry how she had foolishly managed to put everything at risk.

She pushed back from her desk with a grunt. The call to Henry was inevitable. She might as well get it over with. Her cell phone didn't work here, so she would have to use the landline.

She walked to the end of the hallway, past the eighteenth-century French wallpaper that Jonny would undoubtedly rip out, to a small door set into the paneling. She yanked it open and, feeling for the light switch, went down a set of steep, enclosed stairs. When she got to the bottom, she kicked the door. As always, it was stuck.

She kicked it again and it opened. The stench of something slightly rotten rose up into the air. Pandy coughed. Dead mice. She leaned across the couch and unwound the two windows. They opened smoothly, but brought in a handful of dead leaves. Pandy brushed the leaves away and looked around.

The den, as usual, was in its gloomy half-light. The windows in this room were small and high, meant to save on heating. She went to the wall and flipped on the light. The gloom could be explained by the dark plastic paneling that someone had stuck on the walls in an attempt at renovation.

She opened another door and went into the mudroom. Unlike the den, no one had ever attempted to renovate the mudroom, but the appliances, at least, were recognizable. There was a washer and dryer, a big farmhouse sink, a toilet, and most important of all, heat, generated by a potbellied stove in the center of the room.

Arranged around the stove were a picnic table and two old Barcalounger armchairs that had started out a hideous orange but had now faded to a dirty tan.

Leaning against one wall was the tall, narrow mirror where she and Hellenor had checked themselves before they left the house. If Hellenor looked too strange, Pandy would make her change.

The mudroom and the den. Where Pandy and her family had

spent most of their time. Because the TV was in the den, and the phone was in the mudroom. The phone was located on a small shelf next to an old answering machine, which still worked. Next to the shelf was a large corkboard where their mother had left herself notes. It still held an assortment of old birthday cards and photos.

Pandy sighed and picked up the receiver. Henry was going to kill her.

She glanced at a photo on the corkboard: her and Hellenor on one of the many Halloweens in which Hellenor had insisted on being Peter Pan and Pandy had been forced to be Wendy.

Pandy frowned. She hated Wendy.

She put down the receiver. She couldn't tell Henry. Not *right this second*. She had to think. Henry was right; she needed to clear her head.

She looked back at the photograph. Hellenor, with her short boy-cut hair, green tunic, and bow and arrow. Hellenor, who had managed to avoid just the sort of trouble Pandy was in right now. Hellenor, who had chosen not to become emotionally encumbered by marriage, children, or even a relationship.

And now Hellenor was perfectly happy.

Goddamned *Hellenor* had no worries. *And boy, oh boy, wouldn't she just love to be Hellenor right now*, Pandy thought bitterly as she marched back up to her room.

∞

Several minutes later, having changed into a pair of baggy shorts and a T-shirt—her only old clothes that still fit—Pandy stuck her phone into her back pocket and headed down the path that led to the boathouse. The veined marble stones skirted the boxwood maze and ended at a set of wooden steps, at the bottom of which was an ornate Victorian structure with a cupola and a large teak deck.

At the top of the stairs, she paused. It was hotter than she had expected. The air was still. There would be thunderstorms later.

Pandy went down the stairs and around the boathouse to a dock where a shiny red canoe was always tied. She got into the boat, sat down, unhooked the rope, picked up the paddle, and pushed the boat away from the dock.

The lake was shaped like a gourd, with a narrow chute at one end, enclosed by marshes where all the little turtles bred in the early summer. It was to this marshy underworld that Pandy now made her way.

She paddled briskly for a minute or two, and then, exhausted, put the paddle back into the canoe and let the boat drift to the center of the lake.

The air was deadly quiet.

Pandy looked around. The sun had gone behind a cloud, and the lake was like a mirror. She remembered how her mother had always told them that the skating mirror under the Christmas tree was a miniature version of this lake.

She leaned forward, put her face in her hands, and began to cry.

∞

She didn't know how long she cried, but it was long enough that when she heard the first crack of thunder, she wondered if she had the strength to make it back to the boathouse. The whiteness of the cupola was suddenly in stark contrast to the gray-black clouds that had gathered behind it. Pandy noticed that there was a tinge of green to this now-rumbling mass.

She picked up the paddle and began rowing as a sluice of cold, hard rain blew across the side of the mountain. It was suddenly as dark as night; when she reached the dock, Pandy's fingers fumbled with the rope until she gave up on tying up the boat. She stood cautiously, her arms outstretched as she attempted to balance on the tippy canoe. She had one foot on the boat and one on the dock when she felt an electric tingling and heard a deafening crack.

And then, just like in a movie, a jagged, bright white bolt of lightning split the boathouse in two. Suddenly she was airborne. She knew she was up in the air because the trees were upside down. And then they weren't, and she was lying facedown in the muddy grass.

She must have blacked out, because she had the distinct sensation of being in a dream. Or rather, of being in the particularly nasty nightmare that she had all the time: trying to get onto the elevator, but the doors wouldn't open.

And then, miraculously, her eyes opened, and she knew she was still alive.

She was lying on her stomach halfway up the hill. A spark must have hit the stairs, because now they were burning. Rising onto her hands and knees, she clawed her way up to the top of the hill. It felt like she was climbing the face of a mountain.

When she reached the top, she stood up and looked back. The front of the boathouse was an enormous bonfire; soon the whole thing would go up in flames. Moving as fast as she could, alternating between a brisk walk, a slow jog, and several moments when she had to stop altogether, she realized this fire was the last straw. She couldn't imagine how much it would cost to rebuild the boathouse. Then she remembered that she was never going to be able to rebuild it, because she'd never again have the money.

The boathouse was gone. And pretty soon, other pieces of Wallis House that couldn't be replaced would go, too...

Enraged, she stumbled into the mudroom. She picked up the phone, but it took her three tries to dial 911.

Finally, someone answered. "What is your emergency?"

"Fire," Pandy said, hacking as if the inside of her throat had been burned as well.

"What's the address?"

"One Wallis Road. The...big mansion on top of the mountain," she choked out. She felt like she was going to black out again.

"Oh. That place. Hold on."

The operator came back on. "It's going to take them half an hour to get there. Is everyone okay?"

"Thirty minutes?" The boathouse would be nothing but ash by then. Pandy started to cry.

"Ma'am? Is everyone okay?" the operator repeated. "There isn't a body burning in there or anything?"

Pandy found she couldn't speak. Possibly she was going into shock.

"Ma'am?" The operator's voice was suddenly sharp. "Hello? Is anyone hurt? Was anyone in the boathouse?"

Pandy's insides squeezed shut as she tried to contain the shaking that was building up in her body like a pending explosion.

"To whom am I speaking?"

Pandy took a deep breath and, managing to stifle her scream, moved in front of the mirror. Her eyes widened in surprise. Her face and body were streaked with black soot and her clothes were in tatters. Her hair was burned off at the roots. Who *was* she, she wondered wildly. Her eyes landed on the photograph of Hellenor as Peter Pan…

"Ma'am? To whom am I speaking?" the operator demanded.

Pandy opened her mouth and, confused, nearly said, "Peter Pan." But she knew, somehow, that that wasn't right, because Peter Pan was actually…"Hellenor Wallis," she gasped. It was the best she could do.

She let the phone drop from her hand as she heard the operator demanding to know the name of the person who was burning up in the boathouse.

She stumbled across the mudroom to a narrow cabinet. She reached up to the top shelf and took down a large bottle of whiskey. She unscrewed the cap, took a gulp, and then, as the whiskey hit her system with a jolt, she came to slightly and went back to the phone. She picked it up. "Hello?" she slurred. "It's PJ Wallis." And then the tsunami that had been building inside her

210

suddenly came spewing out. Bile, black ash, and whiskey sprayed the floor.

The shock of this purge suddenly made Pandy feel better. The clamminess receded. She picked up the phone and hung it up, wanting to take advantage of this brief moment in which she felt slightly more mobile. She grabbed the bottle of whiskey and wobbled up the back stairs.

From where, only a short time ago, she had originated on some kind of mission. Unfortunately, she now had no idea what that was.

She wove down the hallway to her room, stripping off her garments as she went into the bathroom. Taking another gulp of whiskey, she sat down on the edge of the tub. Her hands were trembling as she turned the tap to run the hot water.

She got in, lying flat on her back in order to cover herself as quickly as possible.

As the hot water began to trickle in, her muscles began to relax slightly.

She sat up and took another sip of whiskey.

"There's a body burning up in the boathouse," she said aloud in the kind of silly voice that would have made Hellenor laugh. Hellenor. If she really had burned up in the explosion, Hellenor wouldn't be laughing. She'd be sad. But at least she would inherit everything Pandy owned, including the rights to Monica.

Monica. Pandy groaned. She put her head in her hands. And suddenly, she was stone-cold sober.

Now it was all going to come out. The truth about her marriage; how she'd given Jonny money. Everyone would say it was because she was so desperate to hang on to him, she gave him whatever he wanted. And then they'd whisper behind their backs that she'd deserved it. She'd made more money than her husband, and certainly that merited some kind of punishment.

She took another swig of whiskey, got out of the tub, and lurched for a towel. Whatever happened, she'd just have to deal with it. She dried herself off and then used a corner of the towel to wipe the steam from the mirror. She stared at her reflection. What she saw nearly caused her to go into shock again.

She was basically bald. Or would have to be, soon. What remained of her charred hair was a patchwork of crinkled, blackened strands of uneven lengths that would clearly have to be shaved.

For a brief moment, she could only shake her head in wonder at the viciousness of this particular run of bad luck. It wasn't enough that her book had been rejected and she would have to explain to the world why she couldn't write Jonny his check. She was going to have to do it as a bald woman.

Suddenly, she was exhausted. She dropped to her knees in a fatigue so deep, it threatened to overwhelm her. And in this fog, she remembered that she still had to deal with the fire department.

∽

They arrived, having been informed that Hellenor Wallis had reported that her sister, PJ Wallis, was burning in a fire. Pandy took one look at the grim-faced volunteer firemen and realized she simply didn't have the energy to explain the mix-up. She would take care of it in the morning.

It was so much easier to go along with the notion that it was vaguely true.

"And your name is Hellenor Wallis?"

"Yes," she said.

"And your sister was in the canoe—"

Pandy tried to say no, but her teeth were chattering so much, she couldn't get out another word. She pulled the blanket she'd wrapped around her head and shoulders closer as three more men came up the drive, shaking their heads.

They'd found what they presumed was Pandy's cell phone, now a twisted, charred piece of unidentifiable material. They explained that they were truly sorry, but because the house was so remote it

212

wasn't technically in the jurisdiction of the township and they could only file a report.

And then the nice man with the gray mustache told her that she would need to make a citizen's report to the local coroner. She could do it on their website.

When she haltingly explained that the house didn't have an internet connection, the man must have felt sorry for her, because he offered to file a paper report instead, in which he would describe the fire. The coroner's office would be out in a day or two to comb through the ashes when the site had cooled.

Pandy nodded, propping herself against the wall in utter exhaustion. By then, of course, it would all be sorted out. Finally they left, their red taillights flickering down the drive like fireflies.

When the last one had winked its red eye, she turned back to the house, determined to do what she'd been needing to do *forever*, it seemed:

Curl up into a little ball and go to sleep.

She stumbled into the mudroom, kicked off her boots, and fell onto the couch in the den. She pulled the acrylic comforter her grandmother had knitted over her. As the world slowly blinked out around her, her mind circled down into long-ago memories. Like the night twenty years ago. When she and Hellenor were sitting on this very couch. When they'd gotten the news. In addition to the house, she and Hellenor had each been left fifty thousand dollars.

"Spend it wisely," the lawyer had said.

Pandy's brain clicked off like a light jerked by a string.

She slept like the dead.

PART THREE

CHAPTER FIFTEEN

THE DREAM was always the same:

It was Pandy's birthday, and SondraBeth Schnowzer was there, her face pressed next to Pandy's as they laughed in the flickering orangish light from the hundreds of birthday candles on Pandy's cake.

The dream vanished as Pandy gasped and hinged upright, the afghan clutched under her chin.

Where was she?

She took in the gloomy atmosphere and sighed. She was in the den. In Wallis. Her book about Lady Wallis was dead, and now the boathouse had blown up. *Another great beginning to another fabulous day*, she thought bitterly as she went into the kitchen.

She filled the electric kettle and clicked it on. She opened the cabinet, and, from among several different types of tea, she and Henry being aficionados, removed a sachet of double-bergamot Earl Grey.

Strong tea. She had that tiny thread of Englishness in her bones that believed the right cup of tea might possibly make everything better, no matter what the situation. Catching a whiff of the still-burned strands of her hair, she realized that in this case, "the situation" was as simple as being alive.

And that has to be something, right? she reminded herself as she

217

poured hot water over the tea bag. In any case, for the first time in a long time, she was happy to feel her body. It actually felt like a bonus, as opposed to a large steamer trunk.

She sighed and dropped the tea bag into the garbage. She was alive, but the boathouse was gone. There had been an explosion. The volunteer firemen had come. And now she was supposed to go on some website to report that she was dead. Except, of course, she wasn't.

It was just like life, she thought, meandering back into the den with her tea. Bad things came in threes.

What's next? she wondered, plopping down on the couch and absentmindedly pulling out the knob on the TV. As the old television sprang to life, Pandy gathered the afghan around her and wished she could go back to sleep.

Forever. She yawned as her eyes slid toward the screen...

And once again, she was wide awake. And here came bad thing number three:

She was dead.

For there, on the screen of the old black-and-white TV, was that old black-and-white author photograph of her from ten years ago, when—she realized with a start—she had been *so much younger.*

"PJ Wallis, a longtime Connecticut resident, has died at her home in Wallis," said the announcer; the same announcer Pandy recognized from when she was a child. "She was known to many as the creator of the popular character Monica. She was forty-six years old—"

"Forty-five!" Pandy shouted automatically.

And then her image was gone, replaced by a package of Depends.

"That did not just happen," Pandy said aloud.

She stood up, uncertain about what to do. Surely, what she'd just seen had to be a mistake. Otherwise, Henry would have called.

Or would he? As she went into the mudroom to pick up the receiver, she remembered that the TV only got the local station. Apparently that nice fireman had filed his report, but perhaps the news hadn't spread. Henry likely didn't know she'd been declared dead.

She dialed Henry's number. He answered with his usual drawling "Hellooooo?"

"*Hello?*" she demanded. "Have you noticed that I am *dead?*"

"Now why on earth should something that convenient happen to you?" Henry asked. "I saw a tweet from *Publisher's Daily* that the author PJ Wallis has been reported dead by her sister, Hellenor…"

"And?" Pandy continued.

"That was it. Since we both know that Hellenor is in Amsterdam, I could only conclude this particular 'Hellenor Wallis' was actually PJ Wallis *playing* dead."

"And why would I do that?" Pandy asked archly.

"To remind me of how wonderful you are, and how terrible it would be if you really *had* died."

Pandy laughed. And then she remembered the boathouse. "Actually, Henry, there *is* a tragedy. The boathouse. It was struck by lightning, and now it's burned to the ground. I know how much you loved that boathouse. Remember that scene in *The Philadelphia Story?*"

"That's one of your favorite movies, not mine. In any case, the boathouse doesn't matter. The important thing is that you, my dear, are alive." Henry gave a low chuckle. "Although I can't say your publishers feel the same."

"What do you mean?" Pandy's eyes narrowed.

Henry cleared his throat. "Based on their reactions, it's rather a shame you're *not* dead. Your demise seems to have caused a small stir. One actually called at seven this morning to discuss it. Of course, he expressed his condolences. But he also pointed out how good it would be for your sales."

"And what did *you* say?"

"I didn't see the need to get into the details about Hellenor's likely identity. I simply said that I'd get back to him when I found out more about the accident. It won't hurt him to think you're dead for a few hours."

"You're such a sneak," Pandy said admiringly. "*Of course* my death would be good for my sales."

"Now, darling. Don't get too excited. You're not actually dead—yet."

"It's almost a shame I'm not," she said, reminded of Jonny. She glanced in the mirror and sighed. She seemed to have aged two decades overnight. She was literally gray. Her skin was still smeared with soot, and her hair—her *hair*—

She turned quickly away from the glass. She had worse things to worry about than her hair. "I need money, Henry. And fast."

"You *have* money."

"No, I do not. I need money desperately."

"I don't understand."

"Oh, Henry." She grimaced at the mirror and noticed that her teeth were also sooty. She sighed. She was going to have to tell Henry the truth: She hadn't made Jonny sign a prenup, and Jonny had lost all the money she'd given him in a bad restaurant deal.

Henry would be furious. And it would turn out that he would have been right about Jonny all along.

"Pandy?" Henry coaxed.

"It's just…" Pandy took another look in the mirror and noticed her charred bra strap was showing through where her T-shirt had torn. "I'll tell you all about it when you get here, okay? And can you *please* bring up my clothes? I can't fit into my old ones, and the clothes I'm wearing have been literally turned to ash."

With a grim goodbye, she hung up and made her way up the back stairs to her bathroom. She plugged the sink and ran the hot water, grabbing a washcloth and soap and scrubbing her face and head until all the blackened clumps came away.

The sight of her once-beautiful hair, now charred and smeared on the damp washcloth, almost made her cry. She threw the washcloth into the trash, and spotting the bottle of the whiskey next to the tub where she'd left it the night before, picked it up and took a swig.

She dried her head and looked in the mirror.

A charred sort of frizzle stood up along the top of her head like a rooster's comb.

She took another slug of whiskey. The second shot made her fight down the urge to vomit.

When that passed, she opened the cabinet and took out a can of shaving cream and a razor. She aimed the can at her head and pressed the button.

The shaving foam made a cap. A clownish kind of cap that reminded her of the Marx Brothers. If she added Hellenor's safety glasses, she'd look just like Groucho. She took another swig of whiskey. She ran the water, picked up the razor, and began shaving.

As the razor drew lines in the foam, she realized that the first thing she would have to do when she got back to New York was to buy a wig.

She put down the razor, tipped her head, and splashed water over her scalp. The slick surface under her hands nearly made her sick again. She dried the top of her head.

And lifting her face while she mentally braced for the inevitable, she looked in the mirror.

She gasped.

She was expecting it to be bad. But *this*?

Who *was* she?

No one. Without her hair, she looked anonymous. She could be anyone, really. She could even be a *man.*

Grabbing the towel, she pulled it over her head. This was the final indignity. "Bad thing number four," she howled aloud, throwing herself onto her bed.

She rolled into the dip of the old feather mattress. And then, as generations of little girls had no doubt done before her, she cried and cried and cried.

Sometime later, she sat up and dried her tears.

She'd had her emotional indulgence. Like every Wallis child, she'd been taught that feelings, no matter how bad, were unlikely to change reality. Meaning, don't just sit there feeling sorry for yourself. "Take action," her father would have said.

Besides, it was relatively simple: She was bald. She needed hair.

It was possible that in the jumble of old costumes in the Victorian theater there was a wig. Possibly several. But they would be like Old Jay's bed: You wouldn't want to sleep in them.

She would have to wear a hat instead. The best selection of hats could be found in one of Hellenor's old rooms; specifically, in the room Hellenor had once dubbed "the lab."

Panting slightly—a reminder that she was in terrible shape— Pandy made her way down the long second-floor corridor, then up another flight of stairs to the children's wing, where she opened the door to the schoolroom.

At one time, if something was burning, exploding, or boiling over, chances were it was coming from this room. Pandy would burst in screaming to find Hellenor, dressed in a white lab coat and wearing safety glasses, holding a smoking test tube.

"Yes?" she would ask curtly.

"Mom's worried you're about to burn down the house."

And Hellenor would say, "Maybe someday I will."

Back in the days when Hellenor was so angry.

And maybe, because of Hellenor, Pandy had been angry, too. Because of Hellenor, she didn't see the world the way little girls were supposed to—all sugar and spice and everything nice.

Indeed, while the other girls at school were busy learning how to be girls, she and Hellenor were busy learning how to be feminists. They were determined to rail against a world in which being a woman meant being a second-class citizen, without proprietary rights over your body, your thoughts, your soul, or your very being.

They hated what they would come to know as sexism so much that after "Monica," Pandy had begun another series called "World Without Men." But then she discovered boys.

Hellenor didn't. Instead, she decided to annoy everyone and dress like a boy. Hence the collection of men's hats for nearly every occasion, along with an assortment of other "manly" garments she'd dug up from one of the attics and hung from a pegboard on the wall.

Pandy picked out a gray fedora and put it on. She wandered over to Hellenor's lab table and picked up a pair of safety glasses. Trying them on, she glanced in the mirror and frowned, reminded that her clothes were burned and she was going to be reduced to wearing not just one of Hellenor's hats, but her clothes as well.

Walking to the closet, she extracted a flannel shirt and a pair of the men's black suit pants Hellenor used to favor. Hellenor had been a little taller, so Pandy had to roll the trouser legs up over her knees. Discovering an old pair of Hellenor's construction boots, she figured she might as well put those on as well. They'd be useful when Henry arrived and they went out to inspect what was left of the boathouse.

Once again, she looked in the mirror. And here was more irony: Now she really did look like Hellenor. Or what Hellenor might look like now.

This was the final insult. She hoped Henry would get there soon.

She marched into the library and, standing in front of the painting of Lady Wallis Wallis, shook her head. People were stupid. How could someone *not* want a book about Lady Wallis? She had all the courage—if not more—of a modern-day heroine, but her life had been real, and she'd actually had a hand in shaping the future of America.

And she was beautiful. That still wasn't *enough*?

The whole world sucked, she decided. No one had any imagination anymore. Feeling impatient for Henry's company, she decided to go up into the cupola to see if she could spot his car.

She went up three flights of steps, around a landing, and then up another flight. Above her dangled a white rope with a carved wooden pull. Pandy tugged it, and a wooden ladder unfolded.

Pandy climbed up and looked around. Old Jay's lookout, as they used to call it, was built inside the enormous eight-sided cupola. Posted in front of each large round window was a telescope.

The views were amazing. Through one telescope, you could see two states away, to the still-snowy tip of a mountain. You could also see down to the gas station, which was handy, because then you knew if anyone was coming up Wallis Road.

Pandy lowered her eye to one of the telescopes.

She froze.

Coming from between two pine-covered hilltops were what appeared to be helicopters.

She lifted her head and took a step back. That was strange. No helicopters ever came to Wallis. There was no place for them to land.

Perhaps there had been some kind of terrorist attack?

She bent down to look through another telescope. Several cars and what looked like two white news vans were pulling into the parking lot of the gas station.

And then she saw SondraBeth's custom navy-blue Porsche coming up the drive.

⊙

Monica.

In the frenzy of trying to deal with her own problems, Pandy had forgotten about Monica. She'd forgotten about SondraBeth Schnowzer. But apparently they hadn't forgotten about *her*. And just like Frankenstein's monster, here came disaster.

Apparently word of Pandy's death had spread after all. Sondra-Beth—*Monica*—in mourning, paying her respects to the family of the deceased, would make for a dramatic photograph and, without having to speak a word, would send the proper message: She was grief-stricken over the death of her creator, PJ Wallis. Which would have been enormously flattering—if PJ Wallis actually *were* dead.

Pandy hurried down the staircase, and reaching the second floor, peeked out the front window. A cameraman and a woman with a device in her hand were standing in the middle of the rose garden. Now, this was just too much. Henry would be furious. Incensed, Pandy went through the French doors that opened onto a deck shaped like the prow of a ship. She walked to the edge and shouted down angrily. "Excuse me!"

"Yes?" The woman looked up.

"You're standing in my rose garden."

"So?" the cameraman asked, resting his camera on his shoulder.

"So you're standing on at least two hundred years of history. Now will you please *move*."

The woman gave Pandy a dismissive look and rolled her eyes.

"Hello?" Pandy repeated sharply. "I asked you to get out of my rose garden."

The cameraman swung around, and out of habit or aggressiveness, took several shots of her in rapid succession, as if Pandy were the target in a video game.

"We're trying to get a photograph of Monica," he said pointedly, lowering his camera.

The woman looked up at Pandy curiously. "Are you PJ Wallis's sister? Hellenor Wallis?"

Hellenor? For a second, Pandy could only gape at the woman. Then she felt the breeze on the back of her neck. She'd forgotten she was bald. No wonder they hadn't recognized her. "No," she snapped. "I most certainly am *not* Hellenor—"

She broke off and frowned past the intruders to the hill beyond. A squad of cameramen and reporters were now pounding up the rise like soldiers about to plant a flag on enemy territory.

And then the Porsche swung back into view. The mob suddenly organized, pointing their lenses at SondraBeth's car and snapping away until the car disappeared around another hillock. Then they lowered their cameras and relaxed.

Pandy, on the other hand, didn't.

She was going to have to greet the world looking like this?

She ran into the bathroom and peered again in the mirror. Was this fate's ultimate insult?

And suddenly, she was furious. She pulled the fedora over her ears and strode out into the corridor. Now, thanks to SondraBeth Schnowzer and Monica, the whole world, including Jonny, was going to see her looking like this. The photos would be everywhere—and Jonny would laugh his head off.

And then, word would get out about the truth regarding their marriage, and the whole world would jeer about that as well...

Christ. Where was Henry when she needed him?

"Hellenor Wallis?" she heard a voice call out.

Pandy jumped. She hurried to the window at the end of the hall and yanked it open. Leaning out, she spotted SondraBeth's navy-blue Porsche parked in the kitchen lot reserved for family and deliveries.

Unlike the press, SondraBeth knew where to park. Back when they were friends, Pandy and SondraBeth used to come up to Wallis and have a ball.

Pandy banged down the back stairs, went through the den, and flung open the door to the mudroom.

Sure enough, SondraBeth was already in the mudroom, on the phone. She was wearing a tight-fitting black T-shirt and skinny black jeans. Slung over her shoulder was some kind of loose, baggy, unconstructed garment that swirled behind her like a shadow. Wrapped around her face like insect eyes were multifaceted iridescent sunglasses.

"I wish I could fire someone for this. I really do," she was saying.

Pandy cleared her throat. SondraBeth turned her head and raised her dark glasses. She looked briefly at Pandy and quickly held up one finger. She went back to her call. "Can you hold on for a second? Pandy's sister, Hellenor, just walked in. Thanks." She turned back to Pandy and put her palm over the receiver. "I'm so sorry, Hellenor. I probably should have called to let you know I was coming, but I wasn't expecting to be followed by all this press. Apparently my phone has a tracking device. I'm just trying to clear a couple of things up. I won't be more than five seconds." She nodded at her assistant, who was standing respectfully at the other end of the room.

She went back to her call. "I need to speak to PP, okay?" she said sharply, and hung up.

SondraBeth looked Pandy up and down and smiled. Stepping forward, she took Pandy by the shoulders. Bending her knees slightly to stare into her face, she said, "Hellenor. I'm so honored to meet you, and so sorry about your sister."

Pandy's jaw dropped. Was she joking? SondraBeth didn't recognize her?

Pandy moved her face closer. She squinted at SondraBeth. "Squeege?" she asked cautiously.

"Squeege!" SondraBeth exclaimed. "That's what Pandy used to call me. And I used to call her Peege. But of course you would know that. I'm sure she's told you *everything*."

SondraBeth looked straight at Pandy as her eyes narrowed knowingly. Pandy wondered if SondraBeth was trying to give her a message. Trying to somehow hint to Pandy that she recognized her but couldn't acknowledge it.

SondraBeth smiled grimly. "In that case, I suppose you know all about Jonny."

"Jonny!" Pandy said, emitting a harsh laugh. Her lips drew back into a tight line, and in a voice that insinuated that she understood, she said, "You could say I do."

SondraBeth paused, again peering at Pandy closely. Seeming satisfied by what she saw, she nodded briskly. "Then you know what a bad guy Jonny is."

"You could say that." Pandy followed SondraBeth out of the mud-room and into the kitchen.

"I tried to warn Pandy before she married him that he was a bad seed." SondraBeth swung open the refrigerator door, took out a bot-tle of water, and unscrewed the cap. "But you know how stubborn she could be when it came to men. And now she's gone, and it's too late. I'm never going to forgive myself for letting a stupid fight over a guy get in the way of our friendship."

"SondraBeth?" the assistant was now cautiously standing in the doorway.

"Yes, Judy?" SondraBeth asked.

"PP in three."

"Thanks." SondraBeth began walking back to the mudroom. "The upshot is that all kinds of awful shit is going to come out about Jonny. I know you can handle it, but I just want you to be pre-pared. Pandy always said you were the kind of woman who would never get taken in by a man. And you're exactly as Pandy described you." SondraBeth gave Pandy another quick up-and-down look, re-minding Pandy that she was dressed in Hellenor's clothes. "A true individual." SondraBeth picked up the phone. "PP?" she barked.

Did SondraBeth really think she was Hellenor? Pandy frowned and went past SondraBeth to the fuzzy orange armchairs. She sat down with a plop and stared through the back window at the makeshift camp that had been set up outside. She glanced back at SondraBeth, who was still on the phone with PP. PP, she remem-bered, probably knew a ton of stuff about Jonny. And recalling what SondraBeth had just said about her ex-husband...She looked up to find SondraBeth's assistant leaning toward her with an outstretched hand.

"Hi, I'm Judy." Judy was pretty, with round cheeks, brown eyes, and long hair that appeared to be natural. "I'm so sorry about your sister."

Bemused, Pandy shook the young woman's hand.

"If you need anything—" The young woman broke off to tap the piece in her ear as she turned away.

Pandy leaned back in her chair and shook her head. For a moment, she felt like she'd been thrust into some kind of alternate universe. Where she actually *wasn't* Pandy. She closed her eyes briefly and laughed at the idea.

Then she sat up straight.

Because the thought was sickeningly scary. Flashing back to the explosion, she could taste the metallic grit of dirt in her mouth, smell the scent of scorched earth and scorched hair. She took a deep breath. The fact was, she very well might have died. But somehow, she had not. And now it was like the universe was playing a joke on her: *What would happen if you tried to tell everyone that you were you, and no one recognized you? Who would you be then?*

She reminded herself that she must still be shaky from the explosion. There was SondraBeth talking on the phone. And at the other end of the room, two men in dark suits and earbuds had come in, asking Judy for the bathroom.

Everything was fine. This was simply a case of mistaken identity. One that Pandy was going to clear up right now. She pushed up from the armchair and went over to Judy.

"Actually, I'm Pandy," she said. Judy smiled at her indulgently. Pandy turned to the two bodyguards, who were also looking at her, amused.

"I'm PJ Wallis."

The bodyguards shrugged and looked at Judy, who also shrugged. Pandy rolled her eyes and went outside.

This was interesting. No one cared if she was Pandy, because all they cared about was Monica.

Pandy frowned as she took in the scene in the parking lot. Two SUVs were parked next to SondraBeth's car; black-clad assistants were bustling in and out of them, and a couple of people were on walkie-talkies. If it weren't for the fact that PJ Wallis had supposedly just died, the scene would be exactly like another boring day on the set of *Monica*.

In which case, she might as well have a cigarette. Or two. She inhaled the fresh morning air and detected the harsh scent of tobacco smoke.

One of the chauffeurs was smoking next to an SUV. Pandy went up to him, giving him her very best smile, and said, "Excuse me. I am PJ Wallis. And I would like a cigarette."

The man smiled at her like she was a dotty old thing, which reminded Pandy again that she was bald. Apparently, no one was going to believe that she was Pandy until Henry arrived. The man handed her his pack. He cupped his hands for her to catch the flame from his lighter. "You the sister?" he asked.

Pandy took a step back, inhaled, exhaled, and smiled.

"The sister's lover, then?" the man said.

Pandy shrugged. It didn't matter. Henry would come, and everyone would know the truth.

She took another drag on the cigarette and began wandering down the drive. Perhaps she could meet up with Henry before he arrived, unprepared, at this mess. She strolled past some photographers who were milling about on the lawn. She supposed she and Henry could gather them together and announce that she was indeed Pandy, but this particular breed of press were like herd animals. You had to know how to control them.

She took another pull on the cigarette, continuing down the drive. The lady reporter and the cameraman were now standing off to the side.

The woman turned and saw her. "Oh, hi there, Hellenor," she drawled, as if they were now best friends. "So I hear you're a big Monica fan?" she asked in a friendly manner.

Was she kidding? "The biggest," Pandy said, annoyed. "You could say that I know every sentence and each line by heart."

"Is that so?" the woman asked.

"Actually, yes," Pandy said. She dropped her cigarette, grinding out the butt beneath her construction boot. "Because the fact of the matter is that I *am* PJ Wallis—"

"Hellenor?"

Pandy turned to find Judy coming down the drive.

Judy touched her arm. "Listen. Would you mind doing one thing? Can you walk to the place where PJ Wallis blew up?"

Pandy squinted down the drive. The whole squad of paparazzi had moved down to where the boathouse had been. This really was too much. It was one thing for her publisher to think she was dead for a couple of hours, but quite a different matter to announce it to the world.

"Now, listen, Judy," Pandy said firmly.

"I know, I know," Judy said quickly. "You're not happy about all this press. But neither is SondraBeth. She wanted this to be private. She was hoping you and she could have a long visit. Reminisce about Pandy. Talk about the old days and the future of Monica. Maybe even plan a special memorial. But then the studio got word, and the press, and now PJ's death is out of control—"

Pandy cleared her throat. "Judy," she tried again. "PJ Wallis isn't dead. There's been a huge mistake and *I'm* PJ Wallis."

"Oh, *I* get it," Judy said with a knowing laugh. In the husky tones of a former college party girl, she added, "Like what you did back there with the reporters? That was hilarious, fucking with their heads like that." Judy raised her palm to give Pandy a high five. "You, Hellenor, are fucking crazy. I'm so glad you're cool. It makes everyone's job so much easier."

She tapped her earpiece and nodded once, then took Pandy's arm and began leading her firmly down the hill.

Where the hell is Henry? Pandy thought angrily as Judy pushed through the paparazzi that were circled around SondraBeth like pagan priests around a sacrificial lamb.

She was standing on a patch of grass near what was left of the structure: a few charred pieces of wood scattered around a large rectangular patch of mud. The piece of fabric Pandy had seen SondraBeth holding earlier was now covering her body like a shroud. She jerked her arm back to take Pandy's hand.

Pandy looked around at the camera lenses aimed in her direction like faceless black eyes and decided she'd better go along with the charade. She tore her eyes away from the cameras and looked at SondraBeth instead.

SondraBeth was staring at her with those shining green-gold eyes. And suddenly, Pandy realized this was going to be just like that time on the island when Pandy had caught SondraBeth in the marsh with the herons. She was going to do what she needed to do, and she was going to act like nobody else was there.

SondraBeth dipped her head. She pulled Pandy forward a step or two into the mud. Hissing under her breath, she said, "Your sister meant everything to me, Hellenor. The two of us used to be best friends. The best friends two girls could ever be." She paused and looked Pandy straight in the eye. "And now I'm hoping we can be friends, too."

Pandy stared back. Was it possible SondraBeth honestly didn't know she was Pandy? Pandy decided to try to give SondraBeth a message back:

"I think that can be arranged," she said, with a meaningful nod.

SondraBeth gave Pandy's hand a quick squeeze before she dropped it and strode, silent and alone, through the mud to the center of the rectangle where the boathouse had been. She raised her arms, and suddenly, the flashes stopped. The crowd held their collective breath, as if wondering what she might do next.

Into the silence came the lone caw of a crow.

SondraBeth lay down on her back. She extended her arms and, sweeping them up and down, made angel wings. Then she rolled forward onto her knees, and with her head bowed, slowly stood up. She turned around and began walking back toward the driveway. As she walked, she peeled the fabric from her body, carefully folding the muddy material in her hands.

Reaching the grass, she stopped for a moment to allow her people to catch up with her.

"Did you know she was going to do that?" Pandy heard someone whisper as they hurried toward SondraBeth.

"No," someone else whispered back.

SondraBeth turned her head and looked back at Pandy. And then, as if making a sudden decision, she walked toward her.

"Come with me," she said. Her voice was quiet and splintery.

She disappeared into her swirl of assistants, and suddenly Judy was by Pandy's side. She touched Pandy's arm in a friendly girl-to-girl manner. "We've just heard from PP. He wants you to come back to New York with SondraBeth. He wants to meet you."

Judy began drawing Pandy along with her, nodding her head and smiling conspiratorially. "You'll stay in the basement guest room in SondraBeth's townhouse. It's fantastic; it has its own separate entrance."

And the next thing Pandy knew, the bodyguards had surrounded her, and she was being bundled into the back of an SUV. *I need to call Henry!* she thought wildly as the doors slammed shut and the car started forward with a jerk. As Wallis House disappeared around the mountain, she had a startling thought:

She had just been kidnapped by her own creation.

CHAPTER SIXTEEN

A GOOD OLD New York City pothole woke her up.
She bounced and hit the back of the seat. Once again, it
felt like her head was on fire.

It wasn't, but the place where she had hit her head two nights
before, when she had fallen off the couch during the party in her
apartment, was suddenly reinflamed.

That had happened on Wednesday. Was it a mere forty-eight
hours ago when she was still innocent? When she was still happy?

When she was still PJ Wallis?

"Hellenor, are you awake?" Judy asked. She was seated in the
row ahead. She turned and looked at Pandy across the top of the
seat.

The lump on the back of Pandy's head throbbed. She winced.
Pain. Good, sharp, come-to-your-senses pain. There was nothing
like it in an emergency.

"Yes," she answered, through gritted teeth.

"Would you like some water?" Judy asked.

When Pandy nodded, Judy motioned to someone in the second
row to hand her a bottle. Of course. Everyone was trying to be nice.
Trying to make poor, bereaved, weird Hellenor feel better.

If only people had treated Hellenor like that before.

Pandy grabbed the bottle of water and drank thirstily.

234

"Hey, I've got good news for you," Judy said. "Your sister's first Monica book is number one on Amazon's bestseller list."

"Is it?" Pandy asked. She rubbed the back of her head, and nearly screamed when she felt only the slightest stubble. Its texture was like velvet. It would take years for her hair to grow back.

"I think that would have made your sister so happy. Don't you?"

Pandy took a deep breath. "Would you mind if I used your phone?"

"Of course not," Judy said. "Please, call anyone you like. But if it beeps, will you hand it right back to me? Because it could be Sondra-Beth."

Pandy nodded. She touched Henry's number on the keypad, but it went right to voice mail. Of course. Henry wasn't going to answer his phone, especially from an unknown number. She groaned. He must have arrived in Wallis by now. Looking out the window, she spotted those outlying brown brick buildings in the marshes of the Bronx.

Judy's phone began singing: an aria. "It's SondraBeth," Judy said, holding out her hand for the device.

Pandy handed it back. She couldn't believe that SondraBeth had allowed her former best friend to be taken back by van while she drove her goddamned custom Porsche to Manhattan. If she and SondraBeth had remained friends, Pandy would have been traveling in the front seat with her.

But apparently SondraBeth either still didn't know Pandy was Pandy, or had a reason to keep up the ruse.

Road trip, she thought ironically as she tapped Judy on the shoulder for the phone. Judy looked back at her, mystified, then spoke into the phone to SondraBeth. "I think Hellenor wants to speak to you. Do you mind?"

Does she mind? Pandy thought. She had better *not* mind, she thought as Judy handed her the phone.

"Squeege?" she demanded. "Now listen. I'm happy to see your townhouse. In fact, I've been dying to see it ever since it came out in

Architectural Digest. But someone needs to get in touch with Henry. He's probably at Wallis House by now—"

"Shhhh," came a soft whisper.

"Excuse me?" Pandy said.

"Breathe with me, Hellenor."

"I am breathing."

"No. I mean, really breathe with me. Inhale through your nose and exhale through your mouth."

"SondraBeth," Pandy said, in a panic, "is this a yoga thing? You know how much I hate yoga. I can't even touch my toes!"

"You sound just like your sister. I have to go now."

"But—"

SondraBeth clicked off, and Pandy was left staring at a blank screen. She handed the phone to Judy, slid down in her seat, and crossed her arms. For a moment, she was truly speechless. How long was she going to have to play this game?

Pandy looked back out the window and glared. The SUV was now on the Henry Hudson Bridge. Down below, the water was twisting and shining like a Mardi Gras snake. Then it disappeared behind a hump of green, and they were turning a corner.

And once again, there it was: the Monica billboard.

Judy leaned across the seat and held up several strings of glittering gold, green, and purple beads.

"San Geronimo festival," she said as she lowered the beads over Pandy's head. "Welcome to Manhattan."

"Thanks." Pandy turned her head to stare at Monica until she once again disappeared.

She fingered the beads around her neck.

Monica was still missing her leg.

∞

Twenty minutes later, the van arrived at SondraBeth's townhouse: a white cube famously designed in the 1960s by a now-forgotten architect. Located on East Sixty-Third Street, it could be reached via a parking garage a block away, thereby allowing its resident to avoid detection by the paparazzi. It was this route that the van took, pulling into a space under the townhouse marked PRIVATE.

Judy led Pandy to an inconspicuous metal door with a code pad. The door opened into a short cement corridor. At one end was another door; across the landing was a flight of steps leading up to the first floor of the townhouse.

"The basement," Judy said, pressing a metal card onto the lock.

The door buzzed open, revealing what appeared to be a sort of bachelor pad. The carpet was an industrial gray, as was the fabric on the large, squishy couch and two overstuffed armchairs. On the wall was a large-screen TV; neatly arranged on the shelves below were a variety of clickers and gaming consoles. Two heavy glass ashtrays were stacked next to a digital clock.

"I think you'll be really comfortable here," Judy said. Her headset beeped. "SondraBeth will be back in fifteen. In the meantime, Peter Pepper would like a word. He's the head of the studio."

"I know who he is," Pandy snapped. "And in the meantime, I would like to use the facilities."

Annoyed once again by this Hellenor business, Pandy stomped down the hall to where Judy had pointed. She passed through a bedroom with the requisite king-sized mattress and even larger TV and into a bathroom the size of a small spa. *Good old PP*, Pandy thought, looking around at the sunken Jacuzzi tub, steam room, and separate his-and-hers toilet stalls.

Now *he* was an interesting development, she decided, going into the "his" stall. She supposed his presence made sense. Naturally the head of the studio would need to be on-site to stage-manage any potential situations concerning *Monica*. On the other hand...

Pandy went to the sink and washed her hands. Patting her face with water, she shook her head.

He might be here because of the clause in her Monica contract.

It stated that in the event of the death of PJ Wallis, the rights to Monica would revert back to her sister, Hellenor. It had been Henry's idea to insert the clause, his worry being that if Pandy happened to die young, like her parents had, there would be no preventing someone from someday being able to do whatever they wanted with Monica—including using her to sell soap.

She and Henry had dubbed it "the Golden Ticket." But in any case, it didn't matter. Because she *wasn't* dead. And she certainly wasn't Hellenor.

"Hellenor?" Judy asked, knocking on the bathroom door. "Are you ready?"

"I guess so," Pandy said, glaring at her still-unfamiliar reflection in the mirror.

Now all she had to do was convince everyone else.

⁂

PP was waiting for her upstairs, seated on a stool in front of a long island in the center of an open-plan kitchen.

"Hellenor," he said, springing to his feet. He clapped her right hand in both of his and squeezed. Hard.

"Ow," Pandy said.

"Would you like something to drink?" he asked.

"Sure. I'll take a glass of champagne," she said sarcastically, taking the stool next to him.

"That sounds good. Chookie?" PP called out. A guy wearing a white chef's uniform came through a swinging door. "Would you mind getting Ms. Wallis and me a glass of that nice pink champagne SondraBeth always has lying around? And something to eat, perhaps."

Chookie nodded and vanished into the kitchen, but not before surreptitiously giving Pandy a horrified look, reminding her that she was still dressed in Hellenor's clothes.

It didn't matter. PP, she was sure, would soon understand that she was Pandy.

Glaring at Chookie's retreating back, she turned to PP. He, too, was looking at her curiously, beaming with the sort of forced grin people slapped on their faces when they didn't know what to think. "Tell me about *you*, Hellenor," he said. "I'm told you live in Amsterdam?"

Pandy smiled sardonically. Apparently PP *had* been briefed about Hellenor. "You know I do. So why are you asking?"

"Excuse me?" PP said.

"I suppose you're going to ask next if I wear wooden shoes."

"Actually, I was going to ask if you spoke Dutch. But then I remembered that most Dutch people speak English."

Pandy rolled her eyes. She wasn't sure exactly what PP was up to, but he seemed to really think she *was* Hellenor. She needed to straighten him out on that one right away.

"Now, listen—"

PP held up his hand. "Of course, we can talk about Pandy. If you'd like."

"Well, I—"

"Your sister was funny. And…pretty." PP cleared his throat. "In any case, that was her problem. You can't be funny *and* pretty in Hollywood. Because if you're going to be funny, you have to be willing to risk looking stupid. Or even *ugly*. But then, you're no longer pretty. Get what I'm saying?"

"Yes, I most certainly do." Pandy crossed her arms as Chookie came back through the swinging door bearing the champagne, placed a glass in front of each of them, and disappeared again.

Pandy breathed a sigh of relief as she picked up her glass and held it to her lips. Pink champagne was her favorite drink, and now it was a reminder that she was *not* Hellenor. That all would be fine.

PP lifted his glass. "To Monica," he said.

Pandy nearly choked, but PP didn't notice. He kept on smiling away, as if nothing were strange. "Tell me," he said conversationally, "how much do you know about Monica?"

"Are you kidding me?"

"Were you a fan?" he asked cautiously.

"I guess you could say that," Pandy snapped.

"Good. What was your favorite Monica movie?"

"Movie? What about *book*?" Pandy demanded. She took a larger gulp of champagne. As usual when it came to PP, she was feeling increasingly insulted.

"Book, then. That's even better. You're a *real* fan." PP smiled and put down his glass. "I assume you've read them all."

For a second, Pandy could only gape at him in disbelief. "I know them inside and out."

PP nodded.

Pandy put down her glass as well. "Now, listen, PP," she repeated. "You do realize—"

"Shhhh." PP patted her hand and glanced at the swinging doors.

Right on cue, Chookie came through, setting down a silver tray with tiny sandwiches before retreating once more. Pandy pushed the tray away and looked at PP imploringly. "I am PJ Wallis. I *created* Monica."

PP stared at her briefly. Then he shook his head.

"I'm—" Pandy tried again, but PP put his hand on her arm to stop her from talking. "There's been a huge mix-up," Pandy said desperately. "And no one will believe me."

Suddenly she had a terrible thought: If she couldn't be PJ Wallis, she might *as well* be dead. She slumped onto the counter. When would this nightmare end?

PP patted her on the back. "There, there," he said, as if speaking to a child. "It's going to be okay. You were so overcome by the death of your sister, for a moment, you thought you *were* her." He stared at her curiously and then smiled knowingly. "Oh, I get it," he said. "You were *joking*. You're funny, too. Just like your sister."

Pandy wanted to cry. She reminded herself to stay calm. Sondra-Beth would arrive soon, and she would know that she was Pandy.

"I truly am sorry about your loss. I always liked your sister," PP said.

Pandy lifted her head and sat up. "Well, that's funny. Because SondraBeth always said you *hated* Pandy."

PP suddenly looked incensed, as if he'd been caught out. So he had complained about her to SondraBeth after all.

"I don't know where SondraBeth got that idea," PP said. "In any case, I knew her well. Your sister, I mean. She and her husband—that is, her ex-husband—were friends of mine."

Pandy's expression froze. Perhaps being Hellenor wasn't such a bad idea after all. For a few minutes, anyway. In which she might be able to extract information about Jonny from PP.

"Are you still friends with Jonny?" she asked casually.

PP leaned forward conspiratorially. "Frankly, I'd like to strangle the guy. He owes me money."

"You too, huh?" Pandy said, nodding. Apparently Jonny's grifting was more extensive than she'd thought.

"Why do women like Pandy marry men like that? She was so...spunky. Confident. Smart. But then she met Jonny and..." PP shrugged. "Why don't women know to avoid that type of guy?"

"You tell me," Pandy said, sipping her champagne while thinking that PP was cut from very much the same cloth as Jonny.

"Your sister was quite attractive," PP said, clearing his throat.

"Yes, she was..." Pandy suddenly became acutely aware of her appearance: dressed in Hellenor's construction boots and flannel shirt, with her bald pate, she must look like something out of an old *Saturday Night Live* sketch. She flushed in annoyance as she realized that PP was trying to flatter "Hellenor" in order to sway her. Pandy wondered just how far he was willing to go to keep his precious Monica franchise safe.

"Okay, PP," she said. "Let's say I *am* Hellenor Wallis. What then?" She reached for the champagne bottle.

"Well, you're going to be a very rich woman."

Pandy smirked as she refilled her glass, wondering if PP knew about all the money Jonny had taken from her.

"But what about Jonny?" she asked. "What about all that money Pandy supposedly owes him in the settlement?"

"Oh, jeez. *That*," PP said. "Jonny is a bit of a problem, and believe me, I understand. But eventually he'll go away. And in the meantime, we're planning to make lots and lots of Monica movies."

"More Monica!" Pandy said with false cheer.

PP patted her on the shoulder. "As I said, eventually you'll be a very rich woman. Thank God for Monica, right?" he added as Judy came through the door.

Pandy sighed.

Judy turned to Pandy. "Hellenor? Can I bring you back to the suite? SondraBeth will be down to see you in ten."

∞

Back in the basement, Pandy flopped onto the bed. She turned on the TV, figuring she might as well catch up on her so-called death while she was waiting for SondraBeth.

It was the usual news loop: a live report from the San Geronimo festival, and then there it was, an update on her demise: PJ Wallis, creator of Monica, reported dead in a tragic fire at her childhood home in Wallis, Connecticut.

And suddenly, there *she* was on the screen...with *Jonny* at a black-tie event—the same event where SondraBeth had warned her against him. And she was so naïve that she was actually *smiling*...

The screen cut to a close-up of a fan laying a pink plastic champagne glass on an already large pile that also contained stuffed animals. The camera pulled back to reveal her building.

"Hundreds of fans gathered outside her apartment..."

"No!" Pandy shouted at the TV. This could not be happening. Her so-called death was not supposed to be her next big moment. Her next big moment was supposed to have been about her new book, *Lady Wallis*. And there he was again: the cause of all this trouble—Jonny.

Now he was pushing through the crowd outside her building, trying to get in. Pandy groaned. Of course he would know that Pandy had left the Monica rights to Hellenor. His lawyers had been over every single one of her contracts with a fine-tooth comb.

Jonny would know that if Hellenor decided to execute her rights, there would be no more Monica—and no more money for Jonny.

And now Jonny knew Hellenor could ruin him.

CHAPTER SEVENTEEN

A s PROMISED, we're going back live to the San Geronimo festi-
val," said the voice from the screen.

Right now, Jonny must be furious, Pandy thought gleefully. And
for a second, she was happy. Then she looked back at the monitor.
Three young women were jumping up and down and screaming, rais-
ing glasses of pink champagne to Monica.

"Hellenor?" Judy's voice came over the intercom. "SondraBeth
in one."

"Thanks," Pandy said. Remembering that Jonny's fury over her sup-
posed death would be short-lived, she went out into the living room.
The suite had a damp smell, as if someone had just turned on the air-
conditioning. It was still stuffy, so Pandy tugged open the window.

The view was of a small stairwell. Pandy heard voices and stuck
her head out.

SondraBeth's back was to her. She was having a heated discussion
with a rubbery-faced man in a T-shirt. SondraBeth said something
and the man laughed, his man-boobs jiggling under the fabric.

Pandy frowned, recognizing the man's voice. He was Freddie the
Rat, part of the old Joules crowd. Apparently SondraBeth had re-
mained in touch with him.

Pandy withdrew her head. She heard a short knock and went to
the door.

SondraBeth was standing on the threshold. She had changed her outfit, and was now wearing high-tech white workout gear with silver piping. In each hand was a shopping bag bearing the Monica logo.

"Hellenor," she said, striding into the room.

Oh no. Pandy sighed. *Not this again.* She clomped to the door in Hellenor's old construction boots and shut it firmly behind her. "Squeege," she began.

"I'm *so* glad you're here," SondraBeth said warmly.

"I'm glad *you're* here, too," Pandy said as SondraBeth turned away to head into the bedroom. "I've been waiting for you," Pandy said, annoyed. "We need to clear some things up. Like the fact that I'm—"

"I don't have long." SondraBeth dropped the shopping bags on the bed and gave Pandy her most brilliant Monica smile. "There's been a change of plans. The Woman Warrior of the Year Awards are today, and thanks to your sister's sudden death, they want me to present the award to you."

"To *me?*" Pandy gasped. She looked at SondraBeth. Was it possible SondraBeth really didn't know she was Pandy? "That is not going to happen."

"Why not? It happens all the time," SondraBeth said. She pawed through one of the shopping bags and held out a tissue-wrapped package to Pandy. "People die, and other people start giving them awards for having once been alive."

"But that's just the problem. I'm *still alive.*"

SondraBeth pushed the package toward her. "Of course you're still alive, Hellenor. But it's Pandy who's getting the award. You're accepting it on her behalf."

Pandy groaned.

"First things first," SondraBeth chirped, pushing the package into Pandy's hands. In her friendliest Monica voice, she said, "In appreciation of how special you are, I'd like to gift you with a few of my favorite items from the Monica line."

Pandy threw the package back onto the bed. "Now, listen—" she snapped, unable to contain her frustration.

"Here, let me help you." SondraBeth picked up the package and inspected her incredibly sharp nails. Using her middle finger, she neatly sliced through the tissue paper and then, with a flourish, held up a garment.

It was a beautiful white hooded robe, made of the softest, lightest, coziest material Pandy had ever seen. She picked up the sleeve and felt the fabric. "It's beautiful," she said with a sigh.

"Isn't it?" SondraBeth said mournfully, at last dropping the Monica routine. "It's just the kind of thing your sister would have loved. I remember all those times when the two of us would be lounging around in our robes—"

"Still hung over," Pandy added.

SondraBeth shot her a sharp glance. "Will you try it on? For me?" She smiled imploringly.

"Okay," Pandy said. She wasn't sure what SondraBeth was up to, but the robe was too tempting to resist.

She draped the hood over her head, went into the bathroom, and looked at herself in the mirror as SondraBeth came in behind her. The hood did not disguise the fact that she was bald, and now she looked like some kind of newt. Or rather like a spa refugee with huge, scared eyes.

And suddenly, she was sick to death of this farce.

"Now listen, Squeege," she said, tearing off the robe and throwing it onto the floor. "If you have to tell me something about Jonny—"

"Jonny." SondraBeth grimaced. "Now you listen. The truth is that in the last few years—well, your sister and I weren't exactly friends. I'll explain why, someday. But in the meantime, I never got the chance to tell her the truth about Jonny."

SondraBeth leaned past her to reach into the top of the medicine cabinet. "It's nasty stuff, but Pandy always said you were the kind of person who wouldn't be swayed by sentiment. Unlike Pandy herself. I always told her she was too emotional about men, but she wouldn't listen."

"Is that so?" Pandy said archly.

SondraBeth laughed as she removed a lighter and a pack of cigarettes, which she shook at Pandy. Pandy took one.

"But since you already know Jonny's a bad guy…" SondraBeth stuck a cigarette into her mouth, lit it, and then lit Pandy's. Sondra-Beth inhaled and exhaled quickly, like someone who hasn't had a smoke for a while. "I happen to know that Jonny owes the mob a lot of money."

"What?" Pandy began coughing. SondraBeth patted her on the back.

"I know. It sounds shocking, but you have to remember that Jonny was in the restaurant business. He borrowed all this money from the mob. But that's not the worst of it."

"There's more?"

SondraBeth nodded, and with the guilt of someone who knew she shouldn't be smoking, she took another furtive drag. "That guy who was just here, Freddie the Rat? Your sister and I used to hang out with him. A long time ago."

"I know all about Freddie," Pandy sighed.

"Well, Freddie knows all about Jonny. And he told me that if there weren't any more Monica movies… if Monica were, to say, *die*"—SondraBeth took another drag—"the mob would go after Jonny for the money he owes them, because they'd know his source of funds had dried up."

"What are they going to do? Kill him?" Pandy asked sarcastically.

"Don't be silly," SondraBeth said. "They're not going to *kill* a famous person. They don't operate like that."

"How do you know?" Pandy asked.

"Because they do *business* with famous people. It's like being a drug dealer, okay? You don't want to kill your clients."

"Holy shit," Pandy said, remembering the Vegas guys Jonny had mentioned; those mumbled phone calls in the bathroom.

"But it's way more than that," SondraBeth continued. "He's been cheating the union guys, too. Who are part of the mob."

"You mean those people who make deliveries to his restaurants?" Pandy gasped.

"Hey." SondraBeth's eyes narrowed. "Don't tell me you're in the restaurant business, too."

"I'm not. I know all about it because *I was married to Jonny.*"

"*What?*" SondraBeth nearly dropped her cigarette. "You too?"

"I'm Pandy!" Pandy shouted. "Christ, Squeege. We've seen each other naked. Remember that time on the island? You invited me to come and visit you, and then you convinced me to invite Doug there. And then you *stole* him," she shrieked.

"I did not!" SondraBeth jumped back in shock.

"Excuse me?"

"That's not the way it happened. Technically, he wasn't her *boyfriend*," she said quickly.

"What difference does it make? Because after you had sex with Doug, you sent him to me as *a present.*" Pandy's voice rose to a screech. "And then, you acted like it was no big deal and *I* was crazy. Like I was the crazy one who fucks their best friend's boyfriend behind their back! And you want to know another thing?"

"There's more?" SondraBeth demanded.

"The last time I looked at you, I saw evil. *Pure evil.* I saw a serpent come out of your head and swoop down toward me. Well?" Pandy demanded in reaction to SondraBeth's still-startled expression.

And at last, SondraBeth's eyes widened in recognition. She took a deep breath. "Well, yourself," she said. She took another cigarette from the pack. As she raised her hand to light it, Pandy saw her hand was shaking.

And suddenly, Pandy felt dizzy, too, as if she was about to swoon in fear, anger, and excitement. The history she and SondraBeth had between them could fill a novel—yet, at this point, they might as well have been bookends on the opposite ends of the longest bookshelf in the world.

She looked at SondraBeth, who was looking back at her as if she couldn't comprehend what Pandy had become.

What she'd *done*.

"Why?" SondraBeth asked, her voice full of hurt. "Why didn't you tell me? Why did you let me go on like a fool, acting like you were Hellenor?"

"I never said *I* was Hellenor," Pandy said sharply. "It was everyone else—"

"Oh, please." SondraBeth crossed her arms in disgust.

"I seem to recall that you were the one who invaded my space, 'sista,'" Pandy continued. "If you remember, I was happily alone in Wallis, waiting for Henry to arrive so I could change my clothes, find a wig, and get back to being Pandy, when *you* showed up with your paparazzi circus."

"So it's *my* fault, huh? I interrupted your plans?"

"What plans?" Pandy shouted.

"Pretending to be Hellenor. How long were you planning to keep it up?"

"I wasn't planning to keep it up at all!"

"You knew about the mob, and you were planning to kill Monica!"

"Of course I wasn't," Pandy replied. "Why would I want to kill Monica?"

"You tell me."

When Pandy continued to shake her head, SondraBeth spoke to her like she was an idiot. Stating the obvious, she said, "You wanted to kill Monica to get even with Jonny."

"Honestly," Pandy said, "it never even crossed my mind."

"Well, I suppose it's not going to happen now," SondraBeth said, frowning. "Now that I know you're Pandy."

Pandy lit up another cigarette. "You sound kind of disappointed."

"I'm just shocked, that's all." SondraBeth took another cigarette and looked at Pandy assessingly. "I do understand why you did it. If I had a husband like Jonny—"

"Well, aren't you lucky. You never have," Pandy replied. *Now* it all made sense. This wasn't about Jonny. It was about Monica. SondraBeth had believed she was Hellenor and, knowing that Hellenor had the rights to Monica, had obviously brought her here to convince her to make more Monica movies. Just like PP.

"Either way, what difference does it make? Because I'm alive." Pandy took a mournful drag. "Why should you care about what happened between me and Jonny anyway?" she asked suddenly. "After all, you certainly didn't care about me and Doug."

SondraBeth took a step back and sniffed. Looking as if she was recalling that terrible moment on the island when they'd fought about Doug, she said, "Oh, I get it. You're still mad."

"About what?"

"Doug Stone?" SondraBeth said tauntingly.

Pandy laughed snidely in return. "Of course I'm still mad. It's not the kind of thing *I'd* ever forget."

"Of course it isn't," SondraBeth said.

Pandy laughed this off. "Why *did* you do it?"

"You really want to know?"

"As a matter of fact, I do." Pandy crossed her arms.

"Oh, Peege," SondraBeth said. "You always made these things bigger than they were. There was no conspiracy, nothing. I was just jealous. Don't tell me you haven't been jealous of *me*." She tossed her head.

"When?" Pandy challenged.

"The mayor's party? When I was invited and you weren't?"

"I guess Doug told you," Pandy said. "Well, so what? Maybe I was jealous. But that doesn't mean you're entitled to steal *my guy*."

"Of course not," SondraBeth sneered. "Because as usual, you, PJ

Wallis, are a far better person than I am. Because *you* grew up with all the *manners*."

"Not this again," Pandy said warningly.

"Listen, I made a mistake," SondraBeth said. "I honestly didn't think you'd be that angry about it. You said that you were done with him. I thought you felt the way I did. Like he was kind of a Panda-Beth toy."

"What?" Pandy screeched.

"Oh, calm down, Peege," SondraBeth said. "I'm joking. Haven't you learned to stop being such an idealist? Surely you know that these kinds of things happen in life. You just hate it when they happen to *you.* Anyway, I was never in love with Doug."

"I thought you two were supposed to be *soul mates*," Pandy sneered.

"Well, I found out pretty quickly that we weren't," SondraBeth said, marching back into the bedroom as Pandy followed her. "Especially when I discovered that my so-called soul mate was fucking everything, everywhere, and everyone was covering up for him. And then, it was too late. It was all over the tabloids that we were together. And then you went and married Jonny."

Pandy frowned. "What's that got to do with it?"

"Nothing," SondraBeth said, leaning back on the bed. "It's just that when you and Jonny got married, the studio decided it would be a great idea if *Monica* got married as well."

"Are you saying your getting engaged to Doug was the studio's idea?"

"Did you think it was mine?" SondraBeth asked.

"Why didn't you say no?"

"Because I liked having sex with him, and it was good publicity. For Monica. In fact, I almost went along with it—*for Monica.* But in the end, I *couldn't* do it. I didn't love him, and I couldn't go through with that much of a lie.

"Why *did* Monica have to get married, anyway?" SondraBeth

continued in exasperation. "What happened to the old PJ Wallis? The PJ who said Monica would never get married, because *she'd* never get married."

Pandy winced. "I fell in love, I guess. And now, because of Jonny and his debts, I have to write *another* Monica book. And now that I'm divorced, Monica is going to have to get divorced, too. And then she's going to have to try online dating."

"Dating again? She's forty-five, for Christ's sake," SondraBeth said. "How much more of her life does she have to devote to dating? The woman who *plays* her certainly doesn't have time to date. She doesn't even have time to pick her teeth with a tooth-pick."

"I fucked up. Okay?" Pandy snapped.

"How?"

"I can't say," Pandy said between gritted teeth.

"What did you do?" SondraBeth demanded.

"Something incredibly stupid." Pandy glared. "I never made Jonny sign a prenup, and then I gave him hundreds of thousands of dollars for his restaurant in Vegas. And now *I'm* broke and will probably have to sell my loft and write a million more Monica books."

"Why did you give him all your money?" SondraBeth said as Pandy began to cry.

"I knew I shouldn't have, but I felt guilty," Pandy sobbed. "Because my career was going great, and Jonny's...well, it *should* have been going great, and he was *acting* like it was going great, but it wasn't. He was losing money. And then, when he couldn't pay it back, I was forced to write another Monica book. And then Monica had to get married, and now she'll have to get divorced..." She hic-cuped as she glanced at the TV, which was running the news loop of PJ Wallis's death again. "Or worse. Maybe now that *I'm* dead, Monica will have to die, too."

"So this is all Jonny's fault."

"And now I still can't do anything about Jonny. Because I'm *not dead*," Pandy said, shaking her fist at the screen.

SondraBeth looked at the monitor and back at Pandy.

And then she got that look in her eye.

"Peege," she said in that familiar wheedling tone of voice that had been the beginning of so many misadventures. "You don't know how badly the union guys want to teach Jonny a lesson."

"SondraBeth?" Judy's voice came over the intercom. "I need you to get ready."

"Thanks, Judy," SondraBeth called out gaily as she pressed the button.

She picked up her phone and smiled. "I'm going to call Freddie. I think I know how you can still be Pandy *and* get back at Jonny." And as she pressed his number, she gave her the old PandaBeth grin. "All you have to do is stay Hellenor for a few hours."

∞

Five minutes later, they were still arguing.

"No." Pandy got up and stubbed out her cigarette. "It would never work," she added sharply. "Besides the fact that it's ka-ray-zee, I could never get away with being Hellenor."

"But you already *have*," SondraBeth pointed out. "Even *I* thought you were Hellenor, until you mentioned that snaky thing coming out of my head." She paused and looked at Pandy sympathetically. "Sista, you're bald. Do you know how different that makes people look? It totally changes the proportions of the face. Even the photographers didn't recognize you."

"Which was annoying," Pandy admitted. She crossed her arms. "On the other hand, even if I *were* Hellenor—"

"Freddie said the union guys have a big surprise planned for Jonny at the leg."

Pandy moaned and flopped into an armchair. *The leg*. In addition to the Woman Warrior of the Year Awards, which Pandy had

253

forgotten about, given her rotten last few months, the unveiling of Monica's shoe was also today. It was a new thing the studio was try-ing. According to SondraBeth, this was the reason Monica's leg had been late:

It was getting its own day.

"SondraBeth." Judy's voice came through the intercom. "We need you to get ready."

"We don't have much time," SondraBeth hissed. "All you have to do is go to the Woman Warrior of the Year Awards as Hellenor, accept the award, announce that you're killing Monica, and then, while the mob grabs Jonny, we'll go to the leg event, where you go back to being Pandy."

Pandy groaned.

"You, PJ Wallis, have picked a very good day to die," SondraBeth said, sounding as if Pandy were the one who had hatched up this plan in the first place.

"Can I at least call Henry?" Pandy asked.

"Sure." SondraBeth tossed her the phone. And in her very best Wicked Witch of the West voice, she added, "Remember, you only have five minutes to decide."

And then she was gone.

⚭

Fucking Squeege, Pandy thought, stomping back to the bedroom. This was perhaps the real reason they hadn't seen each other for so many years: When they did, crazy things happened. Bad things. Em-barrassing things. Things that almost made you glad you didn't have a mother to tell.

She plopped down on the bed and looked at the packages. At least they hadn't done any cocaine. So all in all, nothing was *that* bad, yet.

And then she quickly pawed through the packages, just to make sure SondraBeth hadn't hidden a little "surprise" in the bag. After all, she had just seen Freddie the Rat, and it *was* the kind of thing...

But she was happy to see that the bags only contained more of those luxuriously soft workout clothes.

"Hellenor?" Judy sounded more urgent this time. "We need *you* upstairs in *three*."

Right, Pandy thought. She stripped off Hellenor's clothes and pulled on a set of navy-blue workout gear with MONICA outlined in silver on the back.

And then she heard Jonny's voice. It was coming from the TV. There he was, *again*, in front of her building. But this time he was talking to a reporter.

"Who is Hellenor Wallis?" he asked. "That's what I want to know." Turning to face the camera, his still-handsome face arranged into his trademark sneer, he added, "I know you're out there, Hellenor. And I'm looking for you."

Jonny was looking for Hellenor? Well, he was about to find out that some people were looking for him, too.

Pandy clicked off the TV. She was going to pocket the phone when she remembered Henry.

She *had* to call Henry. At least to let him know where she was. She tapped in his number, preparing to lie her ass off.

∽

While the phone rang and rang, Pandy found herself praying that Henry wouldn't answer. But he picked up just before it went to voice mail.

"SondraBeth?" he asked cautiously.

"Henry! It's *me*," Pandy squealed with, she realized, way too much enthusiasm.

"You're kidding," Henry said drily. "I thought you were dead."

"So does everyone else," Pandy chortled. "It's all been a huge, huge mistake."

"Yes. So I can see from the devastation at Wallis. No wonder you fled. As you're calling from SondraBeth's phone, I assume she's in the vicinity?"

"Oh yes," Pandy said reassuringly. "She's upstairs. And I'm downstairs in the guest suite of her townhouse."

"And does this mean you and SondraBeth are once again fast friends?"

"What makes you say that?" she asked casually.

"That misadventure the two of you had in the mud this morning? Just like two little pigs."

"You saw that?" Pandy acted surprised.

"How could I *not* have seen it? It's been broadcast all over Instalife. SondraBeth Schnowzer rolling in the mud with you standing behind her, dressed like the construction worker from the Village People."

"I had to wear Hellenor's clothes. Because I couldn't fit in my own," Pandy said, beginning to get annoyed. "Not to mention the fact that I am *bald*." She took a breath and added contritely, "In any case, I did try to tell everyone I was Pandy. But no one believed me. It was like one of those really awful what-if games. Like what if everyone *thought* you were dead, but you *weren't*?"

"This day just gets worse and worse, doesn't it?" Henry said. "I have only *just* left Wallis. It took me an hour to get the paparazzi off the property. Can you imagine what it would be like if you really *had* died?"

"I'm beginning to have a very good idea."

"Hellenor?" Judy's voice came over the intercom.

"Sorry, Henry, but I have to go."

"Sit tight," Henry said. "And don't do *anything* until I get there."

"I won't," Pandy said as he clicked off. She felt bad about lying to him, but hopefully it would all work out and Henry wouldn't have to know how foolish she'd been about Jonny.

She knew how disappointed he would be in her if he did find out.

"Judy?" she said. "It's Hellenor. I'm ready."

CHAPTER EIGHTEEN

S HE WAS more than ready an hour and a half later, when the SUV
was speeding down the West Side Highway on the way to the
Woman Warrior of the Year Awards. Having put herself into the ca-
pable hands of the in-house Monica wardrobe and makeup team, she
was now wearing a black leather jacket, black pants, and black
patent leather loafers.

Judy was seated next to her in the third row. In the second row
were SondraBeth and PP. In the first row, meaning the operational
part of the operation, were a bodyguard and a chauffeur who could
double as another bodyguard if necessary.

"Meaning he carries a gun," PP had informed her.

Pandy had nodded solemnly. Normally, this sort of information
would have upset her. She would have had to ask what sort of person
she was, to allow herself to be transported around Manhattan with
two men bearing arms. There seemed to be something ethically off
about it. But she was in no position to ask questions. Indeed, she
ought to be grateful she was around men with guns, after that threat
Jonny had made on TV.

Which hadn't gone unnoticed by the team. "Hellenor?" Judy
asked, looking down worriedly at her device. "What's this thing on
Instalife about Pandy's ex-husband looking for you?"

"Jonny is a real scumbag," SondraBeth replied smoothly, jumping in before Pandy could answer. Ever since Pandy had gone up to wardrobe and makeup as Hellenor, SondraBeth had barely let her out of her sight. She seemed to have her ear tuned to any potential conversation in which Pandy might inadvertently reveal the truth.

"It's just that he seems like a real crazy person. Like an actually insane, psychologically challenged kind of person," Judy said.

"Well, he is. Wouldn't you say so, PP? After all, you were friends with him," SondraBeth said smugly.

"I wasn't exactly friends with him," PP said. "We were friendly. I was just doing business with him, that's all. Trying to make some money."

"And how'd that work out for you?" Pandy asked snidely.

SondraBeth snickered under her breath. "Exactly."

"Frankly, if you were any kind of man at all, I'd think you'd want to punch the fucker," Pandy said, just loud enough so that Sondra-Beth could hear and PP probably couldn't.

"Har har har," SondraBeth laughed loudly. Dressed in her full Monica regalia, she could barely turn her head. She was so decorated with hairpieces and layers of Spanx and silicone cutlets that she might as well have been a marquess in the court of Louis XIV. "Hellenor didn't mean that," she added. "She's totally against violence. As we all are."

She shot Pandy a warning look. "In any case, I'm sure karma will get Jonny. No one can escape from it."

"Actually, it's the tax man," Pandy said. "No one can escape from the *tax man*."

"Which reminds me," PP said, scrolling through his device. "Thanks to that little stunt you two pulled this morning—that rolling-in-the-mud thing—you're going to have to be sure to emphasize that Monica is very much alive."

"Of course she's alive," SondraBeth tittered. "Why would anyone think she wasn't?"

"The Instaverse is claiming that when you rolled in the mud, you said, 'I buried Monica.'"

"What? Like John Lennon and the White Album?" Pandy snorted derisively.

"'I buried Paul.' Very *good*, Hellenor," PP said approvingly. "Maybe you can be a studio head someday." He turned back to SondraBeth. "When you give Hellenor the award, be sure to state specifically that Monica is alive."

"She is *alive*. She lives!" SondraBeth called back to Pandy jokingly.

The light turned green and the car started forward with a jerk.

"Ow." Pandy touched the bump on the back of her bald head and winced.

∽

Twenty minutes later, the SUV was at last pulling in through the gates of Chelsea Piers. After being stopped by several guards, they were told to wait. The event didn't begin for another hour, but there were already hundreds of photographers on the bleachers along the carpet, sitting like Hitchcock's black crows on the telephone wires outside the children's school. Cordoned off behind metal barricades was a bigger mob of fans, some, Pandy noted, with plastic champagne glasses strapped to their heads.

This was going to be interesting.

Eager for a glimpse of Monica, a splinter group had broken through the barricades and was now approaching the car.

Sensing danger, the bodyguard got out and stood with his arms crossed in front of SondraBeth's door.

"What do we do now?" Pandy asked.

"Wait," SondraBeth said.

"For what?"

"For someone to come and get us."

Pandy looked out the window and grimaced. The group was now

surrounding the car. A face was squished up against her window for a second before it was swept away by the bodyguard. Pandy almost thought she'd imagined it, but for the greasy smudge left on the glass.

The horizon began tilting as Pandy started to feel the beginnings of a panic attack. Big crowds scared her; she always imagined being trampled.

"Hellenor? Are you all right?" SondraBeth's voice seemed to be coming from too far away.

"Have some water," PP said, handing her a bottle.

"It's all the fans," SondraBeth said, turning a quarter of the way to address PP. "I used to feel that way, too, remember? Like a fraud. I'd be in the car, my heart pounding, sweat pouring from my underarms, and I'd think, what if I get out there and they *see* that I'm a fraud? That I'm not *really* Monica? What if the crowd thinks they're getting Monica, and discover they're getting SondraBeth Schnowzer instead? What if—"

"They tear you limb from limb?" Pandy asked, half jokingly. The question wasn't necessarily facetious. Another group had squeezed between the metal barricades and was now approaching the car.

Plink! A plastic champagne glass hit the rear window.

Pandy screamed.

"Check your face. That's what I always do," SondraBeth advised, looking in the vanity mirror.

And then the police came and shooed the crowds away, directing the driver to a guardhouse where the backstage entrance was protected by a metal gate in a chain-link fence. Pandy breathed a sigh of relief as the SUV pulled up to a loading dock that led to the backstage area. The water she'd chugged had made its way to her bladder, and now she had to pee. She sat up in anticipation of bolting from the car.

The door to the SUV swung open. SondraBeth rose slightly on bent knees and, ratcheting herself around to face the open door, assessed the situation.

"I'm going to need a ramp," she said.

"She needs a ramp. Someone get her a ramp," came the sound of male voices shouting from below.

Pandy sighed deeply and pushed back into her seat, squeezing her thighs together. This *was* annoying. SondraBeth was blocking the door. Pandy couldn't go forward or backward until someone got that damn ramp.

This was why she hated showbiz.

"Maybe you could change your shoes?" Pandy asked, wondering how much longer she could hold out for the bathroom. "Maybe if you had on different shoes, you could get the hell out, and then we could *all* get the hell out."

"No," SondraBeth hissed angrily. "This is it. This is *the outfit*. I can put it on once, and then it has to stay on *as is* until I take the whole thing off. *Get it?*"

At that moment, the ramp arrived.

"Got it!" shouted a voice, and slowly, helped on either side by two burly men with shaved heads, SondraBeth inched forward onto the loading dock.

And then she unfolded, snapping open black metallic panels on her long skirt. Pandy watched, mesmerized, as she slowly raised her arms, the fabric undraping to reveal what looked like two iridescent black wings.

"Christ," PP said, coming up behind Pandy. "She looks like a gi-ant fly."

Judy spoke into her headset and in the next second they were surrounded by various crew and producers and assistants. SondraBeth was led to her dressing room.

Hellenor Wallis was shown to the green room.

Bypassing the spread of fruit, candy, and sandwiches, Pandy ran to the ladies'. Just as she was pulling up her pants, there was a knock on the door. "Hellenor? It's Judy. They need you to do press. Are you ready?"

Pandy smiled.

"I'm ready," she said.

∽

"Do you think when your sister sat down to write *Monica*, she ever in a million years imagined it would be like this?" asked one of the journalists who were clustered around Pandy in the green room.

"No, I don't think she did. I don't think anyone could," Pandy said, looking, she hoped, appropriately sad.

"She would have loved it, don't you think?" the journalist asked.

"Yes, she really would have." Pandy's eyes slid over to the large-screen TV, on which there was a shot of the Monica billboard, now covered in cloth and a series of ropes and pulleys. MONICA SHOE UN-VEILING, read the caption.

"And what did PJ Wallis have in store for Monica? Besides her new shoe?" the journalist asked.

Pandy tore her eyes away from the image of the billboard. "The truth is, Pandy had just finished a book that *wasn't* about Monica."

"I see. And what about this rumor that Pandy's ex-husband, Jonny, thinks you're not really Hellenor?"

Pandy cocked her head. She knew Jonny was looking for her, but this last piece of information was new. "I've heard he's not the sharpest knife in the drawer."

"If you had a message from PJ Wallis to all those Monica fans out there today, what do you think it would be?"

Pandy stared straight into the camera and glared. "That's easy: Don't ever get married."

"Thank you, Hellenor."

"Hellenor?" someone else said. "Can we get a shot of you with the Monica shoe?"

"The Monica shoe is here?" Pandy asked.

"From now on, those shoes go everyplace SondraBeth goes. She's got to wear them to the unveiling," Judy explained. She spoke into her mike. "Can someone bring me the Monica shoes, please?"

In the next moment, the stylist's assistant appeared, holding a pair of fringed red suede spike-heeled booties stuffed with tissue paper. Pandy held the booties up on either side of her face and smiled into the flashes.

"What do you think about the big memorial service SondraBeth is planning for your sister's funeral?" another journalist asked.

Pandy's smile stiffened.

The photographers shot off a few obligatory snaps and turned away.

"A memorial service?" Pandy said to Judy. She spun on her heel and began marching down the hall to SondraBeth's dressing room.

"Hellenor?" Judy said, hurrying after Pandy. "You can put down the booties. I need to return them to wardrobe."

Pandy ignored her, rapping on the door with the cruelly sharp heel of one of the booties. "SondraBeth? I need to talk to you."

"Come in," SondraBeth purred.

"Hellenor?" Judy said, catching up to her. "Is everything okay?"

"I need to talk to SondraBeth alone. It's about my sister, and her *death*." She turned the knob, pushed inside, and shut the door firmly behind her.

SondraBeth was standing in the middle of the room. The hinged skirt was attached to a stiff black bodice covered with tiny rhinestone M's.

"Oh, good." SondraBeth reached out her arms for the booties. "You've brought me my shoes."

"Monica's shoes," Pandy said. SondraBeth took the shoes and toddled the few steps to the makeup counter to deposit them. She turned stiffly and swayed back toward Pandy, slowly lowering her arms. "So talk," she said as she held up her nails and examined them.

The sight made Pandy gasp. Each of SondraBeth's fingers

sprouted a different miniature masterpiece of a famous building. Pandy picked out the Chrysler Building, the Eiffel Tower, and the Space Needle. She tore her eyes away and plopped herself onto a folding chair. "What's this I've just heard about you planning a memorial service for Pandy?"

"Oh, that." SondraBeth smiled and pointed the Empire State Building at her. "It was just something that popped into my head."

"When?" Pandy glared.

"Just at that moment. The journalist asked me if I knew anything about a memorial service, and I—"

"Well, pop that idea right back *out of* your head. Because at the end of the day, I will once again be alive. Meaning there isn't going to be any memorial service."

"Of course there isn't. But if I told the journalist that, it would look fairly suspicious, don't you think? PJ Wallis dies, and there's no *funeral?*"

"I guess." Pandy narrowed her eyes. "I just want to make sure that we're both on the same page. Right after the Woman Warrior of the Year Awards, I go back to being Pandy."

"SondraBeth?" Judy knocked on the door, then opened it an inch and stuck her nose in the crack. "They need you in rehearsal."

SondraBeth slowly made her way out into the hallway.

"How's she going to walk across the stage in that getup?" Pandy hissed to Judy.

"She doesn't have to. The stage is revolving."

"Like a turntable?" Pandy was aghast.

"They call it a lazy Susan. Don't worry, you'll be fine. You only have to be onstage for a minute or two," she said over her shoulder. Quickly she walked away to where SondraBeth was being lifted onto a trolley to be driven to the stage. Judy hopped into the seat next to the driver. "Don't go far, Hellenor. We may need you as well."

"Okay," Pandy agreed.

She inhaled deeply, trying to calm herself as Judy and Sondra-Beth sped around the corner. She took a step to follow, but her legs felt as if they were made of rubber. How big was this production going to be? It had to be large if there was a revolving stage. Heart pounding at the thought of having to get up in front of all those people, Pandy decided she'd better have a cigarette to relax. Stumbling through the nearest exit, she nearly knocked over a girl holding a tray of champagne.

"I'm sorry," Pandy said.

"I probably shouldn't be standing in front of the door. Come in. Would you like a glass of champagne?"

"Well, sure." Pandy took a glass and stepped to the side, nearly bumping into a mannequin dressed as Wonder Woman.

Pandy laughed as she straightened the dummy. She smiled fondly at the mannequin of Joan of Arc placed next to Marilyn Monroe. She was in the Woman Warrior Hall of Fame, a somewhat hokey display that was a traditional part of the awards. Attendees were meant to wander through the hall during the cocktail hour.

The crowd was beginning to trickle in. Pandy stopped to shake her head at poor old Mother Teresa's ragged costume. She and SondraBeth had come to these awards together, years and years ago when they were still friends. They'd done a tiny line of cocaine in the bathroom, "for Dutch courage," SondraBeth had said, and then they'd strolled into the display.

There was a tap on Pandy's shoulder. Three young women were standing behind her.

"Sorry to bother you—"

"But are you Hellenor Wallis?"

"You are. We saw you on Instalife this morning!"

"Can we get a photo?"

"Well, sure." Pandy smiled, and then remembered to wipe the smile from her face.

"Your sister meant everything to me," the first girl murmured, tilting her head next to Pandy's and holding out her device for a selfie. "She was my idol. I wanted to be just like her."

"I need a picture, too!"

"Just one more? I'll die if I don't get a photo."

A crowd of women was gathering around her. Two handlers broke through, trying to shoo them away. "Ladies, please."

"But I came all the way from Philadelphia!"

"I don't mind." Pandy smiled reassuringly. For a brief moment, she was back in her element. Motion the woman closer, arm around the shoulders, heads cocked together, *smile!* Next.

And the ladies kept coming. "*I love* Monica. I love her *so much.*" Their eyes a little glazed. "I hope you love yourself just as much," Pandy replied, wanting to shake them and tell them not to hold too tightly to a fantasy.

She imagined this was how SondraBeth must feel every day—literally heady—her head swelling from the attention, the frenzied excitement, the irresistible fawning. And in the middle of this bubble, the oddest feeling—the guilt of a hypocrite.

"Hellenor." Judy was suddenly beside her, pulling at her arm. "We have to go. They need you in rehearsal, too."

☙

"Right this way," said the PA, leading Pandy along a ridged mat secured with reflective green tape. She guided Pandy to a set of metal stairs and quickly ushered her to a small platform, in front of which was an enormous round disk covered in tape.

The dreaded lazy Susan.

"You'll step here," said the PA, hustling Pandy onto the disk.

"Hello," SondraBeth called out. She was standing in the center of the disk, waving stiffly.

"Hi," Pandy called back. SondraBeth looked like a bride on a wedding cake, save for the fact that she was dressed in black.

"You will walk to SondraBeth," the PA said briskly, as if she was not in the mood for any nonsense. Urging Pandy along, she said, "And then you will stop and accept the award from her."

Pandy halted in front of SondraBeth, who pantomimed giving her the statuette.

"And then," the PA barked, "you will turn and walk forward to the podium—" She walked a few steps ahead to demonstrate where Pandy should go. "And you will stop. And you will say..."

"I am Hellenor Wallis...," SondraBeth said from behind her.

"I am Hellenor Wallis," Pandy repeated.

"And all the screens will be lit up in a circle around the room—"

"There are screens?" Pandy asked nervously.

"So we can take questions." The tech producer's voice came through a speaker that sounded like it was right above her head.

"There will be questions?" Pandy called out to this invisible man.

"Not for your segment. All you have to do is accept the award, and say thank you on behalf of your sister."

"That's it? I don't get to say a few nice words about her?" Pandy asked.

"We're on a tight schedule," the PA said, taking her arm once again. She walked Pandy to the other side of the platform. "The stage will be revolving. You'll stand here, so we can broadcast you on the screens, and then when you reach the platform where you got on, you'll get off and head backstage through the Hall of Fame, which will be closed off to the public by then. Got it?" she asked sharply.

"Hellenor?" Judy said, motioning from the platform. "There's someone here who needs to see you."

"Jonny," Pandy gasped, recalling how he'd threatened to find her. By now he must know she was with SondraBeth at the awards; it was all over Instalife.

Judy smiled. "It's Pandy's agent."

And there he was: Henry. Standing at the bottom of the stairs.

∞

"Well, well, well. What do we have here?" Henry asked, circling around her. Pandy grimaced and automatically put her hand over her bald head.

"Excuse me, Ms.—" Henry turned to Judy.

"Judy," Judy said. "I'm SondraBeth's right hand."

"Is there someplace"—Henry glared at Pandy—"that *Hellenor* and I can go to speak *privately?*"

"You can use SondraBeth's dressing room. They need to keep her next to the stage until the show begins. It takes too long to move her," Judy said over her shoulder as she led them back into the Hall of Fame.

This time the hall was packed. The high-pitched screeches of women who'd already had a bit too much champagne filled the room like the calls of exotic birds.

"Henry!" a voice shouted.

Pandy turned to find Suzette barreling toward them, with Meghan, Nancy, and Angie in tow. Judging from the way they were tottering on their heels, Pandy guessed they'd already had a couple of glasses of champagne. And then Suzette threw her arms around Henry as tears sprang from her eyes.

Within seconds, they were surrounded. Pandy was being pulled in all directions by her grieving friends.

"PJ Wallis's sister!"

"Poor Pandy. She was so *alive.*"

"Impossible to think she's gone."

"How could this happen?"

"So young, too."

"Literally the best woman—the *best* woman in New York—"

"Thank you. Thank you."

The buzz in the hall grew louder. *PJ Wallis. Icon. Great loss.*

Hellenor Wallis. Pandy's sister. Over there. You can see the resemblance.

"Excuse me," Henry said, yanking on Pandy's arm, bringing her back to reality. Following Judy, he marched her through the exit door and into the backstage hallway.

"Here you go," Judy said, unlocking the door to SondraBeth's dressing room.

"Thank you," Henry said. He pushed Pandy into the room, closed the door, and locked it. He crossed his arms. "Explain."

"I don't know where to begin."

"Try."

"SondraBeth convinced me. It's only for a couple of hours. She said if I killed Monica, the mob would go after Jonny—"

Henry looked away, held up his hand, and gave a quick shake of his head. "You're going to exercise the clause because of Jonny?"

"It's only for a couple of hours," she said pleadingly. "In between the Woman Warrior of the Year Awards and the leg event. Look," she said, pointing at the red booties. "There they are. Monica's shoes."

"You are going to kill Monica at the Woman Warrior of the Year Awards and then bring her back to life at the Shoe Unveiling?" Henry's voice was beginning to sound thunderous.

"Yes," Pandy said quietly.

"Who is she, Tinker Bell?"

Pandy shrugged.

"You can't just go around killing creations and then bringing them back to life," Henry snapped.

"Why not?"

"Because it's cheap. It's soap opera—"

"It's *drama.* Monica will die, Jonny will get a talking-to from the mob, and when all that is taken care of, PJ Wallis and Monica will rise up like two phoenixes from the ashes, and everyone will love them again!"

"You're sacrificing Monica and risking everything you've ever achieved for a *man?*"

"I'm doing it for *me.*"

"No, you are not. You're doing it to get *even* with a *man.* Meaning, once again, you have allowed your actions to be dictated by a man."

Pandy had had enough. "You're a fine one to talk."

Henry paused. He inhaled, exhaled, and then glowered threateningly. "So you're going to use *that* as an excuse."

"Why not?" she said sharply.

"If that's so, then you, my dear, are pitiful. You're not the Pandemonia James Wallis I know."

"Maybe that Pandemonia James Wallis doesn't exist anymore. Maybe she's been too beaten down to continue. Just like her sister, Hellenor."

Henry drew himself up to his full height. Pandy's heart sank. She and Henry hadn't had a fight like this for years. Perhaps ever.

Henry held up his hand. "I can see you've made up your mind. In that case, I suppose congratulations are in order. Your publisher has agreed to publish *Lady Wallis,* but only because you are dead."

"You were the one who told me to stay dead for a couple of hours."

"I told you to do nothing. Now, because of this spectacle, your publishers will cry fraud. So if you don't clear this up immediately, as far as I'm concerned, you *are* dead."

"Fine," Pandy said coldly, crossing her arms. "They weren't going to publish the book anyway. Which gives me more of a reason to get even with Jonny."

"And how do I fit into this scheme?"

"Just go along with it for a couple of hours. Remember—you owe me."

"Very well," Henry said. He turned his back and opened the

door. He shot one more warning glance over his shoulder. "Don't say I didn't caution you. And when things don't work out as you've planned, don't come running to me!"

He went out, slamming the door behind him.

"Henry!" Pandy said. She opened the door and looked up and down the hallway, but he was gone.

Judy, on the other hand, was right there. "Hellenor?" she said. "We're going to need you onstage in ten minutes."

Pandy shrank back into the dressing room. She leaned over the makeup counter and stared at herself in the mirror. Who was she? Henry was right, she thought despondently. By killing Monica, she was once again making her life all about Jonny.

She glanced at Monica's shoes.

Henry was wrong, she decided. And grabbing Monica's shoes, she took off her own shoes and put them on.

She stood up. The curved heel was tricky, but the booties them-selves were light, embracing the foot like a glove. Pandy turned to stare at herself in the mirror. Thanks to the six-inch heels, she was now towering.

Leaving the dressing room, she crossed the corridor and strode confidently into the Hall of Fame. She swung open the door, and was again surrounded by her friends.

"There's Hellenor," Nancy called out, pointing and sloshing champagne over her hand.

"Hellenor! Hellenor Wallis." Suzette's enormous yellow diamond was suddenly glittering in her face.

"We were Pandy's best friends."

"And we need to be best friends with you, Hellenor."

"We need to talk to you."

"You need to listen."

"It's about Jonny."

"He called every single one of us this morning. Wanting to know if we'd seen you."

"He kept saying he was going to find you, and that when he did…"

"He was going to make sure you spent time in jail."

"He said you'd committed *fraud*."

"But in the meantime, he's looking for you."

"Now listen, if you need us, we'll be at the Pool Club right after this."

"Hellenor!" Judy screamed from the just-opened doorway.

"I'll leave your name at the door," Suzette hissed.

"I gotta go," Pandy said desperately. Her friends! How she missed them. And yes, she *would* meet up with them at the Pool Club afterward. After the leg thing. Where she would come back to life.

CHAPTER NINETEEN

*B*Y ENTERING *this area, you agree to be photographed and recorded. You acknowledge that your image and likeness may be distributed throughout the universe into all eternity including, but not limited to, the past, present, and future. You also acknowledge that you have no privacy, at least not by any current definition of privacy.*

A dark, velvety mist, lightly perfumed—sweet lily of the valley and white clover—wafted through the air. Standard party space reconfigured into a fantasyland where women ruled. Where they made the decisions. Always the good ones. Where they celebrated each other in the way the world—meaning the men—should celebrate them, but didn't. Meaning for their strength and their courage and their hard work and their contributions. But not, goddammit, for what the world—meaning the men—tried to tell them was their only value; namely, their beauty and their ability to bear children.

"And now, it's time for the Woman Warrior of the Year Awards," the announcer said.

The rest was a blur. Pandy wasn't sure how much time passed, but the next thing she knew, she was being pushed toward the stairs by two men, who helped her up. And then, somehow, she was on the stage. Except that this time, it actually was revolving. The lazy Susan. The crossing of which required every skill, it seemed, but laziness to survive.

Like balance.

Standing with her arms out and legs slightly apart, she tried to do what the stage manager had told her to do: focus solely on what was in front of her. Namely, SondraBeth. Or rather, Monica. Turning around and around on the center of the platform, like the pretty black bride on a black wedding cake.

A spotlight lit up the path to Monica, who was beckoning, *Come with me.* It was just like in her dream; she and Monica were going to be together again...

Pandy took a couple of tentative steps forward and heard a smattering of kindhearted laughter from the crowd. The sound brought her back to earth. She was on a revolving platform and she was about to receive an award for her sister, PJ Wallis, because she, PJ Wallis, was dead.

She must move toward the light. Focus on what was in front of her...

She heard the crowd laughing again. She lifted her head and looked around, taking in the neo-dark audience lit up with neon flashes from a thousand silent devices. And she remembered: She was funny onstage.

She—PJ Wallis—was *funny.* Even PP had said she was funny. And not only that, he'd said Hellenor Wallis was funny, too. Funny was the one thing Pandy and Hellenor had in common. Remembering that she was funny made Pandy feel more confident. She could do this. She took another few steps, and once again, the crowd chuckled in encouragement. Pandy gave up on the stately approach in favor of the comedic, and SondraBeth picked up on it. She was smiling down on Pandy with her most beatific Monica grin.

"Hello, Hellenor," she said in her rich timbre. The audience exhaled a blast of approving applause.

"Hello," Pandy said to the crowd, holding up her palm in a stiff wave. The platform lurched. "Wow. This is like being on one of those Japanese game shows. *Takeshi's Castle*," she said.

Titters of appreciation; not everyone understood the reference. She should have named one of those network shows instead.

"Yes, it *is*, Hellenor," SondraBeth said. And taking a beat to absorb the positive energy in the room, she sang out to the audience, "Ladies and gentlemen, I give you *Hellenor Wallis*."

A roar. Pandy's first impression was of how different it was to be on the receiving end. The rush of love she felt. The happiness. And all of a sudden, the statuette was in her hands.

It was surprisingly cool. Smooth and cold, like a cube of ice. And heavy. A crystal sculpture of a woman wearing armor, bow and arrow raised above her head. As if leading the charge into the future.

And then she was standing in front of the lectern.

Two words came to her: "*Non serviam.*" She tried to look out into the audience, but between the camera flashes and the screens, the room was now a womb of darkness. She could see only the microphones. "I will not serve. Especially not a man. Thank you."

"Speech!" came a cry from the audience.

She turned to look back at SondraBeth, who was beaming encouragement like sunshine. Suddenly, Pandy found her footing.

"This is so unexpected," Pandy said into the mike. She held the statuette briefly against her cheek, then carefully placed the Woman Warrior on the Plexiglas podium. As she took a deep breath and looked out at the expectant audience, she realized what SondraBeth had meant in the car about playing Monica: She was the ultimate impostor.

But every woman feels like an impostor, she reminded herself, glancing down at the statuette. Probably even the original Warrior Woman herself had. Until someone showed her she wasn't.

And suddenly Pandy knew what she was going to say: yes.

Yes to the accolades:

"Thank you for this award."

Yes to the acclaim:

"My sister really deserved this."

And *yes* to seizing the moment:

"I wish—" She looked up, her eyes beginning to adjust, seeing forms and faces. "I wish my sister, PJ Wallis, were here to accept this. This award would have meant everything to her."

Would have? Did. *Does* mean everything. She was giving her own eulogy. She didn't have to guess how she might feel. She *knew*.

"Most of you knew my sister as the creator of Monica. Or even as the real-life Monica. And while she was that, she was so much more. An artist. A writer. A person who lived and died by her work. A person who gave everything to her work. And, like so many of you who give it your all, she also knew about the struggles. And the disappointments."

She took a breath and hearing murmurs of approval from the audience, she continued.

"But PJ Wallis never gave up. And that is why this award would have meant so much to her."

On the screens around the room, a close-up of the statuette, the Warrior Woman's bow and arrow raised high, followed by a shuffling of images of herself—PJ Wallis—through the years. Followed by that iconic image of Monica.

"Monica!" someone cried out.

Pandy sighed. "Good old Monica," she said as she looked at Monica—hair flowing, striding across the top of the New York City skyline. "Monica meant everything to Pandy." Pandy paused, allowing for the smattering of applause to die down, and continued.

"Sometimes, Pandy wondered who she would be without Monica. But then she realized, when you ask yourself that question, what you're really asking is: Who would you be without a *label*? And we all have them: Mother. Wife. Single Girl. Career Woman. Soccer Mom.

But what do we do when we find that our label no longer applies? Who do we become when our label expires?"

A gasp swept through the audience like a fresh breeze.

"Well, ladies, it's time to let go. It's time to let go of those labels. It's time to let go and let grow."

"Let go and let grow!" came several shouts from the audience, as the words "Let go and let grow" appeared on the screens.

"Let go and let grow," Pandy repeated, her hand resting on the top of the statuette. "And while Monica isn't real, PJ Wallis *was*. A real woman with real aspirations. A real woman who aspired to what women aren't supposed to aspire to: to be the best. And to be recognized for her talents. And not by the standards of male hubris, but by the standards of excellence. To be free from the confines of what society and culture say a woman may or may not be. Can a woman be ambitious without apology? Can a woman dedicate her life to her work without apology?"

"And can a woman say thank you?"

SondraBeth's voice was right in her ear.

Pandy turned her head. Glaring into a white-hot spotlight, she realized the black chess piece that was Monica had moved across the board and was now leaning next to her, clapping.

The audience, Pandy noted, was also clapping, politely, with a sense of relief.

Pandy took a step back. She understood: Her fifteen seconds were over. She turned to look for the steps.

"Hold on," SondraBeth said, coming forward and taking Pandy's arm. And then cocking her head as if she had a hidden earpiece, she said into the crowd, "Mira from Mumbai would like to comment."

Mira's face appeared on all the screens. "Hello, ladies."

"Hello, Mira," the audience called back.

"I am the head of the international feminist organization Women for Women. And I would like to say that after a while, Monica no longer belonged to PJ Wallis. Nor does she belong to Sondra-

Beth Schnowzer. Nor does she belong to even the audience, which is mostly women."

"What do you mean by that, Mira?" SondraBeth asked.

"I am saying that Monica now belongs to a corporation. She is owned and controlled by an entertainment corporation that decides whether or not and how to make money off this entity that was created by PJ Wallis. I hope PJ Wallis made a lot of money from her own creation, but I suspect she did not."

Knowing murmurs from the audience.

Mira continued. "We have done many studies that show us that when a woman contributes in the entertainment industry, she is not rewarded justly. Because women may do what they do and be geniuses, but it is still men at the top who make the decisions, including how much money the women will be paid. It is the men who are lining their pockets with the efforts of women. It is men who have made millions, maybe billions, from Monica."

Close-up on SondraBeth, face as still and proud as the features on the Warrior Woman statuette.

"Wow," SondraBeth said. "That's a very interesting take. And here is Juanita from South America."

"I would like us to consider what men do with that money. Here, they use money to make war."

"Thank you, ladies," SondraBeth said emphatically. "It takes a very brave woman to point out how the system really works. Money is to men as cheese is to mice. If you're missing some cheese, you'll usually discover a man's been eating it."

The screens were now blinking like Christmas lights: women from all over the world eager to weigh in.

"And let's remind the audience that even though PJ Wallis is dead, it's still a *man* who will continue to profit," SondraBeth said scoldingly. She turned to Pandy.

Every eye was now on Pandy, and the attention was like a blow. And then she felt a rush. Like her soul had literally drained out of the soles of her feet and she was now merely a thin, hardened shell.

"And that is why Hellenor has something very important to announce," she heard SondraBeth say.

Pandy tried to open her mouth and found that she couldn't. She realized she was in the throes of a particularly bad case of stage fright, and now all she wanted to do was get off the stage. Somehow, she managed to lean into the microphone and whisper, "Due to the death of PJ Wallis and to unfortunate circumstances, there will be no more Monica."

"In other words," SondraBeth said, leaning into the microphone next to her, "Monica is dead."

"We have to…" Pandy's chest squeezed tight. She couldn't breathe. "Kill Monica, please…" She was having a heart attack. No, she was having a panic attack.

The frenzied roar of the crowd spun away into silence as a time balloon inflated inside Pandy's head. She saw lips moving in slow motion, a pink plastic champagne glass suspended in the air above the stage. Her own arms raised in triumph, clutching the Warrior Woman statuette in her hands. Around and around she went. Monica. Finished. Jonny. Ruined. And for one brief moment, she actually believed she had won.

And suddenly—*pop*. The balloon in her head exploded and the noise and reality came thundering back, engulfing her in an enormous wave of rage.

"Let Monica live!"

The pink plastic champagne glass landed on the stage. Then another. And another. One hit the back of SondraBeth's head. She didn't move. Her always-perfect Monica smile was now slightly lopsided, as if arranged by the hand of a mortician who couldn't quite get the expression right.

Pandy took a step back in confusion as the roar of the crowd came racing toward her like a tsunami. "Long live Monica!"

"Let Monica *live!*"

Pandy looked again to SondraBeth. Her Monica smile was back in place, but her eyes had a life of their own, darting from screen to screen.

And suddenly, Pandy *did* understand.

The crowd was going to kill them. Tear them both limb from limb. Which meant—she was going to die twice? In one day? Was that even possible?

Another champagne glass whizzed by her head and landed on the stage behind her. SondraBeth caught Pandy's eye.

"Run, Doug, run!" she hissed.

And they did.

Or tried to, anyway. They shuffled to the edge of the platform, where, thank God, Judy and a posse of men were waiting. People were moving rapidly, the way they do when they sense a storm is coming but have yet to discover how bad it's going to be.

"Now listen," SondraBeth whispered into Pandy's ear as the posse moved to get them out of the theater and back to the dressing room. "Make a stop in the Hall of Fame. Grab two costumes, and meet me back in my dressing room."

"But—" Pandy broke off as the heel of a man's shoe ground into her ankle. She was being trampled.

"My dressing room. In five," SondraBeth said as she went through the door.

Pandy ran toward Mother Teresa, grabbed the head scarf, and put it over her own head. She lifted the robes of the old mannequin, and they came off in a swirl of loosened threads. She spied a burka on another mannequin. She tugged on the headpiece and the garment flew off in a single stroke. Clutching the fabric, she ran down the hallway and into SondraBeth's dressing room.

SondraBeth was standing with one bare leg up on the counter. Following her gaze to the end of SondraBeth's leg, Pandy suddenly understood why SondraBeth could barely walk: her boots were taped to her ankles with electrical tape.

Pandy gasped as SondraBeth cried out, "Shut the door!"

While SondraBeth's body was still cocooned in her Spanx, her Monica costume was hanging in shreds from her shoulders.

"How'd you—" Pandy gasped.

"Get out of the costume?" SondraBeth held up her fingers and displayed her buildings. "These." She went back to doing what she'd been doing before Pandy walked in—expertly slicing away the electrical tape to free her feet. "We need to get out of here," she said calmly.

"What do you want me to do?"

"Take off that leather jacket and put on Mother Teresa's robe." She fell back slightly as her foot came out of the boot. "And hand me that burka," she added.

Pandy had the burka in one hand and the robe in the other. "Which should I do first?" she asked, terrified.

"It's like the air mask on an airplane. Put your own mask on first. And *then* help others."

"Okay," Pandy said, taking off her leather jacket. Her pulse was beating at the base of her throat. She slipped the tattered blue robe over her shoulders and handed SondraBeth the burka.

"Good," SondraBeth said, sliding it over her head and freeing her other foot at the same time.

"Are we going to the SUV?" Pandy whispered. Already the Monica shoes were killing her.

"We're making an emergency exit." SondraBeth looked around quickly, as if making sure she wasn't leaving anything important behind.

"What about the Warrior Woman?" Pandy asked.

"She stays here. A PA will get it." SondraBeth slid her feet into a pair of running shoes.

"Knock knock," Judy said urgently.

"Coming," SondraBeth said. She unlocked the door and Judy opened it, holding it just wide enough for the two of them to slip out.

"Food court," Judy said into her microphone. She walked briskly ahead of them, talking into her mike while beckoning them along. There were more people in the hallway now, and they looked worried. The way people look when something bad has happened and all they can think about is how not to get blamed for it.

"Keep your head down and stay next to me," SondraBeth whispered.

Judy opened another door, and they were hit by the sweet smell of meat and dough and cheese. Suddenly they were in a bustle of humanity; paparazzi shoving food into their mouths while tapping their screens and hastily gathering up equipment for the next assault. A man shoved Pandy so hard, she nearly fell. "Out of the way, granny."

Next to her, SondraBeth was chugging along determinedly. "Keep moving," she said, steering straight into the crowd massing toward the main entrance.

Pandy heard the bellowing shouts of policemen trying to control the unruly crowd.

"Ladies and gentlemen," one of them yelled, trying to get the crowd to turn away. "Monica has left the building!"

"Monica collapsed," she heard someone say. "Ambulance on its way."

"Missing, I heard—" said someone else.

And then they were being pushed. Shoved and bumped and stepped on as the crowd spun them out the revolving doors and into another mass of angry, screaming fans, holding up their devices and craning their necks for a better view—of what, Pandy couldn't say. But the crowd wanted something, and she was a mere impediment to their view.

She was going to be crushed.

Pandy felt her rib cage implode as her knees buckled beneath her.

And then her face was pressed into an endless pillow of flesh; it was up over her ears, suffocating her—

"Get off me. Off of me!" A terrified shriek, followed by the push of two greasy hands the size of small pizzas. Pandy rocked back, thrusting her own hands at SondraBeth, whose hands were right there to grab hers—her razor-sharp nails digging into Pandy's flesh like a predatory bird.

Pandy screamed. And then something came over her. She didn't want to die. Not like this. Seizing SondraBeth's arm, she lowered her head and twisted forward and out like a corkscrew, until, with a mighty push, she broke through the pack.

They emerged into more chaos: sirens and the pounding *whoop*, *whoop*, *whoop* of emergency vehicles. "Step away from the entrance!" blasted through a loudspeaker. Cops and firemen were running into the crowd. The driveway was clogged with vans and town cars; the SUV that had brought them here was nowhere in sight. Up ahead, two men were trying to close the gate in the chain-link fence.

"Run!" Pandy shouted.

Her legs, supported only by the cruelly curved heels of the red booties, felt like she was running on matchsticks.

"What the hell just happened back there?" Pandy asked, making her way to the fountain. "The audience was loving us. And then you said Monica was dead...and all of a sudden they went wild. We could have been *killed* back there."

Pandy pressed the button on the stand. The fact that water came out at all felt like a small miracle. She drank thirstily.

Directly ahead was the Hudson: a sparkling expanse of greenish brown. On the other side were the gleaming high-rises of Hoboken. It was a warm enough day for a large sailboat to be making its way down the river, skimming over the wake of the clanging Circle Line ferry, its passengers arranged like wooden toy people in the top. Then one helicopter passed overhead, while another rose up from behind the George Washington Bridge. Tilting forward with mechanical determination, the second one began speeding its way down the Hudson.

Pandy turned back to SondraBeth. "It's a good thing we're really *not* killing Monica. I don't think either one of us could survive the bad news." She patted her face with Mother Teresa's head scarf. "Was that supposed to happen?"

"What?" SondraBeth asked, not looking up from the device.

"That mayhem," Pandy said as the helicopter flitted down to Chelsea Piers and then turned around, heading back in their direction.

"I hope you're calling Judy," Pandy said anxiously, hurrying to SondraBeth's side.

"Judy knows where we are," SondraBeth said distractedly. "The phone has a tracking device."

"Then what are you doing?" Pandy demanded.

"I'm checking the Instalife feed." SondraBeth grinned wickedly as she read the headlines aloud: "'Real-Life Monica Missing: Possibility of Foul Play'...'Is Monica a Feminist?'...and wait for it..." She held up her hand. "Here it is: 'Monica Declared Dead!'"

She held the phone out to Pandy. There was the classic shot of

Monica striding over the skyline of Manhattan, but someone had cleverly drawn a coffin around her. And for the first time in her life, Monica didn't look so happy.

"Ding-dong, the witch is dead! The wicked old witch. The Monica witch," SondraBeth sang out.

Pandy frowned and handed the device back to SondraBeth. "Do you have to be *that* happy about it?" she asked, sitting down to loosen the laces of the booties.

"What do you mean?" SondraBeth asked.

"I don't know. Monica is dead. I sort of feel like we should be *sadder*."

"Oh, Peege," SondraBeth said, sitting down next to her. "Monica *isn't* dead. Or won't be in a couple of hours, when she comes back to life at the leg. And in the meantime, we should be celebrating."

Monica's shoe suddenly came away from her foot and Pandy smiled victoriously. "Because now the mob goes after Jonny!"

"He's gonna get his!" SondraBeth set the phone down and gave her a high five.

"Excellent," Pandy said, picking up the phone to check the headlines.

And then all of a sudden, it was out of her hand and SondraBeth was running pell-mell toward the end of the pier, the phone banged into her splayed left hand like a ball in a catcher's mitt. She came to an abrupt halt, and winding her arm behind her back, she hurled it into the river. It sliced through the air for a good forty feet before reaching its apex and plunging unceremoniously to its watery grave.

"What the fuck?" Pandy shrieked.

"The *tracking device*. How do you think the paparazzi followed me to Wallis?" SondraBeth shouted as the helicopter roared overhead. "We're too visible here. Come on."

SondraBeth pulled the hood of the burka over her head as she knelt to help Pandy get Monica's boot back on.

Pandy's feet were screaming. "Are we going to have to run again?

I should have changed back into my own shoes," she shouted, glancing up at the helicopter. Apparently they hadn't been recognized, as it began spinning away.

"No. This time we walk," SondraBeth said. "Keep your head down and don't look anyone in the eye."

A cavalcade of police cars came racing down the West Side Highway toward Chelsea Piers, flashing blue, white, blue, white, blue, like a flag. Pandy froze. She had a vision of herself being arrested dressed as Mother Teresa. There would really be no explaining that one.

"Are we going to be arrested?" she gasped, drawing back.

"What are you talking about?" SondraBeth said as the police cars sped by. "I'm a very valuable asset. But I'd like to keep the paparazzi off our trail. So far no one is looking for Mother Teresa and her burka friend. Not yet, anyway."

And glancing quickly over her shoulder, she hustled Pandy across the West Side Highway.

Unfortunately, Pandy wasn't able to get far. She managed to make it half a block, to the loading dock of one of the storage joints, before she had to pull up short to catch her breath.

"I don't understand," Pandy said, loosening the laces on the shoes again. "We have no money and no cell phone. And I cannot walk any farther in these goddamned Monica shoes. Can we please borrow a phone from someone and call Judy?"

"Don't worry. We will. Hey," SondraBeth said. "Remember the Alamo? Remember *Jonny*? We should be painting the town red."

"*Now?*" Pandy asked, looking around. This part of Manhattan was so deserted, there wasn't even a deli.

"Not here." SondraBeth laughed. She walked to the corner of Tenth Avenue and put her hands on her hips. "Someplace no one will know us. What about one of those Irish bars?"

"You mean one of those places where they use that stinky rag to wipe the bar? And the peanuts contain traces of male urine?"

"That's the ticket, sista," SondraBeth said, slinging her arm around Pandy's shoulders. She looked down at Pandy's feet. "But first, we need to get rid of those shoes."

And with Pandy wincing along, they passed through three long blocks of crumbly brown buildings standing stubborn against the sea of change. At last reaching Seventh Avenue, they headed south, hugging the storefronts that offered everything from homeopathic remedies to tandoori specialties. SondraBeth stopped suddenly in front of a store with two dusty mannequins in the window, one wearing a 1950s ball gown and the other a sagging silk peignoir.

∞

Pandy held her breath as they entered the slightly humid air of the shop. She looked around cautiously, then exhaled. The place was largely unchanged from all those years ago, when she and Sondra-Beth used to shop there for vintage clothing that they could turn into party dresses. Pandy looked up at the shelf over the glass case that held the cash register. Even that old stuffed toy monkey was still there, dressed in his dusty red felt shorts.

"Hey," Pandy said, grabbing SondraBeth's arm. "Look. The monkey in the moleskin."

"PandaBeth!" SondraBeth hissed, looking around for the proprietor. Dressed in a frayed Japanese robe and smelling strongly of cigarettes, he was the sort of New York City person who has seen better days, and yet continues on in a determined time warp.

SondraBeth slipped past him, and motioning for Pandy to follow, began piling various items on her outstretched arms. A glittery skirt, a denim shirt. Two feather boas. "Whatever happened to PandaBeth, anyway?" she asked.

"Well, I'm not the one to say," Pandy said, frowning at the growing pile, especially when SondraBeth added a blue wig. "You were the one who ran off with Doug Stone. Who, by the way, had the temerity to inform me that *you* hated *me*."

"Ha!" SondraBeth snorted. "He told me you were trashing me all over town. He was more like a girl than I was. He was constantly in front of the mirror. He would go over his schedule every evening and plan his outfit for the next day!"

"Asswipe," Pandy exclaimed, yanking back the curtain to the dressing room. It contained two rusty folding chairs and an old mirror propped up against the wall.

"When our engagement ended," SondraBeth continued, lifting her arms and wriggling out of the burka, "there was so much bad press, I didn't even know if I *should* play Monica anymore."

"I know," Pandy said, completely distracted by the act of trying to squeeze herself into a tattered sequined party dress and a pair of ancient silver dancing shoes.

"But of course, I knew *that* was never going to happen," Sondra-Beth went on. "And I *thought* about calling you then, but you seemed to be so happy with Jonny." SondraBeth slid her feet into a pair of cowboy boots. "I knew there was no way you'd ever want to be friends again—I mean, what girl wants to be friends with the girlfriend who told her that her husband was a shit?"

Pandy frowned at the blue wig SondraBeth had tugged onto her head. "But why didn't you call me *after*? When Jonny and I *did* split up?"

SondraBeth clapped a cowboy hat onto her head. "Why didn't *you* call *me*?" she asked. She met Pandy's eyes in the mirror. Pandy suddenly felt guilty.

"I didn't think you'd want to hear from me." Pandy frowned at the blue wig. "Because of the stupid way I'd acted with Doug. And then, according to the press, you and Doug were the ideal couple. And then after you guys split up, you were so busy. With Monica. And Doug said you hated me."

"I never said I hated you."

"Then what did you say?" Pandy asked, thinking about what Doug had told her about how without Monica, SondraBeth would have been nothing. "After all, if it was only about Doug, why didn't you get back in touch?"

"Because I guessed Doug had said something about what I said about you."

"Which was?"

"Nothing," SondraBeth snapped. "But you have to remember, I was the one who was working her ass off for Monica. And meanwhile, you never even came to the set. You had Monica, but you still had a life. Even if Jonny was a scumbag, at least you had the chance to act like you were in love with him."

"Act like it?" Pandy asked.

"Don't you understand?" SondraBeth glared at her. "*Because of Monica*, you were the last girlfriend I had. The last girlfriend I had *time* to make. And after that..." She shrugged. "I had no time. I was scheduled. *Am* scheduled."

She tossed Pandy a couple of feather boas as she yanked open the curtain and went out.

Pandy took one last glance at herself in the mirror before she hurried after her.

The proprietor was standing behind the glass counter, his gaze focused on the small TV above his head. "And how are you going to pay?" he asked, briefly tearing his eyes away from the screen.

"With these," Pandy said, heaving Monica's shoes onto the counter.

The proprietor glanced at the shoes and looked back to the news loop. He picked up one of the shoes and asked casually, "Is Monica *dead*?"

Pandy could barely glance at SondraBeth, who gave her a warning look as she held out her hand for the pile of twenties the proprietor was counting out.

Pandy tried to hold it, but a terrible eruption, an explosion, was rising up through her insides...She fell onto the glass door and swung out onto the sidewalk, convulsing with laughter.

Five minutes later, they were sliding up to the bar at McWiggins's. The interior was shaded and, as most of these places were, somewhat gloomy.

Pandy looked around and wondered if this was indeed the best place to kill a couple of hours. The Pool Club would definitely be better. On the other hand, she was tired and thirsty. "I'll have a beer," she said to the bartender.

"What kind?" The bartender looked at her challengingly. Pandy wasn't sure if it was because she was a bald middle-aged woman, or because she was a bald middle-aged woman wearing a blue wig and a tattered sequined dress.

"Two Heinies, draft," SondraBeth said. "And two shots of Patrón. Silver."

"Coming right up," the bartender said in a surly tone of voice.

"What would you do if there were no more Monica, anyway?" SondraBeth asked, leaning over the bar to rest her head in her hand. "With that speech you gave at the Woman Warrior Awards, it sounds like you're ready to move on."

The bartender slid two shots and two beers in front of them. SondraBeth lifted one to her lips and, giving Pandy a thumbs-up, sent it down the hatch.

Pandy sighed as she held her own shot up to her lips. "I love Monica as much as you do, but while Jonny was trying to take me for every penny I'd ever made from her, I *did* create a new character." She frowned, thought of Lady Wallis, and downed the shot, which caused her to cough into her napkin. "But because of Monica, no one wants her. And the weird thing is, she's sort of like Monica. I mean, she's pretty glamorous. She was friends with Marie Antoinette. Can you imagine what it would be like to find out that your best friend had her head chopped off?"

Pandy grimaced and motioned for another shot.

"I think it sounds fabulous," SondraBeth said as the bartender gave them refills.

Pandy laughed. "In any case, Henry said that they would only publish it if I were dead. And since I'm not—" Pandy shrugged. "Having a book rejected is horrible. It's like having a baby and when you show it to people, they tell you to stick it back in your uterus." She snorted, realizing she must be feeling the effects of the shot. "What would *you* do if there were no more Monica?"

"I'd go live on my ranch in Montana."

"Wha—?" Pandy said into her beer.

"That's right." SondraBeth nodded. "I wouldn't even be an actress anymore."

Pandy wrinkled her nose. "You wouldn't?"

"Nah," SondraBeth said, motioning for another round of shots. She emitted an ironic laugh. "Thanks to Monica, I *still* don't know what I want to be when I grow up."

"Really?" Pandy asked as the new round arrived.

"Sure," SondraBeth said, taking a shot. "If it hadn't been for you and Monica, who knows how my life would have ended up? But then Monica came along. And it was such a great opportunity. And then it was *all* about Monica..."

"But *Montana*?" Pandy asked, slurring slightly. "I thought you said you hated the place."

"I did. But I went back a couple of years ago when my father died. And my mother and I kind of made up. Mom, as it turns out, loves Monica. And when I was finally successful..." SondraBeth put down her empty glass. "She kind of had to admit that she was wrong about me as a child. I *wasn't* going to end up in jail after all."

Pandy laughed. "You were never going to end up in jail."

SondraBeth raised her eyebrows. "I got pretty close a couple of times. I ran away from home, remember? I became a stripper. It could have turned out that Mom was right."

"I remember," Pandy said gently. "You told me about it. That night on the Vineyard."

SondraBeth laughed and sipped at her beer. "I was so afraid to tell you because I thought if you knew, you'd think there was no way I could be Monica."

"You know better than that," Pandy said. "Come on, sista. Remember how I told you I didn't have the best childhood myself? How my sister tried to kill herself when she was sixteen? And then my parents died. And then—" Pandy inhaled sharply, catching herself before she said more. Just like that time on the Vineyard, she'd almost spilled her biggest secret. Which wasn't hers to tell.

"You never told me *that* story about Hellenor," SondraBeth said.

"It was nothing," Pandy said quickly, waving it away. "It was a long time ago. She's fine now."

SondraBeth shook her head musingly. "I always thought it was going to be you and me, you know? That somehow, we'd be the ones steering this Monica thing. How'd we lose control?"

"Men," Pandy said.

"Men." SondraBeth's eyes narrowed.

And then they both looked up at the bar's TV.

This time, they didn't look away. It was the same news loop, but now it was all about Hellenor.

"Last seen with SondraBeth Schnowzer—" A shot of SondraBeth in her black wedding dress, staring blankly into the camera, then a close-up of Pandy, looking terrified—"An outbreak of chaos"—wide shot of hundreds of women shouting into their devices, handbags swinging, ankles buckling, tablecloths torn from tables as they ran toward the exit...

And then another close-up of Pandy at the Woman Warrior Awards: "Authorities seeking information about the woman who claims to be Hellenor Wallis—"

And then to Jonny again, in a new clip: "I'm onto you, Hellenor. I'm looking for you—"

And finally, a live shot of the Monica billboard. "Due to the mysterious disappearance of SondraBeth Schnowzer, the studio is considering canceling the Shoe Unveiling."

"Now that really would be a shame," said the announcer.

"And now, live, back to the San Geronimo festival."

SondraBeth didn't look at Pandy as she casually put down three twenty-dollar bills. "Keep the change," she called out to the bartender, who nodded.

And once again, they were running. The lyrics from the Talking Heads' "Life During Wartime" played over and over in Pandy's mind as she dodged hot dog stands, small fuzzy animals attached to leashes, zombie humans attached to their devices, old people on bicycles, electrically silent taxis, flattened cardboard boxes, trucks, police cars, and an ambulance or two.

They ran all the way to Union Square, darting between the booths in the farmers' market, into the center of the square. Where, finally, Pandy stopped panting heavily as she tried to catch her breath. Above her head, screens mounted on the tall buildings flashed tickertapes of useless information. The national debt. What was trending. The most famous person on Instalife. The number one photograph. And with the exception of the national debt—insurmountable, immutable, and dependably growing—Monica was at the top of the list.

Monica was everywhere. Pandy could never outrun her, never outgrow her, and most of all, never kill her.

Monica was totally *fine*.

Monica was safe.

On the other hand, with Jonny still on the loose and blabbing to the press about Hellenor, Hellenor might not be.

CHAPTER TWENTY-ONE

S ONDRABETH caught up with Pandy on Eighth Street. "What the fuck?" she shouted.

"Jonny." Pandy turned, her eyes blazing. "He's still on the loose."

She began walking again, heading diagonally through Washington Square Park, past the old men playing their endless games of chess. Jonny looking into Hellenor's background was the one part of the equation she hadn't considered when they'd cooked up this scheme to get even with him. In her attempt at revenge, she'd stupidly put Hellenor at risk. Jonny asking who Hellenor was; the authorities looking into Hellenor's background? That was not good.

SondraBeth grabbed her arm. "What's this about?"

"I can't say," Pandy said stubbornly.

SondraBeth looked at her closely. "It's about Hellenor, isn't it? What's the big secret? Is Hellenor some kind of axe murderer?"

"Please," Pandy said. "She's just someone who wants to live her life a certain way, and I've always tried to respect her wishes. She's my *sister*." Pandy reached Houston and, looking left and right, began crossing against the light.

SondraBeth walked briskly next to her. "Okay. I get it," she said. "I won't ask questions."

"Great. Just help me find Jonny before he says anything more about Hellenor."

"What about the leg?"

"This is more important than those union guys," Pandy muttered.

Jonny, she figured, must still be in front of her building, looking for her. At least he had been ten minutes ago, when she'd seen him on one of the screens.

Halfway down her block, however, she was forced to stop. The base of her building was cluttered with the debris of flowers, Monica dolls, and pink plastic champagne glasses. A large group of women were holding up hand-lettered LET MONICA LIVE! posters.

"Are you a Monica fan?" one of them asked Pandy.

"Yes, actually I am."

"Will you sign the petition?"

"For what?" Pandy said, looking around for Jonny.

"To let Monica *live*."

A black town car pulled up to the curb. The back window slid down and Freddie the Rat stuck his head out.

"Freddie!" SondraBeth exclaimed, rushing the car. She and Freddie had a brief conversation, and then the window went up.

"Well?" Pandy demanded as the car drove away.

"Freddie says he's sure Jonny will be back. I mean, where else would he go, right? He's looking for Hellenor. Naturally, he would think that you'd come here."

Pandy frowned, recalling what he'd said on the screen. "He's at Gay Street," she said quickly.

Gay Street. Where Henry lived. Where Jonny had been before. On the day of that fateful snowstorm. When they fell in love.

Jonny knew Pandy would go there to hide out. It was the perfect place for a showdown.

∞

Sure enough, there he was, on the stoop of Henry's house.

"Look at him," SondraBeth said, flattening herself around the curve of the street so Jonny couldn't see them. "He's just standing there. He's like a sitting duck."

Pandy peeked around the corner at Jonny. He was as handsome as ever. It was such a shame he was so pathetic.

"Like taking candy from a baby," SondraBeth said. And straightening her cowboy hat, she turned into Monica. Monica, with her country-girl swagger. Her confidence. Her innate belief that everything would always go her way. In her very best Monica voice, SondraBeth started toward him, saying, "Oh, Jonny? It's me. It's Monica..."

"No, wait!" Pandy said. She marched down the sidewalk in her sequined dress. As she ripped off the wig, she got right in Jonny's face and said, "Now look here, Diaper Boy. It's me, Pandy. So when it comes to Hellenor—"

Jonny's eyebrows shot up. And then he smiled, as if he'd known this was going to happen all along.

"I knew you'd come here." He started circling her like a boxer.

"Because I know my own fucking wife, right?" he continued. "And what a creep she is. I knew you'd pull a stunt like this to get out of paying me. You're a big fucking cheat. And I'm going to make sure all the world finds out. That, and the fact that the only reason I married you was because I thought you were Monica." He broke off, gave her one last vicious sneer, and began walking away.

"Huh?" Pandy said, gobsmacked.

Jonny stopped, turned around, and strode back to ridicule her further. "And what are *you* going to do about it?" he jeered. "Nothing, right? Because you never *do anything*. You're just what I said you were—a weak, judgmental woman. You think you're so high and mighty, like you'd never make a mistake. Well, you just made a huge mistake, baby. Who is Hellenor Wallis?"

Pandy blanched.

"Well?" Jonny demanded. He took her by the shoulders and

shook her, hard. "Does Hellenor Wallis even exist? Or did you make her up, too?"

"I—" Thoughts spun around in her head while Jonny went on mercilessly:

"Oh, I'm sorry. Did she die, too? How convenient." He gave her another violent shake that made her teeth rattle.

The edges of Pandy's vision went black. "It wasn't like that," she choked out.

"Then where is she?"

"I don't know."

"What do you mean, *you don't know?*" Jonny emitted a harsh laugh. "What were you planning to do when they tracked down the real Hellenor?"

Thwack! A pointy-toed cowboy boot hit Jonny square in the forehead. He let go of Pandy and spun around. And there was good old Squeege with her arm pulled back, ready to give Jonny another thunk if necessary.

"Come on," SondraBeth said as she hailed a taxi.

Pulling Jonny from the front while Pandy pushed him from behind, they bundled him into the backseat, where he was lodged between the two of them.

Just like the ham in one of his famous jambon sandwiches, Pandy thought smugly.

"What the hell!" Jonny snarled.

Heading toward Soho, Pandy took in the colorful beads of the San Geronimo revelers reeling past the car. "You know what?" Jonny blared, like a megaphone at a parade. "You were a really bad fucking wife. Did I ever tell you that? Okay, you were good in bed. At first. But that's about it."

"I can't take this," SondraBeth said. "Hey, driver, can you turn up the radio?"

"You turned into a goddamn nag," Jonny continued. "And then, when I saw where you came from…you fucking Puritan bitch! Pretending to be broke, when you had that estate in Connecticut!"

He continued cursing her until three blocks later, when they reached the backstage loading dock of the billboard on Spring Street. As they emerged from the taxi, Pandy saw Freddie the Rat edging forward through the crowd. She and SondraBeth got out, and Freddie quickly came forward. The two men who were with him unceremoniously yanked Jonny from the backseat.

"We got it worked out," Freddie the Rat said to SondraBeth as the men hustled Jonny away, the heels of his Italian loafers leaving skid tracks along the pavement.

Freddie turned to Pandy. "Nice to meet you, *Hellenor*," he said with a wink. He hurried after his guys. "Hey, Jonny," he called out. "You ready to take a little ride?"

And suddenly, Judy was there. "SondraBeth? Hellenor?" she asked. "We need you to get ready."

∞

They emerged on the roof of the building, where the Monica billboard rose straight up above under a murky, darkening sky.

Judy handed Pandy a paper cup of coffee. "You've unleashed a monster," she said. She gestured toward the front of the building, at the crowd that was massed on the streets below.

"Look at all those people!" SondraBeth said.

And turning to look, Pandy discovered PP running across the rooftop toward them.

"Where the hell have you been?" he shouted at SondraBeth. And then, spotting Pandy next to her, he turned on her.

"And you, Hellenor Wallis," he said, all puffed up like a plastic G.I. Joe doll. "I was *wrong* about you. You are just as bad as your sister." PP looked from Pandy to SondraBeth as he took another deep breath. "And this time," he said threateningly, "you'd both better make sure to tell everyone that Monica is *alive*..."

"Or else what?" SondraBeth demanded.

"I have a list of infractions from the police department," PP bleated, shaking his device. "Jaywalking, fencing stolen items... I'm going to take these expenses out of your Monica money."

SondraBeth gave him a nasty smile. "Oh, can it, PP. It's not up to you. It's up to *Hellenor*, remember?"

"Are you ready?" Judy said, tapping the mike.

⌒

And then they were on the elevator platform that would take them up to the stage. Pointing to a panel, Judy reminded everyone that they should press the green button to go up and the red button to go down.

Someone pressed the green button, and with a small lurch, they were suddenly moving up, up, up into the sky, satellites twinkling like stars across the landscape. SondraBeth stood on the edge, gripping the railing and staring fiercely out over the landscape. For one second, Pandy saw the girl she'd fallen in love with on the billboard all those years ago...

And suddenly, she knew.

The platform bounced slightly as it came to rest against the back of the small stage.

"You planned this," Pandy said as they were hustled out of the elevator and onto the narrow backstage platform.

"Planned what?" SondraBeth blanched.

"This whole killing Monica thing. That's why Freddie the Rat was at your townhouse. You still thought I was Hellenor back then. You were going to convince Hellenor to kill Monica."

"What are you talking about?" SondraBeth gasped.

"You did all that staging—rolling in the mud, murmuring that Monica was dead, while thinking I was Hellenor..." Pandy shook her head. "Why didn't you just *say* you didn't want to play Monica anymore?"

"Because I didn't want to disappoint you."

"You know that's not true," Pandy hissed.

"So what?" SondraBeth said. "I didn't have the courage to admit it. I don't *want* to be Monica anymore."

"Are you ready?" Judy asked. A section of the billboard dropped down in front, opening Monica's mouth to reveal the stage. Pandy felt a gust of wind, and then it grew into a wave of approval from the audience below.

"In any case, it doesn't matter," SondraBeth hissed. "When I realized you were Pandy, I knew it was over. Still, we got even with Jonny. And that's all that counts."

"But why not just tell PP that you don't want to play Monica anymore?" Pandy asked as someone put a microphone in her hand.

"You know why." SondraBeth laughed harshly. "It's in my contract. The studio can fire me, but I can't quit. My contract with Monica is like the worst marriage ever. Monica can get rid of me anytime she likes, but I can't leave her. *Ever.*"

"Welcome to the first annual Monica Shoe Unveiling!" Pandy heard the announcer's voice boom out into the open crowd.

And then Pandy was on the stage. She took one look back at SondraBeth as she was drowned out by the shouts, whistles, and cheers from the audience below. The roar of the crowd was like an animal demanding attention.

And Pandy was happy to give it to them. Buoyed by the crowd's rush of expectation, their desire to witness a miracle, Pandy raised one arm like the Warrior Woman herself. Holding the mike to her lips, she screamed, "Kill Monica. Please!"

And just as promised, Monica's leg began to rise. First the hard shiny toe, and then the cruelly curved heel, and then there it came: yards and yards of red fringe waving like triumphant streamers in the air. And as the leg rose, so, too, did Jonny. For suddenly, there he was, dangling from a harness attached to several pieces of fringe.

The crowd began to laugh. And laugh. Suddenly, Pandy was

laughing, too. The leg rose up another five feet, and jerked Jonny like a puppet, his arms and legs flailing.

SondraBeth came to stand next to Pandy, and the crowd went crazy, hooting and cheering as she clapped, the microphone between her hands. Eventually, when the noise died down, she walked to the edge of the stage. Taking a wide stance in her cowboy boots, she said, "Ladies and gentlemen. Let me introduce you to Jonny Balaga. Resident *scumbag!*"

Deafening boos. Pink plastic champagne glasses were tossed in Jonny's direction.

"And just to make the event even more special, this, by the way, is *not* Hellenor Wallis," SondraBeth said, turning to Pandy. Raising her arms in triumph, she shouted, "This is PJ Wallis—the creator of Monica—in disguise!"

Another huge roar of approval, like the crowd was about to witness a boxing match. SondraBeth paused to let the rustling die down to a hush. She put her arm around Pandy's shoulder. Looking out over the crowd, Pandy followed her gaze, right across the rooftops to a huge screen that had been set up to project their images.

On the screen, Pandy saw SondraBeth lift the microphone to her mouth. "My best friend PJ Wallis and I cooked up this little plot to get even with Jonny, who is Pandy's ex-husband."

"Ooooooh." Wide panning shot of the vengeful crowd. Then another close-up of SondraBeth. And in her very best, naughtiest Monica voice, she said, "Because Jonny has been a very, *very* bad boy. Isn't that right, Jonny?"

Spotlight on Jonny. And there *he* was, up on the screen, dangling like a marionette. What could he do? He waved.

"I think Pandy has some things she'd like to say to him," Sondra-Beth said, her voice echoing against the tall buildings. Before Pandy could refuse, SondraBeth passed the microphone off to her and returned to stage left.

And once again, Pandy was all by herself. Staring out into the hot, salty lights.

As if in encouragement for what she was preparing to say, the leg jerked, and Jonny bounced and swung, holding on to the straps. The crowd laughed again as Pandy looked at Jonny and thought:

There's your happy ending.

"Hey!" Jonny shouted, waving.

"Boooo!" the crowd shouted back. Pandy looked at Jonny, dangling like the fool in the failed deus ex machina, and realized that once again, Henry was right. This *was* all about Jonny.

And then the strangest thing happened. She looked again at Jonny and felt absolutely nothing. Like she'd never even known him. Like they'd never been married. Like he simply didn't *belong*. Not in her life, anyway.

And then, like water rushing in to fill an empty space, she felt sorry for him.

She looked at SondraBeth, smiling out at the crowd, dressed in her cowgirl spangles, and felt sorry for her, too. And then, gazing across the rooftops, she caught sight of herself on-screen, and felt most of all sorry for herself.

She walked to the end of the platform and leaned over the edge, toward Jonny, the height causing her stomach to clench in terror. "The truth is, I did disguise myself as Hellenor. And I did try to kill Monica. And I did do it for revenge. On that man."

A large burst of applause. Pandy nodded in acknowledgment. "I was weak, and I fell in love. I knew I shouldn't have, but I did. Because even though I knew better, some part of me felt that I deserved *that* happy ending." She pointed to Jonny. "And for a short time, I thought I had found it. Until I realized that that man could never give it to me."

"Boooo," the crowd said, throwing pink plastic champagne glasses at Jonny. The leg jerked higher, and Jonny grabbed at the straps.

Chapter Twenty

WATER. I need water!" Pandy gasped minutes later, lurching after SondraBeth. They were in one of those new parks that had seemingly sprung up overnight on the Hudson River. "What the fuck?" Pandy said, slowing down to a laborious clop.

She looked around. The grass was fresh and clean, as were the hard plastic forms molded into table and chair configurations. Lowering herself onto her hands and knees, she attempted to crawl across the grass to the chair forms, but gave up halfway and flopped down on her stomach instead.

"I need water," she groaned.

SondraBeth was standing above her, the top of the burka pulled back from her head like a priestess's robe. "We did it!" she shouted.

"We did?" Pandy sat up.

"We killed Monica!"

"Are you sure?" Pandy asked. The knob of pain on the back of her head was pulsating again, as if it had a life of its own.

"Give me my phone," SondraBeth commanded.

Pandy struggled to her feet and reached into her front pocket. "Water?" she asked, holding out the phone in exchange for information.

"Drinking fountain—that way," SondraBeth said, grabbing the device and pointing in the direction of the Hudson.

"And when that man didn't give me my happy ending, I thought the right answer was revenge."

An intake of breath, like the dry rustling of leaves as the crowd considered this information.

Pandy continued, strolling to the other side of the platform, grateful to be away from the sight of Jonny. "And while revenge might seem like the right answer, at some point during the past forty-eight hours—in which I've been involved in an explosion, suffered a case of mistaken identity, and accepted an award for being dead—somewhere along *that* journey, I realized that revenge against a man because he didn't give me my happy ending wasn't the answer. Because a happy ending with a man is never going to be *my* happy ending. Nor is it going to be Monica's happy ending. But that's okay, because every woman's happy ending doesn't have to be the same. And it doesn't have to involve a man."

Heart pumping in her chest, Pandy looked across the stage at SondraBeth. SondraBeth caught her glance and threw it back to her with that old PandaBeth smile.

"Because there are some things that matter more than a man," Pandy said, gaining momentum as she walked across what felt like miles and miles of stage to reach SondraBeth's side. "And those things are friendship—and being true to yourself."

Gazing out past the shimmering screens and into the bright lights of the city, she saw herself as an eager young woman taking it all in, her heart and soul aching to belong, believing she could conquer all obstacles. It had been a long struggle, but she had painted the town every color of the rainbow.

And then she knew what she had to do.

Pandy looked up at the giant image of Monica and smiled ruefully.

"And so, as much as we both love Monica, we've allowed ourselves to be Monica for too long," she continued. "Maybe it was because we wanted too much. Or maybe it was because we were scared. Or maybe it was because we fell in love with the wrong men."

Pandy shook her head at Jonny, who was still dangling from his straps as a fireman on a ladder tried to grab his ankle.

"But none of those reasons matter," she said, slinging her arm around SondraBeth's shoulder. "Because the truth is that this woman—SondraBeth Schnowzer, whom most of you know only as Monica—doesn't want to play Monica anymore. And I don't want her to, either."

The crowd, at last, went silent.

Into the silence came a lone voice. Perhaps it was the voice of a Hellenor, or even of a SondraBeth or perhaps of a Pandy herself—the voice of any woman who was sure she didn't belong and was sick of trying: "Kill Monica. *Please.*"

And then, like the fresh breeze that presages the arrival of better weather, a tinkle of laughter came from the audience. It grew and grew until it was rushing like the gathering waters of spring, racing downriver from the mountains to the sea. The noise of laughter commingled with those cheery notes from the Monica theme song, and SondraBeth and Pandy began singing along. And for one last moment, it was all a blur...

Until reality came flooding back in. Specifically in the form of wincing foot pain. Pandy's feet felt like those of a young girl after a long, exhausting day spent pounding the pavement. Back then, her feet had been able to go on forever. With a sigh of relief, she realized that unlike the young woman she'd once been, it was okay to leave the party before the blisters set in.

She turned to Judy.

"Are you ready?" Judy asked, glancing quickly over her shoulder to where SondraBeth was still onstage, and probably would be for quite a bit longer. "Do you mind going down alone?" she asked, motioning for the stage manager to help Pandy onto the elevator.

"No," Pandy said. "I don't mind."

She stepped onto the platform and, pressing the red button, went back down to earth.

Where PP was waiting. "Goddammit, PJ Wallis. I should have known this so-called 'Hellenor' was you. Now let me tell you something. If you think you and SondraBeth are going to get away with this little stunt, you're wrong. You have absolutely no authority to kill a creation that no longer legally belongs to you. The studio already has a pack of lawyers lined up to deal with the two of you…"

Pandy held up her hand. "You know what, PP?" she asked. She paused to think of what she really wanted to say. And just like the Senator squeezing those imaginary balls, she realized the message was simple but effective:

"Fuck you!" she said with an exuberant shout.

And feeling quite pleased with herself, despite knowing that her career in the movies was probably over, she exited the building through the same door she'd entered. Where she ran right into Henry on the sidewalk.

"Well, well, well. What have we here?" he asked, looking her up and down appraisingly.

Pandy glared at him. "I thought I was *dead* to you."

"I said if you went *through with it*, you would be dead to me."

"You know what?" Pandy said. "I'm too tired for this. You should be grateful to me. I may not be Lady Wallis, but at least *I* managed to keep *your* secret."

"And I managed to keep yours as well." Henry reached into his breast pocket and withdrew a folded letter. "While you were busy prancing around Manhattan like a moldy Monica, I was busy making us money. From your new character."

"Lady Wallis?" Pandy gasped.

"This, my dear, is a commitment letter from your publisher to publish Lady Wallis, whether or not you yourself are alive."

"Oh, Henry!" Pandy flung open her arms and hugged his narrow shoulders. "I knew you could sell Lady Wallis if you just tried!"

Henry sighed. "I suppose I have as much invested in her as you do."

"Yes, you do. And you're an angel," Pandy declared. She started to head up West Broadway.

"And where," Henry demanded, starting after her, "do you think you're going?"

"To the Pool Club, to see Suzette and the others," Pandy said innocently over her shoulder. "Now that I'm Pandy again, I've got a whole lot of explaining to do."

"I would like to remind you that now that you've sold your Lady Wallis novel, they're going to want another one. Immediately. Which means it's a school night."

Pandy stopped and put her hands on her hips. "Now listen, Henry. I told you, I've had *enough*. I've been rejected, blown up, blown off, and most of all, I've had to pretend to be *you*. And as much as I love you and as far as I'm willing to go to keep your secret, I want a night off."

Henry paused. Then he shook his head and laughed. "That old secret? The next thing I know, you'll be claiming that *I'm* the reason you did all this."

"You are *one* of the reasons"—Pandy paused for effect—"*Hellenor*."

Henry sighed. "Hellenor was such a long time ago."

Pandy rolled her eyes. "It wasn't that long ago. Okay, maybe you're right. It was twenty-five years ago when Hellenor went to Amsterdam—"

"From whence I emerged," Henry said proudly. "You have to admit it *is* silly," he added, taking her arm. "You pretending to be me. And then trying to kill Monica. It's the daftest thing you've ever done."

Pandy laughed, looking over her shoulder at the Monica billboard. Jonny had been removed, and Monica at last had her leg.

"In any case, I'm not looking for my happy ending anymore.

307

In fact, I think I'd like to avoid endings of any kind for a while." Pandy reached the corner and sniffed. Smelling the sweet childhood perfume of cotton candy, she exclaimed, "It's the San Geronimo festival."

"Don't tell me you just noticed. Oh no," Henry said, balking at the corner like a mule.

"Why not?" Pandy insisted. "I want to go. And remember, you still *owe* me."

Henry sighed. "I suppose I could accompany you. As long as I'm not dragged to that dreadful watering hole known as the Pool Club." He shuddered. "Compared to that, I suppose having my craw stuffed with cotton candy is preferable to being forced to listen to the *caw* of those crows you call your friends."

"At least you didn't say 'crones.' Come on, Henry." Pandy laughed. And possessed of that spirit in which one could take as many acts as necessary to complete a full life, she grabbed her former sister's arm, and together they went into the glittering neon lights.

Acknowledgments

There were many people who helped me along the crazy creative journey of writing *Killing Monica*. Thanks to everyone who sat tight and waited patiently as my imagination ran wild…

Thanks to the brilliant Heather Schroder of Compass Talent, my tried-and-true agent and partner in literary crimes, who trusts her guts and instincts and always believes. This book would not be possible without you.

Thanks to Deb Futter for her sure-handed guidance and for knowing what, where, when, and most of all, *how* to get there.

Thanks to Leslie Wells, whose deep wisdom and grace helped us steer this boat back up the river and safely into the harbor.

Thanks to Jeanine Pepler of AKA LIFE, whose bright spark of positivity and unwavering belief in any possibility is forever inspiring.

And to Jeanine's team at AKA: Laura Nicolassy, Brooke Shuhy, Marina Maib, Allison Meyer, and Chloe Mills.

Thanks to Matthew Ballast, our very own "Henry," along with the other terrific folks at Hachette: Brian McLendon, Elizabeth Kulhanek, Anne Twomey, and Andrew Duncan.

Thanks to Richard Beswick in London and Ron Bernstein in LA.

A huge thanks to Dawn Rosiello, who makes order out of chaos.

And a special thanks to my intern, Jennifer Foulon, who put up with all the zaniness and bought her first pair of Jimmy Choo shoes.

ABOUT THE AUTHOR

CANDACE BUSHNELL is the critically acclaimed, international best-selling novelist whose first book, *Sex and the City*, was the basis for the HBO hit series and subsequent blockbuster movie. She is the author of seven novels, including *Trading Up*, *One Fifth Avenue*, *Lipstick Jungle*, and *The Carrie Diaries*—with the latter two made into popular TV series of the same names. Through her books and television series, Bushnell has influenced and defined two generations of women. She is the winner of the 2006 Matrix Award for books (other winners include Joan Didion and Amy Tan) and a recipient of the Albert Einstein Spirit of Achievement Award. Bushnell grew up in Connecticut, and attended Rice University and New York University. She currently resides in Manhattan and Connecticut. For more information, you can visit CandaceBushnell.com or follow her on social media:

Facebook.com/CandaceBushnell
Twitter/Instagram: @CandaceBushnell
Pinterest.com/CandaceBushnell